the girl who stayed

TANYA ANNE CROSBY

PRAISE FOR THE GIRL WHO STAYED

"A beautifully written, page-turning novel packed with emotion."

— #1 *NEW YORK TIMES* BESTSELLING AUTHOR BARBARA FREETHY

"*The Girl Who Stayed* is a deeply moving story. I am fascinated by the concept and by Tanya Crosby's stunning storytelling."

— STELLA CAMERON, *NEW YORK TIMES* BESTSELLING AUTHOR

"*The Girl Who Stayed* defies type. Crosby's tale is honest and sensitive, eerie and tragic. It's a homecoming tale of a past ever with us and irrevocably lost forever. A haunting vision of that chasm between life and death we call 'missing.'"

— PAMELA MORSI, BESTSELLING AUTHOR OF *SIMPLE JESS*

"An intense, mesmerizing Southern drama about a young woman who returns to her coastal home to put to rest the haunting ghost of her sister's tragic past. Told in the rich, lyrical style of Siddons and Conroy, *The Girl Who Stayed* is a woman's story of discovery and acceptance, redefined by Tanya Anne Crosby's dramatic storytelling, sharp characters, and well-defined plot. A must read for any woman who believes she can never go back home. Fabulous, rich and evocative!"

— *NEW YORK TIMES* BESTSELLING AUTHOR JILL BARNETT

"Crosby tugs heartstrings in a spellbinding story of a woman trying to move beyond her past."

— *NEW YORK TIMES* BESTSELLING AUTHOR SUSAN ANDERSEN

"In one word, exceptional!"

— LITERARILY ILLUMINED

"The ending was brilliant. The dramatic tension soared in the last section, building to a completely unguessable and unforeseen twist which grips the reader and completely holds your attention until the very very last page."

— BIBLIOMANIAC

"I thought this book was incredible, it was heart pounding, intense, and really bittersweet."

— COMFY READING

"A captivating novel of new beginnings. Beautifully rendered and quite atmospheric, this poignant yet ultimately uplifting story will stay with readers long after the last page is turned."

— Book Reviews and More by Kathy

"This book is really good. Really really good."

— Good Girl Gone Redneck

"Thought provoking, emotionally engaging and filled with psychological twists.... If you enjoy contemporary fiction, this is a book you'll certainly enjoy."

— Queen of All She Reads

"I couldn't stop reading. *The Girl Who Stayed* is a compelling and enjoyable read."

— Book by Book

"A really great read – it was entertaining, suspenseful and tragic all at once."

— Ms. Nose in a Book

"A gripping, multi-layered story."

— Laura's Reviews

"*The Girl Who Stayed* is a girl who will stay with you."

— Worth Getting in Bed For

"The ending surprised me and made the book memorable for me. If you enjoy suspenseful novels with a lot of depth, this is the book for you!"

— PALMER'S PAGE TURNERS

"*The Girl Who Stayed* is a raw, sometimes gut wrenching, emotional read. Powerful and compelling."

— CMASH READS

This one I wrote for myself, with abiding thanks to all who inspired me, angels and demons both. No one more than my husband, Scott Thomas Straley, whose faith in me burns brighter than my own. And to my children—my daughter Alaina in particular, who listened to me go on and on about things like the complexities of pluff mud and, with her curiosity and insight, found ways to help me delve a little deeper into the muck.

PROLOGUE

HANNAH'S BIKE

There was a feeling Zoe sometimes got . . . as though something were about to happen. She didn't know what or when, but it clung to the day like a cold sweat—a blind intuition that originated somewhere else . . . not in the gut . . . deeper . . . in the bones.

That's how it started, then as now.

They found Hannah's bike in the dunes near Breach Inlet, the silver handlebar glinting hard against a waning sun. More to the point, *Zoe* found the bike.

The pale-blue Schwinn lay twisted on its side, the black rubber of the left handlebar buried at least two inches deep so that sand spilled from the bar's interior once Zoe lifted it to walk it home.

Whether her sister dropped it there hard enough to drive the bar down into the sun-bleached sand, or whether it lay so long, undisturbed, that sand, driven by coastal winds, piled up and into the rubber hole was uncertain. Zoe only knew her sister worshipped the bike as much as Zoe did her first typewriter.

A few weeks earlier, when the bike's pristine blue paint was desecrated in a headlong collision with the fire hydrant on the corner of Middle Street and Station 26, her sister was devastated.

"No!" Hannah had screamed. Half dazed, scrambling to her feet, she'd been far more concerned over the scratches on her bike than she ever was over her skinned and bloodied knees. With scrapes from her thighs to her ankles, she'd brushed herself off and hurried to right her fallen bike. "Stupid tourists," she'd said, sounding like their dad.

"You're bleeding," Zoe had said.

"I don't care."

"But it's getting on your shoes."

"I don't care," her sister had said again, brushing her palm over the fender of her bike to test the finish.

At home, Zoe found a Band-Aid and placed it on Hannah's bleeding knee, worrying a bit because the edges wouldn't stick over a wound still dripping with blood. Solemn and filled with purpose, Hannah had been too busy searching for something out in the garage to bother washing herself off. Blue metallic paint, Zoe realized after a while. Tight-lipped, her sister searched until she found what she needed on a high shelf, where their father kept the construction materials for his model planes.

It seemed to Zoe that Hannah had felt much the same way about the scars on her bike as Zoe did after discovering the S on her typewriter showing signs of wear. Except that with those older model typewriters you couldn't easily change the keys, and while it was possible to touch up bike paint, the marring of such perfect machines seemed in those last days of innocence like the death of an era—the same way it felt to get a C after years of As and Bs, or blood stains on a brand-new pair of white Converse sneakers. In retrospect, neither she nor Hannah ever truly understood the concept of loss until Zoe hauled Hannah's bike up out of the dunes and wheeled it home.

Alone.

From that moment forward, Zoe understood only too well.

Later that day, with her sister's bike parked carefully in the driveway, Zoe sat at the kitchen table, tilting an empty saltshaker back and forth, wondering why her mom put rice in the salt, but never in the pepper. As her mother paced the kitchen, and her brother Nick rode shotgun in their dad's red Ford pickup, probably yelling out the window for Hannah, Chief Hale wanted to know why Zoe had thought to check the beach when nobody else had.

Zoe didn't know; she just had *a* feeling.

What Zoe wanted to know was why Chief Hale was asking dumb questions, when he should be out there searching for her missing sister. From Zoe's seat at the kitchen table, she could hear choppers hatcheting the air outside.

Guilt did the same thing inside her brain.

It was warm that day—warmer than most days in December. So of course no one bothered to check the beach. Who would think to swim so late in the year? Especially there, where everybody knew the currents were so deadly.

In fact, there was a sign that read "Deadly Currents," but no one who lived on the island needed any dumb sign to know it was a bad place to swim, no matter what time of year.

And yet her sister had been drawn to people and to places that were less than prudent. There was a sort of fever in Hannah's eyes whenever she pushed boundaries—something she did often, especially on her pale-blue Schwinn.

For example, they weren't supposed to cross the bridge onto the Isle of Palms, but sometimes Hannah did, stopping at the bait-shop gas station. Each time she would buy a Coke, pop the top, and stand outside, sipping victoriously until the time came to get back on the bike and head back home. Her sister had that certain middle-child lack of responsibility, with maybe a little something to prove.

But the one thing Hannah was never reckless about was her bike. That day out on the beach, the kickstand was up and the bike lay carelessly on its side. It wasn't as though her sister had left it standing and the wind or some brat kid pushed it over and it fell. No, it was cast aside without any real thought for what lay beneath, ready to scratch the shimmering paint. The bike lay in one of those twisted death throes, like the ones portrayed on TV, with the body outlined in thick white chalk. Except, of course, they didn't do that for bikes.

To everyone else it made perfect sense that Hannah wouldn't have bothered with a kickstand there in the shifting sand, but Zoe knew her sister better than that. Hannah would have found a spot where the sand was packed hard enough to support the weight of her precious bike and then she would have tested and retested the footing before walking away—slowly, like a mother with a teetering toddler.

So *why—why* was Hannah's bike lying twisted in the sand?

That was something Zoe never discovered.

1

"ENE, MENE, MUH"

The cell phone on the passenger seat gave a rude squawk. It rang on and on but Zoe ignored it, as though the act of doing so might buy her more time.

Compelled to look at every blond head she passed by—inside cars, along the bike ramp—it crossed her mind that Hannah would have loved biking over the new bridge—the third bridge to span the Cooper since the island's colonization. Originally, there had been two, standing side by side.

Zoe dated a guy once who'd claimed his grandfather helped build the first Cooper River Bridge. He was an oddball, talking incessantly about an ex-girlfriend, who just happened to look a lot like Zoe. Hearing this had made Zoe look at him differently, not the hunky guy he'd appeared to be, but the obsessive stalker beneath, who'd rather kill and stuff an ex-girlfriend than lose her. Regrettably, this image was further reinforced by his *other* favorite topic, which happened to be the family business, a mortuary. Not taxidermy, but close enough.

So one night, while crossing the Cooper—about three miles worth of mindless chatter—he'd gone back and forth between telling Zoe about this look-alike ex, explaining the process of embalming, and regaling her with tales of his grandfather's escapades during the building of the first bridge. Of course, at the time, both bridges had been past their prime, and even without stories about cadavers and look-alike exes, it was creepy enough driving over a swaying expanse of groaning, creaking metal—in the dark, mind you. Suffice it to say, the date hadn't turned into a second and even now, Zoe couldn't remember his name.

Bart, maybe.

The bridge Bart's grandfather had worked on was built around 1929, the second in 1966. The Silas Pearman Bridge was constructed to relieve load limits on the Grace Memorial Bridge, but both had been narrow enough to make driving over them harrowing, especially after the lanes were opened to two-way traffic.

It wasn't like that anymore. The first two bridges were demolished and a third went up—the Arthur Ravenel Jr. Bridge, a cable-stayed, eight-lane overpass that included pedestrian and bike lanes. This bridge was named after a retired US Congressman, although if you asked anyone the name of any one of these three bridges, they'd give you the same answer: it was the Cooper River Bridge.

The point being: on that old bridge, especially at night, you drove all the way across, shoulders tense, black skies overhead, black river below, ignoring the headlights that appeared as though they were coming straight into your lane. There was nowhere to swerve off to, nowhere to escape—unless you wanted to ram through thick sheets of metal and off into the river below.

Once on the bridge, you were at the mercy of oncoming drivers and your choice—the only choice—was to stay the course, fists gripping the steering wheel, holding your breath, hoping today wasn't your day to end up in the grill of an oncoming vehicle. And all the while, you could feel the bridge shuddering beneath you.

That's how Zoe felt right now: Tense. Expectant. No choice but to move forward. Hoping to avert impending disaster.

Back when Zoe's great-grandparents first purchased the house on Sullivan's, they'd had to take a ferry. It was a short hop from the peninsula in plain view of Fort Sumter. Edgar Allan Poe once wrote that the island, little more than a splinter of land, was "separated from the mainland by a scarcely perceptible creek, oozing its way through a wilderness of reeds and slime." Zoe loved his description, unflattering as it was, because it was the way she saw the island too—full of secrets whispered through dense tangles of sweet myrtle . . . secrets kept, no matter how long or hard you searched.

Leaving the bridge, shoulders tight, Zoe passed repurposed buildings and shopping centers that appeared as though they'd already lived out one commercial lifetime during her absence and now were preparing for a dubious rebirth, with freshly painted facades and empty parking spaces out in front. The hamburger joint she and her friends had satisfied munchies at was gone, converted into a ratty tire shop. But the Page's Thieves Market was still there, with the vintage street clock still guarding the porch, like a shiny silver sentinel.

They sold houses now as well—at least that's what her brother said. Maybe she could enlist their help.

The last few times Zoe had come to Charleston she'd stayed with her brother Nick, never bothering to check on the house. She left Sullivan's on the day she turned eighteen and never looked back, except to return long enough to bury her mom. Her dad was already gone before she moved away, puffing on unfiltered cigarettes every minute of his miserable life, until the smoke cleared and he was no more. Throat cancer. But like she told Nick, Rob Rutherford was dead to her long before that.

Of course, Nick led a Hallmark life, like the one they'd always believed they'd shared . . . back before that day in December, back when all the neighbors crowed about their perfect family.

Beautiful children. Beautiful parents. A house with a foundation as old as Charleston. How lucky they were.

How lucky they were.

That house. It had weathered Hugo, withstood the sea, but never made it past Hannah Rutherford's disappearance—or, more to the point, her family hadn't survived. The house on the feral lot on Atlantic Avenue, with the screened-in porch was standing still ...

Zoe pulled into the familiar driveway, stopping the car where she remembered parking Hannah's bike all those years before. The engine idled like an old man with hiccoughs. She pulled out the keys and palmed them, clutching the metal so hard the teeth cut into her skin. The scar on her forehead itched, but she tried to put it out of her mind. Seated in the driver's seat, Zoe took a moment to survey the dirty white bungalow.

It was older now, not so old as some. The wood and cinderblock siding needed a good coat of paint. The yard had returned to scrub. The native sweet myrtle had overtaken the lot. It clambered toward the house, clawing desperately at the siding. In one spot, it managed to stab meanly through the porch screen.

Fifteen feet high in some places, the shrubbery on the right side of the lot obscured the neighbors' house from Zoe's vantage in the drive. On the other side, a six-foot-high row of red azaleas were in full bloom—blood-red blossoms dripping from every branch.

On the front side of the screened-in porch remained a baseball-sized hole in the mesh. Zoe remembered when it happened. She and Nick had been throwing the baseball out in the yard, just the two of them. Wearing her dad's stiff glove, she'd made a sad attempt to help her brother improve his game.

Standing in the front yard, her brother had looked sullen, ready to give up. "Come on," Zoe had said. "You're so much better than me."

The comparison hadn't cheered him. He *was* better than Zoe, but Zoe rather sucked. "I'm no good, Nicky. Why don't you ask Kevin to come throw with you?"

Kevin was Nick's friend who'd lived over on Goldbug Avenue —a kid whose family still ate dinner together and who sometimes went fishing with his dad.

Her baby brother had given a half shake of his head, as though the effort might be more than he cared to make. He'd dropped the ball into his glove, then picked it up again, dropping it yet again, probably wondering why their dad was inside yelling at their mom. Again. Or maybe he'd simply been wishing he had a brother instead of a sister—one sister. That was key. By that time, Hannah was already gone, her twin bed donated to a new mom from church, whose three-year-old had outgrown his crib.

There was something about the look in Nicky's eyes that had made Zoe feel his life—all that he could be—hung in the balance.

It had been hot and humid that day, not unlike today. The hair had stuck to the back of Zoe's neck. The inside door shut tight to keep the argument contained within, probably hadn't improved either of her parents' moods.

Staring into his glove, Nicky had continued dropping the ball, picking it up again, decisions being made . . .

"It's my fault," Zoe had reasoned. "I'm not very good, Nicky. Let's just do it again."

Her brother had seemed to consider this. His wavy, blond hair was sweaty at the ends, dark—as dark as his somber brown eyes. At nine years old, he was already becoming a crusty old man. Shifting uneasily from foot to foot, Zoe had pounded her fist into the oversized glove the way she'd watched them do on TV.

"Come on," she'd coaxed. "I'm ready now. Come on, Nicky Boy!"

Nicky Boy. That was the name her dad would have used— mostly when he was in a good mood. But good moods had become few and far between.

A half smile had turned her brother's lips then, a little gleam in his eyes that brought to mind Casey at the bat. He'd taken a ready stance, thinking, thinking, aiming . . .

Rearing back, he'd set the ball loose. It flew over Zoe's head, powered by all the anger he'd had mustered up inside, ripping through the flimsy screen, and crashing into the inside window, shattering glass.

No longer contained, her parents' voices had risen to a crescendo. Zoe's brain had refused to recognize coherent words and phrases. She and Nicky had given each other wary glances, and then their father had exploded onto the screened porch— red face, tan khakis, silver keys. He'd flown out the screened door, toward his pickup, mouthing obscenities, and Zoe had pretended to be a statue until Robert Rutherford was safely inside his truck. And then, just to be certain, she hadn't moved until after he'd peeled out of the driveway, kicking up gravel and shells in his wake.

And now, seated in her own car, with the windows rolled up, Zoe stared at the hole in the porch screen. The mesh was curled with age, never repaired. One month after Nick ripped the screen with his baseball, Hurricane Hugo had thrown more than base-balls at the house. It managed to stave off that assault as well, but as far as the will to set things right went, it pushed any remaining resolve over the edge, never to return.

Across the street, a brand-new triple-story house on stilts had gone up since Zoe left the island. Only because she was checking the housing market, she knew it was now in foreclosure. Sitting empty, with its lovely peach facade, it was a million-dollar oops for somebody. Somewhere near two dozen homes remained of the original dwellings that once complemented the old military base. A few of the island houses were as ancient as Fort Moultrie, but not included in the registry as original base housing.

Fort Moultrie was where Edgar Allan Poe was once stationed. All these years later, the man had a street, a library, and a pub named after him. In return, he had immortalized the island in his story "The Gold-Bug"—not Goldbug, as some dummy had named one of the back streets on the island. Only a writer would get the difference. And there, behind Goldbug Avenue, up against the salt marsh, was Raven Drive. Here, you see, was a going theme. Probably not because of it, though certainly not in spite of it, this pinprick of land on a splinter of sand was worth more than Zoe could walk away from. So here she was, at their "Kingdom by the Sea," appropriately named by her great-grandmother in honor of Poe's Annabel Lee. *Clever.*

Very clever, indeed.

The wooden sign out on the porch hung stock-still, despite the proximity to the beach, as though the world itself held its breath to see what Zoe would do.

Breathe in.

Breathe out.

It's just a house.

Zoe opened the car door, stepping out. Heavy and oppressive, the island heat smacked her full in the face. She moved through it, stepping through a time warp . . .

1986

"Where's your sister?"

Sand crunched beneath Zoe's sneakers as she sauntered into the kitchen. "I dunno."

"Supper is ready soon."

Technically, in the South, supper referred to a light evening meal while dinner was considered to be the main meal, whether or not it took place at noon or later in the evening. Lunch, on the other hand, was like a supper eaten at noon—a lighter, less formal affair. Her mother never seemed to get that straight, but

Zoe learned the right way from her Nana. "What are we having for dinner?"

The scent of pot roast filled Zoe's nostrils, an immediate answer to her question, although her question was far less a matter of inquiry and more a matter of deflection.

"Food," her mother said, with just a hint of a German accent. It didn't mesh all that well with the Southern words she tried to use. Nor was her diction and locution precisely correct. "What happened, you two? Y'all are peas in a pod, Zoe, fess up."

Zoe furrowed her brow. Her sister was out on the beach searching for turtle eggs with her *new* best friend, despite that messing with turtle nests wasn't allowed. There was no telling Hannah anything anymore. Unless Zoe wanted to sit on her sister to keep her out of trouble, there was nothing else for it. Gabi was a troublemaker. Zoe didn't like her very much. "Don't worry, Ma. Nothing happened."

Her mother gave her a discerning glance, one that implied she didn't quite believe Zoe, but Zoe knew instinctively she would drop it, and she did, returning her attention to peeling the onions for the roast. Her mother was all too often distracted.

"I'm hungry." Zoe gave the kitchen a once over, searching for something to abscond with. A handful of carrots sat on the counter, near the stove, but they weren't yet peeled. That wasn't what she was in the mood for anyways, especially after watching Hannah scarf down a bag of Bugles she and Gabi had swiped from the bait-shop gas station. Both had been wearing Bugle claws when she'd found them, one over each finger, and growling and pawing at the air in front of Zoe like angry bears. Zoe was pretty sure Gabi had stolen the bag, but Hannah didn't seem to care her friend was a "bad seed." That's what their Nana called ill-behaved folks, and Gabi was most certainly ill-behaved.

A few months before, Gabi Donovan had moved in next door with her "meemaw and papaw." As far as Zoe could tell, the Donovans were too old to keep up with all their many cats, much less a "bad-seed" granddaughter and Zoe wished Gabi would just run away, like all the Donovan's cats.

"Poor Gabi," Mama would say, but that's not the way Zoe saw it.

Poor Zoe. Poor Hannah. Even poor Gabi's "Meemaw and Papaw"—cranky geezers that they were. But never, *ever* poor Gabi. Gabi was meaner than a junkyard dog—another saying her Nana had, coincidentally, often used in reference to Gabi's grandparents. Like granddaughter, like grandmother, Zoe supposed.

"She's with Gabi," Zoe felt compelled to say. It wasn't tattling, exactly. "I don't know where they went. Maybe the beach." Probably Hannah would tell Gabi all about their secret quest, and that possibility made Zoe's stomach ache. She wasn't hungry anymore.

Her mother sighed, apparently not liking Zoe's answer but, as Zoe expected, her mother wasn't willing to leave her kitchen long enough to do anything about it, so Zoe made a dash for the living room, hoping there would be something on TV besides the Iran-Iraq war. For months after the president bombed Libya, news interrupted all her favorite shows. "It's close to dinner," her mother said quickly. "Please go find your sister, Zoe."

Zoe skidded to a halt as the pads of her feet hit the carpet her mom and dad argued over way too much. Her dad wanted to rip it out, return the floor to the original wood, as it was when he was a little boy. Her mother thought the carpet deadened the echo that made her feel as though she were walking through a mausoleum.

Zoe didn't care one way or another, except that the carpet looked a lot like the matted hair on her troll doll. "Do I have to, Mama?"

"Yes, you *have* to. Go find Hannah, Zoe. Supper is ready soon."

Zoe slid her mother an annoyed glance. It was supposed to be supper *will be* ready soon, not supper *is* ready soon. Zoe wouldn't care so much that her mom didn't talk like other moms if she weren't always so distracted. Grumbling, she spun about and marched across the kitchen, toward the back door, resenting the task but too dutiful to disobey.

Hannah, on the other hand, she would have pretended to go. She wouldn't have uttered a word in complaint, eager for the opportunity to jump on her new bike and go riding up and down the street without any aim at all. Her sister never had to do *anything*, ever. It was tough to toe the line, tougher yet to watch her sister never do anything she was told to do and never get in trouble for any of it.

That's why Zoe sometimes had bad ideas. Sometimes she wanted to pull out all of Hannah's hair. Sometimes she wished her sister would get on her bike and keep on riding and never, *ever* come back home. But mostly, when Gabi wasn't around, Zoe didn't know what she would do without her little sister. Her mother said they had a love-hate relationship and that was probably true because at the moment Zoe hated Hannah with all her heart. She wished her sister were never born. Nick wasn't half the trouble her sister was.

∿

Present

OF ALL THE times Zoe had imagined her sister walking out the door and never coming home, not once did she ever truly expect it to happen.

Her gaze was drawn toward the house next door, where Gabi Donovan had arrived like a hurricane and less than a year later was hauled away, literally kicking and screaming. Zoe couldn't remember where she'd gone, but thought Gabi's grandparents had sent her to live with an uncle. Zoe never saw Gabi again, and that was soon enough for her . . . especially after what the little bitch had said.

Even now, all these years later, it made Zoe angry. Everyone claimed they hadn't believed Gabi, but a seed of doubt had been planted just the same.

Moving cautiously up the front steps, Zoe examined the stairs. The wood was rotting and needed to be replaced. This close to the ocean, if you didn't keep wood treated and painted, it didn't last very long. On the top step, careful to avoid the rot, Zoe turned to survey the yard. From here she could see over the sweet myrtle and azaleas into the neighbors' yards. On the one side, the house was newish, built sometime after Hurricane Hugo. The other house—Gabi's house—was exactly as Zoe recalled. Like theirs, it was a relic of the island's military past. Although well kept, it was nothing like the sprawling beach houses that had cropped up in recent years. It was a mishmash of styles—part cedar siding, part cinderblock, part board and batten.

At thirty-nine, Zoe had not yet lived long enough to forget the pain of standing here on this porch step, waiting for her dad's pickup to pull into the driveway.

She pictured him now as she'd seen him that life-altering day, sliding out of the passenger seat, his expression full of confusion and fear. In the short time since he and Nicky had left the house, her dad had aged. He appeared years older as he emerged from his truck, his gaze somber, his lips thinner. His gaze had honed in on her mom, never on Zoe, as though to see her might have somehow broken his back.

Standing next to her, her mother had worried dry, cracked hands. "Did you check the Mound? You should check the Mound, Rob. I tell the kids never go there. But Hannah doesn't listen."

That day had been a first for many things. It was the first time her dad had looked past Zoe, as though both his daughters disappeared that day. It was also the first time Zoe recalled her mother ever acknowledging Hannah's impetuosity. And it was the first time her father had ever snapped at her mother in front of the kids.

"Not now!" he'd said, storming past, into the house, slamming the door behind him. Marge had followed him inside.

Zoe had pulled Nicky into her arms as he'd ambled up the steps, partly because she'd needed a hug and partly because she'd sensed Nicky shouldn't follow them inside. That day, as she and her brother had stood embracing on the front porch steps, the first threads of their family tapestry began to unravel.

Or maybe it began before that day? That probably wasn't something a ten-year-old would know. Or a six-year-old for that matter. Hannah was only eight the day she'd disappeared.

Zoe examined the house next door. Like Kingdom's, the paint job was faded, but not so much that it had become an eyesore. The low-pitched roof was in better shape than Kingdom's, and the oaks were majestic enough to conceal any of the house's imperfections. The patchy grass was cropped short, and the mailbox stood straight, painted with numbers that could easily be read. Above the house numbers, there used to be a sign with the house name, but Zoe could no longer remember what it was. The sign was no longer there. Crazy house. Loony bin. That's how she thought of it now.

Not that "Kingdom" was any better.

For a while, she'd used a local firm to handle rentals for their property, but the broker seemed more inclined to rent it out to high school seniors. Considering the scars on the island house and their lack of incentive to fix the place up, Zoe was never overly concerned by the prospect of renting it out for much. But considering that the island had ordinances against overnight rentals, she had anticipated somewhat more thoughtful tenants. The condition of the house had suffered as a result.

It was unrentable in its current condition.

Of course, Nick couldn't be bothered to care one way or the other. Her brother made it a point to stay clear of the house, and

Zoe couldn't decide whether his decision was driven by a sense of self-preservation or a desire to appear like something more than his tarnished roots. A spark of anger flared. He and his lovely wife lived in a cute little cottage in Summerville, with a perfectly manicured, chemically enhanced lawn that he saw to himself, just as far away from the salt spray of the ocean as he could manage. His wife looked like a model straight out of a Sears catalog—even after two kids, and she was a teacher so she could rush home to be with their little darlings every day after school.

Perfect.

Pristine.

Zoe was pretty sure Beth had no knowledge of the things that had transpired here in their Kingdom by the Sea. She ran her fingers across the stair rail. It was shedding years of bad paint jobs, like a molting snake, but, unlike the stairs, the rail was sturdy. Still it would probably have to come down since it was attached to the stairs. Flakes came away at her touch as she looked inside through the screen. Over the years, the blue ceiling of the porch had faded to a Confederate gray, as though rebelling from years of neglect. The house had an expectant aura—a ringing silence that felt more like a scream.

The furniture, what little remained, was familiar to Zoe: a sturdy white rocker that once belonged to her Nana. With ten years of tenants, it was surprising no one had stolen the damned thing. To begin with, they'd left the house fully furnished, hoping to appeal to vacationing families. It was never intended to be a year-round rental.

Next to the rocker sat an odd little octagonal table that had once shouldered a vase with roses from her mother's garden. Even after Hannah, Marge had kept her resolve to fill that tulip-shaped vase. Old English roses were her favorite, complicated flowers that were perfect despite messy blooms.

Zoe knocked awkwardly on the screen door, not altogether certain why—maybe to ward away ghosts? Or maybe to alert the homeless who might have taken up residence inside? There was no one living here now, although some part of Zoe hoped leaving it empty would curry some favor with the Universe. The place had terrible karma. It bore an aura as dank and dark as one of Poe's fetid tales. Although in reality, leaving the house empty was more a matter of avoidance than any sense of altruism, because Zoe wasn't anyone's savior, not even her own.

Searching for the door key at the bottom of her purse, Zoe thought about her car. It needed a tune up. Chris was the one who usually handled such things, but since he wasn't going to be around anymore, she resolved to do it soon.

She didn't need a man in her life.

The screen door wasn't locked. There was a simple latch inside the door that couldn't be hooked from the outside, but the lighting was better outside, so Zoe continued searching out on the steps. After just a few moments under the sweltering sun, she reconsidered the wisdom of placing the key on her keychain, although she probably wouldn't do that. It was one thing to come back here to take care of business, yet another to incorporate the house into her life. Somehow, placing a key on her keychain implied a certain permanency she wasn't willing to consider.

Finding the key beneath a pack of gum, Zoe pulled the door open, finally stepping into the shade of the screened-in porch. Without a breeze, the room wasn't all that much cooler out of the sun, but that was the great thing about living near the sea: ocean breezes were godsends in the muggy May heat.

In the early days, before Hannah went missing, her mom would have been at this door before the three of them ever started up the drive, waiting to usher them inside, with promises of cold lemonade or cookies. Sometimes both.

A vision of the three of them—Nicky, Hannah, and Zoe—accosted her now. Hannah laughing over something—always something—Nicky elbowing his way past Zoe to see what treat their mother had in store, and Zoe meeting her mother's fragile gaze, as though to issue an unspoken apology: *I'm sorry I wasn't here to help today. I'm sorry you look so sad whenever we leave. I'm sorry mom, because it seems you lose your world every morning at 7:00 a.m., each time we walk out the door.*

Zoe had sensed the loneliness her mother felt, sending the last of her brood off to school. And Zoe, being the eldest child, had been careful to be sure Nicky always held her hand when crossing the street. The two of them looked both ways, while Hannah barreled ahead, heedless of oncoming traffic. Luckily, there hadn't been all that many cars around back then. Even now, the island was mostly locals, while nearby Isle of Palms catered to tourists and folks who thought it was funny to brave a swim at Breach Inlet.

"Dead tourist!" her dad used to exclaim whenever he'd spied the orange-bellied Coast Guard choppers overhead. Nearly always it had been because someone thought the rules of nature didn't apply to him—usually some strapping military dude, head shaved, tattoo on one bicep. Her father had never seemed overly aggrieved by the prospect, but Zoe had always felt solemn, thinking of somebody's mother crying into her hands. Of course, after Hannah, her dad never cracked that joke again—or any joke for that matter.

Absently reaching into her purse, Zoe plucked out the pack of chewing gum, prying one out of the pack. Dropping the rest back into her purse, she unwrapped the piece of gum in her hand, put it into her mouth, and crumbled the silver wrapper, dropping it back into her purse.

"Can I have a piece?"

"Where's yours?"

"I gave it to Gabi."

"Then no. You can't have one."

The memory eddied like a vapor, ready to be swept away. It was easier not to remember. Except that, like the heat of jalapenos on a burger, even after you'd plucked them all away, it left Zoe with a smoldering sadness.

Despite the stagnant air, the porch was aerated enough not to smell closed up. Still, she detected a hint of mustiness in the air—only a hint. It would be worse inside, but Zoe went for the door anyway, determined to get this over with. The sooner it was over, the sooner she could get on with her life. Even now, she sensed the ghost of Hannah's bike parked out on the driveway. The somber weight of her grief was still heavy in this island clime.

The master key slid into the lock easier than she expected. You'd think by now the keys were old enough to warrant a little wriggling, but without any effort, it seemed to Zoe that the house was so anxious to see her it removed all barriers to her entry.

So here we are . . .

Zoe pulled the door open and stepped inside.

Like many of the bungalows on the island, it was an elevated single story. The front door dumped you straight into the living room and behind that sat the kitchen. Another long corridor acted as a tributary, spilling you into various rooms—four bedrooms, two bathrooms. From the outside, the dormers appeared to be upstairs rooms, but they peered out from an insulated attic. When Zoe was young, she remembered talk about converting the attic into an upstairs suite but, of course, that never happened.

The curtains, thick sheets of yellowed-ivory material, were drawn against the early morning sun, casting the living area into shadow.

Zoe made her way over to the front window, drawing open the curtain. The thick, sticky material offended her fingers. One day her mother up and replaced her grandmother's thin, lacy ones that tended to billow in with the breeze with thick ones that hung like theatre curtains off stiff wooden facades—as though to conceal everything inside from prying eyes, thereby curtailing all Good Samaritans from friendly neighborhood interventions.

At least that's the way it appeared through a child's eyes, and it was an impression that never left Zoe. It clung to her even now, like the cigarette smoke that stuck like amorphous carbon layers to the yellowed curtains.

"*Why do you keep on her like that, Rob?*"

"*She's got a shitty attitude and a shittier mouth. I want her to learn her place.*"

"*A woman's place, you mean? Like mine?*"

"*Goddamn you, Marge. This ain't about us. It's about a mealy-mouthed teenager who ain't smart enough to keep her goddamned trap shut.*"

Silence.

"*Admit it.*" *Soft sobs.* "*You blame her, Rob. You blame her; she knows it. This is why you can't leave her be. Of course she's mouthy. She struggles the same as you and me.*"

With a great, big tug, Zoe ripped down the curtains, determined to replace them once and for all. They were dirty, old. It grossed her out to think how many tenants had fingered them before her. Sunlight burst into the room, stabbing its disapproval into all the dark corners.

2

The place was a wreck. Even knowing what she would find inside, the prospect of handling it all alone was daunting. Nick's tone gave her no doubt he meant every word. "Hire it out. Burn it down, Zoe. I don't care what you do."

Zoe gripped the cell phone so hard the joints in her fingers began to cramp. "Really? You don't care, Nick?"

Her brother's answer was spoken softly, devoid of emotion. "No."

Anger clouded reason, but Zoe kept her tone calm to mirror Nick's. "Oh, you care. You just don't want to spend any energy dealing with it."

For a moment, silence greeted her accusation.

"Look," he said. And this time, Zoe detected a hint of annoyance—a fact that gratified her because it proved her brother was human. "I don't have time to deal with it . . . not like you."

Presumably because Zoe's life wasn't as ordered as his?

She'd come six hundred miles, dropped literally everything—for more reasons than this, but that wasn't something Nick could possibly know. On the other hand, her brother never even bothered to show up after the police called to let him know the house had been broken into. "Make time," she said. "This isn't just my responsibility; it's yours too. This house belongs to both of us."

The days of sheltering her baby brother were over, Zoe decided. She'd created a monster with her reluctance to allow him to share the burdens of their upbringing. She'd kept him preoccupied in his bedroom, playing board games while the shouting persisted outside their bedrooms. She'd anticipated questions that never came, reassuring him when reassurance was scarce. As a result, Nicky was pretty handy with his invisibility cloak, casting it easily over anything he didn't care to see. The house was under his cloak now, and maybe Zoe was as well because, clearly, her life wasn't as pretty as his.

"Damn it, Zoe. I told you a long time ago I don't want anything to do with the place."

"Yet you'll take the money once it sells?"

Silence filtered over from his end of the line. Zoe forced herself to wait for his response, because this wasn't really about money. It was never about money.

"If you need it more than I do, keep it."

Zoe's skin prickled over his charity—an unintended back-hand slap. Her brother wasn't mean. She knew he didn't intend to belittle her, or make her feel small, but that's exactly how she felt right now. The scar on her forehead burned. A cold sweat broke out over the back of her neck. She didn't want or need to keep the money from the proceeds of the house. She wanted her brother back—her last living relative. Was it so wrong to want Nick to be her rock, just this once, instead of the other way around?

She was tired of being strong through every ordeal, though if she said as much to Nick, he would probably tell her to stop weathering life as though it were a perpetual storm. Zoe was certain he saw her travails as problems of her own making. Her chest ached with sobs that couldn't be freed. "You know that's not what I want," she said quietly.

But he had to know that.

Zoe had always looked after Nick, putting him first, even at her own expense. And then one day, he'd seemed to pick himself up and carry on with little effort, while Zoe continued to stumble through each and every day.

There was probably some truth to the fact that she shouldered too much, even things she had no business shouldering. But Nick's brow was untouched by worry, while fine lines etched permanent inroads into hers.

But that's what you want for him, isn't it? You want him to be "happy" despite everything? This is all you, Zoe. You accomplished exactly what you set out to do.

The other end of the line remained silent, so intensely silent that she wondered if she'd dropped the call. The battery on her cell was low. "Nick?"

His voice sounded terse. "Yep."

In a way, this was a test. At least that's how Zoe saw it. Either everything she ever wanted for her brother was a lie, or she had to allow him to live his life without the burdens she bore.

"I don't know what to tell you," he said, his tone firm.

He wouldn't be joining her on the island; that much was clear.

Zoe also noticed he didn't bother to ask about Chris, which was fine, because she didn't want to talk about him either.

"Don't worry, Nick, I'll take care of everything." Zoe resisted the urge to add, *like I always do,* because it wouldn't help matters any. Even without the afterword, there was a note of passive aggression to her response that she wholeheartedly despised.

She felt the rift widen between them. It was up to Zoe to keep it together, because no matter how much she had done for her little brother, Nick was very good at preserving his peace. She should take a page out of his book. She just didn't know how. "Tell Beth I said hi," she said, withdrawing from the battle.

"I will."

"And the girls."

A smile returned to her brother's voice. "You should tell them yourself sometime. They'd love to see you."

"I will," Zoe promised, and then said goodbye, ending the call.

In her frustration, she kicked at a pile of empty beer cans she'd swept to one side of the kitchen, scattering them across the floor, and then she said a few well-rounded curse words. The clang of tin reverberated through the empty room, the sound as hollow as she felt.

The sky was falling and Zoe had nowhere to run.

Some part of her was furious with Nick, but more so with herself. She recoiled from the edge of her anger, knowing instinctively that one easy slice would open a vein. She took a few purposeful breaths, clawing away at the invisible chains constricting her chest. "You're fine. This is doable. You can do this, Zoe."

She was turning forty this year. So why did she feel like an angsty teen? The entire situation disgusted her.

A sheen of moisture manifested between Zoe's breasts, pooling, until a bead of sweat glided down, tickling her skin. She clutched at her blouse, telling herself it was only the heat.

She wasn't losing it.

She was fine.

First things first.

Once again Zoe lifted the phone, this time to dial the police. Once she had the appropriate person on the line, she went through the story: She was returning their call now that she was back on the island. She'd already called the real estate management company. They'd washed their hands of the entire ordeal. Technically, Zoe had discontinued their services two months past. Now the kitchen window was smashed. The sheer quantity of trash might be due to accumulation over time, but the cans of Coke and the dabs of exhausted cement-gray chewing gum stuck to the cabinets, along with the bags of chips and cigarette butts all over the kitchen floor, all suggested something else. Kids were partying in the house, hence the broken window out back, where the tangle of sweet myrtle bushes were at their thickest. It was a jungle back there, literally, with wild, unkempt briars, concealing more than her mother's curtains ever did.

The police came promptly, as small town cops were wont to do. Zoe barely had time to snag the Oriole's cap from her passenger seat and jam it on her head before the police-grade white Ford Explorer pulled into the driveway. She recognized the man wearing the chief's badge. He was about her father's age. Approaching the truck, Zoe tugged down the bill of her cap.

Chief McWhorter slid out of the driver's seat and gave Zoe a look like the ones her mom used to give her when trying to determine Zoe's guilt. Or maybe Zoe was being paranoid—as though it were somehow her fault she'd acquired the scar now concealed beneath the cap. Because, of course, scars like this didn't happen to decent, God-fearing folks. They were white trash badges of courage, and she wasn't particularly brave, nor was she trashy. Like a seedy knife wound, she hid it, even from close friends, embarrassed by the unlovely gash. She wore baseball hats for the first time in her life, which didn't actually hide the scar. But that was the one bright side about Nick's refusal to come: he wouldn't see her face, and therefore she wouldn't have to to lie about it.

The chief's ice-blue gaze zoned in on Zoe's hat. Well-worn, supple and faded, it didn't belong to her. She could claim she'd borrowed it, but since she never intended to see its owner again, it was more appropriate to call it stolen. She tugged down the bill to hide the indisputable evidence of Chris's latest tantrum, a one-inch vertical scar that disappeared beneath the bill of her cap.

"I knew your parents," the chief said. "Good folks. Welcome back."

He gave her a playful wink and Zoe cringed. She'd spent too many years listening to Chris tell her that *all* men *only* wanted in her pants; she was stupid to believe otherwise. In fact, it was

Chris's MO. He never met a pair of jeans he didn't want to stick his dick into. Her hand lingered near the bill of her cap. "Thanks."

"I understand you need to file a report?"

"Yeah," Zoe said, feeling inexplicably vulnerable. Nevertheless, she invited Chief McWhorter into the kitchen, where he inspected the broken window, toeing the glass on the floor with a scuffed black boot.

He checked the back door, particularly the knob. "Doesn't appear as though it's been tampered with," he suggested, returning his attention to the window. "Probably came in through there and unlocked the backdoor."

Zoe crossed her arms. "Maybe, but it wasn't broken before."

Chief McWhorter reexamined the window, as though he'd never laid eyes on it before. Zoe wondered who it was who'd answered the vandalism call.

"Before when?"

Zoe braced herself for a battle. "Well, I have to assume it must have been fine after the last rental?" She refrained from pointing out the why; that it was the Sullivan's Island Police Department who'd delivered the eviction notice for her. Regrettably, the last tenant was a full year in arrears and it had taken a court order to get them out, a fact that still gave her visions of homeless children warming little hands over trashcan fires, never mind that the weather in November could push eighty degrees and more.

"You know that for sure?"

Zoe met his challenge, throwing one back. "Wouldn't you guys have noticed when you came to get the keys?"

He scratched at his chin, contemplating her question. "I suppose we should have." His eyes narrowed a little. "Remind me again when that was?"

Suspicion tinged his questions. Zoe realized it must be protocol, if not habit. She had the distinct impression he must know all the answers already. With a population of fewer than two thousand, there wasn't much that transpired here on the island Chief McWhorter wouldn't know about, which was in part why she felt laid bare.

"A week or so before Thanksgiving."

Chief McWhorter nodded, studying the trash piles. "Ain't no tellin' how long it's been this way or who broke the window. Could be a bunch of kids found it this way and came in to party. You know how it is." His gaze flicked over the bill of Zoe's cap.

Zoe *did* know how it was, but his question felt like a judgment on her character. He turned to make his way out of the kitchen before she could respond. "When did you get in, Ms. Rutherford?"

Zoe's answer was a bit less gregarious. She tightened her grip on her arms. "A while ago."

"Awhile as in hours or days?"

"Hours."

He looked back over his shoulder. "Guess this ain't quite the welcome you anticipated?"

It was *exactly* the welcome she'd anticipated, but she followed him out of the kitchen without a word, feeling cross. Walking through the house, with the power off and the raw guts of her past exposed, was like a personal autopsy with an audience. Maybe Chief McWhorter couldn't see the entrails of her past strewn everywhere, bleeding out, but Zoe missed nothing, and his questions, protocol or not, weren't improving her mood.

He held a heavy-duty flashlight in his left hand, one that could easily double as a baton. He waved it into gloomy corners as he led the way through empty rooms. "So . . . y'all back to stay?"

It was only Zoe; nobody else. She might have corrected him, except that in these parts "y'all" wasn't necessarily plural. The scar on her forehead itched ferociously. Why did the answer to his question feel so mercurial, when the truth was that she wanted to be as far away from this place as was humanly possible? "Not sure yet."

Throughout the house, random pieces of familiar furniture remained, some broken, some not. One by one, under Zoe's direction, the management company had discarded ruined heirloom pieces, deeming them deterrents to a viable rental contract. What remained now was mostly junk.

In her parents' bedroom, only an ancient black telephone remained—the kind you had to dial, although it wasn't plugged in. It appeared as though it had been yanked out of the wall in some vintage horror flick and then abandoned where it lay, near the closet. The image of a woman accosted her—sobbing, dragging the phone inside to whisper frantically into the receiver . . . But that wasn't a memory—or so Zoe hoped.

The curtains in this room were similar to the one's hanging in the living room, except that these were once ocean blue, faded by years of the sun's daily scrutiny. Zoe knew this only from memory because, like the porch ceiling, they were now a dirty gray. The floor here was wood, never carpeted, which was good, but there were scratches on the floor where beds, one after another, had found purchase, probably some with rough metal frames and no casters. Even now, it seemed the floor sank beneath the weight of some invisible berth. The wall behind it was pocked, as though repeatedly hammered by headboards—certainly not her parents. Still, the thought brought a warm flush to Zoe's cheeks as the light from Chief McWhorter's flashlight skated over the hammered sheetrock. He didn't bother to look back at her, so he couldn't see Zoe's naked thoughts. His flashlight continued to probe the room. As though it were a living, breathing entity, Zoe had the impression of the house being frisked. Next thing you know, like a cartoon character held upside down, it would be shaken ruthlessly, joggling out secrets for all the world to judge. "Looks like the place has taken a bit of a beating," was all he said.

"Looks like," Zoe agreed.

With nowhere left to go, she turned to lead the way back through the dingy house. Despite it being early yet, Kingdom lived in the shadow of its neighbor to the east, another relatively new three-story beach "cottage" on stilts.

"Y'all plannin' to stay the night?"

Once again, Zoe itched to correct him—some deep-rooted need to reassure him that Chris wasn't coming around, which was perfectly ridiculous, because he didn't know Chris. "That's the plan," Zoe said. "If I can get the electricity back on."

"Tell Regina I said hey. Might win you some favor. I pulled her cat off a roof last week." He swung the light of his flashlight to and fro and Zoe decided that flirtation was simply part of his nature. Near the living room, in the darkest part of the house, he stopped, blocking her path.

Uncomfortable with her position, Zoe had to restrain herself from brushing past him, into the living room where there was more light and a door within sight. She bit anxiously at her bottom lip.

"I gotta be frank, Ms. Rutherford. We'll handle it however you like, but we're likely looking at a misdemeanor here. Despite the broken window and the trash in the kitchen, there's no sign of criminal intent," he explained. "Kids'll be kids. Even if we can ascertain who was actually in the house, ain't no telling how the window got broke. Could've been a rock for all we know. If you ask me, a good week's worth of cleaning and a bit of paint'll do the place wonders."

Zoe tapped a finger at her elbow, anxious to skirt past him—the report as well. Suddenly, it all seemed too much trouble. His advice rang with truth.

Paint was a good call, she decided. She had more than enough saved for minor repairs. Before leaving Baltimore, she'd pulled out all the money from their joint checking accounts and opened a new account at a bank she knew served the island. It was her money, after all. Chris should be grateful she'd left him with rent paid and enough cash to get by until he got another paycheck. Hopefully, this was the last place he would search for her. After eight years together, she was certain he knew she despised this place—as much as she despised him. Maybe even as much as she despised herself.

Then again, there was a good chance he would try to find her instead of putting his own life back in order, because to Chris, clinging to Zoe would be the path of least resistance—except that this time, Zoe was stronger in her resolve.

She studied her immediate surroundings, eager to get the job started. Turning toward the chief, Zoe tugged down her cap, nodding. "All right, do you by chance have a direct number where I can reach you, if necessary?" She moved past him to lead the way to the door.

"I'll get it before I go," he said, swinging his flashlight toward the floor. "Watch that board."

Stepping over a random two-by-four, Zoe led the way out onto the front porch, where the hole from Nicky's baseball remained, framed by a rusted screen. She opened the screen door and stepped outside, relieved to be out in the daylight. This was the thing no man truly understood about a woman's plight. No matter where she was, who she was with, or who she was, there was always a bit of apprehension over being alone with a man. At least for Zoe there was. She was perfectly aware of his strength and advantage. One wrong guess about a man's character could land her in the emergency room, or worse.

She knew this from experience.

Zoe watched Chief McWhorter descend the stairs and head toward his vehicle, his stride purposeful. He didn't look back and Zoe half expected him to get into his truck and leave, overlooking the number she'd asked him for. But he didn't. He opened his car door, rifled around for a minute, then returned to Zoe, bearing a card in hand.

"Belongs to my son," he explained. "My number's on the

back." He handed the card up to Zoe, and once more eyed her ball cap. This time, given his vantage, she knew he spied the scar, but he didn't say a word.

"Take care now," he said, turning to go. Then he paused, turning around to face Zoe. "Hey, we had two women turn up missing last month, maybe you heard?"

Zoe nodded. She'd heard, but the truth was that as close to home as it might appear to be, there was more to fear in the place she'd left. "I did," Zoe said. "Thanks for this." She flashed the card between them.

"If you want, I'll give my son a ring," he said. "He could swing by later to board up your window, probably do it for free. He can give a quote for glass."

Zoe nodded. "Sounds great."

"Alrighty then," the chief said and looked back at Zoe's car, parked out in the driveway before his truck. It was loaded to the seams. "I don't suppose you've got a gun in all that mess?"

In only in a handful of states would that be considered a casual question. Unfortunately, South Carolina was one of them —no permit required to purchase rifles, shotguns, or handguns. Zoe crossed her arms, digging her thumbs painfully into the inside of her elbows. "No, sir," she said, pushing herself up on her tiptoes. "I don't believe in guns."

He gave her a tight little smile.

Zoe cocked her head and gave him a little smirk. "If I did, there'd be a trail of dead boyfriends in my wake." She gave him a shrug. "But hey, I've got a frying pan. Cast iron. Leaves a pretty good dent."

The chief's smile widened. He winked yet again. "Girl after my own heart," he said. "Alrighty, Ms. Rutherford. I'll leave you to it. Seems to me you know what you're doing." And with that, he left and Zoe lingered a moment on the front steps to watch him go. She shoved the card into her back pocket without looking at it.

As the police car drove away, a silver Camry eased into the driveway next door. Zoe stood watching from her porch step, arms still crossed. Out of the driver's seat swung two long legs, followed by the lean form of a man. His hair was gray, shimmering under the sun as he walked toward the house, pulling a bad leg behind him. He didn't bother to look Zoe's way and, after a moment, she walked back inside after her keys, intending to go directly to the electric company to see about the power. As much as she hated this house, a hotel room didn't make all that much sense.

As he'd said she would be, Regina from the electric company was helpful—especially once Zoe dropped Chief McWhorter's name. The girl blushed profusely as Zoe provided identification. She paid the minimal sum remaining in arrears, then left. Afterward, Zoe swung by the grocery store, and then by the gas station to fill up her car. By the time she arrived back at the house, the power was already on.

In small towns people generally did what they said they would do, and, therefore, expecting the chief's son to swing by as his father said, Zoe made use of the remaining daylight hours, unpacking her car and placing everything in what used to be her father's office. Locking her car doors was becoming problematic, because she sometimes couldn't get the electric locks to work. Unfortunately, that was something else she would have to fix, but if there was a line for all things broken in her life, it was safe enough to say the car door locks would be last in line. However, leaving all her worldly possessions in an unlocked vehicle—the few things she'd seen fit to shove into her car while Chris was still at work—didn't seem prudent.

"I can't do it anymore," she'd told him two weeks ago, her voice soft, deflated, and resolute—more so than ever.

There was no surprise when he'd snagged the first thing he could reach to lob at her—a terra-cotta pot that had left pieces wedged in her forehead. She could still feel the shards at night, tiny razor-edged blades, and when she placed a finger to the healing spot, she thought she could feel them wriggling beneath her fingertip. Sometimes, while she lay in bed at night, she would press a finger against the wound just to feel the stab against her new flesh—a brutal reminder to harden her resolve.

"It'll leave a scar," the nurse had said, while stitching up the wound—this, after fishing out all the minute pieces of clay still embedded in her skin. He'd winked flirtatiously, but Zoe was sure it was an act of pity. "It adds character," he'd said, as Zoe lay still on the hospital bed, alone, because the man she'd lived with for more than eight years had refused to come in, worried more because Zoe might report him to the police.

His mom had stayed in the waiting room, because Zoe wouldn't allow her to come back, some part of her wanting both mother and son to worry a little about what she might do.

"I'm sorry," Chris said as he'd dropped her off at the emergency room door, his voice filled with worry. "I don't want to lose you, Zoe."

But it was his mother who'd helped Zoe out of the back seat of the car, pressing a blood-soaked kitchen rag to her forehead. Zoe had ignored Chris' rationalized apology. Stumbling out, she'd leaned against his mother for support, feeling woozy, while Chris had looked on, both hands firmly on the steering wheel, like a getaway driver in a heist.

"I'll wait," he'd said. When Zoe didn't respond with her undying gratitude, he'd added, "Should I expect a cop to come knocking on my window?"

Zoe had swallowed, saying nothing in response, unable to reassure him.

The truth of the matter was that a visit from the police was exactly what Chris deserved. But what bothered her most was that he still didn't know the first thing about her. She *still* wanted to believe the best of him—that, ultimately, he'd intended to miss, and that her head had simply gotten in the way. It was reasonable, after all—if you overlooked the dozens of other small *accidents* he had inflicted upon her. It had become an undeniable pattern, and still Zoe needed to prove something to him—that some people were worth loving. *That she was worth loving.*

But why did she need to be loved by someone who was so clearly incapable of it? Even more disturbing was this: she didn't love Chris either. She'd stayed with him because she was afraid of what would become of him after she left—because he was a bigger mess than she was. *When* she left, mind you, not *if she left.* Even as concerned as Zoe was about Chris's welfare, leaving was never in doubt. How screwed up was that?

One day, after he'd lost yet another job, Zoe had walked in on him, lying naked on their bed, with his gun—a Smith & Wesson, nickel-plated 9mm pistol—in his hand, resting precariously at the edge of the bed, as though he couldn't decide whether to lift it to his temple or shoot the first person who walked in through the door. "I should just do it and be done," he'd said brokenly.

Zoe had turned around and walked away, because she couldn't stay.

"That's right! Fucking leave," he'd shouted at her back. "You've always had one foot out the door anyway, Zoe. Just go!"

Some part of her had wanted to turn around, but she couldn't do it, because it reminded her of another time, a moment she had never shared with anyone, not even her brother, and especially not Chris.

Why?

She didn't know.

~

1990

ZOE WALKED out of the bathroom to find the house silent. Her mom was out grocery shopping. Nick was playing with his friends. Her father sat in his bedroom, alone. He must have heard some telltale sound Zoe made, because he knew it was her and called her by name.

"Zoe," her dad said, his tone stern, low. And sad. So achingly sad.

She froze, terrified by the tenor of his voice. Attention from her father rarely boded well, but his voice sounded particularly ominous today.

"Come here, Zoe."

Standing alone in the hallway, Zoe wanted to scream *no*. She wanted to yell for her mother. She wanted to race outside into the light of day, where secrets were impossible to keep. But she did none of those things. With a heart that beat too hard for her not-yet-mature breast, she slowly turned toward her parents' bedroom door, a portal to hell right there in their Middle American home, complete with glowing red light projected by the oversized orange lampshades, one on either side of the master bed.

Rob Rutherford was seated on the edge of his bed, made military style—the sheets folded into hospital corners, and then tucked under the mattress, all the way up to the head of the bed. In spite of the fact that he was seated on the bedspread, the covers were stretched so tight there wasn't a single crease. He was polishing his gun. It lay in pieces all shiny on the flowered spread. Her father said nothing as Zoe came to stand in the doorway, watching him pluck up sections of polished metal, one by one, to re-assemble his gun.

Zoe had no idea how long she stood there. She recognized a fathomless sadness in her dad's eyes, coupled with an inexplicable anger. She couldn't quite determine which of these things she was more afraid of—his anger that was so often directed toward her, or the broken man, who truly had no one responsible left to fix him.

That someone like her father—the tall, handsome, larger-than-life soldier he had once been—could snap like a twig beneath bare feet was inconceivable. That her mother, the gentle ally she had once seemed to be, could turn all her grief and loss into silence was implausible.

Zoe had little knowledge about guns back then. She had no idea what sort it was her father held in those hands that presumably had once changed her diapers. It was a handgun, that's all she knew—one with a barrel that looked large enough to a teen's wide, fearful eyes to shoot a cannonball through, like those big black iron balls that sat mounted in pyramids at Battery in Charleston; Civil War era projectiles that were monuments to hate and fear. The gun was a testament to these things too, but it was held by someone she'd once looked at through a child's innocent eyes. The broken soldier had once been her hero.

"Where's your mother?"

He already knew where her mom was.

Something about the look in his eyes gave Zoe pause. She knew to watch her mouth. He wanted her to smart off to him right now. In fact, he often baited her that way, because he wanted Nicky to hear his only remaining sister be the *smart-mouthed little bitch* he often referred to her as. He wanted her mom to see that he was well within the rights of his parental duties when disciplining Zoe. But this moment, they both understood Zoe would keep her mouth shut. They both knew she only ever took the bait whenever her mother was near.

Right now, there was no one around to save her. The house felt like that tomb her mom feared it would become.

Clear, sparkling liquid formed in her father's eyes. Zoe would have called them tears, but it didn't seem possible that he could be subject to these signs of human frailty.

More than that, Zoe didn't want to need to comfort him.

Once her dad's gun was fully reassembled, he looked up at her, water glistening in his eyes, and he said something entirely inconceivable. He said, "Do you know how easy it would be for me to pull the trigger, Zoe?"

Bam.

Zoe felt the question like a blow to her gut. She said nothing in response, but her head grew dizzy and her heart hurled itself into her throat, lodging there. Her pulse ticked throughout her face, until she could feel it clear into her jaw, even through her teeth.

She didn't dare move.

Daren't respond.

Even the notion of speaking made Zoe's heart pound harder.

"I should put both of us out of our misery," he said quietly, as though he were weighing options.

Zoe stared at him with a sense of horror, understanding that he meant every word—that he could do it. And just to prove it, he leveled the gun at her. That's when Zoe looked straight down the barrel. Her legs turned to jelly. Her palms began to sweat. Her throat grew thick with fear, as she stared down the barrel of her father's gun, and then she lifted her gaze to his sad, sad hazel eyes, wanting inexplicably to go to him, to comfort him, because it seemed to Zoe that her dad had never needed comfort more than he did in that instant.

But he had the gun.

One wrong move would see her brain matter splattered all over the wall behind her. She had no clue where her backbone came from—or even how the words escaped her tight throat. Despite feeling woozy, she let go of the threshold and said, devoid of emotion, "If you shoot me, Daddy, you'll have to shoot me in the back."

Daddy. She said it like a five-year-old child. *Daddy,* as though there could be love.

She waited a moment, praying there was something left of

the senior chief petty officer that would prevent him from plugging an innocent kid in the back—never mind that Zoe was his daughter. Her feet seemed glued to the floor, but she pulled one free and turned and walked away, slowly at first, and then, as she realized he wouldn't pull the trigger, she slid around the hall, out of his line of sight. She went straight back to her room, closing the door. Why she didn't leave the house, Zoe would never know, but she sat on her bed for who knew how long, listening to her father cry in his bedroom, half expecting to hear the boom of his gun go off, and thereafter walk inside to spy the mess he'd made.

Maybe that's why she stayed?

To clean up the mess.

Because that's what Zoe was most inclined to do.

~

Present

As promised, Chief McWhorter's son arrived with enough wood to board up the kitchen window. He took measurements for the glass and was finished with the job by the time the sun began to set. His name was Ethan. He was around Zoe's age, but unlike his dad, he didn't seem to notice Zoe was of the opposite sex.

Soft-spoken and matter-of-fact, with a gaze as direct as his father's, Ethan asked Zoe to show him to the broken window.

Zoe didn't bother with the hat in his presence, tossing it on the counter over by the kitchen sink. There she stood, watching him work, her gaze focusing on his hands. Big, masculine hands, a bit unkempt. Chris kept his nails neatly manicured. He'd probably had as many manicures in a single year as Zoe had had in her lifetime.

Ethan was halfway through with the window job before he said, "Mind if I ask ... how'd you get that?"

Even without checking to see the direction of his gaze, Zoe understood what he was referring to. The question hung in the air a long, uncomfortable moment, like guilty smoke before a quitting smoker, refusing to dissipate. Even though it was no longer visible to the naked eye, the scent of scorched tobacco crept into everyone's airspace.

Zoe met Ethan's gaze and found his blue eyes devoid of pity or judgment. He ran dirty fingers through his shoulder-length hair, brushing it out of his face.

Here and now, the truth seemed a bit less damning. "I wound up on the wrong side of a terra-cotta pot," she said, joking.

Ethan lifted a brow. He was sharp enough to read between the lines. "I hope you lobbed a bigger one back."

Zoe smiled wryly. "I was busy trying not to paint the ceiling red."

He visibly shuddered over the image she presented. "Damn," he said, but that was where he left it. He dropped the subject as he completed his task. "You don't remember me?" he asked after another long while.

Zoe squinted her eyes, as though somehow that effort might repaint his face as it was in his youth.

"Don't sweat it," he said, saving her from having to respond. "I was a few years behind you. Now, Hannah . . ." he trailed off, as though suddenly thinking better of whatever it was he was about to say.

And there it was, again, that disquieting silence—that sense of discomfort whenever Zoe's and Hannah's names were mentioned in tandem.

"Anyway," he said, changing the subject. "This should do ya." He gestured at the boarded up window. "I'll come by later this week to put in a new sheet of glass."

"How much?"

Now he gave her a wink, like his dad. "This one's on me, Zoe. Call it a housewarming gift, but if you go breaking any more windows, I'll have to charge y'all double."

His offer squeezed the breath from Zoe's lungs. Tears stung her eyes, closing her throat. Zoe shut them down. "Thank you. I . . . I appreciate it."

"No sweat," he said, and then he picked up his tools and left.

3

MEA CULPA

Notifications annoyed Zoe. She hated smartphones for that reason, all those tiny red circles with screeching little numbers: 488 unanswered emails, twenty-two Facebook notifications, all from strangers—zero for Twitter, because Zoe had unfollowed everyone—and seven voicemails. Every new ding chipped away at her nerves. When finally she clicked through them all, there were seven remaining blue dots next to Chris's name.

Zoe might have been better off erasing all seven messages, but there was something to be said for knowing what challenges lay ahead. The first started off with a bang: "Lying cunt—think you're so smart? Don't think I won't find you."

With approximately one minute and forty-three seconds remaining in Chris's message, Zoe jerked the phone away from her ear. She deleted the rest of the message without listening to it and then started to delete the remaining six. A little voice told her to keep them—in case she needed evidence. Judging by the time stamps, which were progressively shorter between each message, she knew the rest would be equally or increasingly angry and abusive. If something should happen to her, she wanted the police to hear Chris's threats in his own words.

Eight years she'd spent with that man, every day of those eight years a trial, and yet Zoe had stayed. This was the impetus for everything now: discovering why she felt such a need to punish herself on a daily basis. Considering the fact that she was already daydreaming about exit plans three months into their relationship, the question was: *Why?*

Why didn't she leave? Why did she stay? Why? Why? Why?

The air was charged with anticipation—not the good kind. Something bad was hanging around, something dark. If she did everything exactly right, she might inch past and manage to escape.

Zoe had no choice but to leave him. She and Chris were headed toward disaster. If the gash on her forehead wasn't proof enough, that nagging feeling her Gullah grandmother would call "a knowing" simply wouldn't go away. Even now, it clung to her nerves like the yellow film on her mother's curtains.

With trembling hands, Zoe set the phone down on the old Formica counter, turning to survey her mother's kitchen. The trash was all gone now; you could see the old white-and-gold checkered tiles. By itself, the floor wasn't distasteful, but coupled with all the yellow appliances and the mustard-yellow walls it was vintage at its worst.

She could still envision her mom standing over the sink—Marge washing dishes with that look of utter distraction upon her face. There were burn marks at the edge of the old enamel, where her cigarettes had loitered, waiting for a puff—the same as her kids, except that none of her children had the added allure of all the five hundred ninety-nine potentially addictive substances in a single cigarette.

The house had never had a dishwasher, despite the kitchen having ample space, and Zoe was aggrieved to admit that, as a teenager, it had never once occurred to her to step up and take her turn at the sink. Somehow, Marge had seemed to belong there.

Only looking back at it now, Zoe was horrified to admit that she had cast her own mother into cheap gender roles—never mind that Marge had forged those casts herself. Still in this respect, Zoe hadn't been any better than her father, whose time at home was generally spent holed up in his office. Zoe always had the distinct impression he'd resented being in his own home.

It was only later she'd understood why.

A white farm-style table used to sit against the far wall, with five chairs surrounding it. The sixth chair sat before her father's desk in his office.

"Who wants to face an empty chair at dinner?" he'd asked the day he took the extra chair away, much to her mother's dismay.

"Oh, Rob! Where will guests sit?"

Even then, before Hannah went missing, the tenor of her father's voice had been full of rancor. "Since when do we invite guests to dinner, Marge?" *Dinner.* Her father got it right.

Blinking, Marge had dried her ever-wet hands with the sunflower yellow dishtowel and said plaintively, "The children have friends."

"Yeah? So when's the last time they invited one over?"

Her father had been right, of course. Not even gregarious Hannah had ever invited anyone to eat with them. Most of Zoe's friends used to hang up the instant her dad answered the phone.

That day before dinner, the chair he'd carried away had belonged to Nana. After her sister disappeared, another chair vanished. Only this time, her dad took that one out back and put an axe to it, chopping it to splinters while holding back tears he'd refused to shed.

As Zoe watched him destroy the chair from the safety of her bedroom window, it occurred to her then that her dad had loved Hannah in a way he wasn't capable of loving Zoe. Hannah had been his favorite—more so than his only son, whom he'd crowed about, but treated more like a trophy than a flesh-and-blood child. Zoe wondered if that was because Zoe loved Nicky best.

Her feelings for her sister had been equally maternal, given that Zoe was the eldest child, but they had been tainted with something else . . . something Zoe didn't want to explore. Considering the job ahead, she studied the kitchen.

The old refrigerator used to be gold as well. Now there was a smallish white one in its place and judging by the angle at which it sat, either the floor was sagging or the screw-in legs were off kilter. It was more than likely the legs, because the floor was only about thirty years old. Tomorrow would be soon enough to crack open the fridge to see what lay in store. There might be a science project in there and there was only so much shriveled up food matter Zoe could deal with in a twenty-four-hour period.

At her back, on the counter, the cell phone rang again. Shoving off the counter, she made her way into the living room, without bothering to check the caller ID. If *he* wanted to play hide 'n seek, she didn't intend to give him the first clue.

"You can't find me!" a child's voice sang from Zoe's past.

Barely perceptible, after years of mental erosion, her sister's ghost sat huddled behind the living room door.

The screen door had been closed and locked, possibly to keep two-year-old Nicky from wandering outside. The heavy white door was left ajar to lure in a sweet ocean breeze. This was before they'd built the screened-in front porch.

Hannah's skinny body had scarcely fit behind the door so that the door remained halfway shut, or halfway open, however you chose to view it. An orchestral rendition of the Beatles "The Fool on the Hill" had drifted out from under the closed door of her father's office down the hall.

"Na, na, na," Hannah had called out, giggling.

At four years old, her sister giggled all the time. That particular moment she could barely contain her glee. Her pudgy fingers had protruded through the doorjamb and Zoe's first thought had been that her sister was bound to get her fingers pinched. Unfortunately, Hannah's responses to her big sister's cautions had been all too often ignored, despite Zoe being two years her senior.

Zoe never meant to hurt her sister.

Purposefully, she'd moved toward the door, closing it gently, barely enough to put pressure on Hannah's fingers— so that she might figure it out on her own. She shouldn't put her fingers into doorjambs. But just at that instant, Nick had come wobbling around the corner, tripping past the curio table, crashing into Zoe. As one of her mother's vases dove to the floor, the door had closed on Hannah's fingers. The sound of breaking glass had accompanied her sister's shriek of pain. Zoe had hurled the door open, too late to save the tip of Hannah's index finger. It was lopped off, her hand bloodied.

Their father had stormed out of his office to investigate. Marge had rushed out of the kitchen, dishtowel in hand. At the sight of so much blood, her mother had screamed along with Hannah. Back in her father's office, the same orchestra had switched to a frenzied version of "A Hard Day's Night."

"Zoe did it!" Hannah had shrieked. "Zoe did it!"

A noxious cloud of guilt had descended over Zoe.

She hadn't meant to hurt Hannah. Her dad yelled, "What the hell were you thinking, Zoe?"

Zoe had stood with shoulders tensed, watching her mother wrap Hannah's hand in the dirty dishcloth, mulling over her father's question: *What the hell were you thinking, Zoe?*

Hannah had continued to wail, "Zoe did it on purpose!"

Some part of Zoe had wondered if in fact she had. Even at six, she must have known how it would turn out?

Their father had swept Hannah into his arms. "I'll take her," he'd said tightly.

To the hospital, he'd meant. They would have to go all the

way to St. Francis, across the Cooper River Bridge, because there wasn't anything closer.

He'd eyed Zoe with cold eyes; it was the first time he'd ever looked at her that way. Before that, Zoe had often spied something bitter behind his gaze, but he'd always shuttered it quickly, the look in his eyes shifting to something more like apathy.

The entire time her father was gone, her mother sat numbly on the couch, wringing bloodstained hands, while, at the artless age of six, Zoe had attempted to decrypt her own motives. In the end, all she could remember was that terrible sense of guilt, coupled with worry over her baby sister's mangled hand. That was her first taste of how one misguided action could end with frightening permanency.

Many years later, after Gabi Donovan's accusation, Zoe's father brought up that incident with the door. "She's always resented Hannah," he'd told her mother. "Remember the door? For all we know, she did it, like Gabi said."

They'd whispered in their bedroom, behind closed doors, but Zoe had heard their words, filtering up through the vents in her room.

"How can you say that, Rob? She's your daughter."

Her mother's question had been punctuated by a sharp silence.

"So was Hannah."

"I don't believe any word of it."

"Yeah, well, get it through your thick skull, Marge. She's never coming home."

Silence for another interminable moment, and then her mother had begun again. "You act like you know what happened." There had been a trace of accusation in her voice, a hint of something, and then Zoe heard a sound she would come to recognize only too well, although nevermore perpetrated upon her mother.

Thereafter, Robert Rutherford's anger had been diverted

toward his eldest child.

Shrugging off the memory, Zoe moved across the living room to the window.

The house was deserted but, like hidden data on a reformatted computer, memories crowded every inch. Even standing inside the house, she could smell the brine in the air.

Outside, a wind gust fluttered the oaks. The fronds on the slender palmetto across the street danced frenetically against an inky sky, like bicycle streamers. Her Nana's rocker on the front porch pushed into a gentle rocking motion, as though still occupied.

Atlantic Street was a last bastion before the ocean's end, a line drawn in the sand to keep the tide at bay. But those who lived here understood it was laid down with a prayer. One mean tidal backhand would see it all crashing into the sea, every last brick and grain of sand. No manmade barricade could withstand nature's wrath. They were merely obstacles, not unlike a hand lifted to shield your face.

Out on Folly, across the harbor, down a ways, a washed-out strip of beachfront remained to remind folks of this truth. If you took to the air, you could see footprints of old houses that once stood erect and proud, but now were nothing more than manufactured shapes drowned beneath tumbling waters. The wood that once covered these timber skeletons was now little more than driftwood, forever afloat. Or riddled with wormholes, lying prayerfully upon a bed of oily sand. And still more houses went up—like the one across the street. And men, like Neanderthals, beat their chests, blithely mounting surfboards to cruise the salted streets.

It was on an evening like this Zoe had spent her first night without Hannah.

That night, each sound had sent her scurrying to the bedroom window. She didn't sleep at all, and in the morning, despite a soul-sucking weariness, had opened her eyes, hoping to spy her sister's dirty blond hair nestled against the Berenstain Bears sheets she couldn't see fit to outgrow. Zoe recalled staring at that empty bed with a feeling not unlike the one plaguing her now, and despite the early hour, it was probably in that instant Zoe had first realized with perfect lucidity that her sister was never coming home.

She'd understood it the way she now understood Chris's threats were not idle . . .

Clutching the living room curtains with white-knuckled fists, she whispered, "Hannah . . . where are you?"

In a shallow grave?

Lying somewhere beneath shifting sands?

Listening to the pulse of the sea?

The only one thing she knew for certain was that Zoe *did not* kill her sister, no matter what Gabi Donovan had said—no matter what her father had wanted to believe.

But she *was* guilty.

Guilty because, as with that morning when she'd pinched Hannah's fingers in the doorjamb, there were times she wished her sister had never been born.

Not dead.

There was a difference.

Dark feelings rushed up unexpectedly from uncharted places in her soul, and although Zoe might deny it to everyone else . . . she could never lie to herself.

Her sister had been a ray of sunshine from the instant she was born—hadn't everyone said so? Whatever guilt she bore was only compounded by the knowledge that Hannah hadn't deserved Zoe's enmity any more than she'd deserved whatever fate had allotted her.

A therapist once told her that she would never stop sabotaging herself until she found a way to come to terms with the guilt she harbored over her sister—not merely Hannah's death, but the hidden anger Zoe felt over her sister's very existence.

That was the first time anyone had ever called her out on those feelings—feelings Zoe couldn't acknowledge even to the watcher in her head.

She'd fired the therapist, of course, insisting she loved her sister, and therefore the therapist's assertions must be bullshit. And yet Robert Rutherford had been living proof that ambivalence was not only possible between sentient beings, it was as real as the warm glass in front of her nose.

Pressing her forehead against the window, Zoe watched her breath cloud the glass and wondered idly where she should sleep.

Her parents' bedroom was the most obvious place. There was a small, private bathroom back there. She couldn't stomach the thought of sleeping in the bedroom she'd once shared with Hannah, but Nick's room was the farthest from the bathrooms. It was silly to consider that small, cramped bedroom, simply to avoid the other two.

Was it any wonder it had taken her so many years to return to the house?

Here, there was little she could do to escape the past. Memories rushed at her like linebackers, ready to plow her into the ground. Releasing her death grip on the curtains, Zoe went after the blankets in the spare room.

THE FOLLOWING MORNING, an airless Tuesday, Zoe woke with an unexpected sense of purpose. Now that she was back on the island, it seemed appropriate to pursue not simply answers, but all new questions. Her life was a mess—then and now. She suspected the house and all things surrounding it were at the core. It was pointless to deny as much, considering that she couldn't point to one healthy relationship in all her life, not even the one she shared with her brother.

Chris had never been her confidante, not even in the beginning. He was more a child to be cared for, which was hideously dysfunctional, considering that the only thing worth anything in that relationship was the sex, and even that wasn't particularly wholesome. Zoe hated to think about the boundaries she'd crossed during their on-again, off-again relationship.

The first task after waking: she tackled the refrigerator, emptying it, washing it down, inside and out. To her way of thinking, the fridge was the first order of business, from which all other tasks flowed.

Of course, she couldn't function on fast food, so a trip to the grocery store was in order, and then the hardware store, because she couldn't just show up the first day back on the island and knock on her neighbor's door, asking to borrow a hammer and nails.

During the course of the morning, Zoe's cell phone rang overbearingly, so she abandoned it in the car at each of her destinations. By the time she arrived home again, it was after 3:00 p.m.

After stocking the clean fridge, she spent about thirty minutes wiping down counters, doorknobs, faucets, and then, afterward, she mopped the kitchen floor. Her mother had said a dirty kitchen was a sure sign of mental illness and/or bad parenting.

Marge must certainly have known. She'd had both those areas covered, except that her kitchen was meticulous up until the end.

Memories of her mother were no longer pleasant, Zoe acknowledged. They were too often fraught with grief and pain. Still, she had to give her mother this: instead of using her kids as crutches, she'd found her solace in pills. In the end, those pills destroyed her liver.

Pushing thoughts of her mother, father and Chris out of her head, Zoe kept busy cleaning the house, down to, and including all the dirty, dark corners and the tops of the windowsills.

Down at the baseboards, she thought she detected a hint of

pluff mud, even after all these years. The sulfurous scent of
Charleston's swamp mud was distinct and unsettling. If you were
unused to the smell, it was enough to pucker the nose. It stank of
death and decay. Thanks to Nana's Gullah stories, there was a
time Zoe had attributed a far more sinister meaning to that
sulfurous scent.

Sometimes—especially as a child—she'd suffered night
terrors—dreams that played stubbornly, even after her eyes were
wide open. Zoe learned to control them, a bit like counting sheep.
As shadows in the room played havoc with her imagination, she
corralled her dreams, playing out the scenes in her head.

But worse than the dreams was the occasional sleep paralysis
—a transitional state between wakefulness and sleep, where
Zoe's limbs felt paralyzed. It didn't happen often but in those
moments she understood she was asleep. She could see the room
as it was, as though she were wide awake. Still always, beyond her
peripheral, there was a dark figure lurking and Zoe couldn't get
away. She couldn't scream. Couldn't move.

One morning before school, when her head wouldn't come
off the breakfast table, her Nana had asked, "What's the matter,
chil'? Ere the Boo Hag ridin' ya?"

Her dad had complained, "Mama, don't fill her head with
nonsense."

"What nonsense, Robbie?" Nana shooed her son out of the
kitchen. "You get on out now an' let me speak wit' my grandchil'
all alone."

Once he was gone, her grandmother had placed Zoe's first
cup of coffee in front of her on the kitchen table, and said, "It's all
true, chil'. Don't you pay yo' daddy no mind. It would do him a
lotta good to realize this heah ain't all there is. You understand
what I'm sayin', chil'?"

Zoe hadn't, but Nana was quick to explain. According to the
Gullah, she'd said, folks had a soul and a spirit. Souls left the
body at the time of death. If it was a good soul, it went to Heaven.

But a person's spirit was a different thing. The spirit stayed behind to watch over loved ones. If it was a bad spirit, this was called a Boo Hag, or maybe sometimes a slip-skin hag.

Boo Hags were undead creatures that fed off the energy of the living. During the day, they stole peoples' skins, wore them about like clothes. At night, they shed their disguises and went in search of new victims to ride. They didn't just belong to the Gullah culture; in other circles they were known as vampires or succubi.

"They's wicked little sneaks," Nana had said. "Get all up into y'all's house through cracks beneath the door, and once inside, they sit on you and steal away your breath whilst you sleep. And that's God's truth."

To Zoe, the very idea of this was more terrifying than any dream she might have conjured on her own, but Nana had been quick to reassure her, "Don't worry, chil', you'll know when they are near. The air gets all muggy an' begins to stink."

Never mind that it was *always* muggy in Charleston and they were literally surrounded by the ripe scent of swamp mud. So by Nana's own description, there must always be a Boo Hag running around. Clearly, Nana had thought so too. To keep those spirits at bay, the tops of Kingdom's windows had all been painted "haint" blue—like the porch. Tiny bowls of sea salt had been placed in every room of the house, because, of course, a salted hag couldn't return to her true self. Why this was so, Zoe didn't know, but she guessed it must be related to tossing salt over your shoulder to ward away bad luck.

But also, in Hoodoo folk magic, water and sky were considered crossroads between heaven and earth, and therefore barriers between the living and the dead. In the South, this was the reasoning behind the "haint blue" ceilings of Island porches. Painted a soft blue-green that mimicked the color of the sea, it kept spirits from crossing the threshold into the home. This was still done today, even if only because your mother and grandmother did it too.

As long as Zoe's Nana lived, no one had ever touched those salt bowls. Only Nana ever knew what to do with them, if anything at all. Presumably, you might grab a fistful of salt and toss it at the Boo Hag to get her off your chest, but it could also be that the salt's presence alone was like stringing garlic over your bed to ward away vampires.

After Nana died, the salt bowls all disappeared. The little blue dishes thereafter had been relegated to the cupboard in the kitchen, to be used on occasion for dips or sauces. However, the blue tops of the sills remained, except that now they were so faded by the sun they too appeared gray.

Much later, Zoe learned the ever-present scent of pluff mud was due to bacteria and decomposing organic matter in the muggy Southern climate. And the sleep paralysis was a result of disrupted REM sleep, where muscle paralysis is induced by the brain to prevent sleepers from acting out dreams and sleepwalking. It was a common occurrence and during this time the brain often kicked in a defensive reflex to warn of potential dangers, thus manifesting a lurking terror. Sleep paralysis was linked to disorders like narcolepsy, migraines, anxiety, and sleep apnea. Zoe suffered two of the four.

Thankfully, her night terrors were mostly gone now

There was nothing to fear here, she reassured herself; it was safer than the place she'd left. Pausing in her cleaning, Zoe pressed a finger to her scar, searching for the tiny hard lump.

ON THURSDAY, Ethan McWhorter arrived with a sheet of glass, ready to install. Zoe left him inside to work and took a broom outside to sweep off the front porch. From there, she swept down the steps, all the way down the brick sidewalk her father once laid.

Finding it intolerable to sweep over stubborn tendrils of

beach grass, she sank to her knees to yank out the straw-like sod. It was easier to keep busy rather than deal with her unsettling thoughts or worry about Chris's threats.

She kept envisioning him on his way down from Baltimore, cursing her the entire way. By the time he got to Charleston he'd be fit to be tied.

What would she do if he showed up? What would he do? Would he knock politely—like a stranger—on her parents' door? Or would he burst in, surprising Zoe in her bed?

Anything was possible.

Next door, her lanky neighbor emerged from his nondescript house and moved toward his car, his limp a little less pronounced than before. He looked over at Zoe, and Zoe waved, though once again he turned his head and Zoe frowned.

Annoyed that he would snub her friendly gesture—a gesture that didn't come easily for Zoe—she tugged at the grass between the bricks with renewed vigor.

He had that long Donovan face and aquiline nose. What did she expect? As a rule, except for Blabby Gabi, the Donovans had all kept to themselves. Both her parents had groused plenty over their neighbors' peculiarities and it was Zoe's father who'd planted the row of sweet myrtles to block the Donovan house from view. Native to the area, hardy as they were, he'd known they would provide a natural barrier so he wouldn't have to see "that old coot next door."

The sweet myrtle bushes: that would be Zoe's next task, unless she wanted to spend the money to hire landscapers, but that wasn't necessary. Here, so near the beach, there wasn't much of a lawn to be manicured. If it weren't for the gnarly bushes, she wouldn't even bother but, as it was, the house had zero curb appeal.

Next door, the silver Camry quietly pulled away and Zoe returned her attention to the bricks, clearing away the prickly beach grass.

Ethan emerged from her house. "You're gonna get blistered out here. Sun's hotter than you think."

He stood on her front porch, like a golden surfer god. He had *that look* going on, with the messy blond hair and ocean blue eyes. His deep blue and gold shorts could easily be mistaken for a bathing suit, and his faded baby-blue T-shirt was blanched from the sun or maybe too much bleach. Could be either one. The open-toed sandals made a distinct devil-may-care statement but were highly impractical for a guy installing glass. If he happened to drop a sheet on his foot, he'd have a few less toes, and what might that do for his balance on the surfboard?

Zoe eyed the sandals as he came down the steps. She was more than well-acquainted with the island weather. She didn't need him to look after her. Maybe he ought to consider his own self before throwing around advice. She rose to her feet, dusting sand off her hands. "All done?"

He nodded. "Yep. All done." A fine sheen of perspiration was visible on his brow as he whisked off his hat.

Zoe left hers on. "How much do I owe you?"

He looked back at the house as though he could see through her walls into the kitchen. "Well . . . I used an odd piece of glass I had on hand, so we'll call it good at twenty . . . if that works for you, Ms. Rutherford?"

Despite the queasiness it gave her to hear herself referred to in the same manner her mother was once addressed, Zoe smiled and nodded. "Suits me fine," she said and started toward the house to grab her purse.

He followed behind. "So . . . how long y'all plannin' to stay?"

Zoe shrugged. "Long as it takes."

"I was only wondering 'cause, well, you don't have a stitch of furniture up in there. I've got an extra bed, if you need it. Comes with a mattress, gently used."

On the top step, Zoe turned to face him, her hands going to her hips. "How much?"

He looked up at her, hat in hand, snapping it against his leg. "No charge. It belonged to my ex-roommate. He left the thing when he got married. It's just in the way."

Zoe searched his face, half expecting him to make some lecherous joke in reference to her potential payment, but he seemed so sincere.

He shrugged. "Figure it's the right neighborly thing to do," he said, in case she doubted his integrity.

Zoe wasn't hurting for money, but she wasn't in a position to spend frivolously. While a new bed and mattress might not be entirely useless, the thought of spending any money for one to be used here, in this house, seemed a total waste. Eventually, she would have to move it all back out. However, sleeping on a wood floor, even with pillows and a blanket, wasn't all that appealing. "If you're sure you don't need it, I could use it."

He grinned like a teenage boy. "It's all yours," he said, and Zoe thanked him, ducking inside to find her purse to pay him for the glass. A little belatedly, she realized she'd left her purse in the kitchen all the while he was working on the window. Eying his handiwork, she fished out her wallet, opening it to look inside. Her cash was untouched.

Zoe's gaze returned to the window. The job was well done, and as large as the sheet of glass was, she doubted he'd used some odd piece for the repair. Everyone had ulterior motives, she assured herself. She just didn't know what Ethan McWhorter's were as yet, but whatever they might be, there certainly wasn't any harm in borrowing his bed. If he wanted to charge her less for a job because she had breasts, well, that was entirely his problem.

Zoe returned to the front porch stoop to find Ethan waiting where she left him. She handed him a twenty and a ten, with the bills folded over.

He didn't bother to count the money, shoving the bills into his front pocket, unaware that she'd given him more. "I'll be back in two shakes," he said. "It's not far. Just over a ways in old Mt. Pleasant."

Zoe's brows lifted. "That's *right* neighborly," she teased. "Considering that we're not exactly neighbors."

"Yeah, well, I was born down the street." His hands went to his hips, as though waiting for Zoe's next volley.

She didn't have a clue why she was firing off warning shots, except that Ethan McWhorter gave her a nervous feeling in the pit of her gut. "You mean literally? You were born down the street?" He'd made it sound as though he were Hannah's age, and she knew for a fact there were no hospitals in the area back then.

"Yep, literally, 1979. Mom's water broke out on the beach. By the time they carried her back, got her to the car, I was already on the way. She said I was an impatient little dude, but I don't think it's true anymore." His lip curved slightly at one side. "Anyway, if you want to get technical about it, we can call it a gesture of goodwill to a past and future neighbor?"

Zoe smirked. "With one small hitch."

"What's that?"

"I don't intend to stay."

There was something in the way his eyes scanned the property that told Zoe he didn't view this piece of land the same way she did. "That's too bad," he said after a moment, but he couldn't begin to fathom the extent of Zoe's loss.

"Anyway, I do appreciate it," Zoe said, taking a step down as he turned to go, startled by the unanticipated impulse to ask him to wait.

"I'll be back," he promised.

"Yeah, all right," she said, and stood on the front porch step, watching him slide into his truck, trying to decode the feeling of relief she felt over the simple knowledge that he meant to return.

4

THIRTY YEARS

How many DNA samples were present in bathroom grout after nine and a half years as a rental property? There was no telling how many folks, or what sort of body fluids were spilled over these floors during the years Zoe was gone.

As intensely as she loathed the idea of bleach, it served a purpose, and she was beginning to share her dad's disenchantment with carpet. Bleach was not possible in the living room, not without leaving the carpet looking like a bad dye job on an old lady. Unfortunately, nothing short of ripping it out and replacing it would remove the odors that had seeped down into the thirty-year-old pad. Apparently, as much as her father had disliked carpet, he'd loathed, far more, the parting of green from his wallet, because it was the same dirty-gold carpet her mother had installed after the deluge of Hurricane Hugo.

With fingers that were raw, Zoe assaulted the troll-hair material with an industrial-grade carpet cleaner, hoping for the best. In the end, she had a semi-clean carpet, and a house that smelled overall of industrial waste, the scent so tenacious it permeated her hair and clothes.

By the end of the week, seven contractor bags filled with

assorted trash sat on the front curb, not-so-pretty maids all in a row. Perhaps it wasn't so many as she thought, considering the number of fat bags of designer clothing she'd left for Chris to donate, but too many when you considered that the house was supposed to be empty, and all the trash in the bags had been left by trespassers. Cigarette butts, beer cans, a pair of bloodstained underwear, enough semen-filled condoms to impregnate a powderpuff football team, an old T-shirt, also stained, and sundry items that had been discarded in the interim since the management company had abandoned their contract.

By Saturday the house was habitable, if not entirely presentable. From thereon, it would be a painstaking effort toward further improvement, beginning with the daunting task of repairing the front steps—daunting only because Zoe didn't have a clue how to begin. The only thing she'd ever used a drill on was a jar of grapefruit juice—one of those stubborn screw-on caps that wouldn't come off, no matter how much she banged it on the counter, or how hard she torqued it. Determined not to be thwarted from her morning glass of juice she'd retrieved a dusty electric screwdriver from the garage and drilled a hole in the top of the metal cap. She was pretty certain she ingested a little aluminum with her juice, but at least she'd gotten her vitamin C that morning.

Living with Chris had barely changed her circumstances. For all intents and purposes Zoe had lived alone, fending for herself, and it often became painfully apparent how woefully unprepared she had been for that.

Among the things her parents taught her were: how to keep out of sight—an utterly useless task if two people were expected to end up in the same bed at the end of the day; how to gap spark plugs; and the practical application of Bondo.

Her father had taught her the latter two skills, after purchasing a beat-up Pinto for Zoe to drive to work. The lesson on spark plugs had likely been an honest attempt by her dad to resuscitate his parenting skills. He'd believed one should work for everything one had, and that included her beat-up car, despite it hanging together on rusted bolts. To Rob Rutherford's credit, he did purchase the car for her, although it had cost him less than a month's worth of beer money. Later, once Zoe discovered the car's neat little design flaw—a rear-seated gas tank, positioned between the rear bumper and axle—she secretly believed her dad had been trying to kill her. That seemed to be an ongoing theme with the men in her life.

A mental image of Chris cornering her in the dining room wheedled its way into her thoughts.

THEY WERE BOTH DRINKING. Zoe couldn't remember how it began. By the time they were finished shouting at each other, she was wedged in the corner of the second floor dining room, her back against the ledge of the half-wall that lay between her and the stairs, Chris faced her on the opposite side of the table. Made of wicker, the table had a glass tabletop. He could easily tell which way her feet were pointed, even if her body language feinted in the opposite direction.

"You think I'm stupid, Zoe?"

The look in his eyes was confused—the same look her dad had the morning with his gun. The only way out was over the ledge, across the stairwell, and into the living room, one flight down. The stairwell itself, nestled between the two rooms, led down to the garage, two stories below. Zoe sobered at once. "No, Chris. Calm down."

"Fucking bitch," he said, teetering toward anger. She never knew what to say in these moments, and once it got to this level, her unfaltering calm was like a slap to his face. On some level, he must realize he wasn't being rational, but it only served to anger him all the more. Yelling wasn't the answer either. Both paths led to the same place. Chris swept chairs aside and Zoe clambered onto the ledge, with barely enough time to push off the edge. Powered by fear, she propelled herself across the narrow stairwell, toward the couch on the other side of the dividing wall.

Her leg rammed the ledge of the half-wall on the other side. Pain shot through her thigh. Bouncing over the wall, she spilled onto the leather couch eight feet below, then onto the floor, narrowly missing the coffee table on the way down.

Blinded with pain, Zoe lay clutching her leg as Chris scurried down the stairs. When she opened her eyes he was hovering over her, brushing hair away from her face.

"God damn. Are you fucking crazy, Zoe? What the hell were you thinking?" Her father's voice came out of Chris's mouth.

Zoe couldn't speak. Her leg was bruised to the bone, blood already seeping into the tissue surrounding the injury, so that the muscle atrophied for months after, leaving a noticeable dent in her thigh that was visible even through her clothes.

He kissed her on the cheek, half stroking, half pulling her hair. "Why you gotta piss me off so much?"

Zoe's throat closed, obstructing the flow of words. Tears clouded her vision as Chris scooped her up into his arms, pulling himself to his feet. "Don't worry, baby, I'll take care of you," he said and then dumped her into their bed, crawling in beside her. Zoe cried herself to sleep.

ZOE STOOD STARING at the front porch steps, wondering where to begin. Considering that there were only nine steps leading up to the porch, it didn't appear all that insurmountable, but this was not among the skillset she had cultivated from her parents.

Of course, she'd learned other skills throughout her lifetime, and no doubt her parents were often directly or indirectly responsible for her continued education, but mostly Zoe learned her lessons the hard way.

Like the time she'd tried to wallpaper the kitchen, barefoot, on wet floors—wet because she'd been submersing the wallpaper into a trough and slopping water everywhere. With sticky water dripping from her toes, she'd stood on a metal ladder and tried to cut out an outlet hole with a steel-handled knife. Smart, right? The zap she received had sent sparks clear through her toenails. And that lesson was particularly inexcusable, having been born the daughter of an electrician. However, considering that not even Nicky had learned these lessons under their father's tutelage, Zoe's near electrocution should be perfectly comprehensible.

As for the lessons Zoe had learned from her mother, these comprised crucial values, not the least of which included honesty, kindness, and compassion. But while Marge had been all these things and more, she couldn't quite be considered loving. Her mother would never have shared a diagnosis with her children, nor was it certain she ever received one, but she had most likely been clinically depressed.

But one lesson Zoe did learn from Marge, and she'd learned it well: a woman needed a career, and here Zoe excelled. There was no way she'd ever allow herself to become so dependent on a man that she didn't have choices.

Zoe was good at what she did—so good that she never needed to take a job she didn't want. But her marketing skills weren't going to help her fix the front porch steps. Lucky for her, she had two good hands and she knew how to wield a hammer and how to use nails. And since, contrary to popular belief that Southerners were nosy neighbors, no one around seemed to be paying much attention to anyone else, her foibles should be safe enough from prying eyes.

Even her next-door neighbor was blind to her presence. Every time he appeared, Zoe waved at the man as he marched forth, with blinders on, limping to and from his car. For sure, he was a Donovan, she decided—a fact that, once noted, nearly derailed her already faltering architectural inclinations. If you weighed both on a scale—the need for new stairs vs. the need to learn what happened that day in December—the stairs would lose every time.

So that following Monday, perhaps still avoiding the front porch steps, Zoe decided to pay a visit to Chief McWhorter.

Little more than a stone's throw away on Middle Street, the police station sat behind a brand-new fire station that had been built sometime after Zoe quit the island. Not as fortunate as their fire-fighting brethren, the police station was nestled at the far end of a small cluster of short, beige trailers. Inside, Zoe found Chief McWhorter nursing a cup of black coffee, poring over paperwork at his desk, although according to his secretary, he was "on his way out the door."

"It's all right, Patty," he said, waving Zoe into his office.

The woman—Patty—gave Zoe one of those looks—not so much one of irritation as one of wariness. They were about the same age. It was possible she recognized Zoe, but she didn't look all that familiar.

Chief McWhorter's office was tiny. The blinds on the windows were open to the parking lot. Outside, across the gravel drive, there was a clear view of the Mound—the mysterious vine-covered remnants of gun batteries Butler and Capron, where Zoe and the rest of the neighborhood kids used to slide down on cardboard boxes into the bamboo groves below, until Nicky nearly took an eye out on a shaft of broken bamboo.

Beneath the Mound lay a maze of spidery tunnels that had been sealed off during the nineties.

Chief McWhorter looked at her expectantly.

"Hey," Zoe began, "I wanted to thank you." She held her purse in front of her like a shield. The fact that it bore a designer label was purely accidental. She'd bought it at an outlet, unwilling to spend much for a receptacle to hold ChapStick and leaky pens. "Ethan's been great," she said. "He fixed my window and donated a bed." She smiled nervously, unconsciously lifting a hand to the brim of her hat. "I think maybe he took some pity on me."

The chief scratched the back of his head with a long finger. He screwed his face a bit. "I'd be willing to wager he didn't do it for pity's sake, Ms. Rutherford." Still his gaze returned to Zoe's hat, and once again, he was at a vantage to spy what lay beneath the bill. Zoe's scar began to itch obnoxiously. Ignoring it, she eyed the brown folding metal chair in front of Chief McWhorter's desk.

"Please, sit," he offered. "What can I do for you?"

Her brain jamming with questions, Zoe slid into the metal seat, tucking her purse into her lap, resisting the urge to shimmy the cap down to relieve the itching once she was there. She sucked in a breath before speaking. "Chief McWhorter . . . I know . . . Well, I know you know . . ."

She peered down at his desk, more than uncomfortable suddenly and read the upside-down headline on the paper positioned on his desk: SEARCH FOR MISSING WOMEN INTENSIFIES. She blinked, thinking irrationally about Hannah.

"Well, I know you know what happened . . . back then."

His gaze followed hers to the paper and then returned to Zoe's face, steadily assessing her. "I know a few things, Ms. Rutherford, but I presume you mean the business with your sister?"

Zoe nodded, the back of her neck growing warm.

Chief McWhorter sat back in his chair, bringing his coffee cup to his lips with a daintiness that was incongruous with his sturdy build. "You know I didn't handle that case," he said, on the off chance she didn't remember. "Chief Hale was in charge at the time."

Zoe nodded.

"But I know."

Zoe nodded again.

"It's pretty near impossible to keep things quiet in a small town, Ms. Rutherford, much less a department the size of this. It's not every day folks go missing."

Zoe's gaze shifted to the paper on his desk.

Technically, it wasn't true, evidenced by the headline splashed across the page. To date, there were two new missing-persons cases. No one knew where the girls had gone. And this much Zoe knew, from her own digging: every forty seconds, a child went missing, more than eight hundred thousand kids every year, eight million worldwide. The simple fact that it had been thirty years since Sullivan's Island had become a pinpoint on the missing children's map was probably more good luck than bad—unless your name happened to be Rutherford.

Several years ago, Zoe felt compelled to check public databases. There were a few available to the public, but mostly used by law enforcement, medical examiners' and coroners' offices. Originally, her sister's name was not on any of those lists, until Zoe submitted it.

Anyone could submit a name at any time. The files were retained indefinitely, until the individual was either located or the record was canceled. Each year, like clockwork, Zoe got an email from NamUs, asking her to sign in and renew her account. At this point, she was pretty sure her sister's bones would never be found.

Outside the office, the phone rang. The receptionist intercepted it. Zoe heard Patty speaking quietly. "Well, he's got someone in his office right now," she said, and then laughed low. "Alrighty then, no worries, I'll put you through." She forwarded the call. The phone on Chief McWhorter's lit up, but he ignored it, letting it go to voicemail.

As he sipped his coffee, he remained silent, studying Zoe. "You spent some time with Amy Lowndes, didn't you?"

It wasn't an accusation, but there was a hint of something in his voice.

After Gabi's accusation, Zoe spent six months with a therapist, who'd tried her damnedest to determine whether Zoe was suppressing memories. In the end, Amy Lowndes had decided Zoe was telling the truth, but her stint with a therapist was enough to cast a long shadow of doubt over Zoe's character.

Even worse, the entire ordeal had cast a veil of uncertainty over Zoe's memories, making Zoe question every impression she harbored in her foggy brain. She believed she loved her sister, and before that day in December, she'd believed they were happy. She'd believed their life was normal. But in the end, nothing about their life on Atlantic Avenue had been normal, so how could she not question everything else?

Nodding, Zoe stared down at her purse, trying to find the right words. Even without looking at him, she felt Chief McWhorter's gaze on her face. "I didn't do it," she said quietly. "I loved my sister, Chief McWhorter."

It was the chief's turn to nod. He gave her a long one. "I don't think anyone in this office ever believed you were responsible, Ms. Rutherford. But this was thirty years ago. What is it you think I can tell you that you don't already know?"

Zoe's hand reached up for the bill of her Oriole's cap. She tugged it down sharply, held it a moment, then let go. "I want— no, need—I need to know how closely you looked at my dad . . ."

Inevitably, whenever the subject came up, folks who remembered the gossip surrounding her sister's disappearance were often cowed by Zoe's direct gaze. She could only imagine the source of their discomfort: Sympathy? Suspicion? Pity? Maybe all these things combined?

Chief McWhorter held her gaze, his pale-blue eyes empathetic. He seemed to sense Zoe's quiet desperation. He leaned forward to set his cup down, pushing it aside. "Ms. Rutherford," he began, his tone laden with discomfort.

"Zoe," she offered. The more personal she made it, the less likely he would be to blow her off. She understood that principle instinctively. In fact, she was counting on it. How many times had she been on the verge of losing a client, and then managed to save the day, simply by using their first name in a genuine way?

Nevertheless, he shook his head, and Zoe had the impression he was going to send her away empty handed. Panic flared.

There was nowhere left to go. She understood this now, despite it going against all logic. As anyone else might view it, Zoe had plenty of places to go besides Sullivan's Island, South Carolina, but she understood deep down that all roads led here.

"Please . . ."

The sting that came to her eyes surprised even Zoe. Until this instant, she hadn't realized how much she needed the answers to her questions—or even that she had questions left unexplored.

If she was ever meant to be a better person, to live a better life, everything depended on what happened from this moment forward.

The chief blew a tired sigh. He reached for his cup again. "Your father didn't do it," he said. "I don't remember the details after all this time, but he didn't do it, Zoe."

Zoe sat back, processing the statement. *He didn't do it. She didn't do it. So what happened to Hannah?* Her gut burned. "Is it possible for me to access the files?"

The chief pursed his lips, once again scrutinizing her.

Could he see behind her eyes? Did he have any inkling how close she was to tears? Her vision blurred as she removed her Oriole's cap and set it down on the desktop, exposing the angry cut on her forehead, red and ridged even after weeks of healing. She wasn't entirely sure why she bared it. It wasn't premeditated, but once it was done she realized she needed to lay herself bare before this man. She needed him to look her straight in the eyes and understand how thoroughly her past had wounded her.

The unknowns were like splinters buried in her skin,

festering every day of her life, no matter that Zoe endeavored to ignore them. Like the itching at her forehead, it refused to be set aside. And, more to the point, like those rotting steps on her house, this is where she knew she must begin to root out all the septic truths that were poisoning her day by day.

Zoe felt moisture beneath her armpits, but her hands were cold—as though she'd dipped them into a bowl of ice.

She caught Chief McWhorter staring at her forehead and she could tell he was trying to determine what to say next. She was no longer a member of this community. The offense leading to this particular injury wasn't any of his concern—as long as it hadn't occurred in his jurisdiction. And it hadn't. But Zoe was here now. As she sat in the chair facing the Sullivan's Island chief of police, she knew she wasn't going to leave this island until she came to terms with her past.

For a long interim, Chief McWhorter's eyes remained focused on her scar, and then he said, "This is a quiet community. That"—he indicated her head with a nod—"Is it something I need to worry about?"

Zoe could have tripped over a rock, for all he knew. Ran into a wall. Had her guilty demeanor given her away? She sat, considering his question, and more importantly, how to respond. She could take it two ways: either he didn't want the hassle on his watch and he was telling her so, or he wanted to know if she might need someone to look after her. But since he didn't know her, it would stand to reason it must be the former. Although something about the way he was looking at her made her feel it was the latter. In any case, the situation was better served by the truth.

Zoe sat back against the cold metal back of the chair, setting her purse down on the floor beside her, laying aside her shield. Still, how to answer? On the one hand, if she could help it, she didn't intend to see Chris again. On the other hand, she couldn't account for Chris's actions. Certainly, she would take any and all precautions to avoid him, but Chris wasn't stupid, and she couldn't guarantee he wouldn't find her.

"I don't know. Maybe."

A stream of water sprayed the window, followed by an eruption of laughter. Outside, two kids were blasting each other with water guns, glancing nervously at the window to see if their shenanigans would bring the police chief out of his chair.

Ignoring the battery of water against his window, the chief nodded, but this time Zoe spied a measure of resignation in the gesture. "I can't promise there's even a file," he said. "We lost a bunch during Hugo."

Zoe's heart lurched. "If you'll just look, that's all I ask."

Another blast of water hit the window. "Damned kids," he said, rising from his seat. He eyed Zoe pointedly, "All right. I can't promise I'll share it if I find it. But, all right, Ms. Rutherford, let me look into it."

Taking a cue from the chief, Zoe rose from her seat, grabbing her purse from the floor. "Thank you, Chief McWhorter."

"No sweat. Leave your number with Patty. I'll be in touch in a day or so."

AT THE LAST MINUTE, after leaving HomeGoods, where Zoe snagged a few household necessities, she made a left turn instead of a right turn, heading down Ben Sawyer Boulevard toward Carpet Outlet. If all life's decisions could be so simply made, reduced to gut inspiration and natural kinetic motion, maybe she wouldn't now have a scar on her forehead. The rationale here was simple: only the living room had carpet, but it was long past its prime. It was a deterrent to potential buyers, plus it was far more cost-effective to lay down new carpet rather than restore hardwood floors, so she picked out a neutral Berber that seemed practical for sand-covered feet in a high-traffic area, and then set up a time for the install. Whether or not she meant to sell the house, it was nevertheless the right thing to do—like calling the police when your boyfriend cuts a hole in your face.

After leaving Carpet Outlet, Zoe made a second trip to the grocery store, this time with a mind toward a longer-term stay. Although she still didn't have any clue how long it would take to repair the house, it was evident, now that she was here, that it wasn't going to be a quick and easy task—especially without any help.

Thank you, Nick.

Distracted, making mental notes of everything mounted on her to-do list, Zoe lifted up her two bags filled with bare-minimum groceries and headed toward the door.

"Oh, my gosh!" Someone squealed as the glass doors flew open. Zoe half expected to witness a flash mob beginning with the next words "look at her butt." "Zoe!"

Spinning around, arms laden, Zoe found an old high school friend hurrying toward her—the term *friend* here being used loosely, considering that neither of them had made any attempts to reunite since their days at Wando High School.

Zoe moved backward, through the door, out of the lobby as Lori Masterson pursued her—or at least Masterson had been her maiden name.

"Lori," Zoe said, smiling faintly. Any other time she might have actually enjoyed this meet up, but the scar on Zoe's head itched ferociously.

"You're back?"

"Sort of. I'm here long enough to fix the house."

"Oh, yeah?" Lori perked up, her pupils dilating slightly. "So y'all are finally gonna sell?" Dressed for success, she wore patent leather dress pumps in a shade of coral that matched her lipstick and nails.

Funny, Zoe had considered herself so much more sophisti-cated after leaving the island, but Lori looked every bit the big-city executive, slash It Girl. In contrast, Zoe was in blue jeans and a blue wife-beater tee with bleach stains. Abandoned in the muggy heat, the crisp cotton shirt she'd worn as a cover while up at the police station lay wilted in her passenger seat.

Ignoring the irritation at her forehead, Zoe readjusted the heavy bags in her arms, stepping out of the doorway to let an older woman pass her by. "That's the plan."

"Oh, gosh, well, *please* do let me know if y'all decide for sure." She nodded, pointing to the gold-and-white badge she wore on her blouse—a realtor pin, partially hidden beneath the collar of her white blouse, the inside of which was coated with a ring of bisque-colored foundation.

Zoe, on the other hand, wore no makeup at all. Last night, she'd showered before bed, went to sleep with a damp head and, this morning, she sported unflattering cowlicks in all the wrong places. She'd pulled her hair up into a ponytail and then put on her hat, pulling the tail through the hole in the back. No amount of makeup could hide the dark circles beneath her eyes. "I will," Zoe promised. She was itching to get away now—pun intended—hoping to avoid any more questions. Impatiently, she edged backward into the parking lot.

Never one to take a hint, Lori trailed after her, fishing into her purse for what Zoe assumed must be a business card. Her heels clicked daintily across the black tar, and in this heat, probably sank at least as deep as the black rubber of her heel. Somehow avoiding a sideswipe of her bony hip against the bumper of a white pickup, she brandished a bright pink card with a smile as brilliant as the highlights in her hair, and then she handed it to Zoe.

Zoe eyed the pink card, then the bags in her hand and gave a helpless little shrug.

"Oh!" Undaunted, Lori slid the card into the left bag. "Don't forget it's in there," she said, her voice ending on a high note that brought to mind late nights giggling beneath the covers. More oft than not, for Zoe, those giggles had been inspired by Lori's brother Bobby, who later, had kindly accepted the gift of Zoe's virginity. Even so, she broke up with him on the day before their prom because she'd caught him kissing Patty Piggott. But Zoe hadn't been mad for long. She'd figured anyone born with a name like that deserved a few breaks. Although it occurred to her suddenly why that woman at the station had stared at her the way she had. *That* was Patty Piggott.

"I won't," Zoe promised, still sidling backward across the parking lot.

"So how long y'all here for?" Lori asked, pursuing her in earnest now, heels click-clacking at the end of her stockinged limbs. The heat was so oppressive today that even the sight of Lori's pantyhose made Zoe's crotch sweat.

"Not sure. Like I said, long as it takes."

"Oh, but we've *got* to do lunch," Lori insisted. "Are you staying at the house?" Inevitably, her gaze found Zoe's hat.

Some part of Zoe wanted to drop her bags and jerk down the cap, embarrassed by the prospect of being labeled as "one of those women." Never mind what the stats said—that one in four women experienced some sort of domestic abuse at some point during their lives. It made Zoe feel dumb for having stuck around as long as she had—for not seeing Chris more clearly from the start. Or maybe, more incriminating, was this: Zoe had pegged him for that type way back in the beginning, and still, she'd stayed. Reminding herself that Lori had no way of knowing how she got her scar, she tried to ease the tension from her shoulders. For all anyone knew, she'd earned it legitimately.

Then again, maybe Lori couldn't even see it?

Lori's gaze seemed to glaze over, focusing on the logo on her hat. "I see you traded in the Rangers for the Orioles. Bobby will be heartbroken. He married Patty, you know?"

At least she got to change her name. Patty Masterson was a far better moniker. "Good for him," Zoe said and meant it. She and

Bobby had never been destined for more than awkward sex in his car—not that they hadn't both pretended they wanted more.

"Divorced," Lori added, with a wink.

"Oh? Too bad." Zoe meant that as well. At the moment, she had no interest in reviving old relationships. She reached her car at long last. "Well, here I am," she said, setting the grocery bags down on the trunk to locate the keys in her purse—another good reason to put them on her keychain. She was determined to put an end to the conversation once and for all.

Lori held her ground, but thankfully, came no closer, as though finally acknowledging the barriers Zoe was trying to erect between them. "Alrighty," she said with a cute little wave. "Call me."

Zoe unlocked the car, opened the backseat door, shoved her grocery bags into the backseat, and quickly closed the door. "I will," she said, intending to follow through, but only once the house was ready to go on the market. She opened the front car door and slid into the driver's seat as Lori turned away. Zoe couldn't leave fast enough. Even after she backed out of the parking space and set the car into forward motion, she felt the phantom pieces of terra-cotta grinding into the flesh of her forehead.

"It'll leave a scar," the nurse had said. "It adds character."

Zoe didn't want any more fucking character.

5

NOVEMBER RAIN

The sticky, wet sound the roller made as it covered old paint with new, the rhythmic movements, proved profoundly soothing as Zoe painted her way down the hall. She removed the switch plates, popped off the dimmer switches, and set them aside.

She could have hired out the job, but physical labor could be therapeutic. It had been a long time since she had invested herself in this sort of effort.

In fact, she couldn't remember ever painting a house for herself, although once, about five years ago, she helped a friend paint a nursery.

As with boyfriends, Zoe could never commit to a house, so she left walls as she found them—or painted them some shade of ivory, the ultimate noncommittal color. Not even white was so noncommittal. You had to actually like white. You couldn't simply put it up and forget about it, because white screamed for attention.

Much the same way Chris was screaming now.

At the other end of the house, the cell phone rang, a jangly, forlorn sound that bounced off hardwood floors and sailed through empty rooms.

On and on it rang.

Zoe ignored the phone, tempted to let the battery run down. Apparently, he didn't understand words like "quit," "no," or "stop," and since he was the only one calling her at the moment, she could easily let it go.

As part of this endeavor, Zoe had taken a three-month leave of absence, fully intending to return to work, but that's not what she'd instructed the answering service to say.

"I'm sorry. Ms. Rutherford's not available. If you're a client with immediate concerns, her email address is zoe at themarketingstudio dot com."

"Thanks, I have her email. Is there a number where she can be reached? I *really* need to speak with her."

"No ma'am, but I can take your number if you prefer?"

Zoe affected a worried tone. "Will she call me back right away?"

"I'm sorry. Ms. Rutherford is currently unavailable for phone conferences. Please try her email."

The young lady's script was right on cue, without fail. Zoe called back several times, with far more pointed questions, and varying degrees of urgency and attitude. Each time, the girl kept her cool, answering to the best of her knowledge.

The truth was that the answering service didn't know anything, except what Zoe had told them. The girl on the other end of the receiver was a stranger to Zoe, to Zoe's company, and to her life, and that's the way Zoe had intended it.

Inspired by the new carpet, she'd sought a nearby paint store and acquired a few gallons of neutral-colored paint: Ice Mist for the trim, November Rain for most of the walls, Icicle for the bedroom and the living room, and Blue Haze for the bathrooms because, well, Zoe couldn't resist a splash of color.

In the back of her mind, she understood she wasn't painting for herself, but she loved that particular shade of blue. It reminded her of a benevolent ocean, glittering beneath a warm sun. It was a leaded, washed-out, easy blue and by the time the job was completed, the inside of the house would be reminiscent of sand dunes, with glimpses of water beyond the beach. The color she was using now, November Rain, reminded her of wet sand.

Hannah.

"Is that what you see?"

The underside of a dune?

Through fleshless eye sockets?

Zoe stepped back, studying her paint job.

Throughout the years, she'd imagined her sister with shriveled skin, flesh receding from rounded eye sockets, and sand sifting in, like grains through an hourglass. For days now, she couldn't wrench her thoughts away from Hannah.

Who was she kidding? Months, years. Her whole life.

Somewhere along the course of Zoe's endless search, she'd learned that approximately seventy-five percent of the kids who were abducted and murdered were already dead within three hours of their abduction. During the first three hours after Hannah's disappearance, Zoe had probably been seated at the kitchen table, answering questions for Chief Hale. At this point, as she finished up her first coat of November Rain, it had been something like 262,974 hours since her sister had disappeared.

What were the odds she might still be alive?

Probably the same odds she had of ever finding and identifying Hannah's bones. Across the country, coroners' offices held more than forty thousand sets of unidentified remains. Even if there were enough money to test every set of teeth in their drawers, how many man hours would it take?

For years after, until the last face on a milk carton was printed and tossed into the trash, Zoe had found herself standing in the dairy section of the grocery store, lifting up random cartons, just to see if she could find Hannah's face.

How many people remembered the name of the first kid to appear on one of those cartons? Zoe did. It was Etan Patz, a six-year-old from New York with golden hair and a crooked smile. He vanished one day in 1979, walking to his bus stop, two blocks from his house. Like Hannah, his body had never been found.

Thirty-three years later, a former store clerk with a history of mental disability confessed to murdering the boy. The man admitted to prosecutors that he'd choked Etan and placed him, still alive, into a plastic sack, then stuffed the bag into a box and dumped him on a random street.

Despite the fact that there was a day declared in honor of Etan's disappearance—National Missing Children's Day, May 25 —that trial was so far inconspicuous amidst #TheBachelor Twitter headlines and presidential candidate suppositions. No one seemed to remember Etan—except for Zoe.

For her part, she would be following that trial closely, in hopes that his family might finally get some closure because Hannah's story would have no such closure, grim as that prospect might be, and Zoe couldn't decide which fate was worse.

This was the thing: as horrible as it was to picture a man's rough hands wrapped about the small bones of a child's neck, the terror a child must feel, limbs flailing against the assault—eyes bugging, lungs struggling—it was worse *not* to know, and to imagine every other scenario under the sun. In Zoe's head, Hannah died a thousand gruesome deaths, each more hideous than the last.

And then, despite the horror movies playing endlessly in her mind, there was an undying sense of hope that remained, even as the minutes ticked by on the eternal clock. For all those 262,974 some-odd hours since Hannah's disappearance, hope burned, like an eternal flame, flickering ever lower, ever fainter, but never extinguishing. It was wearisome.

In fact, Zoe was convinced her mother died of sheer exhaustion, her dad as well. No matter what ill will existed between Zoe and her father, she knew he had loved Hannah. That was never in doubt. Even now, she knew Chief McWhorter would find nothing on her father. She only hoped—twisted as it might seem—because then it would free Zoe from a cloud of uncertainty. But also because then she would *know*.

For those who'd never lost someone to the unknown, it was impossible to comprehend the day-to-day torment inflicted upon those left behind. Not knowing was like a cancer, black and esurient, eating away at her body and soul.

And yet, despite the endless dimming of hope, Zoe recalled sensing that afternoon, as she sat at their kitchen table answering questions for Chief Hale, Hannah was already gone. Something else went missing that afternoon in 1986, something less obvious than her sister's physical form. That connection she'd had to her sister—that energy that connected two human beings who'd once shared the same womb—was gone. *Poof.* Her mother had sensed it as well. Zoe glimpsed the truth behind her deadpan eyes. That was no doubt why Marge started in on the pills—to numb herself to the pain of loss.

Contemplating her mom's addiction, Zoe set the paint roller down into the trough. It made sense to her—the need to medicate. And yet, she knew enough to know it was nothing more than a slow poisoning. Why put everyone else through a slow-motion suicide? Just get it over with, why don't you? Anger over it still burned at her gut.

What about you, Zoe? Each day for the past eight years, Zoe had placed herself in physical danger. To what end? To punish herself for living? Why else would she have persisted with a relationship that was not only poison to her body, but to her soul as well?

Once she was finished, the hallway looked like the underbelly of a sand dune, dark and wet.

"Whatcha think, Hannah?"

In the answering silence, Zoe could hear the squeaky rotation of the attic ventilation fan. The image of a small pencil box popped into her head, like a tiny thought bubble she immediately popped. She nodded her approval, pleased with the color choice.

The kitchen smelled of paint thinner and fresh paint. Zoe made her way back to the hallway bathroom, turning on the light, looking at the face in the mirror.

There was a splotch of November Rain on her neck. She touched her skin to see if it had dried. Her fingers lingered at her throat, squeezing for a moment.

Chris's face swam before her eyes.

Without Zoe in his life, could he have been a better person? A loving partner, whose first inclination wasn't toward violence? No doubt Zoe's obsession with her sister's death conspired with his baser nature. She realized she wasn't entirely blameless. Whose request was it . . . that first time?

Zoe was broken.

Did she break Chris as well?

Or was he already broken long before Zoe came into his life?

Contemplating the answers to her questions, Zoe stared at herself, at the dark, arching brows, the wavy ash-brown hair, with highlights that were at least four months outgrown. She examined her newest scar, touched it with a finger, even knowing she shouldn't. It was healing, but the tiniest pressure would reopen the wound. Of course she wanted it to go away, but it would be a keen reminder if it didn't.

She turned on the faucet, testing the water with paint-stained fingers. When it was warm enough, she splashed her face, scrubbing the paint off her throat.

What a mess she was. And now the dreams—dreams about Hannah. Probably because she was back in the house. Sometimes Zoe dreamt about the many ways her sister could have died, sometimes they were closer to memories, pleasant drifts to a more wholesome age . . . before their life molted into a sort of hell —like a caterpillar turning into a butterfly, only in reverse— except that, always, Hannah's face was obscured. More and more, even in her most vivid memories, Hannah's face was always a blur.

THE DAY before Hannah's disappearance, Zoe and Hannah went crabbing over on Breach Inlet Bridge. They weren't supposed to do that, but their mother never bothered to leave the house to check on them and their dad was out working on John's Island. The following day, he would do the same only there would be a question as to whether he took Hannah with him. He tended to string jobs together at more distant locations, so that he could get them all done at the same time. On those days, he was gone all day long and into early evening, so she and her sister took a bucket filled with chicken necks they'd stolen from the freezer and headed out to the bridge.

Zoe never particularly enjoyed picking up those slimy necks, but Hannah never seemed to mind. Later, once they showed up at home with a bucketful of blue crabs, their mom would give them an earful, while imagining out loud all the possible scenarios of the terrible things that might have befallen her girls. She might even cry. But then she would put the mess of crabs in a pot and she would cook them until they turned red, and their dad would come home to a meal he might enjoy. They would sit in silence while Rob Rutherford cracked open shells, and quietly severed limbs, sucking out the juices. And then, replete, he would slide back his chair from the carnage, grab a beer from fridge, and head back into his office, only to reemerge whenever he wanted more beer. That was more than enough impetus for Zoe.

On the corner, near the bridge, where her sister sometimes

stopped to buy herself a Coke, they bought snacks at the bait-shop gas station. The shop was gone now, replaced with some fancy new restaurant—a seafood place where folks could sit around and peel shrimp while staring out at the inlet that had claimed so many lives. There was something morbid about that, Zoe supposed, but since some of those deaths were historic—like the ones on the Hunley—at least it could be deemed educational.

The narrow inlet beneath the bridge was about two or three hundred yards wide at its narrowest point, with tidal currents that could sweep a grown man clear off his feet. On the beach nearby, there was a sign commemorating the Marshall Military Reservation, an old Confederate fort commissioned to protect the tributaries behind Sullivan's Island. Supposedly, this was where the Hunley was launched. Carrying nine men, the sub had cranked its way through dangerous currents on its way to take down the USS Housatonic. After torpedoing down the Union war sloop, it resurfaced only long enough to signal shore before heading back down to a watery grave.

Of course, Zoe and Hannah had never discussed the fate of the Hunley. Her sister never learned they'd found it four miles offshore, with its nose pointed toward the island. A crew led by Clive Cussler discovered it there sometime during the mid-nineties, about ten years after Hannah's disappearance.

But she and Hannah would sometimes talk about the currents under the bridge, and both of them had understood the dangers of swimming at Breach. How could you not, when your dad walked about yelling, "Dead tourist!" at the top of his lungs every time he spotted a Coast Guard chopper?

On that particular day, while they were crabbing, Hannah's favorite straw hat blew over the rail, into the churning waters below. Neither of them had considered going after it. They watched it float along the white caps, and scurried toward the other side of the bridge to watch it emerge on the other side and to contemplate its journey.

"Maybe it'll wash up on a sandbar," Zoe had offered. "Someone might find it."

Hannah's eyes had widened. "Or maybe it'll float all the way to China," her sister had said, clearly thrilled by the prospect, despite her disappointment over the loss of her favorite hat.

"Nah," Zoe had said. "It'll get water-logged before then. It'll sink."

Her sister had continued to muse. "Well, maybe they'll catch a shark and find my hat inside his belly, d' ya think so, maybe?" Even before Zoe had a chance to answer, Hannah had laughed excitedly over that possibility, jumping up and down, her hand gripping at the rails.

"Could be," Zoe had agreed, although she really didn't believe it. But it seemed to make Hannah feel better to imagine her hat in some exotic location, so Zoe had let her dream.

"Maybe it'll float into a tunnel?" her sister had persisted.

There were myriad passages all along the island, from Fort Moultrie to Battery Marshall. The ones over at Fort Moultrie were open to the public. Some were cavernous, some narrow, some leading to sealed doors that emerged near the sea. At the Breach Inlet end of the island, the Marshall Military Reserve was now private property, but tunnels existed there as well, beneath the batteries, evidenced by massive steel doors that were built into the dunes. They looked like enormous portals into Middle Earth. Zoe sometimes imagined it was possible to get from one end of the island to the next, all without coming above ground, but many of the tunnels were now flooded and sealed. "Maybe," Zoe had said.

"Gabi says Annabelle's father buried her down there; that's why he couldn't find her."

There had been no need to ask who Annabelle was, or "he" for that matter. For any child raised on the island, it had been a prerequisite to know the bard and his legends. Poe's presence had been ubiquitous. But for those who'd lived in a house named after one of his most famous poems, it was unthinkable not to memorize every word. She and Hannah had made it their life's mission to discover the final resting place of the beautiful, mysterious Annabelle Lee. "Where?" Zoe asked.

"Down in the tunnels."

Hannah's tone had risen at the end as though it should be perfectly obvious, and she seemed pleased to have learned something before Zoe.

As much as Zoe had wanted to solve the mystery—whether or not Annabelle Lee was real and where she was buried—Zoe had equally loathed the thought of Gabi Donovan knowing anything at all. She had rolled her eyes. "Gabi's an idiot."

Her sister had considered that as they'd watched her straw hat catch another current and dart away along the tidal jet. Like a kite that finally caught the wind, it sailed away. The point was this: Hannah would never have considered going after that hat.

If you thought about sandbars like small islands, with inlets flowing in, around and between them, it was easy to envision water rushing out from behind the bars, pushing everything out to sea. Only dummies, or tourists, ever considered traversing the sandbars. Tides in the Low Country were deceptively strong and there was a perpetual riptide there at Breach. Swimmers who loitered on sandbars quickly found themselves stranded and trying to make it back against risky currents. In fact, they were so volatile the land was constantly changing, eroding, reshaping. All along the beachfront, sandbars emerged and disappeared. These were not waters to trifle with, and neither she nor her sister ever did. Like warnings from their parents never to put their fingers into a burning flame, or never to touch a boiling pot of water on the stove, or not to play with firecrackers, especially those with short fuses, treating Breach Inlet with respect was a matter of common sense. This is why Zoe knew her sister did not die there, despite her bike being left in the dunes on that part of the beach.

As for the bridge, Zoe couldn't recall a single fight she and

Hannah ever had there. For all anyone knew, she and Hannah had been irrevocably joined at the hips . . . at least they had been until Gabi Donovan moved in next door. But even after Gabi, she and Hannah had never fought openly with fists or words. It was more a silent war, waged in the confines of their bedroom, each from the safety of their bunkers, until one of them could no longer endure the barrage of silence. Only then came the white flag in the form of two little words: *"I'm sorry."*

"Me too, Hannah."

"You can use my bike any time you want."

"You can wear my T-shirt too; I don't care."

"All right."

"Okay."

A wave of sadness washed over Zoe—like a storm surge, unstoppable. Thirty years in the making, the deluge erupted with heaving sobs that brought Zoe to her knees on the cool tile of the bathroom floor.

SHE MIGHT BE A LIAR, but Gabi Donovan must have known *something*. There was only one way to discover what that was. For the sake of closure, Zoe decided it was time to put enmity aside and reach out to her.

It took her a few days to get up the nerve to walk next door, as though crossing the barrier of sweet myrtle were more akin to climbing a barbed-wire fence, or the once-green lawn, now eroded to sandy patches, was a vast, arid desert in which a wanderer might perish long before reaching the other side.

In fact, there was nothing to climb, nor was the tangle of sweet myrtle all that impenetrable. The lawn had simply returned to its natural state. Sand.

Old man Donovan used to work entirely too hard to keep his grass unnaturally green and free of sandburs, a task that was endless and rather pointless, since the instant he was gone, nature was victorious once more.

For his part, the current owner didn't seem the least bothered by nettles in his yard. Zoe found each and every one as she crossed his property to his front door, stopping every so often to extricate a gnarly bur clinging to her toe or heel.

There were more than a few "ouches" along the way, so he must have heard her approaching before she was standing on his porch. Once there, Zoe nearly lost her nerve, though before she could reconsider, the front door snapped open. She had her leg twisted up, searching for the remaining sliver of a bur. "Hi."

The man frowned, his mouth set in a slightly thinner version of the previous owner's. They were indeed related. Zoe supposed it must be the son—the one who'd joined the military the instant he could in order to escape mean-ass parents—or so her father had claimed.

"What do you want?"

He wore glasses perched at the end of his nose, as though they were bifocals, but Zoe didn't see any difference in the lenses. He was balding, or beginning to, and his skin was supple enough to belie the shock of gray at this temples. His eyes were doleful, save for the slight burn of annoyance in his pale gray eyes.

Zoe extended her hand. "I'm Z—"

"I know who you are," he interrupted. His hand remained firmly on his doorknob, and he glared at hers as though it had breached the air space between them and he were considering slapping it down.

Zoe's hand returned to her side. "Well," she said, searching for something friendlier to say. "I just wanted to say hi."

"So now you have." He glared at her, clearly expecting her to leave, but Zoe had come too far.

"I'm guessing you must be Gabi's uncle?"

For a long moment, the man seemed to assess her. His eyes

narrowed to slits. And then he said, "Gabi doesn't live here anymore."

"Yeah, I know. I hoped you might be willing to give me her number?"

"Gabi's dead."

Something like shock pummeled through Zoe, but she wasn't sure why. Perhaps, more than anyone, Gabi had seemed too mean to die. Still if anyone were headed toward self-destruction it would have been Gabi Donovan. She'd pushed more boundaries than anyone Zoe had ever met. Aside from that, Zoe had spent far too much of her life begrudging Gabi the luxury of breath because it seemed an awful breach of justice that her sister's life had ended so soon, when Gabi flirted with death like an obsessed lover.

"Oh." Zoe met his gaze straight on. "Well . . . can you maybe tell me how? When?"

"No," he said, and then snapped, "Don't come back. I don't have anything more to say about it."

Before Zoe could react to the anger apparent in his tone, he slammed the door in her face.

Incensed, she lifted a hand to knock again, furious over his rude dismissal. It stalled in midair. What good would it do to stand here arguing with some cranky old guy? Clearly, he didn't like her, and no doubt it had something to do with his niece. Either he believed Gabi's lies or he remembered her father's endless rows with his parents. Or it might even be that her dad had been an ass to him in school, or maybe he was simply a crippled old man who blamed the world for all his troubles? In any case, this felt like a dead end.

He reminded her of that prickly old geezer from *Grand Torino*, looked a lot like him too—lean and frail, with all that remained of his toughness there in his eyebrows. A good wind might knock him off his feet.

At least he didn't hide his ugly nature, the way Chris did. All sugary sweet on the outside—in the beginning—until you swallowed his bait, hook, line, and sinker, and then you had the hook set so far back into your mouth that getting free cost a piece of your soul.

Zoe had questions for Gabi, but if Gabi was dead, her uncle probably didn't have the answers anyway. From what Zoe recalled, he was never particularly close to his family.

She made her way back across the yard, trying in vain to avoid the nettles in both their yards, and marveling that even now, the pain they promised wasn't enough impetus to make her wear shoes.

6

Nana Rutherford often claimed there was more than one way to skin a cat, but Zoe often wondered why anyone would ever attempt such a thing. If you examined the concept, the entire idea was not only inadvisable, but had serious karmic consequences. It should have been an ill omen that she even contemplated cat skinning while spying on her neighbor.

From two aisles over, arms laden with rolls of paper towels, toilet paper, and a carton of razor blades, Zoe watched her next-door neighbor through her rolls of toilet paper. Laughing good naturedly, he seemed wholly unaware of her presence, allowing her the luxury of observing him unheeded. He joked with the cashier, paid for a small bag of groceries, and then hobbled out the door.

A woman wearing a blue apron with gold lettering rushed over to hold the door for him. "Sometimes this one sticks," she said, smiling.

"Thank you," he said kindly, then he joked with her as well, leaving Zoe with the inexorable impression that his prickly attitude was reserved only for her, and since she, personally, had never done anything to trouble the guy, she naturally wanted to know why.

Without any clue as to why she was compelled to do it, Zoe fell out of line, allowing the blue-haired old lady behind her to place a bag of navel oranges on the conveyer belt. Moving into the same line her neighbor had passed through, she waited her turn yet again.

The teenager ahead of her bought a pack of gum, along with a Red Bull. The girl's hair was striped with pink, her nails painted black. Her eyeliner appeared as though it had been applied a week ago, before a drinking binge, after which it had never been washed away. Smudged and faded, it left her with a zombie-like appearance, straight from a *Walking Dead* episode. She even had flaky, makeup covered, oniony dead skin that wanted desperately to peel away. Zoe waited patiently for the girl to pay for her items while watching her crabby next-door neighbor limp away toward his silver Camry parked in a handicap space.

Finally, it was Zoe's turn at the register. She set down the toilet paper and the paper towels, then bent down as though to pick up something from the floor. She tended to buy men's disposables razors because they were cheaper. But also because they worked better; she reasoned it must be because the man in charge, was, well, a man.

"Oh, no," she said. "Mr. Donovan must have dropped his razors."

Clearly, they didn't belong to the teenager in front of her, who paused to look back at Zoe with a bored expression before picking up her pace. In a town with so few folks, there was a pretty good chance the cashier might recognize her neighbor by name, although she appeared momentarily confused. "Oh, you mean Walter?"

Zoe nodded. "Yes, right, Walter."

The cashier nodded. "Yeah, don't worry 'bout it," she said, waving a hand in dismissal. "He comes through here near a dozen times a day." Outside, the teenager who'd stood in front of Zoe raced across the parking lot toward the silver Camry now slowly backing out of its parking space, almost as haltingly as he walked.

The girl rapped on the passenger-side window and Zoe watched as the window rolled down. The two exchanged words. After a moment, her neighbor looked toward the grocer's window. He must have told her the razors weren't his, because the girl shrugged and he rolled up his window and drove away as the girl watched him go.

Throughout the entire exchange, the cashier remained oblivious. She rang up the toilet paper and the paper towels. Zoe set the razors down on the conveyer belt. "I'll get them for him," she said. When the cashier appeared surprised, she shrugged. "He's my next-door neighbor."

"Oh! Very nice man," the girl said. But she rolled her eyes. "He makes the dumbest jokes."

Zoe nodded in agreement, as though she must already know this, but she couldn't imagine Walter Donovan making any jokes at all. With Zoe, he'd been a curmudgeon. But at least she was able to verify that he was exactly who she thought he was. Walter. Walter Donovan. That was his name.

"Poor old guy," the cashier said. She poked the buttons on her ancient register. "I think he was wounded in the war."

"Which war?"

The cashier lifted a shoulder. "I dunno, maybe one of those Iraqi ones. Y'all wanna make a donation to Helping Hands?" She pointed to the sticker sheet behind her head. "Walter makes one every time he comes through."

Zoe handed the girl a bill, determined not to allow her grumpy next-door neighbor outdo her as a philanthropist. "Here you go. Take ten."

～

HOPING it would dry by the time she was ready to roll the walls, Zoe resumed painting with the trim in the living room.

The smell of fresh paint infused the air as she covered the trim and doorframes with Ice Mist. Without any furniture to hustle about, the task was easier than she might have supposed. Still, it was backbreaking work, making certain there was even coverage without drippage.

Tomorrow, the new carpet was scheduled to arrive and Zoe wanted to be certain the living room was painted by then. It was better not to have to work around carpet, even with tape and drop cloths.

"Only eejits use tape for trim," she recalled her father saying.

He'd meant idiot, Zoe had realized. Having been a sailor, this was perhaps his way of softening language for his kids, with an international flare—his lone cultural contribution to their education. Idiot became eejit. Fucker was ficker (German). Shit was caca (Spanish). But all bets were off whenever he was pissed.

"Always do the trim first," her father had continued. "Give it a solid coat. Then cut in the color on the wall. Take your time applying. Nature's never in a hurry, but somehow everything gets done."

That morning, it was Hannah who stood watching him drag his yellow brush over the walls. Zoe had simply been passing through. Something about his tone had made her pause. There was a certain kindness he'd possessed when addressing her sister —as though he could have recounted the same instructions over and over again, until Hannah finally got it right. Whatever the quality, it went missing from his voice whenever he spoke to Zoe.

On that particular occasion, Zoe lingered in the hall, watching Hannah chew an enormous pickle—the fat, juicy sour kind, like the ones they served at the movies. How she acquired that pickle had been a mystery to Zoe, but considering that Hannah had often shadowed their dad, it was quite likely she'd tagged along to the paint store and that she'd gotten the pickle as a reward. Such things were not usually part of Zoe's world, probably more Zoe's fault than it was her father's, because her dad had never once actually refused to allow Zoe to tag along. Still, a cloud of envy had enveloped Zoe as she'd watched her sister eat that fat, sweaty pickle.

"Can I try?" her sister had asked as she took a crunchy bite.

Neither had noticed Zoe eavesdropping from the hall. Her dad brushed more yellow paint onto the wall. "We'll see," he'd said, after a moment.

Her sister hadn't argued. Somehow, for Hannah, "we'll see" had meant okay. On the other hand, for Zoe, it had all too often meant no.

"You're too old for that," her dad would say. Or, "It's up to you to set a good example, Zoe." Whatever the reason, the end result had often been a no, leaving Zoe feeling as though she'd misbehaved simply for having asked.

Her sister never seemed to have the least doubt she would get her way. Maybe it had been something about their presentations. Perhaps Hannah had known something Zoe didn't. Maybe Zoe had approached these requests with a naturally argumentative tone that came from too many years of expecting the word *no*. But then, it begged the question: Which came first? The *no* or *that tone*? Zoe couldn't remember a time when her dad hadn't talked to her without that note of exasperation in his voice.

Or there was this: maybe her sister had never truly been invested in the answer, and Hannah would have been perfectly happy either way—happier when she got her way.

After all these years, Zoe couldn't be certain, but the impression she maintained was that her sister had walked through each day beneath a ray of sunshine, even while it was raining.

An ex-boyfriend once said that individuals didn't exist outside of a relationship. The relationship was all there was: "You and me," he would say. "We're one thing together, something else with other people."

The concept merited further scrutiny, except that it was impossible not to imagine certain threads of a person's fabric weaving consistently through all their relationships.

For the sake of argument, her dad hadn't been the same with Zoe as he'd been with Hannah. Nor had he been the same with Nick as he'd been with their mother. Or even with his own parents. Robert Rutherford had been a good son to his mom and dad. He'd been less attentive to Nick than he'd been to Hannah, probably because Zoe had doted on her little brother. But in contrast, he'd been far more connected to Nick than he'd ever been to Zoe or to Marge. Their mother had engendered the greatest apathy from him, and Zoe couldn't remember a single flirty glance that had passed between them. However, one thing was certain: He'd displayed far more enmity toward Zoe than he ever had toward his wife, probably because Marge had learned how to be invisible, while Zoe never mastered that skill.

But then there was Chris, who claimed he was different with all his girlfriends, and that only Zoe infuriated him the way she did. Zoe knew better. She'd spoken to a few of his exes. Each one had her story to tell. It was true that Zoe didn't shy away from arguments and that she probably exacerbated some of their conflicts. But it was safe to say that if Chris was the same with each of his girlfriends, then he, as an individual, was a mean-ass drunk. That's who he was.

His phone calls had abated for now. He must be amusing himself elsewhere. She knew he would eventually turn his attention back to her, because he was as tenacious as a pit bull with a bone. It was a bit less daunting now that some time had passed, and Zoe felt empowered enough to carry this all the way through.

Despite her aversion to guns, she considered buying one, but her sensibilities would simply not allow her to harbor a gun beneath her roof.

No guns, she decided. But maybe she would take a self-defense course after she was through painting? At least it was something to think about.

Her sister's ghost stood beside her in the living room, digging her white Converse sneakers into the yellow carpet. *"Why don't you ask for another bike, Zoe? Then we can ride together."*

"Because dad hates me," Zoe responded. "He won't buy me another one."

"He might."

"No, he won't."

"How will you know if you won't ask?"

Zoe hadn't needed to ask. The word *no* had been spring-loaded on her father's tongue.

Her first bike was stolen from the front yard, a crime for which Zoe had been found guilty and held accountable—if for nothing else than for simply the fact that she'd left it out one too many times, instead of putting it away in the garage. But the garage was her dad's sanctuary and if she didn't park the bike exactly where he wanted her to park it, or if she accidentally knocked off one of his models onto the floor, there would have been hell to pay.

It wasn't so much the constant reminders that Zoe didn't deserve anything new or nice that had bothered her. Of all the Rutherford siblings, she was the most careful of all her possessions. But that bike had had rusted-out fenders and a chain that wouldn't stay on. Her father had bought it at a garage sale for Zoe's eighth birthday and she'd had it for a long time before anyone decided it was worthy enough to steal. No, what had really bothered her was that Hannah got a brand-new bike on her eighth birthday, not a hand-me-down like Zoe.

Wasn't it supposed to be the other way around?

It had been hard to begrudge her sister that Schwinn, because she'd loved it so much. In fact, Zoe hadn't begrudged Hannah anything, but there was probably a little martyr living down in her soul, because she'd refused to beg for another bike or another chance.

Hannah had seemed disappointed in her. She'd wanted Zoe on a bike, instead of walking like a turtle at her side, forcing Hannah to ride in circles while Zoe caught up.

"It was so easy for you," Zoe said quietly to the ghost. But how ridiculous was that? *Easy?* Her sister was likely dead. Gone. Maybe drowned. Possibly murdered. Tortured? Perhaps she was still alive somewhere, trapped in someone's basement.

Hannah's ghost tilted a featureless head. *"If you ask him nicely, he might."*

"Damn it, Hannah, if you're going to haunt me, the least you can do is show your face."

Zoe didn't expect the ghost to comply.

She wasn't crazy.

Keep busy.

It'll all be over soon.

After the living room was painted, Zoe could take her time with the remainder of the rooms. Since the carpet was coming out tomorrow, she didn't bother with a drop cloth. There was no need for precision, only speed. She used a roller over the walls, coming as close to the trim as she dared to go. Later, once everything was dry, she would cut in a coat of November rain, just the way her father had said.

Once the first coat was on—while it dried—Zoe took a moment to pop a handful of olives into her mouth, along with a slice of bread. Her diet could be better, she supposed, but she was in mourning. It was natural to lose your appetite through times of loss. Although what it was she was mourning, Zoe didn't exactly know, because it was far more appropriate to be celebrating with that *eejit* gone—Chris, of course, not Hannah.

Now there would be no more complaints when she forgot to leave her work heels at the door, or when the car was low on gas, even though Chris never once drove her car.

Nor did he ever seem all that concerned about pocks in the bamboo floor whenever he tossed heavy vases at her head.

For Zoe's part, she thought the natural inclination would be to avoid getting low on gas, because the obvious outcome would be unpleasant. Really, who wanted to walk even a mile to a gas station in heels or call a friend for help? But no, instead of the normal motivational incentives for avoiding such hardships, one day she woke up realizing that there was only one true deterrent for everything—Chris's anger. Any and all triggers were possible, and none were evident.

At least with Zoe's father, she'd mostly understood his triggers, and whenever she didn't, it had always come back to this one truth: For Zoe's dad, she suspected she represented a life of captivity with her mother—an unavoidable prison sentence for a man who'd been raised to do the right thing, no matter what.

In retrospect, it seemed to Zoe that her dad had never intended to marry Marge at all. Five months pregnant with Zoe, the two had rushed to the altar to "do what was right"—a deep-rooted theme in the Rutherford household.

"Next to doing the right thing, the most important thing is to let people know you are doing the right thing," her father once said. Of course, he was quoting her grandfather, who in turn was quoting John D. Rockefeller, a self-proclaimed philanthropist.

Her parents had met in Germany, while her father was there on tour. Margit was her mom's real name. Margit Althaus. Poor Margit had returned to America with Robbie, the apple of his mama's eye, and like a snake discarding old, unwanted and imperfect skin, Margit had promptly shed herself of her German heritage only to please her husband and his parents. Of course, this was post World War II, when anti-Germanic sentiment wasn't entirely over. They'd played house with Zoe's grandparents in their Kingdom by the Sea, and lived there not quite so happily ever after, always intending to move out once they found a bigger place.

Of course, that never happened, and not long after Nicky was born, Zoe's grandfather had a massive heart attack, leaving Nana alone. And being the only son, her father naturally couldn't leave his mother to care for the house by herself. So, of course, Nana had kept the master bedroom, leaving Zoe's mother and father to share the next-biggest room—one without a bathroom. Unfortunately for Margit, now otherwise known as Marge, Nana had been a formidable presence in the Rutherford house.

For her part, Nana had cooked what Nana wanted to cook. She'd managed the household, including the children, and Marge's shoulders had slumped ever forward. This would seem like something Zoe might not know, but her grandfather had been obsessed with 8mm film, and he'd used his camera often before his death. For a short while, her dad had taken up the torch, but he'd lacked the same interest and the camera and the film soon found refuge in the attic. However, before that, you could have actually taken clips from videos in which Marge stood in profile, and flip through them to reveal the slow-motion slump of her shoulders.

A bit later, Nana died as well—another massive heart attack her father had attributed to all the "hog fat" Nana used in her cooking. Nana had left a vacancy neither of Zoe's parents were quite equipped to fill—her dad, because he'd been reluctant to do so, never truly having "checked in" when it came to his unwanted marriage. And her mother, well, mostly because she'd already learned to be inconspicuous.

All in all, the era during which they'd lived with Nana was short as lifespans went—a total of six years. But those encompassed most of Zoe's formative years. It had ended on the evening after Nicky's second birthday. Nana said she had an upset tummy and her shoulders hurt. She'd keeled over in the hallway on the way to "go lie down" in her bedroom. She'd broken her nose in the fall and, at six, Zoe remembered staring down at her grandmother lying inside her coffin, purple bruises on a nose covered by a thick layer of makeup that didn't conceal Nana's misshapen knob.

"Nana is in peace," her mother had whispered, a wistful note to her voice, as she patted Nicky's back.

Zoe recalled feeling not so much sad as confused and maybe a little frightened as well—as though she couldn't wrap her little brain around what should happen next.

Looking back now, Zoe assumed it was because her grandmother, for the majority of Zoe's early years, had been the backbone of their family. She'd been a strong, spirited woman, who moved to St. Simons Island during the late thirties to tutor kids in the Gullah community. In return, they'd sent her away with a healthy dose of Gullah superstition and a strong conviction that women could, in fact, make a change in the world.

"Keep ya chin up, chil', heah me?" she would say. "Nobody can break you if you don't wanna be broke."

On the other hand, her mom's response would be something like, "Zoe, honey, stay out of your father's way."

With Nana gone, Zoe had feared her mother would drift down into the dark recesses of the sea, like a shapeless, hapless jellyfish pulled inexorably down by the undertow.

Her dad had stepped up to the plate, however, once again doing the right thing. He'd fixed the garbage disposal, taken out the endless barrage of trash, brought home the bacon. He'd mowed the lawn, gone to work, plunged the toilet, cleaned the gutters. What he hadn't done—ever—was forgive Zoe for being born.

Of course, he'd never actually told Zoe this—not in so many words—but kids were far more intuitive than adults gave them credit for. It was probably for that reason Zoe never wanted kids of her own. Having accepted that she was broken, Zoe didn't believe she could measure up, and she didn't want to live with the knowledge that her kids might see right through her.

Or worse, that she would break them as well.

After a full day's work, most of the trim was completed.

The living room looked new. Zoe cut in the color like a pro, without tape, working faster than she would have thought possible.

Starving now, she washed up, scrubbed the paint from her hair. And then she got dressed and headed to Poe's Tavern for a well-deserved burger and a beer.

A TINY GATHERING of buildings at the corner of Middle Street and Ben Sawyer Boulevard comprised the entirety of downtown Sullivan's Island. Here, like a cluster of Atlantic oysters, squatted the majority of the island's eateries. Down the road a ways, you could find The Obstinate Daughter and the island's namesake, Sullivan's, but tonight, Zoe had a hankering for dark and angsty. Poe's Tavern promised to fit that bill.

A newish addition to the island, the tavern sported an enormous front porch and seating in the front yard—a great place to people watch. Zoe opted for a seat inside at the bar, near the fireplace with the black-and-white mural of Poe's face. She sat, with her back against his mustache, like an Old Time gunslinger with an eye toward the door. Even here, six hundred miles from potential trouble, she wasn't comfortable keeping her back to the entrance.

The ticker on the television screen above the bar announced: POLICE SEARCHING FOR TWO MISSING WOMEN. No one paid the ticker any mind. The sound was on mute. The blond onscreen moved her mouth, but all Zoe heard was the buzz from the bar, a hum that sounded more like angry bees. Tourist season was beginning in earnest. The tavern swarmed with unrecognizable faces, some vaguely familiar, but she wasn't interested in reunions.

Fortunately, this was not the time of year for locals to enjoy the island's eateries—despite Sullivan's being a quieter beach than most. For one, parking here was minimal, and the only available public restrooms were out near Fort Moultrie, at the southernmost end of the beach, where passing ships kicked up unexpectedly high wakes. The north end of the beach wasn't much better: Breach Inlet; enough said.

Nevertheless, it was easy enough to spot the locals. Most didn't sport brand-new sunburns, for one thing. Plus, there was a certain ease of dress that came with knowing you were only a stone's throw from home. No big purses, full of everything a traveling family might need. No camera phones pointed at the murals on the walls.

"Oh my God! You've got to go to the bathroom," she overheard one girl say to another. Presumably, to hear the audio recitation of Poe's "The Gold-Bug"—or perhaps to read one of the graphic novels papering the bathroom wall. It was a neat little gimmick, but probably not deserving of unnecessary trips to a cramped little toilet. Zoe's Poe fascination had ended the day her sister disappeared.

She watched the girls huddle together, chattering vigorously about the precise color and particulars of their newest favorite nail polishes, content to eavesdrop on their conversation.

Too dark? No. I like it that way. Have you tried LeChat's Mood gel? Nah, too expensive. Yeah, it's like eighty dollars for a six-pack. But gotta love the colors. This one's called Frozen Cold Spell; see how it shifts? How cool is that?

Had Zoe ever been one of those girls? She couldn't recall. Nor had she ever had the opportunity to share such benign conversations with Hannah. Looking down at her own short nails and the various shades of paint that were wedged beneath them, she tried to envision Hannah as a teenager.

Her sister's features stubbornly eluded her, but she tried harder. Hannah's hair had always been lighter than Zoe's—especially during the summer, when the sun and salt bleached her ends. Her eyes had been a striking blue—a trait she'd shared with Zoe, but they'd been much bluer than Zoe's—more like their German mother's. And her hair, unlike Zoe's, had been straight as a sheet of glass. Free of damage, it had gleamed in a way only a young girl's might.

Eight years old. That was the age of the face haunting Zoe's memories. It refused to age. Her sister's image was eternally youthful, fading day by day.

On the other hand, although Zoe couldn't seem to make her sister's face transform with age, she also couldn't seem to block more macabre images from her brain. She saw skin that had turned black beneath Hannah's nails, slowly rotting as the years prevailed. She saw tiny fiddler crabs picking away at dead flesh with claws that were far too big for their little bodies. Hundreds danced over her sister's twisted, lifeless form.

And yet she couldn't remember what Hannah had worn the day she disappeared. Her mom said it must have been a blue blouse and a pair of jeans, but Zoe and Hannah had shared all the same clothes and for the life of her, she couldn't remember what went missing from their drawers.

It wasn't as though they'd had much to begin with. Despite the current worth of their island home, their father's job had kept them well fed and properly clothed, but hadn't provided for eighty-dollar sets of nail polish or a closet full of shirts. They'd worn different jean sizes, but Hannah's had all been hand-me-downs from Zoe. The one thing Zoe could clearly remember was Hannah's shoes: she'd worn a pair of white Converse sneakers she'd gotten for her birthday. In Zoe's mind's eye, she could still see the bright white shoes balanced on Hannah's bike pedals, turning round and round—faster, faster—sunlight glinting off the reflectors and the metal shoelace rings as she pedaled away with Gabi perched on her handlebars. The blue-and-white streamers on her handlebars surged to life, like the tentacles of an octopus.

That's what Zoe remembered.

On the other hand, she recalled each second of the long day thereafter. It crawled by like blind ants before the advent of eternity, each minute tiny and complicated.

Selfishly, Zoe wanted her sister around to vent to—to give advice, to tell her not to worry, Chris would give up and go away; he wouldn't bother trying to find her. Then, afterward, maybe, they would sit around and talk about nail polish.

Inasmuch as Zoe considered herself a solitary being—not unlike a hermit crab—sometimes she craved hearing voices that were not her own. She didn't much care what they might be saying, only that mouths were moving and that words were flowing off of other people's tongues. Like chatter from a television in the background. Zoe glanced up at the television screen, where the ticker read: LOCAL POLICE JOIN FORCES IN THE SEARCH FOR HEATHER RODRIGUEZ.

Could these people appear any less fazed?

Zoe glanced up at the television screen. The ticker was gone now, replaced with a Spoleto report. The festival was happening now, downtown, but Zoe didn't have much of a stomach for crowds.

She studied the faces surrounding her. A dark-haired man in one corner sat eyeing Zoe while drinking a bottled beer. His gaze shifted back and forth between the girls behind her, who were now discussing the pros and cons of tanning beds. One said she knew a girl, who knew a girl, who got cancer at age seventeen. The other doubted it was because of tanning booths. Like guns, she argued, suntan beds don't kill. "Dumb people misuse them."

"Right," the friend agreed. "Guns don't kill people, dumb people kill people."

Both girls laughed.

"Speaking of killing. You think those missing girls are both dead?"

"You mean, like, murdered?"

Zoe leaned back to listen a little closer, glad to know the topic wasn't entirely being swept under the table. At least sporadically, people were paying attention.

"I don't know. What do you think?"

"Maybe."

"You remember Britney, right? She knows Heather—says she's always into something."

"Yeah, her boyfriend's a loser, but God he's hot."

"Would you date him?"

"No, but I sure would fuck him."

Both girls laughed again and Zoe sat up, disgusted.

Really, for all anyone knew, those women could have walked out of their homes—as Zoe had—in order to escape intolerable situations.

It was getting dark outside. The lights inside the bar dimmed. Together with the fading light and the conversation, the Poe-oriented artwork evoked a sense of the macabre.

Chief McWhorter had seemed so sure of Rob Rutherford's innocence. Out of everyone, Zoe knew they'd looked closest at her father. Perhaps it was only natural to assume that, if neither she nor her father did *it*—whatever *it* was—then someone else must be responsible for Hannah's disappearance. But maybe her sister had gone out on a sandbar that morning, drawn there for some inexplicable reason that Zoe couldn't discern.

A familiar voice interrupted Zoe's perseveration. "Hey, you, how's the bed working out?"

Zoe lifted her gaze to find Ethan McWhorter standing too close. The seat beside her was empty, but he didn't immediately sit down. He lifted a ragged sandal to the bottom rung of the barstool and pushed an empty beer bottle toward the bartender's side of the bar. In this light, his hair appeared silvery. His blue eyes held a feverish gleam.

"Good," she said, hoping a one-word answer would suffice.

Just for good measure, lest he suspect she might be ungrateful, she said, "Thank you."

"No problem. I'm glad someone's using it. Another week and I'da put the thing out on the curb."

"That would've been a shame," Zoe said. "It's a perfectly good bed."

Ethan and his dad shared a similar mischievous twinkle in their eyes. Zoe had learned the hard way it wasn't a sure sign of good humor. Besides, she wasn't in the market for a man in her life, friend or otherwise.

She sat quietly, making a pretense at wiping smudges from her fingers off her pint glass. After a moment, she set the glass down and pretended an interest in the paint remaining beneath her nails, scraping it out, ignoring the man standing beside her.

As with Lori, Ethan seemed reluctant to take a hint, sliding into the seat next to her, leaving one foot on the bottom rung and another on the floor. He spoke to the bartender.

"What's on tap?"

The bartender seized the bottle Ethan set down. He inspected it, then set it aside. "What'sa matter, Romeo? Bud Light not impressing the ladies tonight?"

Ethan chuckled, a deep, rich sound that sent a reluctant shiver down Zoe's spine. "Come on, man. You're jammin' my game here."

Zoe must have missed some gesture made in her direction, because when she lifted her gaze, both men were staring at her. She gave Ethan a forbearing smile—one that hardly welcomed further conversation.

He and the bartender shared another meaningful glance, exchanging lifted brows. "How about a Pluff Mud Porter?" Ethan suggested.

"Coming right up," the bartender said, darting away.

Zoe stood. "Well, I suppose I ought to be going. It was nice seeing you again."

"Yeah," Ethan said, his gaze sliding to the bill of Zoe's baseball cap. He gave her a long, meaningful nod. "You know my number if you should need anything, Zoe."

"Thanks," Zoe said.

Unsettled by the offer—or maybe more by that sense of knowing she spied in his gaze—Zoe paid the bartender and made her way to the exit. Once outside, she stepped up her pace, sprinting toward home, considering the possibility that Ethan might follow. It was silly, perhaps. He wasn't stalking her, not exactly—in fact, not at all. There weren't many bars on the island. The odds of finding him in one were pretty good. But she viewed his helpful nature with a jaundiced eye. In her experience, people didn't do things for nothing, and he had done more than a little something. That feeling—that vague harbinger of doom—stuck to her like sticky summer air.

Beyond the glow of the local establishments' porch lights, the streets were dark, darker yet with each step she took in the direction of the beach.

Zoe had never worried much about ending up like her sister. What was the saying? Lightning never struck twice in the same place.

Except, yes, it did.

She knew that for sure. One year, it destroyed the CRT on their television set. Her dad fixed it, lamenting how his kids were languishing in front of "the boob tube." Still, he'd replaced it, probably because it was easier than hands-on parenting. A few months later, lightning struck again, killing the boob tube yet again.

Tonight, a thin wedge of moon lit an otherwise black sky. The wind swished through nearby palmetto trees. Shadows rose and fell. For an instant, Zoe imagined footsteps behind her, but she turned to find the pocked, black road devoid of life.

Lifting itself on a gust of wind, a plastic grocery bag swept across the street, impaling itself against a diseased azalea bush along the road. In the distance, Zoe could hear muted voices muffled by the dunes—presumably teenagers out on the beach.

It had been broad daylight when Hannah disappeared. Not night. Still she vanished without a trace.

Those missing women . . . no one knew where either of them had gone. Zoe didn't know much about either case, but she'd read enough to know that both had walked out of their houses on quiet nights, just like this, and no one saw a thing. Like Hannah. *Poof.* Both were gone.

It was less than a block to her house, a straight shot across a wooded lot, but Zoe kept to the road. Picking up her pace, she ran the rest of the way home, hastening to the sound of her sandals beating against the black tar, like a heartbeat quickening on the night.

7

A GOOD MAN

"Boredom's a choice, not a condition," Robert Rutherford used to say to his whining kids—most often to Nick and Hannah over the long, hot summers. As the eldest, Zoe had had more than enough to do, especially once it became apparent that her parents were mostly AWOL.

For someone Zoe generally took such issue with, she often agreed with her dad's nuggets of wisdom. He'd also said, "Character is about how you treat folks who can't do anything for you." And, "The less you give a damn, the happier you will be." He'd also claimed, "Sometimes the wrong choices bring us to all the right places."

None of these were original, but aside from the last of these, Zoe found little to criticize in Rob Rutherford's random moments of parental brilliance. Don't steal. Don't lie. Once again, always, *always* do the right thing. That way, you can sleep like a baby at night.

Be that as it may, her dad had had trouble sleeping. He'd gone to bed early, and somehow managed to wake up with shadows beneath his eyes. Throughout much of Zoe's childhood, he'd had what Zoe came to recognize as that thousand-yard stare—especially after Hannah. Her dad had been a troubled man, whose unhappiness ate at him from the inside out. Zoe knew that because she suffered the same malady. She woke up, every day, with the precise intention of doing all the right things. Still, sleep eluded her as well. Yet for all the bad memories she had of her father, she couldn't find fault in his overall character, except where his treatment of Zoe had been concerned. That gave her hope that perhaps the two of them were simply misunderstood instead of "bad seeds."

"Your father's a good man," her mother would sometimes say with a faraway look in her eyes. The proclamation always surprised Zoe.

Marge must have been able to read her expression, because she would inevitably persevere. "He *is*, Zoe. He goes to work, never goes out, never drinks." As though these things were the sole benchmarks of a good man's character.

And perhaps he had been a *good man*, but not to Zoe—maybe to Hannah and to Nick—but Zoe figured her dad could have benefited from an occasional boys' night out. And beg your pardon, he *did* drink, even if it was only late at night, while secluded in his office.

Okay, so he hadn't gone stumbling about in a drunken stupor, nor had he planted his ass in barstools about town, but Zoe had walked into his office one night to find him toppled backward in his chair. She'd thought he was dead. But it was true; he hadn't gone out much—probably because he hadn't trusted himself. And he hadn't beaten her mother, or his children, save one—a fact that filled Zoe with an odd sense of ambivalence—because, of course, she hadn't aspired for her dad to hit anyone else, but if it had only been Zoe who'd engendered this type of behavior from him, then Zoe must be a bad seed. It only stood to reason. It was just this sort of ambivalence that had left her vulnerable to Chris.

On the one hand, Zoe realized it was unacceptable behavior;

no one deserved such treatment. On the other hand, maybe she deserved everything she got.

After all was said and done, if Zoe was bad, then maybe there was something about Hannah's disappearance that eluded her as well. Maybe because she didn't want to remember. Maybe deep down Zoe knew something more than what her ego allowed her to recall. Maybe that day, with Hannah behind the door, she'd really meant to pinch her sister's fingers. Maybe the time Nicky went down the slide for the first time, she hadn't been there to catch him for some other reason than that she was only six and didn't know to position herself at the end of the chute to wait for her brother to emerge.

That memory accosted her now with a pang. As any good big sister would, she'd helped Nicky up the slide, set him free at the top. His laughter quickly silenced. He'd spun on the way down, smacking his temple, ricocheting into the metal sides. Zoe had watched in horror as he flew down and hit the ground, head first.

Scrambling down the ladder, she'd hurried to where he lay. The impact had left her brother with a knot on his forehead the size of an apple, but in retrospect it could have broken his neck. His face had been purple, his blue lips frozen in a scream that refused to arrive.

Lifting her brother off the ground, Zoe had raced home with Nicky in her arms. All the way home, she remembered battling with a conscience that was telling her she was old enough to know better.

What the hell were you thinking, Zoe?

Zoe didn't know.

Maybe there was a dark lining to her soul. Maybe that's why she couldn't face this house. Or the memories that had been made here. Possibly that's why she'd also put up with Chris for all those years. Because she was punishing herself.

For what?

A sense of anticipation was rising. Somewhere, a massive

hammer was preparing to strike. Zoe sensed it hovering over-head. Feeling restless, she craved a distraction.

And then she remembered the film.

DURING THE FALL OF 1989, Hugo ripped through the Low Coun-try. Wavering between a category-four and category-five storm, it bore down on the island, but before it made landfall, Zoe and her brother helped carry most of their valuables into the attic. With a mandatory evacuation in progress, there was only so much they could squirrel away in the car. Zoe was fourteen that year. Nick was ten.

Marge, too, must have been helping, but Zoe couldn't remember how. In the end, it was Marge who ushered everyone into the blue Ford Taurus. Their old pickup would be abandoned in the driveway, mostly because it needed a new carburetor her father couldn't afford.

Her mom was smoking one Benson & Hedges menthol after another, while her dad furiously packed the car. Whatever didn't fit, he handed to Nick or to Zoe to carry up into the attic, in hopes of salvaging it from the storm surge to come.

The energy that day was a prickly sense of ugly expectation.

Filled with equal parts fear and ignorance, her neighbors all had decisions to make—primarily, whether to stay or whether to go. Despite the fact that staying wasn't supposed to be an option, some folks managed to hide out, with the intention of weathering the storm.

"Get out now. You no longer have a choice," one broadcast said. "This is a mandatory evacuation."

The problem now was that, while hurricanes weren't unknown before Hugo, all the storms they'd weathered in most recent history were less than impressive. David, for example, hailed by the media at one point as a mean category-five storm, had merely slapped Charleston with category-two winds, causing a little beach erosion and minimal flooding. For most folks, there'd only been a mess of branches in the front yard—Nick picked up theirs for two dollars. People tended not to take storm warnings very seriously anymore.

But Hugo, Hugo was so foreboding that Charlie Hall's voice broke as he delivered the newscast. "If you have not evacuated yet, don't try. It's too late." There was a tight sense of grief in his voice. "The storm is almost on us. Get to high ground if you can." And later, these words filled every islander with the fear: "May God bless your souls."

As they waited for the storm to hit, Charlie, apparently fearing the worst, was reportedly hospitalized with anxiety. Everyone prayed the eye wouldn't come ashore south of Charleston, closer to Savannah, so that the northern quarter of the storm, with winds climbing to one-hundred-and-forty miles per hour, wouldn't place the city of Charleston underwater. Hours ticked by in darkness. Windows were off limits.

"Goddamn you, Zoe. You wanna swallow a tree?" her father asked.

Zoe shook her head, moving quickly into the shadows, out of the candlelight, away from windows and doors, and also away from her father.

Minutes before midnight, on September twenty-second, 1989, four years after Hannah's disappearance, Hugo's eye went straight up the mouth of Charleston Harbor, at high tide. A storm surge of ten to twenty feet swept over the city and barrier islands, snapping trees, tossing boats and cars about like toys. It twisted the Ben Sawyer Bridge, rendering it impassible. There was only a single bridge connecting the islands to the mainland and Ben Sawyer stayed down for months after Hugo. People were forced to take boats to and from Sullivan's.

Zoe and her family spent the night at her cousin's house, in nearby Goose Creek, huddled in a pantry beneath a staircase.

They sat there, sweating profusely in the darkness, waiting in dead air. Zoe wasn't sure how long they sat as the eye passed over, but she could hear the drip of a faucet along the pipes somewhere upstairs and mouths panting for air. The first half of the storm descended gradually, but there was nothing like the sound of a hurricane wall approaching. It sounded like a derailed freight train, a rumble that shook heaven and earth. They felt it shudder the stairs. The change in air pressure sucked the breath from Zoe's lungs.

They barely slept that night, and when morning broke, people walked the perimeter of their properties like stunned survivors of a zombie apocalypse. They called the barrier islands north of Charleston "Ground Zero." Her neighborhood looked more like a third-world war zone. Timberlands full of pines were decimated, trees snapped in half like toothpicks. On the island, police kept folks away from their homes at gunpoint, declaring martial law.

Zoe had never witnessed anything more random. One house was reduced to sticks while its neighbor stood defiantly. One woman found a porpoise in her living room. Another man came home to discover his bookshelves intact, with a single photograph face down on a shelf. Their red Ford pickup, with the messed up carburetor, sat nearly where they'd abandoned it, headlights buried into mud-encrusted sweet myrtle bushes.

The Donovans, too, were fortunate, but the house on the other side of Kingdom, recently restored, was ruined after losing its slate roof and having water pour in.

Fortunately, Kingdom had weathered the storm all in one piece. Her father guessed it was because their house was built mostly of cinder blocks. Plus, it hunkered low to the ground. But this also left much of the house with water damage throughout the ground floor. The Barbies Zoe had once shared with Hannah were mangled, with misshapen bodies and muddied blond heads. She found one wedged beneath the screen door—as though it were caught in an undertow, being swept out to sea. Zoe imagined that her sister, enraged, was calling for her lost toys.

The walls were stained with stinking mud. By the time they made it back inside, there was a damp rot trapped in the house.

On their first boat ride over to the island, Zoe recalled looking over the mud-encrusted landscape, searching for Hannah's body. Four long years were gone by then, but Zoe had read about a disaster in New Orleans, where bodies were disinterred after a flood, floating up in a mass exodus from shallow graves. She found herself wondering if Hannah's body would float up from some unmarked grave and happen ashore along the sepia tinted landscape. She pictured dories weaving in and out of tributaries, one butting up against the jellied remains of her sister's body. At last, the mystery of Hannah Rutherford's disappearance would be solved. Of course, this never happened, and Zoe felt guilty for even thinking such thoughts. She told no one —not even Nicky.

Despite the layer of pluff mud caking Kingdom's entire first floor, they found the attic mostly free from damage. Everything she and Nicky had placed up there remained untouched. With the money their dad got from the insurance claim—which after all did include a small sum for the red pickup—they raised Kingdom from the mud, onto piles, and built a brand-new screened-in porch.

THE HOUSE WAS dark as Zoe made her way along the hall, inhaling the scent of fresh paint into her lungs. Tonight was as good a time as any to rediscover what remained of her grandfather's film.

The attic door was a pull-down. After her parents were gone, having made the decision to leave all that remained exactly where it was, she and Nick had removed the lead rope to make the attic a bit more difficult to access—not impossible, only marginally more difficult.

Considering that nothing up there had been deemed important enough to warrant either remaining sibling getting off their duffs to empty it, there had also been no reason to seal and lock the door. Still, Zoe had requested the management company put a codicil in the rental agreement precluding the attic from the available rental space. In retrospect, why anyone would agree to such an oddball request was a mystery to Zoe, but she supposed people were clamoring so much for a house on the beach that they would agree to practically anything. But regardless of the codicil, there'd been nothing preventing tenants from storing their own junk up in the attic, and possibly taking everything when they left. Legally, she and Nick had no recourse; and still, they'd taken a chance, considering everything dispensable. Her brother didn't want any of it. Neither did Zoe. If the tenants should happen to steal it all, she and Nick would have considered it a favor. In fact, it might all be gone. Zoe had no idea what to expect when she pried open the attic door.

A cloud of dust rained down upon her as she tugged down the long-unused ladder. Metal and wood descended with creaks and groans, like an old man bidden to rise after sitting too long in an easy chair.

The smell of age was pervasive once Zoe emerged into the muggy interior of the attic space. She reached up to pull on the bell cord to turn on the bulb overhead. It came on, with a flicker. Dirty light cascaded over the immediate area, fading as it stretched into dusty, cobwebbed corners.

The dormer windows were large, letting in ample light. The screens were filled with twenty years' worth of bugs; she could see them from where she stood. Otherwise, the attic was neat and orderly, boxes stacked precisely as she remembered. One large container was stamped with the words "His Master's Voice." Staring into a daffodil-shaped bell, the RCA dog cocked his head with interest. Another box marked Magnavox was crisscrossed with brittle brown tape. Alongside it were stacked two large wooden crates with lettering that read, "Wholesale Fish Merchants." Beneath that, "Charleston." The second one read, "Sullivan's Island." That was the one that had lured her here tonight. She made her way toward the crate, knowing what it would contain.

Zoe pored through the boxes, sifting through crusty metal 8mm reels. Many were secured with old rubber bands—the kind with tails, so you could pluck them off. As with lizards, pulling only severed the tail, destroying the rubber band's integrity and leaving the film free to unwind with a swoosh. Some of the rubber bands disintegrated at Zoe's touch. A few reels were encased in steel-blue casings. These were rusted together. Prying at them with her fingers wouldn't budge them at all.

Zoe slid the entire crate across the attic floor, perching it near the stairs. Hot and sweaty and ready to be out of the attic, she nevertheless hesitated, turning to assess the attic space as she wondered what else she might have devalued.

Surprisingly, it didn't appear anyone had been up here since they'd removed the lead rope years ago. Except for a few new layers of dust and dirt, it looked the same as it had when she and Hannah used to sneak up together to scrounge around in their grandparents' artifacts. To Zoe and Hannah, this had been a musty museum, where old things came to be forgotten and then rediscovered.

In the back of the room sat her Nana's sewing cabinet. The black enameled machine was in decent condition, with the gingerbread-styled decal set intact and the colors bright and golden. It peeked out at her now from behind rows of boxes.

Her sister's favorite belongings had also found refuge here. Zoe looked for the small pencil box, crisscrossed with electrical tape, applied by her thirty years before. She'd smuggled a few things up here once her mom finally got the yen to wipe free the memory of Hannah's existence from the rest of the house.

Locating the pencil box, Zoe found it untouched, snuggled safely atop the cast-iron treadle stand of her grandmother's sewing machine. Above it, the word "Singer" was carved in ironwork. But then, having seen it, she left it where it was, flicking off the light before hauling the wooden crate downstairs, into the living room. Unfortunately, after this much was accomplished, she lost the desire to search through the reels. She abandoned the box in the living room, intending to move it in the morning before the carpet arrived.

Drawn to the kitchen for a glass of water to clear the dust from her nose and throat, she stood at the kitchen sink, sipping water from a Ball jar, as she looked out at the porch light across the way, trying to remember what it was she'd put in that pencil box.

Her mind was empty. It would be easy enough to go up there and retrieve the box and look, but she didn't want to. She wasn't ready to look inside.

Zoe blinked, surprised to find her cranky neighbor peering back at her, scowling across the yard, like Scrooge. After a minute, he reached out to flip down his blinds, cutting off Zoe's view into what appeared to be his bathroom. The back of their house was built in an L shape. One of the trees she'd trimmed earlier in the week used to block the view. Clearly, he didn't appreciate Zoe's efforts.

Exhausted, finally, Zoe chugged the remainder of the water and then headed down the hall to sleep in her borrowed bed.

8

BAD JUJU

The small patch of "natural" Berber went down without any drama. The installers—two guys, one younger, one older —worked quickly and efficiently, peppering the air with Southern homages like, "yes ma'am" and "no ma'am" and "thank you, ma'am," whenever Zoe offered glasses of water.

While the carpet was laid, Zoe continued painting, moving into the bedrooms. Little by little, the house was transforming— as though a coat of whitewash could erase the past.

She wasn't all that bent on religion, but like her Nana, she believed there was an energy that lingered after people were gone. In this house, that energy was tangible. There was lots of bad juju here—probably dating back to the house's genesis.

Built to house the military, Sullivan's Island had seen its share of death. Fort Sumter hunkered within sight. It was impossible to live here and not consider the island's role in the Civil War. On top of that, the island had also been the disembarkation port for many slaves transported from Africa to the North American Colonies. It was once considered to be the largest slave port in North America. But even despite such a bloody history, the majority of the islanders wore island pride like a Purple Heart. Maybe Zoe would have, too, if her own memories were a bit less dour.

Pondering that awhile, she led the roller into the bathroom, giving it a quick coat of Blue Haze. With the trim bright and clean to match the grout she had bleached, the bathroom looked new. But that was the end of it for the day; she couldn't take the smell any longer. Walking outside for fresh air, Zoe snagged her cell-phone from the kitchen counter so she could call Chief McWhorter.

The woman who answered—probably Patty—sent Zoe directly to voicemail. With a sigh, Zoe hung up without leaving a message and shoved the phone back into her rear pocket, cautioning herself to remember it was there. That was all she needed to do—sit on her phone and have to replace it.

At some point, it would behoove her to get a new number. She was starting to feel that returning to Baltimore wasn't in the cards. Although she didn't plan to stay in Charleston, Baltimore was nothing but trouble waiting to happen. A change would do her good, and her clients would continue to work with her wherever she landed. Why not? Everything she did for them could be done remotely, and many weren't local anyway.

The carpet installers followed her outside.

"All done?"

"Yes, ma'am," replied the youngest of the pair. The elder made a beeline to the white van with the red-and-blue letters stamped on the side. As a whole, their marketing was old and tired, reminding her of a dirty American flag. But whatever worked, she reasoned.

"My brother's getting the work order for you to sign."

Zoe adjusted the bill of her Oriole's cap, considering whether either of them had bothered to wonder why she wore her hat indoors. "Brother?"

"Yes, ma'am," he said again, and then smiled as he wiped the sweat from his brow with his forearm. "Family business since eighty-five."

A year before Hannah's disappearance.

Zoe eyed the truck again, wondering if they remembered the news from the local papers. Probably not; at the time, the kid standing in front of her was likely still picking his nose.

"Wanna come in and check the carpet to be sure it's all good?"

"Sure," Zoe said and followed him inside.

IT SEEMED to Zoe that when Shakespeare claimed parting was such sweet sorrow he must have been talking about the separation of people from their things. After a bad relationship, there wasn't all that much to miss about the person who used to lay next to you in bed, even on a cold night. A heating pad and a vibrator made acceptable substitutes.

Pretty much from the get-go, she'd realized Chris was no great catch. Three months into their relationship, she was already second-guessing it. She remembered lying in bed, staring at the ceiling as he lay his head on her breast, listening to the beat of her heart—or at least that's how she'd perceived the moment. This was before they'd ever moved in together, while each of them still kept separate places. He'd slipped into her house one morning, into her bedroom, without calling, after going AWOL the night before. He'd smelled of alcohol—not vodka or gin or rum, but whatever was left after being sweated out through his system. It had seeped from his pores. Along with that septic odor was something sweeter, the faintly disturbing aroma of women's perfume.

"You're too good to be true," he'd whispered.

Zoe's heart tripped when he'd said it, but he hadn't seemed to notice. It hadn't been a leap of joy, but something more like anxiety. She'd felt trapped already, wanting him to leave, but there in profile, he'd looked so much like a lost little boy with nowhere left to go. So she'd held her tongue as her heart wrestled itself beneath the breast he was caressing.

What had he been doing there anyway? Checking her temperature? Making sure last night's disappearing act hadn't left her cold?

His voice had been hoarse. His breath had smelled of smoke. "I keep thinking you'll wake up one day and realize you don't love me, Zoe..."

Zoe's heart had tripped another beat. She *didn't* love him, but how could she have said that? How could she have told someone who was spilling his guts that she didn't love him? He'd sounded so genuine, so desperate. Did she even know what love was?

In the room that morning, there had been silence. Outside, birds sang in the trees.

Zoe's throat had been too thick to speak.

"Do you love me, Zoe?"

She'd swallowed as he turned to face her, his hazel eyes full of questions. He'd slid a hand beneath the covers, tickling her gently between the thighs...

He'd pushed himself against her, showing her his arousal. The look in his eyes shifted suddenly. No longer a lost little boy, he'd become a confident man who knew exactly how to wield the weapons God had given him. His mouth had twisted into a knowing grin, and even as Zoe was repelled by the odor of him, her nipples had hardened as his fingers slid a little easier between her thighs. She'd lifted her hips, hating herself for the response.

What was it they said about girls who weren't loved by their fathers?

He'd whispered into her mouth. "Zoe, baby ... say you love me..."

At that instant, Zoe had thought she might. "Yes," she'd said. "Yes . . ."

But she didn't. And, this was how it went, over and over, in subtly different scenarios, until one day all the things Zoe had spent her lifetime accumulating became fitting excuses as to why she couldn't leave. Except now that she'd finally severed the umbilical cord to Chris and all their shared possessions, she couldn't remember most of what she'd left behind. It was all simply more stuff to fill up otherwise empty spaces.

Still, the losses of some things were bittersweet.

There was a quilt her mother made—not a true quilt as her Nana might have sewn, with gobs of batting and careful stitches. This one was crocheted—red and white, with polyester squares that were cut from sundry pieces of material—pink, purple, patterned, plain—the only thing they all had in common was that they were cut in the same size and shape. Some of those squares Zoe had recognized as pieces of her own clothing. Some had belonged to her mother, some were from material her mother had snapped up at garage sales. Nevertheless, Zoe cherished that quilt. It had a little burn hole on one of the green patches, left by her mom, even before the quilt was completed. Marge had never repaired it, so, in essence, it was part of the design. Now the quilt was no longer in Zoe's possession. It probably sat, folded neatly, in the trunk at the end of the bed she'd shared with Chris. He'd never liked the quilt. He preferred not to see her "tacky little blanket," he would say, and rather than fight with him, Zoe had put it away.

For her part, that quilt was a reminder that her mom had been a woman, who, despite everything, loved her kids.

No doubt, when Zoe looked back at her youth, it was her mother who'd remained their rock, despite the bomb-shelter look she'd walked around wearing. Without ceremony, dinner always made it to the table, laundry got done, the dishes were washed. Knee scrapes were swathed in iodine and peroxide, T-shirts were ironed and mended—yes, even T-shirts. They were not neglected as children, despite the fact that it had sometimes felt that way.

Emotionally, that was another matter, but it wasn't as though either of her parents had ever received a wealth of affection themselves—neither from their own parents, nor from each other.

But that quilt . . . it was proof that Marge had harbored the same motherly aspirations as every other mom. Leaving that quilt behind was a bit like leaving an album full of photographs to be consumed by a house fire. There was no telling what Chris would do with it once he discovered she was never coming back. But even as precious as the quilt was, it wasn't worth the trauma of trying to get it back. Worse than that, it wasn't worth the risk of returning for it, which would leave the door open to allow Chris back in her life.

As did those who'd abandoned the island on the night Hugo threatened, Zoe made a choice when she left—with one significant difference; she knew beforehand that she was never coming back. Everything she'd left behind would be forever lost.

With little time to spare, she'd taken only what she could carry in ten or less trips out the door. She'd known Chris would be home soon. She'd sensed the storm brewing, long before he darkened their front door.

She hadn't been able to take it anymore. Whatever the reason, their relationship was toxic. If he didn't kill her, with his own bare hands, the stress of their relationship would have accomplished the same thing, only slower—like Marge's pills. It was better to shut the door now and leave it closed forevermore.

Chris began calling again that evening. Every jangle of the phone seemed a new threat. Zoe could see him in her mind's eye, losing his composure, rearing back to hurl his phone. Except that, without Zoe around to replace it, he would merely hold it impotently in midair, his face florid, eyes full of menace, lips curled back in anger.

He could go to hell.

9

BEAN CLAMS

Equally annoyed by the tangle of her thoughts as she was with the one about her legs, Zoe kicked her way out of the bed sheets. Wallowing in the dark, she lay there, pressing two fingers to her forehead against her scar. Two minuscule bumps wiggled beneath her touch. Pressing down gave her a welcome shot of pain.

All the same questions harassed her: Why Hannah? Where did she go? Why did Gabi Donovan accuse Zoe of killing her sister? And *why, why, why* had her own dad been so ready to believe the little bitch? Thirty years later, it was as much a mystery as the life and death of Annabelle Lee.

At heart, Poe's story was about a love that transcended death, but there was never any proof that Annabelle ever existed. There was a local legend about a sailor who fell in love with the daughter of a plantation owner. The father disapproved of the match, so the lovers met in secret. While the sailor was out to sea, the daughter died of yellow fever, and when he returned, the heartbroken dad refused to tell him where the daughter was buried. Some folks were convinced the story was Poe's inspiration for Anabelle Lee. Zoe and Hannah had spent hours investigating the mystery, searching the island for clues, quite certain that Annabelle was entombed right here on Sullivan's. It was a dumb quest perhaps, but such were the things that occupied young girls' thoughts.

Even now, Zoe felt an odd sense of communion with Poe—particularly after having spent much of her adult life in the city where he'd died. He was a patron saint of pre-pubescent goths, the king of woe, the lord of gloom. But there was something innately familiar to Zoe in the essence of his words, a melancholia that went beyond the usual teen angst. The truth was she would rather not relate to a raging alcoholic, who'd found himself alone and forsaken at the hour of his death, but she did. Perhaps it was the keen sense of loss they shared—a loss evident in every word he wrote. Zoe related to his words. They even had the month of December in common.

. . . distinctly I remember it was in the bleak December;
  And each separate dying ember wrought its ghost upon the floor.

HERE, in the wee hours, shadows writhed upon the ceiling of her parents' room. Despite the new wash of paint and the foundation-deep cleansing, the master bedroom, like the rest of the house, harbored ghosts.

With the air conditioning off, the window remained open, admitting a soft, cool breeze. By day, the sun was already intense in the month of May, but these were typically the most idyllic evenings on the island, with cool breezes sweeping inland from the sea.

In the stillness of the night, even a block away, Zoe could hear water slap-slapping at the shore. She could taste salt spray. In her mind's eye, she pictured the moon's sheen along wet sand and the multitude of tiny, indistinguishable shadows that scurried near the water's edge. Sand crabs and beach hoppers digging around small piles of rotting sargassum seaweed. At low tide, millions of bloodworms pocking the sand.

Throughout her youth, Zoe had often sat on the beach in a pair of wet shorts, her long hair drawn into a sticky ponytail, thick with salt and sweat.

If she sat at the tideline, and burrowed a hand into the wet sand, there was a pretty good chance of bringing up at least one bean clam—often more than two.

With a loose fist, Zoe would let the ebbing tide wash away the grains of sand from her palm, filtering out everything but the bean clams. And then, if she held them long enough, until they were shut good and tight—and longer still, until the sound of the ocean drifted to a distant hum—some of the clams would come back to life. Slowly at first, almost imperceptibly, they'd begin to wiggle in her hand. As though testing the landscape beneath their smooth exoskeletons, their tongues slid out to tickle the skin of Zoe's palm.

She would scoot backward from the water's edge, back to where the tide washed over her toes, but no closer. And then she would set the handful of clams down on the sheet of sand to watch what they would do.

She'd never officially timed the intervals where she'd remained quiet, waiting, but these were the moments of her greatest Zen—moments of simply being, when all thoughts and fears were quieted in Zoe's head.

Outside the window, the sound of a car engine approached, then idled off. She wondered before which house the door opened and closed, although she had no real desire to get up and check. Someone was getting home late, but that was none of her concern—as long as it wasn't Chris out there.

Feeling restless, Zoe bounced gently on the bed, testing its resilience—why, she couldn't say. It would be a long time before squeaking beds were any real concern of hers. Still, it was nice to know the bed was sound. Perfect timing to have met Ethan when she did. Too bad she wasn't in any frame of mind for a relationship—or even a friend. There seemed to be nothing wrong with him at first glance.

Then again, that's where Zoe usually went wrong.

There were two schools of thought, one resonating equally as strong as Poe's unhappy tales: it was said that in order to receive good things, you had to be open to them. The second screamed for Zoe to defend herself at all costs. If she circled her wagons, maybe she could avoid more heartache.

In the darkness, she could barely make out the bedposts of the rice bed stretching up toward the textured ceiling, arms raised in supplication. The bed was lovely, made of cherry wood, carved with rice blossoms—hence the name—a bygone symbol of a plantation owner's source of wealth. If he grew rice, then he carved his posts with rice blooms. If he grew cotton, cotton flowers. If he grew tobacco, tobacco blooms.

Twisted as her thoughts were, Zoe wondered if anyone had ever carved slaves into their bedposts, because that had been the real crop here, she thought bitterly.

Groping about the bed, she attempted to locate her phone, where she'd left it last night after peeking at Facebook. She had yet to change her status to "It's complicated"—or whatever it was supposed to say. None of this was complicated, unless she made it that way. The problem was, Zoe always made it that way.

She swept her thumb over the screen, waking the phone. It was 3:31 a.m. The blue light gave the room an electric glow.

"Hannah," she whispered, as though a stubborn litany of her sister's name could change present circumstances. *Hannah, Hannah, Hannah.*

The answering silence left Zoe with an unfathomable emptiness that drove her from the bed. It was early yet. Maybe a walk on the beach would clear her mind and make her sleepy again? With a sigh, she found a pair of shorts in the suitcase still serving as her dresser—a pair of denim cutoffs she hadn't worn in ages, mostly because Chris always said they were much too short. Plucking up a teal blue T-shirt, she shrugged into it, and then she grabbed the sandals she'd tossed into the closet. Old habits returned easily; she didn't bother to lock the door on the way out.

At 3:40 a.m., the skies were free of ambient light. All along Atlantic Avenue, both sides of the street kept front porch lights off from May to the end of October because, here on Sullivan's, as on many of the barrier islands, it was illegal to leave on beachfront lights during turtle mating season. It discouraged loggerheads from nesting and confused the hatchlings from trying to find the sea. In fact, all lights that were visible from the beach were disallowed. If she had to estimate the hour, she could never have done so by comparing the sky here to the one she'd become familiar with in Baltimore.

Salt spray stung the air, and in the distance—not so far—she smelled a hint of pluff mud. By rote, she crossed the dunes at a favorite spot, where the rise sloped more gently and the trudge of countless feet had formed a silken valley, devoid of scrub.

How many salt-crusted sandals had passed this way before? How many times had her sister darted between these dunes, her size-three white Converse sneakers angled toward home? How many barefoot slaves had stumbled over from the moonlit beach below?

As a main port of entry, Sullivan's Island was once the Ellis Island of Southern slave trade. It was no wonder so much of their culture was wrapped up in Gullah traditions and lore. As a teen, Zoe had sometimes blamed their family's troubles on karmic comeuppance and worn an attitude of guilt, much the same way goths embraced Poe's influence, painting their nails black and lining their eyes with liquid gloom. But these were not things Zoe gave much thought to anymore.

On the beach, free from the menace of sand burs, Zoe removed her sandals, dangling them from fingers that were relaxing for the first time in weeks. The sand, still warm, felt glorious beneath her toes.

Drawn to the place where she'd discovered her sister's bike thirty years ago, Zoe turned left, not right, toward Breach instead of Fort Moultrie. The sun was still a no-show as she made her way along the frothing surf.

At low tide, the shoreline was broken, interspersed with warm-water puddles full of briny creatures, all stranded till the tide changed. The worst that might happen would be stepping on a jellyfish. Not all that worried about getting wet, she made her way along the beach, judging the shoreline by the depth of water at her ankles. The sun had yet to begin its ascent, but the darkness was soothing, a bit as it must feel to return to the womb, with the gentle sound of water rushing past her ears. Cool water petted her ankles, as though to say, "Welcome home, Zoe. Welcome home."

It felt good to be home.

Maybe she should have come sooner?

With a sudden sense of certainty that had eluded her previously, Zoe realized this was where she would find her answers.

As though to underline the moment of her epiphany, daylight cast its first blush upon the beach and Zoe realized with a start that she'd misjudged the shoreline.

The tide was coming in, not going out, rolling in shallow-water tidal pools along the coastline. There was a generous stretch of water between her and the beach. She was on a sand-bar, nearing Breach, maybe twenty yards offshore. Instinctively, Zoe understood this was no place to be, but she wasn't particularly alarmed, because she hadn't yet reached the no-cross zone, demarcated by the cement gun casings slowly being devoured by the surf. Beyond that point, currents were more treacherous. Along the narrow inlet, closer to Breach, the water was choppier, churning up whitecaps—a bad sign. She made her way quickly toward the beach, veering toward a foaming ridge of sand that snaked inland.

Everything changed in a heartbeat.

Stepping along the edge, the sandbar caved beneath Zoe's feet, like the eroded edge of a cliff, plummeting her into thigh-deep water. She stumbled, righting herself, and felt a strong pull at her legs, pitching her forward. Her heart lurched. She let go of the sandals as an inescapable riptide dragged her back, toward the sea.

Zoe didn't have the wherewithal to scream. Even if she could have, no one was about to hear. *Stay calm,* she told herself.

Battling a wave of panic, Zoe stabbed her legs into the churning depths, searching for solid ground. Each second's delay found her carried farther out. In some places, the drop offs were more than six feet. Nothing emerged beneath her feet. The water was dragging her back.

Don't fight.

Stay calm.

Think.

Keep your nose above the surface.

Get air.

Tread water.

Swim sideways, parallel to the beach.

But she didn't count on the force of the current or the speed at which it dragged her back. She felt another tug and her heart lurched again—this time mercifully closing her throat. The undertow jerked her down below the surface.

Salt stung Zoe's eyes, burning the inside of her nostrils. She sucked in enough seawater to set fire to her lungs. The current roared past her ears.

Her body recoiled, expelling a rush of air and Zoe felt the need to breath. She fought the urge, her cheeks billowing with the effort to keep air in, to route it to her lungs.

Darkness enfolded her. The dawn light receded to a pin.

Battling the instinct to close her eyes against the burn of salt, Zoe flailed her arms, struggling to pull herself back toward the surface.

Air!

Now!

The remaining breath exited her lungs with an explosion of bubbles. Each pocket caught the pink light above, distorting the view. Instinctively, Zoe inhaled. Water for air. The pain, for an interminable moment, was excruciating.

Hannah.

Oh, God, Hannah.

Her sister's face swam before red-hot eyes, and for the space of an instant, Zoe was aware that she was no longer struggling. She was floating on a pillow of light.

Hannah drifted alongside her, arms outstretched as though to guide her. And then, as swiftly as though someone had turned out the lights, Zoe was sucked down into cold, black nothingness.

10

"Her name?"

"Zoe Rutherford."

Silence.

"Come on, Zoe! Wake up!"

A hand slapped Zoe firmly across the cheek. The sting brought her back to her senses. She heard a chorus of voices, but couldn't comprehend the words. She vomited water, attempted to nod, but her body felt too heavy to move. A face like Gabi Donovan's swam before her eyes. *"Go home, Zoe! We don't want you."*

Zoe sought Hannah's gaze. Her sister's brows were furrowed, eyes sad, but she said nothing to soften Gabi's rude demand.

"We don't want you," Gabi Donovan persisted.

"I promise not to tell."

"Blabbermouth," Gabi sang. *"You're a blabbermouth!"*

Hannah's face blurred over Gabi's shoulder, descending into shadow. Panic squeezed Zoe's lungs. Deep in her heart, she knew this was her last chance to keep her sister close. If she let go—if she let them leave, everything would be lost.

Gabi's face blurred, the whites of her eyes bulging, irises black as pitch. Zoe looked over Gabi's shoulder at her sister's retreating form. "Hannah," she pleaded. "Don't go!"

"Get her into the ambulance," she heard someone snap, and vaguely understood they were referring to her.

Another voice spoke softly near Zoe's ear. "Hang on, honey."

She felt a terrible burn in her lungs, tasted salt and copper in her mouth. Disembodied heads floated overhead. She felt herself lifted, her body whooshed through time and space. All she could think was that her sister was gone and Zoe needed to follow. "Let me go," she heard herself say, but the voice stayed trapped inside her head.

Heavy doors slammed, sirens screamed. Zoe drifted down, into the dark . . . like a spineless jellyfish sucked into a leaden sea.

"Can you hear me, Zoe?"

"Hannah?"

Zoe awoke confused, her lips parched and painful. Her head ached. Her lungs hurt. But still her sister's visage was as real to her now as the white curtains hanging from the canopy above her head.

A black female nurse with a genuine smile and a face free of makeup stood beside her, tucking a blanket over Zoe's shoulders. "Do you need another blanket?"

Zoe shuddered, feeling cold to her bones. Her head felt wooly —a little as though someone had gone through and refiled all her memories out of order. "Where am I?"

"Roper St. Francis. ICU," the nurse said. "We've got you hooked to IVs; don't be alarmed." She patted Zoe's shoulder with a gentleness that made Zoe's throat thick. The tiny gesture of kindness, that brief human touch, left her starved for more. Her teeth chattered. "I'm cold."

"You want another blanket?"

Zoe nodded jerkily. The blanket appeared within seconds, fluttering down over her, providing an immediate rush of neonatal warmth.

Zoe flashed on an image of her mother, tucking her and her sister in after finding them huddled together in the same bed. Her dad would have separated them, but Marge had covered them with the bedspread, smiling as she set a finger to her lips. No kiss, no loving touches on the forehead, but there was love in her eyes. Two doors down, their father had been in his office, music from the motion picture *2001* drifting through the house.

"Better?" the nurse asked.

Zoe nodded, her throat too thick and painful to speak.

"Do you remember anything at all?"

Swallowing a burning knot, Zoe thought about the question. The last thing she remembered, she was hurrying toward the beach. Sand fell away beneath her feet, and then she was in too deep. She nodded. Apparently, she had nearly become yet another Breach Inlet statistic. Even knowing the danger the beach presented, it was so easy to be deceived.

Maybe that's how her sister had drowned. That simple. No great mystery, no stolen child, no murder or terrible accident. Maybe Hannah had simply misjudged the shoreline, following turtle tracks in the sand.

What a crazy coincidence it would be for sisters to die the same way, in the very same place. Crazy, but entirely possible. A few years ago, Zoe read an article about a mom who'd lost both her daughters to shark attacks—different circumstances, but both women had made the ocean their careers. It was the law of odds.

"You're a lucky girl," the nurse said, as though reading Zoe's thoughts. "One of your neighbors saw you go down."

In that instant, Zoe didn't feel particularly lucky; she felt only guilt and self-reproach. She didn't remember anyone else on that beach with her; only Hannah's face peered back at her from the murky depths of memory. She trembled beneath the covers. "Who?" she asked. The word came out sounding guttural.

The nurse smiled, understanding the question. "Mr. Donovan. You can thank him for knowing enough to start resuscitation in the water."

Zoe blinked in surprise. She'd never imagined water resuscitation was possible. Nor could she picture that skinny, cranky old man maneuvering her through churning water, all the while giving her CPR.

The nurse smiled. "He's waiting outside to be sure you're okay. Care to see him?"

"Sure," Zoe said, filled with ambivalence.

The nurse drew the blanket higher, patting her shoulder before hurrying away, leaving Zoe alone behind the curtain.

It would seem there should be an anticlimactic sense of peace, a calm after the storm, but a sense of doom persisted. Zoe waited anxiously.

As the nurse said, she was hooked to IVs, more than one. A wiry stand towered beside her, dripping liquids into her arm. On the same side of the bed sat a cardiac monitor, displaying restless numbers. Despite the blankets that were heaped atop her, Zoe continued to shiver. She supposed she must be in shock but it was too late in the year for hypothermia. She doubted she could have been in the water all that long. Then again, she didn't remember anything beyond the dream of her sister floating along beside her.

It had felt so real. A keen sense of loss overwhelmed her as she acknowledged that it was nothing but a trick of the mind.

A moment later, the nurse reemerged through the curtain, scratching her forehead. "I'm so sorry," she said. "He must have left, but don't worry, we called your husband. He's already on the way." She smiled reassuringly.

Zoe's chest tightened. "Husband?"

The nurse nodded absently as she checked the monitors, looking down at Zoe with furrowed brows. "You'll be in ICU a few more hours," she said, ignoring the question. "Then we'll move you to a room and keep you overnight."

"I don't have a husband," Zoe said weakly.

"If your vitals stay strong, we'll let you go come morning. You're doing great," the nurse said, patting Zoe's arm.

The possibility of Chris turning up at the hospital was all Zoe could think of now. "I don't have a husband," she told the nurse again.

The woman tilted her head. "Boyfriend?"

Zoe shook her head adamantly. She tried to sit. "Please . . . call my brother," she said. "I need to speak to my brother."

The nurse shoved her down with a firm, but gentle hand, her gaze flitting across the scar on Zoe's forehead. "Don't worry, Zoe. Your family's on the way. Please don't get up."

Whether it was the cardiac monitor that gave away Zoe's distress or simply the tone of her voice, the nurse considered the monitor another long moment and then turned to ask, "Is there something you need to say, Zoe?"

"I don't have a husband," Zoe said again, hoping to convey as much as possible without admitting to the world that she was a victim of domestic abuse. Whatever happened here today, she wasn't going home with Chris. She had worked too hard for this separation and now she wasn't going to see it come to nothing simply because she was too stupid to watch her step out on the beach.

"Lay down, Zoe. Relax. I'll look into it for you," the nurse promised, her voice whispery, meant to be soothing. Instead, it left Zoe feeling frantic, as though the woman didn't believe her. "Don't worry," she said again, adjusting something on the IV. After a moment, she left, and Zoe fell back on the bed, exhausted.

Against her will her eyes drifted shut. She conjured a picture of Chris driving from Baltimore, but not even that frightful image or the beeping of monitors was enough to keep her from drifting back to sleep.

11

BLACKBERRY COBBLER

"A re you hungry?" asked a nurse—this one a blond with a smile a shade whiter than her paper-pale skin.

Zoe wasn't particularly hungry but she nodded anyway, thinking that she might as well pick at something, especially if they were going to charge her for it anyway. They'd placed her in a private room overlooking the parking lot. She couldn't see the cars, or the spaces, but she could just spy the rows of lit street lamps illuminating rows of palmetto trees.

Nick arrived a few minutes before her supper did, along with Beth and the girls. Both girls had grown considerably since Zoe last saw them. No more were they bundles of boundless energy and noise. Her brother tested the door, rapping his knuckles on the doorframe to announce their arrival. Zoe smiled, beckoning him in. Beth followed behind, with their daughters in tow. The eldest, Anna, looked like her brother's wife, but Zoe was startled to find Parker had grown into the spitting image of their sister, Hannah, with dirty blond hair a few shades lighter than Nick's and angelic blue eyes, like their mother's. For an instant, the sight of Parker sucked the remaining breath from Zoe's lungs.

As her brother's clan filtered into the room, filling it with their presence, Zoe pressed a hand to her chest.

"How're ya doing, sport?"

Nick's playful greeting belied his dark expression.

"Good . . . I'm good."

Anna greeted her timidly. "Hi, Aunt Zoe."

Parker smiled and gave a tentative little wave.

"You gave us a scare," Beth complained, although she softened the rebuke with a heartwarming smile. Her makeup, as always, was flawless—down to the sixties-era eyeliner Zoe could never get precisely right. To top it off, Beth's hair clearly saw a stylist more often than Zoe's ever did. Her highlights were new, without any roots.

Like a poltergeist, Chris's voice came back to haunt her: *Normal girls make themselves pretty for their man.*

Funny how when they'd begun dating, he'd said he loved the fact that Zoe was a "natural beauty"—his words, not hers. She didn't even care to address the fact that he saw her as a girl, not a woman.

Zoe lifted a shoulder in response to Beth's complaint, uncertain what to say. *I didn't mean to,* seemed a dumb way to respond. "I scared myself as well."

Pulling an aching breath through her lungs, Zoe studied her brother's daughters. "The last time I saw you two, you were only yea high." She lifted a hand, holding it beside the bed, palm side down.

Nick's tone was curt. "They grow a lot in four years' time."

Zoe smiled tightly, chalking her brother's attitude up to the stress of their most recent conversation. She motioned the girls forward to give her a hug.

Anna came quickly, though Parker hesitated, clinging to her mama's hand. Anna hugged Zoe, and Zoe kissed her cheek before she had the chance to move away. Quietly, she returned to her mother's side and then pushed her little sister forward.

Only once prompted, Parker left Beth's side to offer Zoe a belated hug. But she quickly returned to her parents. Both girls' gazes fell away after that. They stared at the bed, at Zoe's feet beneath the covers, at the light above their heads, and for the longest time, at the picture-less TV mounted on the far wall, as though longing for its saving grace. Zoe watched them with an underlying sense of sadness.

They were near the same age she and Hannah had been before Hannah disappeared—eight and ten—but Zoe had been so distracted with her own screwed-up life that she couldn't remember their precise ages. Oh, she'd never missed a birthday, though one year blurred into the next and now, as they stood before her with sweet but solemn faces, Zoe was ashamed to acknowledge how long it had been since she'd last heard their voices. It was no wonder neither seemed particularly overjoyed to see her.

After an awkward moment, with everyone staring at everything in the room except Zoe, Beth sent the girls out in the hall to wait. She gave them each five dollars and told them to locate a vending machine for snacks.

"Spend it wisely," their father said.

Their faces lit more at the sight of the bills than they had over reuniting with their long-lost aunt and Zoe tried not to be hurt.

What did she expect, after all? A few phone calls and birthday cards were hardly substitutes for a relationship. How had she managed to let so much time slip by?

When the girls were gone, Beth leaned a fulsome hip on the bed and reached out to touch Zoe's hand. "Zoe, honey, what happened?"

Zoe shrugged. "Really, I don't know. One minute, I was walking on the beach, the next . . ."

"You're lucky Donovan saw you go under," her brother said, mirroring the nurse's words. "Apparently, he was out fishing when he spotted you out on the sandbar."

Zoe nodded. "So I've been told."

She still couldn't believe that old man had saved her life, when younger and sturdier men had gone down at Breach without much of a fight.

Beth's brows lifted. "They say he's ex-Navy SEAL," she said, looking properly impressed. "I guess you never lose that sort of training." Her gaze then honed in on the scar on Zoe's forehead. She sat uncomfortably for a moment, and then, probably to fill the silence, she added, "Nick thought maybe it happened right there where Ha—"

Nick cleared his throat and Beth hushed abruptly, looking nervously at her husband. She patted Zoe's hand. "Anyway, we're just happy Mr. Donovan was around to help."

Beth's gaze returned to Zoe's face, this time studiously avoiding the scar, and Zoe felt the tension heighten. Clearly, it was not a recent injury, but she imagined the healing stitches raged purple against her bloodless complexion.

"Yeah," Zoe said absently. "I guess I should thank him."

"Unless you were going for different results?"

It took Zoe a moment to realize what it was her brother was implying, and then her brows collided. Her gaze snapped to his. "For fuck's sake, Nick. You don't believe I'd do that, do you?"

He merely stared at her, the question smoldering like coals in his eyes.

Beth shot up from the bed, releasing Zoe's hand. "I'll go check on the girls," she said quickly.

Zoe heard the click, click of her heels recede until the door latched shut. Her gaze remained glued to her brother's. "I can't believe you would think that."

"What do you expect me to believe, Zoe? I talked to Chris."

"Of course you did."

"What does that mean?"

"Nothing except that, of course, he would give you some crazy impression about this. Please tell me he's not on his way from Baltimore."

Nick's brows remained furrowed, his eyes full of questions. "The guy sounded genuinely worried—then relieved. Why would you leave him wondering, Zoe? Why didn't you speak up and tell me what was going on?"

Zoe opened her mouth, and closed it again. She couldn't conceive words to tell her brother that she'd remained in an abusive relationship for eight years too long. Somehow, it didn't seem as though it would help her current case, adding insult and injury to his theory that she had some sort of suicidal wish.

Zoe had always considered herself a strong woman—not the sort who might fall prey to a man like Chris.

The silence was so thick she heard each step outside as people passed by her room. "You didn't answer my question. Is he on the way?"

Her brother's frown deepened. "No. But he asked how you were, said you took the breakup hard."

Zoe lifted a brow, not entirely surprised Chris would spin it so he was the one doing the dumping. "What did you tell him?"

"The truth. I haven't seen you."

"And now that you have?"

Her brother's gaze narrowed. Zoe sensed his invisibility cloak at the ready. "Look," he said, "Whatever is going on between you two is none of my concern. I barely know the man."

Mostly by design, Zoe acknowledged.

Chris wasn't the sort of guy she'd ever wanted to bring home —even if she had a home to bring him back to. But, on the other hand, Nick had never gone out of his way to meet Chris either. Her brother never once came to Baltimore. Only Zoe had ever traveled "home" to reconnect for the holidays, but she'd often felt more like an awkward voyeur into her brother's extraordinary life.

At some point, the contrasts of their lives only managed to

make her feel like an abject failure. She stared out the window, trying to decipher Chris's intent.

It might be a good sign that he was taking credit for the breakup. It was third-grade bullshit, but if that's what it took to keep him away—bolstering his ego with her silence—Zoe was okay with that.

If he came . . . if worse came to worst, she would call Chief McWhorter. The simple fact that she would rather trust a stranger over her brother left her feeling disjointed.

In part, going to Nick for help bucked the natural order of things, because Zoe was the one who was supposed to protect her siblings—a fine job she'd done with Hannah.

Her brother tilted her a look, one that seemed less concerned than suspicious, which only made Zoe feel more inclined to defend herself. "Is there something you should be telling me, Zoe?"

Hearing that particular question again for the second time in one day, Zoe experienced an unexpected rush of anger. "Are you looking for a confession, Nick? You're not gonna get one. I came here to deal with *the house*—something you seem disinclined to do. As for Chris, he's *my* business, not *yours*. But I can assure you I haven't got a death wish. What happened this morning was an accident, not some crazy attempt to follow Hannah to the grave."

Despite the anger in her voice, her brother's shoulders relaxed, apparently mollified by the certainty of her tone. Still, he asked, "Are you sure?"

Zoe felt sick in her gut over the realization that her brother must doubt her very sanity. "Of course I'm sure." The fact that he didn't seem to know her at all—literally, *not at all*—left her feeling wearier than the ordeal she'd faced this morning.

She'd lost her sister as swiftly as she'd lost her footing this morning, but she'd let her brother go ever so slowly. And the worst part of it all was that she had barely noticed, until Nick was so far gone that even a hand between them seemed impossible.

Certainly, the idea of touching him was uncomfortable. Beth felt more at ease with the notion of physical contact than her brother did. He stood at a safe distance, his feet planted slightly apart. "Sorry," he said. "But you've never been able to let her go, Zoe. I wish you'd let the house go as well. We'll get enough for it as it stands."

"Enough for what?"

Nick hadn't bothered to sit, Zoe realized, her gaze flicking over the empty chair beside him. He stood next to the bed, on the side of the room nearest the door, and Zoe felt the rift between them more acutely than ever. Outside, she could hear the girls bickering over something. Beth's voice interrupted.

Her brother peered back at the door, his sideburns perfectly shaped, although graying. Except for the color of his hair, he looked a lot like their dad, with his wide jaw and his prominent Roman nose. As an adult, her brother was handsome, with strong, confident features that were complimented by the wide set of his shoulders and a broad chest. If he hadn't been so inclined toward numbers and accounting, Zoe might have easily pictured him as a linebacker for an all-American team. In high school, he'd worn his hair shoulder-length and carefree to match his attitude, but there was little in his stance now that reminded her of that surfboarding youth. At the moment, his hands were folded in front of him, like a secret service agent, tasked with guarding the president.

Zoe realized his charges were far more precious—his wife, his children, and the life they shared together—a life Zoe was not a part of. He was here, but wary of her and what her presence might bring to their table.

Zoe took a mental step backward, realizing that she wanted all this to change. She wanted to be part of her brother's life. To do this, she would consider searching for a house in Charleston or somewhere else nearby. In the end, she could resent Nick for keeping his boundaries, for handling his losses differently than

Zoe . . . or she could allow him the courtesy of being himself . . . and maybe try a little harder.

She loved her brother, missed his presence in her life. And, in part, she had to wonder if she would have allowed Chris to grow on her, like a cancer, if her sibling relationship had been a little healthier.

Somehow, the answer to that question was a resounding, "No."

Zoe settled back against the pillows. "I'm fine," she reassured him. "I swear it, Nick. It was just a freak accident."

He slid one foot forward, releasing the grip of his hands, unconsciously relaxing, and Zoe smiled, resolved to heal their relationship.

For a moment, she saw him as he was, a little boy ambling up the front porch steps, sliding her a wary look. Zoe craved the feel of him in her arms. That day on the steps, he'd embraced her as though she were his port in the storm.

When did she let go?

When did he?

"Hey, do you remember Nana's blackberry cobbler recipe?" Zoe asked with a smirk, knowing he had never baked a thing in all his life.

Nick cocked his head, like a rooster. "Me?"

Zoe laughed. "Yeah, I didn't think so."

"Why?"

"I'm thinking of baking Mr. Donovan a thank you because, 'nothing says thank you like a warm fruit pie.'"

Her brother smiled at Zoe's use of their Nana's words. He rolled his eyes and blew out a sigh. Zoe imagined it was a natural response to the memories of countless afternoons spent together gathering blackberries so their mom could turn berries into sugary baked goodness. Nick, of course, was too young to remember when Nana died, so his memories didn't include the peculiar dynamics between the matriarchs of their household, but Zoe remembered with a pang in her heart. In that kitchen, everything was always okay, no matter what had transpired outside that room. Despite everything, those ladies had loved their families, and their love was poured, pinched, or folded into every casserole, every pie, and every steaming pot roast they'd cooked. Once Nana was gone, their mother had filled her shoes—at least in the kitchen.

For a good half hour, Zoe and Nick explored the merits of Nana's cobbler recipe—the flawless, buttery crust that melted against their tongues, the ultimate mix of berries, and the tart berry scent that wafted for long hours throughout the house. Zoe always called it a blackberry cobbler, but in fact, Nana's recipe called for raspberries and blueberries as well.

"It was a berry feast," Zoe told him.

"I wish I could recall, though mom's was pretty good."

"It was Nana's recipe. They were much the same."

"I wish I'd known her better."

Zoe knew he meant Nana, but the same could be said about Margit Althaus.

"She was a trip." Outside the room, the girls began arguing again. "Anyway, you always had enough women fighting over you. Sounds as though you still do."

Her brother's eyes smiled, even if it only barely touched his lips. "Beth is pretty good about sharing," he said.

"What about the girls?"

He glanced back at the door. "Not so much."

There had never been any competition between Zoe and Hannah. She tried to imagine what that might have been like.

He was distracted now, with the girls arguing out in the hall. "Why don't you take them home? I'm sure visiting hours are nearly over anyway."

He nodded. "I'll be back in the morning," he said. And then he brought the kids in from the hall to say goodbye. Zoe promised to come and visit when she could.

"Bee, do you have a recipe for blackberry cobbler you can share with Zoe?"

Beth's gaze skidded toward Zoe's in surprise.

Zoe grinned as she readjusted herself to sit a little higher. "I'm going to attempt to bake one for my next-door neighbor as a thank you for not leaving me to drown."

"Oh! Yes! Yes, I do," Beth said quickly. She thought about it a moment, tilting her pretty face and tapping at her chin. "In fact, I'm sure I brought home a couple of your mother's cookbooks back when you two were cleaning out her place." She looked suddenly embarrassed by the revelation, her face turning pink. "I always meant to give them back," she quickly explained. "Figured you might want them . . . after a while."

During those hectic days of clearing out the house after their mother's death, while she and Nick were busy filling contractor bags for Goodwill, Beth had snatched their mom's cookbooks without asking. In the mood Zoe was in at the time, she would have tossed them all out. There wasn't room for everything in the attic, and she'd no longer cared about keeping even her year-books, or mementos from her youth. It seemed an insurmountable task to clear the house of so much junk—generations' worth. She had desperately needed a clean slate. Thank God Beth had looked beyond the ragged notebooks and yellowed, food-stained paper to spot the treasures she and Nick would have abandoned to the trash.

"Thank you," Zoe said and was surprised to discover that she meant it.

12

YOU MUSTA FORGOT

Not to frighten her, they said, but to illustrate the gravity of the matter, the staff at the hospital recounted stories of patients who'd arrived in better shape than Zoe did and then had taken turns for the worse, suffering cardiopulmonary arrest and neurological damage.

Zoe's doctor was only mildly concerned about the possibility of late onset pulmonary and cerebral edema. Additionally, sometimes infections occurred after immersions like hers. Fortunately, by the following morning there was little evidence of any of these complications so, on Tuesday, they released Zoe to go home.

It surprised her to discover that, while the week of her homecoming had come and gone, seemingly without notice, the same could not be said for her release from the hospital. The news of her accident made the local paper. As promised, Nick arrived to claim her from the hospital. He drove her home and let her into a house that had been straightened to perfection in her absence. Beth and the girls scrambled to the front door to greet them.

The windows were open to a balmy breeze. Copious vases, filled with flowers, adorned the kitchen counters. Pies—yes, plural—sat cooling there as well, along with a casserole or three, all with polite note cards tucked beneath the tins.

Despite the lack of furniture in the house, there was a certain hominess to the place that Zoe had never been able to achieve in any of her houses—not those she'd shared with Chris nor any of her own.

With happy giggles, Anna and Parker led her down the hall to unveil Zoe's "new" bedroom, where a tulip-shaped vase filled with flowers had been placed upon the bedside table—also new to the room, although she recognized it. It was the same curio table that had once held her mom's roses out on the porch.

The bed was properly made, adorned with small, lacy pillows that were not previously there—one from each of her nieces, decorated with felt hearts and red glitter.

"Oh my!" Zoe released their hands, tears stinging her eyes as she stumbled into the room, straight to the pillows, inspecting each in turn. Drawn in marker, they sported unique messages: One said, "Welcome home, Zoe," signed "Anna." The other, "We love you," signed "Parker."

Zoe's throat felt too thick to speak. She forgot to breathe. Her lungs protested a sudden lack of oxygen. But each ache and pain was worth it, she decided, as she returned the pillows to the bed, positioning them neatly against the larger shams.

She ran her fingers across the bedspread, the familiar white cotton chamois that had once graced her Nana's bed. It fit well with the new coat of November Rain on the walls. A new set of airy curtains adorned the windows as well . . . simple white cotton. Because the room faced west, the sun in this room was rarely overpowering in the morning. Nick would know this.

Moved by each of these thoughtful gestures, Zoe fell to one knee, groaning as she invited her nieces into a bear hug. This time, both girls came without hesitation, cloaking her with fragile little-girl arms. The ache in her chest might just as easily have been due to her bursting heart as it was the zest of their hug.

Their mother and father stood in the doorway. Her brother Nick, clearly proud of his daughters, reached out to pull his wife into a close embrace. A warm, pleasurable feeling sidled through Zoe at the sight of them.

"Thank you," she said, and refrained from reminding them all that she didn't intend to stay in the house. It was a lovely gesture, one that drove home the dearth of kindness she had been surrounded with in Baltimore. She didn't care to spoil the moment.

"Of course, you're always welcome to stay with us," Beth said, looking up at her husband.

"No, this is wonderful," Zoe said.

Beth smiled. "Nick was pretty sure you'd refuse so we wanted you to at least have a cozy place to recover in."

With a little effort, Zoe stood, wincing as she released her nieces. "I appreciate this so much." This time, both girls remained by her side. Parker fell behind her and sat, bouncing gently on the bed.

"Don't mess it up, Parker," Nick said.

"I won't, Daddy." Her tone was lively. Zoe had to fight the urge to turn around and look, half expecting to find Hannah seated there instead.

"The house looks amazing."

Beth folded her arms in front of her. "Don't thank us. You did most of the work. All we did was straighten up a bit."

For the first time since arriving at Kingdom, Zoe examined her surroundings without jaded eyes. The house did look better. It was clean, with brand-new carpet in the living room. The walls were all pristine. With a bit more work, it would be an adorable beach cottage any young family might relish.

She tried to envision the house with her own furniture but couldn't, in part because she'd already written everything off. There was nothing left of her old life to relocate here.

Zoe had abandoned a couch worth three thousand dollars

that had taken her years to pay off and a limited edition Andy Warhol print lithograph Chris had given her for her birthday using her money, because it was something he wanted. But these were all things that had once prevented her from moving on. Perhaps unfairly, Chris had inherited all Zoe's treasures, but maybe it would be a deterrent to his rocking the boat just now.

Zoe glanced at her cell phone lying on the bedside table where someone probably placed it when making the bed. She had more missed messages, but so far so good; only nine hours from Baltimore and Chris had yet to show his face. With all her stuff it was entirely possible he could be rethinking his position. For once, he had a decent job, and if he sat down and weighed his prospects, he might discover it was never Zoe he wanted. It was the security she had brought. If he merely resolved to set his alarm, he could wake up with anyone he wanted.

Unfortunately, Zoe knew him well enough to know that Chris rarely chose wisely. His ego was boundless. He would take her leaving as a blow to his pride, and there was a good chance he would show up at her front door now that he knew where she was . . . and then what? Reaching out, Zoe turned the phone display over, determined not to worry about Chris while she was enjoying time with her family.

The doorbell rang as her fingers left the phone.

BETH, Nick, and the girls left about six, after the train of well-wishers slowed down a bit.

"Are you sure you don't wanna stay with us a few days?" her brother asked. His look was hopeful, but maybe because he would have liked to see her let the house go, as he'd said. But Zoe wasn't ready to do that, and if she left with him now she might never return.

"You've done enough for now," Zoe insisted. "I'm fine."

She bit back the remainder of what she longed to say—that if he truly wished to help, he could come back and help her clean out the attic, because none of that could remain if they meant to sell the house. However, she'd gotten far more than she'd expected from her brother and his family, and there was a fragile bond restored between them. The last thing she intended to do was prompt him to close that door. She realized intuitively how much this house threatened the picture of perfection he struggled so hard to maintain.

Her brother looked about one last time as he retreated to the porch. He pointed to the rocker. "I can't believe that's still here."

Zoe crossed her arms, giving him a wry smile. "You didn't actually think *she* was going anywhere, did you?" It would have been appropriate for Nana to be haunting the place. "I bet she curses anyone who comes near it with hemorrhoids."

Her brother chuckled. "She was into all that hoodoo crap, wasn't she?"

Zoe smiled and nodded, realizing how much her brother couldn't know; he had been so young when their grandmother died.

"Yep, she was."

In fact, their grandmother had claimed she was a descendant of the Sea Island people, despite of her pasty white skin. At a time when segregation was at its worst, Rosa Beaufain had left the bosom of her family to serve as a teacher on St. Simons Island, where she met and fell in love with a handsome sailor by the name of Simon Rutherford. Given her bold personality, Zoe couldn't imagine her grandmother accepting any form of abuse. Zoe had lots to remember, and even more to share. Oblivious to her thoughts, the girls ran down the front steps into the yard.

"Ow, ow, ow!" Anna screamed.

"Put on your shoes," Beth demanded as she followed her children.

"Look how dark it is, Mama! Look at the stars."

"Stay out of the road, Parker!"

"I'm not on the road. See?"

"I can't see you, Parker. It's dark!"

Anna sat down and started to wail. "Something bit me!"

Beth marched toward the road, sweeping Anna into her arms. "Nothing bit you, Anna. You stepped on a sandbur. That's what you get for taking off your shoes. Come on, we'll find it in the car."

Zoe smiled as her brother lingered on the porch. "You've got your hands full."

He nodded, crossing his arms, seemingly reluctant to go. "If you want . . . I'll fix that porch screen."

They shared a brief but meaningful look.

For Zoe's part, she had come to consider the hole in the screen a bit nostalgically, but it was the first time her brother had ever seen fit to acknowledge the history between them, and perhaps to a lesser degree his responsibility toward the house. Small as it was, the concession gave Zoe a pang of regret over the thought of fixing the screen at all. Nevertheless, prospective buyers wouldn't care one whit about the fact that a sweet little kid blew out the screen one day while throwing a baseball with his sister.

"Yeah," Zoe said. "Just say when."

"How about next weekend?"

Zoe winked. "Sounds good to me."

"All right then. Take care, Zoe."

The admonishment came with a smile and Zoe reached out, tugging her brother into a hug. "I love you, Nick," she said.

He slid his arm around her neck, pulling her close and placing a kiss on the top of her head. "I love you too, Zoe."

LESS THAN HALF AN HOUR AFTER Nick and his family left to make the trek home, another knock sounded at Zoe's front door. There she discovered yet another familiar face standing behind the screen, bearing still another casserole.

"Forgive me if I'm intruding," Ms. Shipman said. And then, as though she didn't quite expect what she would discover after knocking at the door, her eyes widened in surprise. "Oh, my!" she said breathlessly. "My dear, you look just the same."

Zoe opened the door to admit her fifth-grade schoolteacher. Now in her late sixties, the woman had a shock of short white hair. The sight of her filled Zoe with a strange sense of umbrage—after all, it was Ms. Shipman who had told on her for peeling paint off the bathroom walls at school.

Zoe hadn't been one of the guilty. Nevertheless, they'd hauled her into the principal's office and threatened to paddle her, to which Zoe responded by calling her father. That memory pained her immensely: if there was one thing her father had claimed he respected, it was someone who stood up for what they believed in. She'd done the right thing that day, and yet with the principal watching, and with her mom seated in a chair, the secretary looking in through the open door, her father had slapped her hard across the face, calling her a liar.

Zoe pushed the memory away. "How wonderful to see you."

Ms. Shipman nodded. "You're so welcome, my dear. I heard—well, truth is, Maggie Mae heard you had a bit of a mishap. She heard tell on the news, and then she called to tell me."

Maggie Mae was actually Maggie Mae Manly. Behind her back, the kids had called her "Manly Mae." She lived one street over, on Middle Street, closer to the sprawling remnants of Battery Marshall. The fact that Zoe remembered her was less a testament to the fact that she had an excellent memory, and more that Maggie Mae had been a terrible gossip, who'd taken every opportunity to carry tales about all three Rutherford children—a fact that their mother had generally kept hidden from their dad. Zoe smiled. "I guess mishap is one way to put it."

"I don't take the news anymore," Ms. Shipman explained. "It's gotten too depressing. And now they've got those missing girls—did y'all heah about that?"

"Yes, I did."

"That's just too bad," Ms. Shipman said. Her casserole lid rattled atop her pan. "Poor sweet girls."

Zoe preferred to believe both had emptied their bank accounts and walked away.

"Oh lawd," Ms. Shipman said, "You're all grown up, Zoe. It's good to see a familiar face in this house." The woman's entire body shook as she tried to lift her foot to climb the last step.

Zoe reached out to take the casserole from her trembling hands before she could take a spill, but Ms. Shipman tugged it back possessively and Zoe smothered a laugh.

"This heah is my *special* ambrosia salad," Ms. Shipman announced. "Passed down goin' on six generations! My great-great-grandma served it to Robert Mills—you know who that is, right?" Ms. Shipman's voice rose with the question.

Although the name sounded familiar, Zoe shook her head.

"Oh, yes, ma'am, you do," Ms. Shipman argued. "Robert Mills." She said it again, as though it should joggle Zoe's memory. "He was the architect who designed the Washington Monument. I taught all 'bout him in every class till I retired. You musta forgot," she said disapprovingly. And then, without preamble, she chattered on, dismissing Zoe's sin. "Well, if you recall, he designed the Sea Gambit—way back when. Back in those days you had to lease all these homes from the guv'ment. You know about that, right?" She tilted her head at Zoe expectantly.

Zoe nodded, but that didn't stop Ms. Shipman from offering a belated history lesson, as though Zoe's years away from the island had essentially reduced her to tourist status. Carrying in her treasured ambrosia recipe, Ms. Shipman moved into the kitchen, never noticing the new carpet, or the paint on the walls . . . or the scar on Zoe's forehead.

Zoe followed.

Considering her recent ordeal, maybe the scar was to be expected? Zoe might have hit her head on the rocks somewhere. Her brother should have known better, but he'd never asked, nor had Beth. No one had, as though to point it out might be taboo.

Making herself at home, Ms. Shipman pushed two casserole dishes aside, making room for hers on the crowded counter. Oblivious to Zoe's preoccupation with the scar on her forehead, the older woman chattered on. "Way back when . . . good folks just had to pray the guv'ment wouldn't up and take it all away. They could do that, you know? It was written in the bylaws. We were lucky to keep the Gambit," she said. "So were your meemaw and papaw."

Zoe listened, nodding despite never having once called her grandparents by those names. Those had been the names of Gabi Donovan's grandparents and Zoe had never liked them. Nor did she like their cranky son, who nevertheless deserved a thank you, despite the fact that he'd yet to show his face.

In fact, she had to wonder if Walter Donovan regretted his bit of heroism. While flipping through channels at the hospital, she'd caught a brief segment of his unenthusiastic interview on last night's news. A great orator he was not, but he cut the perfect image of a reluctant war hero—a cranky Southern general.

Ms. Shipman caught and held Zoe's gaze. Zoe realized she'd clipped out for an instant. "Not many folks left who can appreciate all the hard work we put into this island—no thanks to Hugo. That's why we're hoping you'll see fit to keep the place."

Zoe wondered who "we" was, but was disinclined to ask—not if it meant prolonging the current conversation. After her unexpected welcome party, Zoe was growing extraordinarily tired.

"Walter Donovan—God bless him—he keeps a tidy yard, but you know these folks you had up in heah, they didn't care one bit about weeding or trimming these bushes. I can see how much work you've put into the place already, Zoe. Believe me when I tell you I don't think those sweet myrtles were trimmed even once during the entire time you were gone. Can you believe it? You know we're not picky about lawns out heah, but that's just plain out of hand."

Zoe wasn't prepared for the unexpected wave of melancholia that crept into her thoughts at the image of some other family setting up residence in her home. She crossed her arms, listening to Ms. Shipman go on and on, without any heart to kick her out. Fortunately, the doorknocker sounded again.

"Oh my, I wonder who that is." Ms. Shipman looked out the back window. "It's awful late, Zoe. You must be tired after all you've been through." She gave Zoe a bit of a glower, but Zoe sensed it was more directed at the person standing at her front door, never mind that Ms. Shipman had only arrived less than ten minutes before—as though ten minutes ago was the cut-off point for good decorum.

Zoe seized the opportunity the instant it was presented. "Oh, gosh, yes I am tired!" she said, turning and rolling her eyes at herself for using the word *gosh*. A week ago she would have easily supplanted it with the F word.

Ms. Shipman followed her through the living room, out onto the covered, screened-in porch, chattering all the way. But her words faded to a drone at the glimpse of the face that now greeted Zoe behind the screen.

13

"Oh my! Ethan, what a lovely surprise," Ms. Shipman said, glancing at Zoe, covering her mouth and giggling like a schoolgirl.

Zoe understood exactly why she was blushing. Ethan McWhorter stood on her front porch step, looking far too comfortable in his sun-kissed skin. She didn't move at once to open the door, even realizing it could be construed as rudeness, so Ms. Shipman reached past her, flinging open the screen door to let Ethan in.

Zoe stepped aside.

"Oh, my! What's this?" Ms. Shipman asked, eyeing the clear half-gallon jar in his hands with the red bow tied about the neck as though it were a diamond in a Zales box. There was a reusable grocery bag slung over Ethan's shoulder as well.

"Just a li'l sumthin', Ms. Shipman," he said, his Southern drawl slightly more pronounced than it was before. He glanced at Zoe, giving her a winsome, blue-eyed wink. "I figure everyone else is bringing Ms. Rutherford flowers and pie, so I wanted to bring something for later." He grinned at Zoe.

Ms. Shipman stuck her nose near the opening of the bag,

trying to peek inside, curiosity getting the better of her. "Oh, yeah? What is it, Ethan?"

Ethan opened the bag wider so she could see. "A sourdough starter, my mama's recipe."

Ms. Shipman flushed even more profusely, her hand clapping her breast. She hooked a finger into the collar of her dress, pulling it away from her neck. "Oh, my, my, Ethan," she exclaimed. "You bake as well?" She turned to Zoe with lifted brows, nodding in approval. "He owns his own shop down in Old Mount Pleasant, and now I hear he bakes as well! Oh, my dear girl, I'll get out of your way and let you young folks visit for a spell. You're in good hands with Mr. McWhorter." Never mind that only minutes before she had sniffed in disapproval over the new arrival at Zoe's door.

Ms. Shipman edged past Ethan, starting down Zoe's rotten steps, reaching up to jangle the house sign from its chains. "You're gonna lose that with a good wind," she warned as she made her way down the stairs. Zoe's heart nearly stalled as she descended, terrified that there was more at stake than a decrepit sign. But Ms. Shipman made it down just fine, crossing the yard more swiftly than Zoe would have expected. She turned to wave before reaching the road. "Oh, and Ethan, won't you tell your daddy I said hello. Tell him I found my glasses up under the front porch. He knows I can't read a thing without them."

Zoe bit her lip. Ethan's father was evidently the town savior, rescuing cats from rooftops and helping old ladies search for reading glasses. Apparently, Ethan was making a concerted effort to follow in his shoes. Zoe was acutely aware of his presence beside her.

"Will do, Ms. Shipman. Are you walkin' home tonight? Might not be a good idea 'til they find those missing women?"

Ms. Shipman batted a hand in the air, dismissing him. "Yes, sir, I'm walkin'. It's a lovely evenin'! I'm not far so don't you go worrying 'bout me. I walk 'bout every evenin' at this hour."

"Well, all right, if you say so, Ms. Shipman. Good night," he said.

Zoe had yet to speak. "Good night, Ms. Shipman," she called out. "Thank you!"

And then it was only Zoe and Ethan standing on her front porch. Zoe turned to face her uninvited guest, for some reason, far less overjoyed to see him than she had been the rest of her neighbors, including Ms. Shipman. She crossed her arms. "Sourdough?"

He gave her a congenial nod. "Yes ma'am."

"You can drop the Southern manners. Zoe is fine."

He smiled at her—a rascally smile. "I was just waiting for permission . . . Zoe."

He pronounced her name with relish, his eyes glinting slightly, and Zoe felt a tiny quiver run down her spine. She ignored it.

"So you had Ms. Shipman, too?"

"Didn't we all?"

"I suppose so. Come on in," he said, as though it were his house. "Let me show you what I brought." He led Zoe into the kitchen and set his jar at the edge of the counter, dropping his bag down in the sink. "Looks like you've got yourself a mess of fans."

"Fans?" It was so far from the truth that Zoe didn't bother correcting him.

He opened his jar, popping the lid and holding it beneath Zoe's nose so she could smell the pungent dough. It smelled faintly of beer.

"It's all ready to use," he said, and then explained the process he'd used to create the starter—something he claimed he was already in the process of doing as a welcome present for Zoe, when he heard the news about her accident.

"From whom?" Zoe asked.

He narrowed his eyes. "Is it who or whom?"

"Whom."

"How come?"

Zoe tilted him a look. "Do I look like Ms. Shipman?"

Rather than take offense at her tone, Ethan laughed, which only made Zoe feel all the crabbier. "Hardly," he said. "But you've got that schoolmarm look down pat—you know the one? That 'I'm warning you' gaze." He shot her a glance with a slightly lifted brow, and then noticed a slow drip on his bag in the sink. He moved the bag aside. "I can fix that for you," he offered.

Zoe pinched the inside of her arms. "What are you doing here, Ethan?"

"Did you ask that of all your guests, Zoe?"

Zoe at once regretted having given him "permission" to use her name. Something about the way he said it sounded too full of promise—promises Zoe wasn't prepared to have him keep.

Fiddling with the faucet nozzle, Ethan adjusted the neck, testing the drip from different angles. His blond hair fell into his face. He tucked the sun-bleached strands behind an ear—a gesture that could have been construed as feminine on any other man, but not on him. The room was so thick with pheromones Zoe could smell them, like the sickly sweet scent of pollen in spring. Once the drip was quelled to his satisfaction, he placed his sack back in the sink and drew out an envelope with instructions, setting it aside on the counter.

"This is for you," he said, slapping it down.

Even without the flirtation, Zoe sensed his visit wasn't entirely neighborly, especially considering that he no longer lived in the immediate vicinity. Based on their meeting at Poe's, she thought he might be taking her disinterest as a challenge, which didn't particularly please her.

"So, here, let me show you how to use it," he said, ignoring her unwelcoming body language.

Zoe refrained from pointing out that she had no baking

supplies, no table and no bowls. If she simply let him do his thing, maybe he would leave.

From the bag, Ethan withdrew a plastic measuring cup, a long spoon, and a bag of bread flour. After this, he yanked the bag out of the sink, set it down on the floor and turned on the faucet. "It's better to leave your water out overnight, get rid of all the chemicals, but this once we'll do it this way." He filled the measuring cup. "You want a good two fluid ounces of water," he said, taking over her kitchen.

Zoe felt helpless to do anything but stand by and watch.

He poured the water into the jar and then, after peering around the kitchen and finding nothing to wipe off his measuring cup, he dried it on his T-shirt. "Sorry about that," he said. "It's clean. I just put it on."

Zoe offered him a smirk, amused despite herself.

"So, now, we measure about two ounces of bread flour." He did that, pouring it into the jar as well, and then he took the spoon and mixed it all up. Afterward, he closed the jar, sealed it tight, and set it aside. "It's that easy."

Zoe uncrossed her arms, lifting a brow. "Just like that? Now the bread appears like magic?" She couldn't help herself. Red flags were going off in her head. He was too comfortable with her, and she was entirely too vulnerable.

He chuckled low. "No, smart ass. *Now* we let it ferment." He washed the spoon as well as the measuring cup and set them both down on the counter to dry.

A sense of panic rushed her, thinking he meant to wait with her until the dough fermented. "Until when?"

He lifted up his bag. "Until tomorrow."

Zoe frowned. "Tomorrow?"

"Yep, tomorrow," he repeated, as though it should be perfectly obvious. "When I come back. So I'll see you then, Zoe." He winked yet again and bolted toward the front door.

Zoe's relief that he meant to leave was tempered only by the fact that he meant to return. "Wait!"

He kept walking, leaving Zoe to follow. He shoved open the screen door and leapt over the rotting steps on the way down.

Zoe halted at the screen door, watching him make his way to the truck parked out on the street, uncertain what to say to prevent him from coming back—at least something that might not offend. He'd said nothing at all about being interested in anything other than friendship, so telling him to get lost was premature. Still, Zoe wasn't comfortable with his attention. Chris was barely out of her life and she didn't care to fill his shoes.

Ethan McWhorter slid into his truck, waving as he drove away, leaving Zoe feeling as sour as his dough.

14

SOUR DOUGH

It was near ten p.m. when the house on Atlantic Avenue finally fell silent.

Once Zoe was alone, she found she missed the bustle. It had been a long time since she'd felt like part of something.

Chris had never liked kids—which was fine, because Zoe never wanted to have any with him. But it also meant that all their friends were childless, and their activities rarely included the din of children's voices. Of course, children couldn't seat their butts on barstools, which was Chris's primary mode of entertainment.

For Zoe's part, her greatest sin was laziness—laziness in regards to her relationship, with a touch of latent self-loathing, indecision, and perhaps misguided self-defensive tendencies.

She'd been lying to herself since the day she met Chris, assuring herself that she was safe with a man like him—safe, because there was nothing about him that made her want to stick around. And yet she'd never left. In her attempt to safeguard her heart with a man she could never love, she'd opened herself up to verbal lashings, black eyes, and scars on her forehead. In hindsight, how safe was that?

Zoe applied for a consulting job once, with a black eye. She'd sat before the company's principles and told boldface lies. It had been her final interview with six of the company's officers. She'd been able to tangibly feel their discomfort. It hadn't been possible for them to look away, when it was incumbent upon them to look her in the eye. The bruising was unmistakable. Zoe hadn't even tried to cover it up. If she could have postponed the interview, she would have, but it simply hadn't been possible, although she did attempt it, telling them she'd been in a car accident. There was something a little less embarrassing about wearing a black eye without apology. "That's too bad," they'd said. "We have to make a decision by Thursday."

"I understand. So let's keep the appointment," Zoe had suggested. "I didn't break anything. Just a little bruised."

"Are you sure?"

"Very. I'll see you at one."

Zoe shown up at 12:50, wearing bold red pumps and lipstick. Looking six men and one woman straight in the eyes, she'd shaken each of their hands and sat down to answer their final questions.

As it turned out the only "bruise" she'd had was the black eye. All seven pair of eyes had shifted uncomfortably when they saw her.

"I'd like to say I went a few rounds in the ring, but the real story is much less exciting," Zoe had joked.

The men in the room had laughed. The female executive looked appropriately horrified.

Donning a face a poker player would have envied, Zoe had told her tale with no small measure of self-reproach. "This is the price you pay when you don't wear seatbelts. I'll know better next time."

One of the men grimaced as he'd asked, "Was it the airbag?"

"The dash actually. The airbag never deployed. The car in front of us stopped abruptly and my—" She never knew exactly what to call Chris. Boyfriend sounded immature and he would *never* be her husband. "My fiancé slammed the brakes."

Somehow, probably subconsciously, she'd still needed to put the blame back on Chris. Whether or not the executives had believed her was still in question. She'd seen doubt nestled in their expressions, but that hadn't prevented them from hiring her.

"The job is yours—if you want it," the woman had said, smiling. She'd bent to whisper, "I figure anyone brave enough to do an interview with a black eye is just the sort of high achiever we require."

Zoe had risen to shake the woman's hand, gripping it firmly, smiling confidently. "I'm all in," she'd said. And then she'd pulled herself together and left. In the end, it was quite probable they'd all believed her. After all, how could a woman who walked and talked with the confidence of a man, be the victim of abuse?

If there was one thing Zoe intended to convey to Nick's daughters, once they were old enough, it was this: respect yourself enough to leave. In Nana's words: *Nobody can break you if you don't wanna be broke.*

Nicky's girls were already getting older. Soon, they would be teens, and soon enough, adults, pursuing lives of their own. If Zoe didn't stick around, she might never realize the joys and pitfalls of being around children. At forty, her prospects were dwindling, and even if they weren't already gone, she had no interest in bringing a child into this world under anything but perfect circumstances. And there again, since perfection wasn't possible, children were not on Zoe's radar.

If she peered at herself beneath a microscope, what she saw was a screwed up individual—functional, but without a joyful bone in her body. Carefree laughter was years and miles away. If she stripped away all the pretty labels—MBA, business owner, consultant—what remained was a broken woman. Zoe was only a shell of herself—like all the discarded husks of crustaceans that littered the beach.

Undressing for bed, she found the box with her grandfather's film tucked away in the bedroom closet. Nick or Beth must have placed it there. She dragged it out, ignoring the soreness in her chest as she repositioned the heavy box. With a grunt, she sat on the floor beside the box and began to rifle through reels, separating them into piles.

Some were too short to watch without splicing onto another reel. The instant you hooked up one end to the projector, the other end would spin right off. She set those aside to worry about later, fully intending to go through them all. She used to watch her grandfather splice the reels, and there was a splicer in the box as well.

She came across a large blue reel marked "Suzie Booty" and set it down, fearful of what it might contain. Her Nana had never concerned herself much with her husband's films, many of which had been taken during his years in the navy. Aside from rare evenings together in the living room, watching Chaplinesque silent movies of bygone eras, most of the reels remained a mystery to Zoe. There was no telling what secrets they held. Some were marked with place names like Thailand, Hong Kong, and Disney. Others were marked simply with a year: 1962, 1970, and 1976.

Her father would have been nine, seventeen, and twenty-three. Respectively, the year her grandfather received his military discharge, the year her father was drafted, and the year after Zoe was born. She supposed there must have been a joyous reunion for her parents after being so long apart, but it clearly hadn't lasted very long.

For some reason, Zoe was feeling oddly sentimental—a mood that was entirely alien to her. For most of her adult life, she had functioned best by looking straight ahead, never behind. It was too hard to linger and watch the could-have-beens and never-weres all line up behind the curtain of her life and peer out at her with solemn, pain-filled eyes.

But tonight—perhaps because it would soon be time to bring the curtain down forevermore—she conceded to a bit of sentimentality.

Quite certain the projector remained in the attic, Zoe pulled the stairs down once again and made her way up into the moonlit loft. Once up the stairs, she yanked the bell cord and stood in the entrance, assessing the order of the room. From the shadows, the pencil box called to her, but she ignored it.

The best place to begin was where she'd discovered the reels, so she directed her search there, knowing her father and grandfather had both kept an orderly storeroom, as befitted their military tradition. There, as she suspected, she discovered the forgotten projector, still stored within its dusty case. She lifted it up and made her way back toward the stairs, clicking off the light.

But here again she hesitated. Dust motes danced along a fat ray of moonlight. Outside, there was a sliver of waxing moon. From here, on nights when her father had worked late, and their mom lay resting in her bed, she and Hannah would sneak up to spy on the beach across the way, like stowaways in the hull of a creaking ship.

Driven to one of the dormer windows, she set down the projector.

Fort Sumter was visible across the channel, a dark speck on the deep-blue horizon. You could barely see it tonight through the fullness of the trees. For a while, after Hugo, all the trees were gone and you could survey the entire shoreline from this attic window.

The house across the street blocked the view as well, but the Donovan house next door had a neat little widow's walk—a true widow's walk nestled up in the boughs of maples and oaks. She tried to locate it through the overgrown trees, and caught a glimpse of the rusted weather vane old man Donovan had placed at its peak.

Back when all these houses were constructed, the widow walks gave unimpeded views over the beach. Zoe wondered how many Civil War widows had watched the bombardments of their husbands' regiment at nearby Moultrie. Across the harbor, Fort Sumter loomed like a ghost from a militant past. In fact, numerous forts had been built on the island, Fort Moultrie, and the Marshall Military Reservation, which included Battery 520, built in the forties as harbor defense for World War II.

As Zoe stood, peering out over the horizon, she was forced to confess that it had long been a fear of hers that Gabi Donovan had told the truth that day.

What if Gabi wasn't lying?

What if Zoe had done something unspeakable?

But Gabi had been a mean little liar. She'd come by that trait honestly. Zoe's dad had claimed her grandfather was a "mean old bugger" and her grandmother a "crusty old bat."

But then . . . Robert Rutherford hadn't exactly been father of the year.

Zoe recalled one particular instance, before Gabi showed up. She and Hannah had dropped their bikes in the Donovan yard, and Mrs. Donovan—the old biddy—had spirited them away, locking both bikes in her garage. She and Hannah had run sobbing to their dad and, for this, Robert Rutherford had risen to the occasion. He'd knocked on the neighbor's door, demanding the return of his daughters' bikes. Without her husband at home to support her, Mrs. Donovan had caved. She'd opened her garage so their dad could retrieve their bikes.

Zoe peered down at the Donovan house now. The lights were all out, except for the lamp in the bedroom, the one connected to the bathroom. She could see the golden aura it produced through the blinds. No one appeared to be home.

Like folks who shut off their lights on Halloween to hide from trick-or-treaters, Zoe figured Walter Donovan must be making it a point to shut down early and stay out of sight, so as not to catch any unwanted attention with all the people coming and going from Zoe's house. Well, cranky old bastard—he was owed a thank you, and Zoe was determined to give him one. And maybe, just maybe, he would soften up enough to talk a bit about his nasty little niece.

EARLY THE NEXT DAY, Ethan McWhorter arrived with a table on his back like a turtle.

"What the hell is that?"

"What's it look like, Zoe?"

For some reason, he tried her patience like no one else. "Let's try this again, Ethan," she said, using his name, without the same intimacy. She pointed at the table. "What is *that* doing here?"

Ethan merely smiled, his perpetual good humor stabbing at Zoe like a sandbur beneath her heel. "Are you going to stand there, barring the door, or are you going to open up and let me in?"

Zoe frowned at him. While his question could be construed as a double entendre, the jury was out as yet as to whether or not Ethan McWhorter was smart enough for that. His beach-bum demeanor didn't lend itself to academic excellence. More likely, he spent his days with a bud between his lips, wondering where the time went. "I'm not sure."

"Well, while you're standing there, not being sure, maybe you can let me slide the table onto your porch? The damned thing's heavier than I thought. Your stairs are crap."

Envisioning the lawsuit that might ensue if he fell, Zoe reluctantly opened the door and moved out of his way. "You know I'm not staying here, right? I don't need, or want, a bunch of furniture I'll have to get rid of later."

"Don't worry, Zoe." He did it again, said her name in that intimate way. "I'm not giving you the table, just letting you borrow it for a while."

Zoe narrowed her gaze at him. "First the bed, now the table—you have an awful lot of extra furniture just sitting around?"

"Actually," he said, looking abashed as he hoisted the table down from his back and set it down on the porch. "I own a repurposed furniture shop. The bed was an antique someone brought in that I didn't wanna sell. So I fixed it up, but I don't have room for it just yet—that much is true."

"So you don't have a roommate who got married?"

He scratched his head. "Well, I do, but the bed isn't his." He changed the subject. "Check it out." He rapped his knuckles on the tabletop. "This is an old reclaimed farm table, lovingly restored."

"Wonderful," Zoe said. She inhaled a breath before speaking again. "It really is wonderful. But, Ethan, why would you give it to me? Do I look like a charity case?"

He leveled a look at Zoe, one that was far less playful than she would have liked, given the nature of her question. His gaze flicked past the scar on her forehead. "No," he said, looking a bit thwarted.

Zoe's hands found her hips. "Then why?"

"Why what?"

"Why would you bring me this table, after giving me the bed?"

He stood, facing her, "Because," he said, with a certain practicality, "You don't have enough counter space, unless we toss out all your lovely flowers. And you can't knead bread without a good surface. Besides, I don't need it right now. Don't worry, I intend to take it back the minute we're done."

Mollified, if only slightly, Zoe's concerns were effectively redirected. Still, she didn't want to make bread with Ethan. Making bread was entirely too personal. But telling him so was an admittance of vulnerability, which Zoe didn't relish. "Very well, take it into the kitchen." She ushered him into her house.

Ethan's full lips broke into a victorious grin. He hoisted the table back up with renewed exuberance. He carried it through the house and set it precisely where the old kitchen table used to sit. Zoe caught a flash of herself, seated there, while Chief Hale towered over her, asking questions about Hannah.

When did you last see your sister, Zoe?

How did you know where to find the bike?

Ethan darted away, returning moments later with a chair, pushing it neatly beneath the table before hurrying away yet again, as though he feared Zoe would call a halt to his bread-making scheme.

She heaved an aching sigh, placing a hand to her chest.

Take a moment.

Breathe.

There was no need for chairs to bake bread, but then, she wasn't entirely comfortable eating pie or casserole while sitting on the floor. There was a part of her that was grateful for Ethan's solicitousness. Still, her comfort level wasn't any of his concern, and she didn't want it to be. What she would have liked to say was that he was the wrong McWhorter, that she would prefer to talk to his dad, who, by the way, seemed to be avoiding her right now. By now, he and Walter Donovan were the only islanders who hadn't shown their faces at Zoe's door.

By the end of Ethan's treks to his truck, her kitchen sported a new vintage farm table with two matching chairs. He laid yesterday's bag atop the table, and this time he whipped out a large bowl, along with various other utensils.

"Did you happen to peek at the dough?"

Zoe nodded. She had, more than a few times, but she hadn't cracked the lid. She didn't dare. Whatever was happening in that jar, it seemed alive.

Retrieving the jar from where he'd placed it yesterday afternoon, Ethan carried it like a precious gem to the kitchen table. "Sweet," he said, after opening the lid. He made a victory fist that was a bit incongruous with the act of making bread, more a touchdown gesture. "It's fermenting nicely."

Zoe decided he was a strange man—a baker, a glassmaker, and a sandal-wearing furniture salesman, who looked like a younger, prettier surfboarding Brad Pitt. Or maybe he wasn't younger and prettier, but he was already growing on her.

"The starter will be good and yeasted by now," he explained, while transferring some of the mix into his wooden bowl. "We're going to do this again, leaving some of the dough behind to use later." He closed the jar, cleaning the excess dough from the rim. "The rest we'll use to make the loaf."

As Zoe watched, Ethan folded in more flour and water into his mixing bowl, explaining that, to do this properly, it should be done in at least two steps, over at least as many days. However, in the interest of getting out of Zoe's hair, he was expediting the process. "This is part of an old starter, one I've been nursing for a good while now. It's good and strong."

Admittedly, Zoe had always wanted to learn how to make bread, but she'd never taken the time to learn. She moved closer to the table to watch Ethan fold in the ingredients. "So what turned you on to baking?"

He abruptly stopped stirring, tilting her an absent look. For an instant, his gaze seemed to drift to another time and place, but returned to Zoe with a wistful smile. "My mama taught me," he said. "I lost the original starter, and boy . . ." He ran a hand through his thick hair. "That pretty near destroyed me."

In all her life, Zoe couldn't recall ever having heard a grown man call his mother "mama." Ethan did so unashamedly, without any sarcasm, and somehow, it didn't seem to diminish him as a man. There was nothing childlike or diffident about Ethan McWhorter. "How'd you lose it?"

"Botched it. Left it out too long. About the time my mom died."

"Oh. I'm sorry."

He gave Zoe a compassionate glance. "Hey, we all lose folks, Zoe. Some of us more than most."

Zoe couldn't tell if he was talking about himself right now, or her. He *must* know her story. It was a small community, with very few secrets.

"Anyway, it's hot out. That should help us along nicely since, essentially, what we want is to turn this into something you'd find in a Petri dish." He grinned. "Hungry yet?"

The imagery wasn't all that appetizing, but even if it were, Zoe hesitated answering, feeling as though Ethan McWhorter had already managed to shanghai her day without much trouble. Worse, she was beginning to enjoy his company. "That's disgusting," she said. "You realize I have things to do, right?"

"Come on, Zoe, you gotta eat sometime," he argued. "Let's walk down to the coffee shop and get a BLT," he suggested. "Tomatoes are good and juicy by now. Once the bread's done, I promise, I'll get on out of your hair."

Zoe's stomach grumbled at the mention of food. Besides, it had been a long time since she'd eaten good Lowcountry tomatoes.

Ethan leveled a look at her with those sultry blue eyes. "I swear it," he said, offering the pinky finger on his left hand.

His fingers were evenly tanned; no evidence of rings, not even a faded band. Zoe laughed, relenting. "Yeah, all right."

They left the house around two, while the bread sat leavening, and made their way toward the coffee shop on the corner of Middle and Ben Sawyer.

The first wave of beach goers were already heading back to their cars, with sunburns that were beginning to blister, coolers that were lighter on their return journey, and children hopping along the burning hot road. Another wave of beach goers—a late crowd, this one without coolers or pink cheeks—headed past them toward the shore.

For most of the way up the street, the silence between them was awkward. Zoe realized she wasn't the most sociable person. But it was difficult to justify hanging onto her irritation when, technically, she might not be around today, except for the good graces of her neighbor. If Walter Donovan hadn't been fishing nearby, if he didn't know the currents the way he did, if he didn't know CPR—if just one thing had been different . . .

Zoe might be with her sister.

How did that make her feel?

A procession of puffy, white clouds drifted across a mottled blue sky. The scent of the ocean was strong today. The afternoon breeze offered a bit of respite from a simmering sun. Beside her, Ethan's sandals slapped lazily at the road.

Zoe watched him in her peripheral, envying his easy demeanor. He smiled at passersby, young and old—not inconspicuously, but with a blinding smile and a heartfelt salute. He was a nice guy. His worst crime thus far was that he enjoyed smiling—and winking—and he did both far too often.

Zoe felt a prickle of guilt over her attitude, which, if she could be honest with herself, matched Walter Donovan's to a tee. If she wasn't careful, she was going to end up being the mean ole biddy next door. "You know . . . I was going to bake a cobbler for my next-door neighbor," she said, breaking the silence.

Ethan cast her a curious glance. "That'd be a nice thing to do. What sort of cobbler?"

"Blackberry. Used to be my favorite."

"Used to be?"

Zoe shrugged. "I haven't had any in a while." To be precise, not since her mother had baked them for her, before she died. Once Marge was gone, not even the second-rate diner variety had graced Zoe's life.

"Maybe you can offer him a loaf of sourdough bread instead?" Ethan suggested. "The recipe we're working makes two."

"Really?" The idea appealed to Zoe. She warmed to the idea of baking bread with Ethan.

"Sure," he said. "Two good-sized loaves." He formed a shape with his hands that looked as though it could have been filled by a football.

Zoe pictured two plump, soft sourdough loaves and roused to the idea even more. "The island hasn't changed much," she said.

He plucked a long strand of sweet grass as they passed. "Yeah, mostly the same folks are still around." He cast her a glance. Zoe felt his gaze on her shoulder. "How long you been gone?"

"Ten years, maybe longer." He stuck the tip of the sweet grass between his teeth to chew. "How about you? Ever think about leaving?"

"Nah," he said. "I love it here." The look on his face revealed that truth. His eyes hooded, like an infatuated lover. "Someday, I'll come back to the island, but for now, I've got a place in Old Mount Pleasant, right above my store."

"Will you buy a new house, or . . . ?"

He cast her a wry smile. "Wait for my dad to kick up his toes?"

Zoe laughed. "Well, I wouldn't have put it quite like that."

He shrugged. "Have you checked real estate prices lately? Hell, no, I'll wait. I'm not in a hurry. Truth is, I hope my dad's around a long time."

"I'm sure he will be," Zoe reassured. "He's in great shape."

He winked at her. "Please don't tell me you're into my father?"

Zoe laughed and shook her head.

"Hey, it's not as crazy as you might think. Dad's pretty popular with the ladies. Ever since mom died, he's had a line of blue-haired ladies ready to make up his bed. Some are actually not all that old."

Zoe laughed again. "I bet."

They chatted easily about Ethan's father. Ethan said he hoped he would meet a nice woman, and that he worked too much. Zoe refrained from interjecting that he must, because he had yet to call her back.

Ethan told her about his store—the fact that he hadn't meant to own one. He'd bought an old house, filled with junk furniture the previous owners didn't want, fixed everything up. One day, he put half the furniture out on the front lawn with "For Sale" signs. After that, little by little, things started showing up. He'd find something offbeat that needed a little love and take it home, clean it up, then turn around and sell it. Soon enough, the entire bottom floor was filled with reclaimed furniture and household items. He'd made the upstairs into a suite, small, but neat—more than enough space for him.

"And your roommate?"

Ethan grinned at her. "He was there maybe two seconds. Long enough to close on a brand-new house."

"What about you? Ever think about getting married?"

He responded without hesitation, shrugging. "Nah."

"Why not?"

"I don't figure that's something you ought to have to think about." He cast her a meaningful glance. "I guess I just never met the right person."

Zoe envied his sense of *je ne sais quoi*. He made life seem so uncomplicated. Maybe a little of it was rubbing off on her; it wasn't until they were done with their sandwiches and on the way home that she realized she hadn't worried once about Chris.

15

8MM

A mong the items Ethan brought in his little sack of wonders was a bottle of Pride Mountain 2006 reserve claret. It was easily a hundred-dollar bottle of wine, but to save the occasion from any nuance of romance, they drank out of red plastic cups. On the other hand, the simple act of making bread felt more like foreplay.

The dough needed a little workout, until it became pliant to the touch. A little wheat germ, a bit of rye, then work it all over again. As Zoe watched, she felt flushed. Her cheeks grew warm.

Kneading the dough across her borrowed table, Ethan turned the loaf over and over. "Now it's your turn," he said, stepping away.

Zoe stepped into position, mirroring his actions, kneading the dough until she could feel it soften. It stuck to her fingers. She peered up at him, raising her brows. He merely laughed and dusted the loaf with a pinch of flour. And then he did something Zoe only half anticipated, stepping in behind her to help her knead the lump. "Like this," he directed, covering her hands with his own. Warm and insistent, they guided her fingers gently over the dough, guiding, but never pushing.

His body heat singed her back. Her heartbeat kicked up a notch, and the tiny hairs at her nape tingled at the feel of his breath.

Outside the window Ethan had fixed, there was a lovely violet sky on display. In the sink he promised to fix as well, water dripped like a metronome in an empty concert hall. Everything was amplified to Zoe's ears. Her heart beat so hard she wondered if he could feel it thumping at her back.

It had been a long time since anyone had touched her so intimately—not even Chris for way too long. Besides, Chris's lovemaking was hardly worthy of the name; his fetishes had grown more pronounced as time went on, as though he were desensitized to normal sex and healthy human interaction.

They'd gone out one night, with the precise intention of initiating Zoe into her first experience with a woman. It wasn't Zoe's fantasy; it was Chris's. Zoe, had become more and more uncertain of her own sense of self-worth after years of being with a fickle man, who, although she suspected of cheating, had never been man enough to admit it and move on. Instead, he'd sworn he loved her, and more, that he needed her—like he needed air to breathe. As time went on, it had taken more and more to arouse him, until the effort thoroughly disgusted Zoe.

As it turned out, finding a threesome had been a simpler task than Zoe might have imagined. They'd hooked up with "Mary," who was eight years younger than Zoe, and far more experienced, to hear the girl talk. Zoe would never know for sure if Chris had set the whole thing up in advance, but after a few tequila shots, Mary had followed Zoe into the bathroom at the bar, pinning her up against the stall, slipping a hand beneath Zoe's skirt. Half drunk, and lonely in a way only someone in a bad relationship could comprehend, Zoe had allowed it.

Even now, the memory of Mary's fingers left Zoe breathless. She'd been powerless to stop it, despite her standing in the bathroom stall of a popular bar. Outside the stall door, drunken women had rapped impatiently.

"Hey, bitches—get a fucking room!"

Mary's hands had skimmed to Zoe's knees, and then she'd knelt, kissing Zoe's thighs, lifting a tongue against Zoe's panties, until she couldn't stand it anymore and she'd pulled Mary back up with trembling hands, dragging her outside the stall, embarrassed. But it had hardly fazed anyone else. The other women had stood with bored expressions, watching a drunken girl in bright orange heels inhale powder by the sink while Zoe repaired her skirt.

Later that night, in the privacy of their bedroom, Chris never touched the girl, but he hadn't touched Zoe either. He'd sat across the bedroom, watching the show, stroking himself while Mary performed rituals over Zoe's body that Zoe would never have dreamt she'd allow. That had been her last time with a woman— her first and last.

Zoe wasn't interested in sex outside a relationship, and since she couldn't picture herself in a lesbian relationship, that meant no more forays into that world. Afterward, Mary had sent her numerous texts, promising untold pleasures. "Guess what? I bought a 2-headed dildo," the girl texted one day. "Just 4 u."

Zoe hadn't responded, but—this was the sad part—until this very day, she'd doubted she would ever meet any man who could kiss her the way Mary had.

At this instant, however, as Ethan molded his hands over hers, coaxing her to knead in just a certain way, she found herself wondering what Ethan's mouth would taste like . . .

It would be easy enough to back up half an inch and find out if he was equally as aroused as she was. Her nipples ached for the feel of his palms. Her underwear felt damp. The flesh between her legs convulsed gently—and all this because he was showing her how to shape a loaf of bread?

"Tomorrow, after it's had a chance to rise, you'll bust the loaf in two, knead it exactly so . . ."

Together, they massaged the pliant dough until Zoe's shoulders were so tense she could have broken off an arm.

"But here's the trick," he said. "You'll want to do this . . . tuck it under . . . pinch it back. That way, you've got a thinner crust when it comes time to bake the bread. It'll hold its shape better as well. But be sure you don't pinch it back too far or you'll crack the crust."

How long had they known each other now?

One week? Maybe two?

This, Zoe feared, was getting out of hand. Her brain experienced a meltdown. She thrust the bread aside and shoved her hands free of Ethan's grasp, shrugging out of his embrace. "Ethan, you have to leave," she said.

Palms coated with flour, Ethan stepped back in surprise.

Zoe's hands trembled. Her knees felt too weak to stand. "I need you to go, Ethan. Right now."

In the twilight, his face visibly paled. "Are you okay, Zoe?"

Zoe held up a hand. "I'm fine."

For a long moment, their gazes met and held, and for an awful instant, Zoe imagined him coming after her, as Chris might have done, bending her to his will.

"Please leave," Zoe begged.

He glanced down at the table, then at his flour-coated hands and shook his head. He didn't bother to retrieve his bag, or wipe his hands. He seemed to realize the seriousness of Zoe's demand. He tucked a dough-covered hand into his pocket to retrieve his keys, and then he left.

WHETHER IT WAS bad juju from her encounter with Ethan, the house, or withdrawals from her brief time with Nick and his happy family, or even simply the fact that Zoe felt lonesome, surrounded by half a dozen vases of flowers, she felt anxious and ill at ease.

It could have been the sandwich she'd eaten, but she suspected stress was ultimately responsible for a lingering belly-ache. The refrigerator, filled with the goodwill of others, turned her stomach merely at the thought.

After cleaning up the mess she and Ethan had made together, and making certain the dough was settled properly in the wooden bowl, covered and sealed with plastic per Ethan's directions, she mounted the projector on the kitchen table, and sat there, quietly cleaning the mechanisms.

Even a minuscule speck of dust could set the film to burning once it was threaded through the projector and subjected to the heat of the bulb. There wasn't much danger of it catching fire while she was paying such careful attention, but once the film was scorched, whatever images it contained would be forever lost.

The task was tedious, but it brought Zoe welcome relief from her pensive thoughts, even as shadows lengthened throughout the house.

She was surprised to discover how much she remembered about working the projector, especially considering how little she'd ever handled the film. Aside from a few times when her dad must have been in a generous mood, he'd restricted everyone from granddad's reels. After so long, they'd lain forgotten in the attic, along with everything else that once belonged to her grandparents. To think how close Zoe had come to letting it all go . . . it gave her a sick feeling that only added to her sense of malaise. These reels, they contained the last moving images of her sister.

Against the silence of the room, the sink nozzle dripped on, a nagging reminder of Ethan's promise. Zoe ignored it, focused on brushing out all of the projector's nooks and crannies, compelled by the knowledge that soon all the ambient light would be gone.

Having chosen a few reels that most interested her, she left the crate in the bedroom, unwilling to haul it out and then take it back. Once the projector was cleaned to her satisfaction, with the last remaining traces of ambient light, she put the parts back together and plugged in the projector, pleased to find the light turned on and the motor whirred with promise. Like a spotlight over a prop in a play on stage, the projector lamp illuminated her kitchen table.

One of the reels spun, the other waited for direction. If you set it in reverse, the opposite reel would turn, leaving the other to follow its lead, but Zoe flipped the switch to a neutral state, leaving the projector light on, so she could thread the film.

It took her several attempts before she remembered precisely how to do it, catching the delicate film on the tiny sprocket holes just right so it could be guided through the proper channel. But she found that, even then, the film was so old and brittle, that if she wasn't careful she'd split the perforation notches, rendering the film and the reel useless, until she could cut or splice it. But like the film, the splicing kit was old, the tape too brittle to work with, so she was forced instead to cut, wasting precious frames. She hesitated to let them go. Holding each discarded clipping to the light, she spied tiny glimpses of Hannah's face.

Was she smiling? Was that a blouse she'd stolen from Zoe's drawers? It looked like Zoe's. And was that a missing tooth or simply a shadow?

For half an hour, Zoe worked under the projector light, half blinded by its intensity. Finally, she succeeded at threading the largest of the reels over the roller arm.

Threading an old projector was a bit like life, in the sense that, if you went to bed and woke up doing all the right things in all circumstances, things were supposed to fall into place. All you had to do was gently feed the film over the roller arm, and it would draw it in, catch the sprockets, and then channel the film into the various mechanisms, pushing it out precisely so that it caught the reel just so, locking the film firmly into place with the sprockets. But if you tried to force the film into the roller arm when any one thing was wrong, it was a complete disaster. If, for example, the sprockets were torn, or if there was old film or dust blocking the mechanism, if the film or reel wasn't facing the proper direction, or if the reel was too small for the roll of film, and just as importantly, if you didn't know which direction to rewind—all these things and more could derail the film. But when all the myriad things that could go wrong didn't, the rewards were significant. It was tantamount to eating a bucket of dark chocolate gelato with sea salt—in bed—with a masseuse waiting to send you off to a dreamless sleep.

Outside her immediate circle of light, the rest of the house remained dark—in part, because there were no lamps to light inside the house. Zoe had been so intent on the projector for so long that she never bothered to get up from her chair to turn on the overhead lights. It didn't matter; she had never been afraid of the dark.

Hannah was.

Sometimes her sister would scoot into the bed beside Zoe, and Zoe would pet her soft, long hair—fine as silk, even when she wouldn't brush it. Zoe, on the other hand, had a mess of tangles that necessitated vigorous brushing, or it would form Brillo-pad-type knots that couldn't be unsnarled, except by tearing out chunks of hair.

She had an image of herself, seated in front of Nana, while Nana grumbled over a knot in Zoe's hair. "Marge, go get me my scissors."

Her mother had leapt up from whatever task she'd embarked upon—crocheting a baby shoe for Nicky, perhaps. Zoe couldn't recall what it was she'd held in her hand until she reemerged from the kitchen with the gleaming scissors, which immediately prompted Zoe's tears.

"Let me try," Marge had suggested meekly. One hand loosely

held the scissors, the other a distended belly that served as temporary housing for baby Nick.

"Hand me those scissors right heah and now," Nana had demanded. "If I can't do it, nobody can."

Zoe remembered peering up at her mother, begging silently for her to prevent the violation of her hair—hair Zoe took pride in, despite the fact that it wasn't soft and golden like Hannah's.

Nana's hand had shot out with silent expectation, palm turned up. Her mother immediately handed over the scissors.

In that instant, Zoe had felt so much loathing in her heart, but not for outspoken Nana as she'd carelessly snipped a huge chunk of Zoe's hair. No, it had been for her mother, because moms were supposed to look out for their daughters.

Practical minded, with too many people pulling at her heart, Nana's love had been far less solicitous. But for her mother, there'd only been Zoe and Hannah. And now the baby, who would lose her attention the instant he could crawl. It was then, maybe in that instant, Zoe had vowed to look after the kid and never leave him to fend for himself. Nicky would come into the world with four females ready to serve his every need.

At long last, the film click-clacked through the projector—a joyous sound—and Zoe pointed the projector at the refrigerator, tilting it as best she could with two uneven front legs. She held her breath with anticipation, unable to recall the last time she was so titillated over the beginning of a film.

Across the refrigerator door raced three-year-old Hannah, hair flying behind her as she chased the family dog. Zoe couldn't remember the dog's name—some mutt with shaggy hair and black spots. It wasn't around long after Nicky began to crawl because he'd tortured the poor beast, nabbing handfuls of its fur at whim. Onscreen, as though aware of this fact, her father sat in a prickly patch of grass, trapping six-month-old Nicky in his arms.

Zoe stared, unblinking, at the slightly off-kilter film, half sliding off the refrigerator door, into the grimy shadow between the appliance and the counter. She turned the lens, searching for a clearer picture, and found it as Hannah laughed. The sound rang through Zoe's memory, despite the film ticking through the projector being the only sound to breach the holy silence. She tried desperately to fill in voices in her head, but she couldn't remember what might have been said—or even the mood. Later, her father had bought a Camcorder that recorded voices, though he'd never acquired the same passion for it as his father had his 8mm film.

On screen, her sister pointed at the dog, saying something loudly, based on the parting of her lips. A sense of longing filled Zoe—so overwhelming that she covered her mouth to prevent an outburst of sobs.

The camera panned to Zoe. At five, she was more reserved, content to watch Hannah chase the dog across the yard. With bright laughing eyes, Nana waved at the camera, offering the cameraman what appeared to be a furtive wink. Across the lawn, Marge sat in a lawn chair, smoking a cigarette for posterity. As though it were an afterthought, she waved belatedly at the camera, and then peered beneath her nails, while Nana, still laughing, chased Hannah around the yard. The only person missing in the film was Zoe's grandfather. Zoe supposed he must be the man behind the camera, though she couldn't recall.

Mesmerized, Zoe sat back in her borrowed chair, staring at the images flitting across the textured refrigerator. The whir of the projector silenced the sound of the dripping faucet; still her gaze was drawn toward the sink.

Zoe blinked.

There, at the window, she made out the vague outline of a face—indistinct, like a photo negative, or the impression you got when closing your eyes after staring too long into bright lights.

Her gaze skidded back to the refrigerator to see if it was a reflection from the film. Her heart lurched as, on screen, her sister chased the dog, her face in profile, no more than a blur of movement across a patchy lawn. She stumbled, directing a pout to the camera, but something her grandfather said returned a smile to her face.

Prickles raced down Zoe's spine. She sat, paralyzed, watching the film, willing her heartbeat to slow, terrified to look again.

Was someone out there? Was it Chris? It didn't look like Chris. It could be that her eyes were still adjusting to the light.

The kitchen took on a macabre aura. Zoe was at center stage, with a peeper in the window as her only audience. Only seconds passed, but it felt like years.

Count to three.

Take a breath.

Swallowing, Zoe forced her gaze to return to the kitchen window.

There was only darkness now, but that didn't mean there was no one out there. All she could see lay within a halo of light from the projector. In her head, Zoe imagined someone backing away from the window, leering from the shadows.

If someone was out there, the last thing she wanted to do was let on that she knew.

The doors. Were they locked?

Zoe's palms began to sweat. Terrified to turn off the projector now, she nevertheless did so, casually, flipping it all the way off, so the kitchen went dark.

She wasn't easily unnerved, but the back of her nape tingled as she rose from the chair, immediately lunging for the door, turning the lock. Without lingering there, Zoe veered toward the living room, heading toward the front door with the intention of locking that door as well.

It could be Chris, though peeping wasn't his style.

At the front door, Zoe peered out onto the driveway. There was only one car sitting there, reflecting the moonlight—hers.

The porch was empty, except for the rocker. It sat dead still. Even Nana's ghost was nowhere to be found.

Here, where no one ever locked their doors, she'd easily fallen into old habits. But there was no one in the yard—not that she could see. Still, she cracked open the front door, rushing onto the front porch, quickly securing the chain on the screen door, before moving back into the house and locking the front door. And then, just for good measure, she moved systematically throughout the house, checking windows and securing every last one. Once the doors and windows were all shut tight, Zoe returned to the kitchen, to the back door and turned on the porch light, peering out into the backyard.

The house was quiet.

Only the breeze stirred outside.

There was no one there. Not even at the Donovan house. Once again, Walter Donovan's lights were out, except for the same lamp shining through his bedroom window blinds. It was possible he had a girlfriend and rarely stayed at home. Zoe knew so little about him or his life.

Back when she and Chris first began dating, he'd always stayed at her house, mostly because, as she discovered later, his apartment had been nothing but a weigh station. One day, she'd awoken to find that he was just another fixture around her house —one that didn't quite belong—like a garage-sale lamp that didn't match anything else, one you constantly thought about tossing out, but for some reason never did.

She reconsidered the need for a restraining order, and wondered how to go about it. But if she took out a restraining order, he would know where to find her, because she was fairly certain you had to give an address, restraining said person from appearing within ten miles of said house, or whatever the wording said.

Nick claimed he never gave Chris her address. Zoe had never once revealed it during their time together. Presumably, all Chris knew was that Zoe's parents had a house on Sullivan's, but it was probably easy enough for him to find the address through public records.

Outside, the neighborhood was quiet and peaceful. A waxing moon smiled overhead. The sweet myrtle bushes shivered softly with an even-tempered breeze. Here, just one block from the beach, the night was as dark as the ocean's bottom.

And now Zoe knew exactly what that was like.

Relief sidled through her. It wasn't Chris at the window. He would have made himself known by now. It could have been one of the kids who'd been using her house as a party zone— someone who hadn't yet realized the house was now occupied. Spotting Zoe inside might have spooked them. It was also possible that she'd spooked herself for no reason at all. She might have merely seen a floater after staring so long into the projector lights.

After a long moment, when nothing stirred, Zoe began to relax.

Leaving the back porch light on, she moved away from the door to search for her cell phone. Less agitated now, she nevertheless wanted to be sure her phone was fully charged and within reach. She found the cell phone in the bedroom, next to the flower vase, and sat on the bed, peering at the display. Six missed calls: none from Ethan, one from her brother, all the rest from Chris.

16

"GABI DONOVAN"

The briny scent the island wore like a cheap perfume filled Zoe with a slowly fermenting apprehension. If it were possible to both smell and taste the ocean at once, without drowning, that's how she felt.

Succumbing to the sea was an experience Zoe wouldn't soon forget, but it was far more terrifying in retrospect, because the most horrific part of the entire ordeal was that, beyond the initial furor of trying to escape, she'd felt a sense of resignation while in the water—a sense of peace. It was only now, this instant, while she was alone with her thoughts, that she could admit she didn't want to come back.

She didn't want to leave Hannah—not without answers.

With the windows shut to the chirrup of birds, and the aging air conditioner grunting periodically, like an old woman forced to clamber to her feet, the air inside was a bit less fresh, a marriage of fresh paint scent with the cloying fragrance of decaying blossoms. In the kitchen, she found scatterings of wilted petals adorning the countertops and the floor, but far from leaving her with a sense of romanticism, it left her with the sense that the house itself was dying, drowning beneath a sea of despair.

It needed more than a coat of paint. It needed love. Even with Zoe's recent improvements, it was in danger of falling into disrepair. Beyond the dilapidated front porch stairs, the eaves were filled with a decade's worth of rotten leaves. The windows needed to be resealed, and then painted and possibly replaced. She'd found evidence of water damage along the hardwood floors, most notably beneath the two-by-four she'd nearly tripped over the day she arrived. While it had appeared randomly placed, it was clear only after she moved it that someone had placed it there to conceal an emerging hole in the floor.

The place needed so much work. After all was said and done, could she find it in her heart to save a house she wasn't sure she valued?

Compelled to tidy up, Zoe swept the petals off the floor and then wiped down the counters—a compulsion, not unlike the one that had probably sent Walter Donovan into the brink to save a woman he didn't know and clearly didn't like. Subjected to reason, his actions might have left her at the bottom of the sea, and for that, she owed him at the very least a loaf of bread.

More than double its original size, yesterday's lump of dough tugged the plastic wrap away from the edges of the bowl. Zoe ripped off the cover, wondering if she had let the sourdough rise too long. But even if she had, she was going to bake the damned bread anyway. She refused to allow yesterday's efforts to go to waste.

Moving the projector and the film out of her way—into the living room, for the time being—she returned the table to the task of kneading bread. Ripping the dough in half, she began shaping each loaf.

Tuck it under . . . pinch it back.

Ethan's voice echoed in her head.

Invading her personal space wasn't Ethan's primary sin. Nor was flirtation, in fact. As long as it had been since Zoe had felt the weight of a man's body pressing her into the sheets, she might have welcomed that. No, Ethan's mistake was something else—what exactly, Zoe couldn't say, because it necessitated looking at herself a little deeper for motives that were less than sane. Really, who lived with an abuser for eight years, then turned around and had a freak out over the idea of spending half a day with a nice guy?

And yet, although he didn't deserve the treatment Zoe gave him, she didn't intend to call and apologize. She much preferred him to stay away, and once she was gone, out of his reach, she would text him and let him know he could come retrieve his things.

Whether Ethan liked it or not, Zoe planned to leave him an envelope with payment for the use of his furniture.

Thinking about Ethan, Hannah, and the house, she kept at the dough most of the morning, stopping only after she had two carefully shaped boules in their prospective baskets—also courtesy of Ethan. Crusted from years of use, she scraped away excess dried dough and placed one loaf into each basket. And then, leaving the bread to rise again, she shoved a few spoons of broccoli casserole into her mouth—straight from the container it was delivered in—before putting away the projector and the film equipment. While she waited for the bread to leaven, she tackled the painting again. Six hours later, most of the walls throughout the house had a second coat of paint and Zoe put the bread in the oven, before tackling the hall bathroom.

As for Ethan, it was heartening to know there might still be nice guys out in the world, but Zoe couldn't help wondering if he might be one of those guys who needed to feel needed. It seemed to Zoe that he hadn't bothered to look at her twice until he spotted the gash on her forehead.

Pity wasn't welcome.

So he was gone. She'd sent him away, but he'd left her with the fragrant evidence of his unending goodwill. Even from where she stood painting in the bathroom, she could smell the bread baking and it took her back to a time when there had been three little Rutherfords running through the house. Nana had been in the kitchen, along with Marge, showing her mother how to properly make collard greens—with a ham hock to give it flavor. You had to use the pot liquor—the soup left over at the bottom of the previous collard pot—because that's where all the nutrients went. But most of all, you had to start collards early in the day, letting them stew with plenty of butter and pork, or else they were tough as old boots, her Nana used to say.

By the time Zoe was finished with the hall bathroom, the entire house smelled like a French bakery with the unfortunate taint of fresh paint.

But she couldn't get over the sense of accomplishment she felt, surrounded by the evidence of her own hard work, and poring over two perfectly shaped boules of sourdough bread. Though now she felt like a heel where Ethan was concerned.

Zoe set the bread aside to cool, thinking it would be nice to deliver one to Walter in some sort of bread bag, the way they did at the bakery. With that goal in mind, she set off to the store, this time making certain the doors were locked.

Upon returning home, she found Walter Donovan's car in the driveway, so she rushed inside to package his gift. Still warm from the oven, she slid one loaf into a brown sack and raced back out the door.

Her stomach fluttered as she made her way up to the neatly kept front porch next door. She punched the doorbell and waited, then rang it again, just for good measure, determining that Walter Donovan wasn't going to hide from her any longer.

Finally, after another ring and a few more knocks, Walter cracked open his front door. He said nothing, merely glared at her.

Zoe smiled. "Hi there . . . I just wanted to thank you." She lifted her loaf of bread for him to see.

He stood, blinking at her. Not a trace of emotion registered upon his long face. After a moment, he said, "Seems to me you ought to know by now that walking out there's a stupid thing to do." His tone was full of censure, and Zoe understood he meant the sandbars. Obviously, she hadn't meant to end up out there. She nodded mutely.

"Folks have better things to do than babysit grown women who ought to have more sense than a grapefruit." His gaze shifted to the brown sack in Zoe's hand. Determined to keep it friendly, Zoe offered him the bread.

"Well, I appreciate what you did . . . so I baked some bread— for you," she said again. "Fresh out of the oven."

Scowling still, Walter Donovan seized the loaf out of her hands. "Well, you're welcome," he said, but then he closed the door in Zoe's face.

Apparently, gratitude wasn't all it was cracked up to be.

Yet it was difficult to stand on moral high ground when she was guilty just the same. She had yet to extend a hand in friendship to Ethan, who'd offered her a much-enhanced version of Southern hospitality. Realizing that she must accept the fact that people made their own choices for their own well-being, she resigned herself to discovering the particulars of Gabi's death all on her own, without her uncle's help.

Shaking her head, Zoe made her way back down his front porch steps, refusing to allow herself a backward glance.

Once back inside her own house, Zoe dusted off her laptop, typing Gabi's full name into the search engine—Gabrielle Renee Donovan.

She remembered Gabi's middle name only because Gabi had made such a big deal about having been named after her dead mother. In hindsight, it was creepy that both she and her mother had died so young.

On Facebook, there was a Gabrielle Renee Fabia, an @gabidonovan on Twitter, but since Gabi was dead, Zoe didn't click these recent profiles.

On the other hand, she did click each and every link that wasn't connected to social media. Finally, at the bottom of the fourth search page, she discovered a link to an obituary, and from there, a short news piece. She blinked in surprise as she read.

As her uncle had claimed, Gabi was dead, but it was the manner of her death that surprised Zoe—and where. She was strangled. In Baltimore. An act of passion, the article said. The man who killed her had choked her so hard with a piano wire that it nearly severed her head. She was found on November 20, 1996 in Leakin Park, one of the most notorious parks in the Baltimore area, infamous for dead bodies. Suspected of her murder, her then boyfriend, a troubled youth with priors, was arrested for Gabi's murder. She was twenty at the time. That was all. No more information was available, although piano wire hardly seemed the sort of thing a person would keep on hand. To Zoe, that felt more premeditated. Neither could she picture a tattooed boyfriend at a baby grand.

For his part, Gabi's uncle was nearly nonexistent on the web, except for a solitary news piece dated July 10, 2003, commending Walter P. Donovan's acts of bravery during the "Shock and Awe" campaign. He was returning to his home in Washington, DC, *not* to the island—little more than a stone's throw from where his niece's body had been discovered since, essentially, Baltimore was part of the Washington Metropolitan Area.

Ostensibly, Walter had returned to Charleston about the same time Zoe left—which would account for the fact that they'd never crossed paths. He was already gone from his parents' home by the time Gabi arrived on the scene and he'd probably left before Zoe was born.

Gabi's death would have also preceded Zoe's time in Baltimore, so despite it being a coincidence, it was little surprise she'd never heard about it. Her grandparents had disowned Gabi in a public display that had had the entire neighborhood talking about it for weeks. On their front lawn, while her "papaw" had loaded Gabi's belongings into his car, Mrs. Donovan had called her a "lying little heathen," and compared her to her "no-good whore of a mother"— who, of course, happened to be their only daughter. Presumably, they'd sent Gabi off to live with the only living relative who would have her—her Uncle Walter.

Thereafter, the Rutherford-Donovan feud had grown as gnarly as the sweet myrtle bushes separating their yards. The foursome had fought over roots infiltrating the Donovan sewers. They'd fought over car tires in the yards. They'd fought over fencing Zoe's dad had tried to put up without a permit. Old man Donovan had seen it taken down nearly at once.

He and his wife had been one of those stubborn couples who'd weathered Hugo here on the island. During the time, while no one was allowed to return, Zoe's dad had been certain some of his tools went missing from the garage. He'd blamed old man Donovan, but he could never prove it. As full of ill will as it might have been, when Zoe's dad had wisecracked that he hoped the Donovans had found themselves washed out to sea as Hugo's revenge, everyone had secretly hoped it might be true. However, upon their return, there they'd been, both of them, tough as nails, seated out on their front porch. All that had been missing from that scene was a twenty-gauge shotgun and a hound dog.

During all the time they'd lived next door, Zoe couldn't remember a single instance where she'd spied either of the Donovan siblings pulling up in the driveway—not for Thanksgiving, Christmas, or the Fourth of July.

Once, while Zoe's father was out back, sharing a beer with a friend who'd come over to help repair their roof, Zoe had overheard him tell the guy that old lady Donovan was so frigid, he was sure she'd spread her legs only four times—twice to get her kids, another two to spit them out. He was sure that alone was enough to make a man lose his marbles.

At the time, Zoe had been titillated by the secret knowledge. She and Hannah had sat up in the attic, contemplating whether or not they would ever want to let a boy "put his thing up in there."

Hannah had said, "No way!" But Zoe had begun to suspect she might—because sometimes, sitting at her desk at school, she'd discovered heretofore unknown sensations that had made her think a lot about kissing boys.

Four-year-old Nicky had overheard their dad's conversation as well. With all the glee of a child who believed he'd accidentally solved all the world's troubles, one day he'd sauntered up to their dad with a hand outstretched. "Daddy," he'd said, "Mr. Donovan's gonna be real happy now."

Robert Rutherford had swiped a greasy forearm across a sweating brow. "Yeah? Why's that son?"

Shyly, Nicky had sidled up to him, revealing what he'd had cupped in his hand: three marbles encrusted with mud—a cat's eye, a clear blue, and a swirl. "Because," he'd said, "I found his marbles."

When their dad looked utterly confused, Nicky had explained that he'd overheard the conversation about Mr. Donovan losing his marbles. That had been the first and last time Zoe remembered hearing her dad let out a belly laugh.

Resigning herself to unanswered questions, Zoe set the computer aside on her bed.

Searching out Gabi's history had only raised more questions —questions that were mostly none of her concern. Even knowing what kind of person she'd been, Zoe couldn't allow herself to judge Gabi Donovan. If not for the grace of God—or someone— she might have ended up yet another statistic herself. Chris's temper led to precisely the sort of behavior that resulted in strangled corpses. After all, there wasn't much separating Gabi Donovan and Zoe Rutherford except a little bit of luck.

17

THE REAL TRUTH

The garage was in the worst shape of all. Zoe opened the doors to air it out.

It wasn't big enough to house a car. Always more of a work-shop, the garage had become a storage area after her father was gone. In all her memory, her dad had never even attempted to put a car inside. Instead, he'd preferred to complain about how badly the salt water rusted out his chassis. Amazingly, the structure had held fast even after Hugo, needing only a few repairs, including the roof, but now it was nearing the end of its days. Inside, it smelled of dead and moldy things.

Zoe was going through junk, tossing it out of the barn-style front doors, when Ethan's truck pulled up in the driveway. He idled the engine a moment, turned it off, and slid out of the cab. Zoe's heart skipped a few beats at the sight of him, but she took a deep breath, pretending he didn't affect her the way he did.

His footfalls crunched over shells, stopping at the garage entrance. He didn't speak at once. He stood peering into the garage, arms akimbo.

"Hey, I'm surprised to see you," Zoe offered, tossing out a

random sandal—Birkenstock. No one in her family had ever worn Birkenstocks, so it must have been left by one of her old tenants. She tiptoed through piles of trash to join him in front of the garage, out in the bright morning sun.

"Don't worry," he said. "I don't plan to stay."

Something like disappointment sidled through Zoe, though how could she expect him to continue pursuing her after she'd asked him point-blank to leave?

A garden snake caught her attention. It slid into an empty flowerbed now sparsely filled with old pine mulch. No flowers. Not even the dried-up remnants of perennials. At the corner of the bed, a scraggly, leafless miniature rose bush with black spot remained. There was little evidence of anyone having cared for this property in years. Someone—not her—had yanked out the tangle of thorn-heavy roses that once filled the bed—a hardy variety her mother had referred to as William Moss. The realization left Zoe feeling bereft, although, in that instant, it wasn't worth exploring.

Barefoot, hoping to avoid burs, Zoe perched herself along the edge of the driveway, where there was a smattering of grass.

"So what are you doing here?"

He peered down at her bare feet, lifting a brow as he met her gaze once more. "You enjoy living dangerously, I see." There was a hint of drollery in his voice, but the twinkle in his eye was gone.

Jokes aside, he didn't realize how close to the truth that appeared to be, even without her recent accident. Zoe shrugged. "Yeah, I know. I didn't mean to start this today. I opened up the garage, and before I knew it, I was inside tossing things out."

Ethan gave a shrug. "They're your feet, Zoe. I just came by to pick up one of those proofing baskets." He sounded embarrassed. "Might not seem like much but it belonged to my mom. You can keep the other one," he said.

Zoe nodded, though she didn't budge from the spot she was standing on. "Of course. The bread turned out great."

Her gaze dropped to the hands that remained on his hips—body language that didn't lend itself to friendly chatter. "That's good. Glad to hear it."

Zoe stood another long moment, waiting, though for what she couldn't quite determine. Maybe she was hoping Ethan would stop looking at her as though she had disappointed him and forget everything she'd said, because she didn't seem capable, even now, of extending herself over the invisible line she'd drawn in the sand.

Zoe watched the garden snake as it slithered through one of the holes of an old cinder block. "Well, okay, I'll go get it."

One arm fell to his side, the other remained on his hip. "Thanks."

He didn't move to follow her. Inside, Zoe snagged the baskets from the kitchen counter and walked back out to find Ethan standing precisely where she'd left him.

Do you want to come in for coffee and bread?

The question hovered on Zoe's tongue, but the words stayed trapped behind her willful lips, refusing to be spoken. She glanced at the baskets in her hand. "I didn't know which was which so I brought both." She offered them both up, feeling unworthy of another gift.

Ethan reached out, taking the crustier of the two. He waved it at her, smiling, sort of. "It's called a banneton," he said. "In case you were wondering."

Zoe didn't immediately lower the other basket. She held it out between them, wanting desperately to say the right thing. But as easy as it might be for others, personal invitations into her life didn't come easily for Zoe. She was afraid to open doors.

Silence grew like kudzu on steroids. If there had been crickets out, Zoe was sure she would have heard them chirping. Instead, she caught the distant tinkle of piano keys.

Beethoven's "Moonlight Sonata" started out low, barely audible, drawing Zoe's gaze to Walter Donovan's picture window.

Muffled behind thick beige curtains, the music built slowly—strangely appropriate to the moment, beautiful and sad—the notes precise, in a way made possible only through hours and hours of practice. The melody was so at odds with the old man whose fingers walked over the ivory keys.

Another anomaly—Ethan's hands inspected the basket he held, his fingers pausing over each little crusty lump, as though to be certain it was still the same as it was before—like a familiar lover. Zoe watched him, shivering involuntarily, imagining those fingers dancing over her skin.

"So . . . you're doing all right?"

Zoe swallowed. "Fine. Thanks."

"Good. Good," he said uncomfortably.

Next door, the melody shifted to something more upbeat, effectively breaking the spell. Ethan took a step backward. "Well, I'll get on out of your way."

"Okay," Zoe said. "Thanks for everything, Ethan." It was the first time she'd ever used his name in a way that wasn't provocative, she realized.

"No problem, Zoe. I'll see you 'round. Take care," he said. And then he turned around and left her standing in her driveway, no winks or jokes. He got into his cab, started the engine, backed out of the driveway, and drove away.

Whether it was the somber piano music playing next door, or simply her mood, Zoe felt glum over this departure—strangely, even more so than she'd felt over leaving Chris.

STICKY WITH PAINT, the paintbrushes sat drying over the sink, growing stiff. Zoe couldn't muster the energy to wash them out. For the second time since her arrival on the island, she'd had herself a good cry.

For the better part of the morning, she sat in her kitchen, surrounded by flowers from well-wishers, feeling as though they had been delivered to a wake rather than offered as a celebration of life. In fact, she was in mourning. She didn't know how to have a relationship, not even a friendly one. The entire time she'd stood out on the driveway with Ethan, she'd had that same sick sense of apprehension she'd had on the day her dad punched her in the gut.

One evening, when Zoe was thirteen, she'd answered the phone. Her mother was lying down after taking a Valium. Her dad was in his office, working, as he usually was. She and Nicky were watching a movie. The phone call had been for Zoe, a boy from school. He'd gotten her number from a friend. It was her first phone call ever from a boy. Terrified of being discovered, Zoe had spoken in whispers, so her father wouldn't hear down the hall. While she was on the phone, her brother walked by. Zoe barely noticed; she'd been so worried about getting off the phone without having to confess she wasn't allowed to talk to boys. Minutes later her father had loomed over her, darkening the kitchen with his presence. He'd glared down at her. "Did you know your brother is sick?"

Fear had seized hold of Zoe's heart. The voice coming through the receiver had diminished to a buzz in her ear. Wide eyed, she'd shaken her head, answering her father.

What came next floored Zoe, literally. Her father had given her a blow to the gut and Zoe folded to the floor. She didn't remember anything more.

Later, she'd been told she was the one who was bad for allowing her brother to vomit up his dinner without any help. The guilt had been Zoe's—not her mother's, who'd managed to sleep through it all. Not her father's, who'd been furious because his son's vomiting had disturbed him at work. Only now, Zoe wondered if maybe her dad had been angry over something else . . . maybe Zoe had been his scapegoat for the anger he'd harbored toward Marge—the wife who would no longer look him straight in the eyes.

Throughout their lives, Nick never took Zoe's side. Ever. Even now, whenever she attempted to talk to him about any of it, he shut her down, demanding that she stop wallowing in the past.

In person, he gave her that look that said he thought she was crazy or maybe just a glutton for punishment.

You like living dangerously, I see.

No, she didn't.

Admit it. You blame her, Rob. You blame her; she knows it.

Maybe there were things Zoe didn't want to remember. Maybe she was responsible for Hannah's death in some way she couldn't recall.

She longed to talk to Gabi Donovan, but now she realized that would never happen—and why did she need that? Did she secretly fear Gabi was the only one who knew the truth?

The real truth?

Knees drawn up, staring blindly at the dripping faucet, Zoe sat on her borrowed chair in the kitchen, trying to recall the precise details of the morning Hannah disappeared. She and her sister had fought.

They *did* fight.

Zoe had wanted to go with her and Gabi. Hannah had said they'd found a new secret place and, naturally, Zoe had wanted to know where it was. On an island with so many secrets—tunnels slithering beneath the ground, old repurposed gun casements and mounts breaking up in the surf—there were endless possibilities.

That day, Zoe had gone searching for her sister, long after she and Gabi had set out together on Hannah's pale-blue Schwinn. Gabi didn't have a bike. She'd talked Hannah into letting her ride on the handlebars—something Zoe knew her sister hadn't wanted to do. And yet she had. Why? Because Gabi had been meaner than a cottonmouth when anyone told her no.

Zoe remembered feeling furious with her sister—as much because Hannah had been doing things Zoe knew she didn't want to do, as it was because her little sister had left her behind. As conflicted as every other relationship might have been, Zoe's role at home was ever clear. *She* was the big sister. *She* was the one who was supposed to look out for her siblings. She was Hannah's example, her leader. Her father had said so.

What the hell were you thinking, Zoe?

Zoe had hated the way her dad looked at her whenever she failed. She'd hated that worried, vacant look on her mother's face. She'd hated feeling so responsible. And worse, she'd hated feeling irresponsible as well.

After Gabi and Hannah left together, Zoe had pouted for a long while, feeling discarded. To the best of her knowledge, she'd never seen either of them again; not until Gabi had been there in her yard, talking to Chief Hale, with her papaw towering by her side.

But that was all Zoe remembered—except for that hateful look from Gabi as she'd stood responding to questions from Chief Hale. And then after . . . Chief Hale had come over to grill Zoe at her kitchen table, as though she'd done something wrong.

It was only later—from her father, no less—that Zoe learned Gabi had told Chief Hale she'd seen Zoe push her sister off the bridge. No one could ever have suspected such a thing, except that it had been Zoe who'd found Hannah's bike in the dunes and then walked it home. Why would she have done that if she hadn't known her sister wasn't coming back for it?

Where's your sister, Zoe?

How is it you knew where to find Hannah's bike?

When all was said and done, her memories of that day were mercurial. The only constant was her pain. *You're fucking crazy,* Chris often said.

Right now, Zoe was terrified he might be right. Certainly, her relationship with him was crazy. She'd never had any physical proof of his cheating but, after they'd been together seven years, they'd stood together in the bathroom one day and he'd taken Zoe into his arms, laughed, and said, "I forget how tiny you are, Zoe."

How could anyone forget the way it felt to hold the person they claimed to love—the person they lived with, slept with every day? Unless she had not been the last person he'd held.

When Zoe confronted him about it, he'd claimed it was all in her head.

It was also "in her head" when she'd found a pair of panties in his car that didn't belong to her—but this had happened far too soon after they'd met for her to doubt him yet. Although she remembered thinking three months was an awful long time for him not to clean his ex's panties out of his car. And then, there was this: Who screwed his girlfriend in his car if a breakup was imminent? In retrospect, nothing Chris had ever said or done made any damned sense, and yet Zoe had struggled to believe him.

Why?

She must have known where it would lead.

What the hell were you thinking, Zoe?

Near the end, she'd told Chris straight up, "If you want someone else, I *want* you to leave. I'm okay with that. Just tell me the truth."

He'd never batted a lash, nor had he looked away. "I love you, Zoe," he'd said. "*You* are the love of my life." Two days later, he'd smashed her forehead with a terra-cotta pot. On the way to the hospital he'd said, "You're the only one who's ever made me lose my temper, Zoe."

Why wouldn't Zoe believe that? That's what her father had claimed as well.

You're a button-pusher, Zoe.

Now she had a scar on her head to prove it.

On the way to the hospital, Chris's mother had sat with Zoe in the back seat of his car, pressing a bloody rag to her forehead. She'd said nothing, the look in her eyes studied, giving Zoe little inkling of her thoughts. If her son had ever done such a thing before, Cheryl Mays wasn't about to tell.

18

"A PEPPER"

There was a story Chris's mother used to tell. It wasn't particularly interesting. Nor was it heartwarming, or necessarily horrific—not in the face of greater tragedies such as child trafficking and murder. It was simply a story, one that sometimes made Zoe grateful for her own family, even with all its dysfunction. It went like this: Three-year-old Chris had been in the back seat of his mother's car—a brand-new white V-8 Camaro that belonged to her linebacker boyfriend. Cheryl and her new boyfriend were going through a fast-food drive-through. "I want a pepper," Chris had said from the backseat.

Translated, this meant Dr. Pepper, Cheryl would explain. "No," she'd said to her son. "They don't have a pepper. You have water."

"No!" he'd cried. "I want a pepper!"

To this, Cheryl had turned with a full-size cup of soda in her hand and tossed it into Chris's face, ice and all. "You should have seen his face," she would say to Zoe, laughing, no matter how many times she told the story. She always made an effort to recreate the horrified look of a three-year-old child whose mother had just buffeted him in the face with ice-cold, acid-grade liquid. "Isn't that funny?"

No. It wasn't—not as far as Zoe was concerned.

In fact, Zoe considered it an act of abuse, despite Chris also laughing whenever his mother told that particular story, always, to illustrate how spoiled Chris had been as a kid, because of course a spoiled kid couldn't be neglected, which had been precisely what Zoe suspected he was—making him a kindred spirit.

But that story was about as funny as a grown man curling up in a fetal position on the couch and staying there for days after a vicious argument with his mom, wherein she screamed at the top of her lungs that she wished he'd never been born.

Clearly, there were varying degrees of abuse, and probably no one got off this planet without a cross to bear. Still, Zoe was certain monsters were not born; they were reared by women with plastic tits, bleached-out hair, and faces painted to harden more than just the resolve of a professional football team.

Contemplating this, Zoe sat on the bottom step of her front porch, systematically deconstructing the stairs, from the top down. Why exactly, without having bought any wood or made arrangements to replace them, she didn't know—except that maybe this was meant to give her the impetus to follow through.

After the stairs were dismantled, she took her measurements to Southern Lumber and asked them to cut stair treads from the cheapest recommended wood.

As it turned out, putting together a set of stairs was much like putting together a jigsaw puzzle. The parts, in all shapes and sizes, were available preformed. She learned about stringers, risers, and treads. The stringers were the "saw-toothed" sides upon which risers and treads were set. She bought two, right and left. Risers were the vertical measurement of each stair, just beneath the tread. For these, she bought cedar, which was what they recommended. The tread was the horizontal section of each stair—the part you stepped on. Using Zoe's measurements, they cut nine of these from cedar as well. Along with the wood, she bought screws, nails, and a good hammer, but she could already see that screwing in the stairs was going to be a bitch and she wished she'd bought an electric screwdriver as well. But, aside from that, how difficult could it be to fit together the pieces of an oversized jigsaw puzzle?

Zoe was hammering in a guide nail to keep one of the risers in place so that she could crawl beneath the porch and hammer it in from the backside, when Walter Donovan suddenly appeared. For a moment, he said nothing, simply stared down at her.

"Looks like you're having trouble."

Zoe looked up at her reclusive neighbor, blinking at his looming form. Dressed in a pair of loose khakis and a dark-blue, long-sleeved shirt, despite the sweltering heat, he towered over her, frowning down like a parental unit—someone's father, forced away from his greasy armchair and a Sunday football game by the antics of a precocious teen.

Zoe's face flushed. She felt the sweat beneath her pits, like a basketball player straight off the courts.

"Maybe a little," she confessed. It wouldn't do any good to deny it. The front yard was littered with refuse and she had barely made any progress.

"Those are drywall screws," he said, pointing to the box she'd been plucking screws out of. "They won't do you any good. You need deck screws." He pointed to a box of nails. "Those'll work just fine, though you're better off using screws. After you install the treads, you'll wanna screw them all down good'n tight and for that you'll need a better screwdriver or you're gonna strip out your screws."

Zoe peered at the hammer in her hand, and then at Walter Donovan, forcing a smile. "Yeah? Well, now you tell me."

His arms remained akimbo, and his frown deepened in

response to her smile. He stood another long moment, blocking the sun from Zoe's eyes.

"The bread was good," he said after a moment, managing to make it sound more like a complaint. Despite that, Zoe perceived it to be a compliment.

"Thank you, but I can't take credit. The recipe is Ethan McWhorter's."

Walter Donovan glanced down the street, presumably toward the police station, which he clearly couldn't see because it was one street up and over. "Chief McWhorter's son?"

Zoe nodded.

"I thought that might be him comin' 'round."

Zoe lifted a brow. "You know him?"

"I know *of* him." Once again, Walter's brow furrowed, looking as awkward as Zoe felt. He pointed halfheartedly at the stairs. "You need help with that?"

It was a grudging offer, but one Zoe couldn't refuse. She grinned up at him, offering him the hammer.

As SIMPLE AS the stair construction might have seemed after her brief lesson at Southern Lumber, Zoe discovered there was much more she didn't know.

From the beginning, she allowed Walter to take the lead, serving more as his "operating-room nurse," handing him nails, screws, hammer, and screwdriver when he requested them. His version of "helping" was hardly the same as her father's, who'd given Zoe direction and let her flounder in an attempt to succeed. What Zoe discovered was that she much preferred her father's method. As it was, she felt like a third wheel on her own construction project. Not that she didn't appreciate Walter's help —she did. But there was something to be said for that feeling of accomplishment you got once a job was complete.

On the bright side: Although Zoe's part in the stair construction was minimal, it gave her time to make a run for deck screws. When she returned, she stood, watching Walter work, prying conversation where she could.

She considered that he might have a touch of Asperger's, but it was difficult to say whether it was that or simply a grumpy demeanor. The grumpy demeanor was Zoe's first guess, but as she watched him work so meticulously in his awkward personal space, she began to wonder whether Asperger's ran in the Donovan family. It would certainly cast Gabi in a whole new light.

After half a day's work together, she and Walter developed an odd fellowship. Still, it surprised her when he peered up from beneath the stairs and said point-blank, "Tell me, Zoe . . . how'd you get that cut on your head?"

Zoe automatically crossed her arms. She gave him a sideways glance. "Let's call it a love tap."

His eyes were unnaturally bright. "Chief McWhorter's son?"

Even the notion of Ethan McWhorter doing such a thing startled Zoe. "No," she said quickly. "Not him, but I doubt he'll be coming 'round anymore."

Walter Donovan nodded. He went back to work, eschewing any more small talk as he focused on torquing screws. Zoe was fairly certain he must own a drill, but he kept on using her screwdriver as though it were his only choice. She guessed he must be enjoying the company, even if he wouldn't admit as much.

He ran his long, lean fingers over the screw heads that were already embedded in the wood, skimming each, going back to each one in turn, stopping to assess one in particular that made his focus narrow.

"What are you doing, exactly?"

A muscle ticked at his jaw.

Tick. Tick. Tick.

Zoe waited.

He eyed her circumspectly, not precisely answering her question. "You should have bought treated cedar," he said. "Now you'll have to seal it or it'll rot in a year's time."

Zoe softened her flippant response with a smile. "Luckily, that won't be my problem."

His pale gray eyes flicked toward her with interest. "You don't intend to stay?"

Zoe shook her head.

He considered that a moment, his fingers returning to the screws, perhaps testing their relationship to the boards, just to be certain that none protruded.

"You'll also need a good high-grade construction adhesive to put below the surface before we install the treads, else you'll hear 'em squeakin' for miles."

Once again, that wasn't Zoe's problem, still, she ceded. "I'll get some. Are you hungry?" If she didn't slow him down, he was going to finish the job by the end of the day, giving Zoe little chance to pry about his niece. So far, she'd remained miles away from that topic, hoping Walter would open that door on his own.

He took his time answering. "Maybe a little."

"Great!" Zoe exclaimed. "I've got plenty of food inside, thanks to our lovely neighbors." She winked at him. "I've even got some of Ms. Shipman's ambrosia salad. How about we stop for a while and I'll fix us a plate?"

Walter didn't say anything to that, but he came out from under the stairs, and Zoe took that as a yes. Still she lingered, just to be sure.

"A glass of water'd be much appreciated," he said.

"Yes, sir, coming right up!"

Zoe raced toward the back door, considering how best to broach the subject of Gabi. The last time she'd mentioned Gabi's name he'd literally shut the door in her face. A sense of excitement filled her at the prospect of talking with Walter about his niece. It wasn't so much that Zoe expected definitive answers, but maybe Gabi had said something that could shed some light on what happened to her sister that day. Her uncle was the closest she was ever going to get to Gabi again.

She brought Walter his water first, and then, heaping more on their plates than either could conceivably eat, she grabbed two forks and carried both plates out onto the front porch.

At this point, the stairs were framed, but there were no risers or treads in place, so Zoe handed Walter both plates and jumped down. She sat next to him in the grass, and he returned her plate. Crossing his legs, he nestled his own plate in his lap.

Forking a piece of ham, Zoe watched as he gripped his fork and set about separating the items on his plate, so that there was at least a quarter-inch of plate surrounding each type of food, like a moat. Potato salad sat in a tiny mound, surrounded by white space, the broccoli casserole as well. The collard greens were shoved over to one side, as though they had been founding wanting and were rejected. He took a finger to the paper plate, making a gully in the side so the pot liquor could run out onto the grass. His meat occupied center stage, and whatever bits had touched other foodstuffs, he pushed into the greens. At last, he took a small bite, beginning with the candied yams. He ate only that, until all the yams were gone, before starting in on the potato salad, moving counterclockwise around his plate, as though he were building toward the meat finale.

In contrast, Zoe's plate was a jumble of food—potato salad shoved against the ham, green pot liquor streaming into the casserole.

"The yard looks nice," he said, complimenting Zoe's hard work. "It doesn't look like the same place."

"Have you seen inside?"

He nodded. "Kids made a goddamned mess, didn't they?"

"You must have been the one who called the police," Zoe surmised, but he furrowed his brow at the suggestion.

Zoe waited patiently for Walter to finish his potato salad and then start the broccoli. "I've been told you're a war hero." She smiled as she took a small bite of ham.

His gaze found Zoe's over his plate. "Not exactly."

"But you were wounded, right? Took a wound to the leg?"

"In a manner of speaking."

"Was it a mine?" Zoe wondered aloud. "I heard there are millions buried out there."

"No." Finally, he forked a tiny bite of meat and put it daintily into his mouth, eyeing Zoe queerly. "I was in the navy."

Zoe didn't want to push, but if she couldn't get him talking about something that placed him in a position of honor, she doubted she could get him to open up about Gabi. "Does it bother you to talk about it?"

"No."

Frustrated, Zoe stabbed a piece of potato, trying to be casual.

Walter looked at her with assessing gray eyes. "Tell me again . . . how did you say you got the cut on your forehead?"

Zoe shrugged.

He waited a moment to drive home his point. "Does it bother you to talk about it?"

Zoe lifted a shoulder. "No, not really."

He smiled thinly, as though it were some sort of verbal checkmate.

However, Zoe didn't want the conversation to end there, so she told him the truth. "My ex-boyfriend chucked a flower pot at my head."

"Why?"

"Because I told him I was leaving."

"And that's why you're here?"

Zoe nodded, confessing at last. The house was merely an excuse, she realized. Now that she was sitting here, looking at the house in broad daylight, a few cosmetic changes weren't going to make all that much difference when it came to the bottom dollar. The land on Sullivan's Island was worth what it was worth, and the house, while it wasn't dilapidated, wasn't worth any more than it had been a few weeks ago. The property, however, would bring her and Nick both a tidy sum—if they sold it. Nick didn't seem to care one way or another about the money or the house.

As Zoe sat there with the unlikeliest of confidants, she found herself opening up about Chris, mostly about their rocky relationship. She gave Walter the highlights, beneath which, like an iceberg, the worst, most-treacherous ninety percent remained hidden under the surface. She realized he sensed what remained unsaid. She could spy the questions in his eyes, although he contented himself with listening.

After a while, it began to feel as though she were the one under the spotlight, being interrogated, not Walter, despite him barely speaking a word. A look here, a look there, were the only prompts Zoe seemed to need to spill her guts after so many years. And once she realized that, she stopped talking and Walter returned to working on the stairs.

19

CALM BEFORE THE STORM

Outside, a fitful breeze rustled leaves in the trees, the sound gently melodic, like chimes. Even knowing Chris was out there, somewhere, the amber glow from the porch light next door gave Zoe an unexpected sense of relief, perhaps stemming from the knowledge that Walter Donovan was within shouting distance.

Reluctant or not, Walter had already come to her rescue more than once, and she had a good sense that if she needed him he'd come running again. It felt good to be back on the island, where even cranky old men felt beholden to their neighbors. In Baltimore, Zoe had barely known her neighbors, except for the woman next door—a nurse who'd gotten chummy with Chris, although she'd had little enough to say to Zoe on any given day.

Glancing over at the Donovan house, she noticed the back of his house didn't receive the same care as the front. The front yard was meticulously cared for, but the backyard was overgrown. The weeds were as high as the bedroom sill. Together, their houses were an odd pair, two relics from the past, surrounded by shiny McMansions.

Out front, she could hear Kingdom's wooden sign knocking

gently against the post. On nights like this, Nana had often warned a storm was on the way—she said she could feel it in her bones. Sometimes they were merely weather tantrums, sometimes full-on gully washers, but Zoe had often marveled that her Nana's proclamations so often came true. She'd come to wonder if old people were living barometers, unnaturally sensitive and able to sense minute climate changes in their joints. Like animals, they grew restless over something they sensed in the air, something unknown to people under the age of sixty-four.

In fact, Nana had also claimed she sensed spirits—a throwback to her time with the Gullah people.

Listening to the wind outside, Zoe stood musing over the kitchen sink, looking out over her backyard, peering into Walter Donovan's house. She could spy him in glimpses, flitting here and there, maybe tidying up.

She wondered how he lived, and whether he kept a spotless home, or whether, like the backyard, he let it go, knowing no one could see it unless he allowed it.

He didn't leave his blinds open much. That he'd done so tonight seemed an extension of his friendship, as though he were somehow allowing Zoe a glimpse into his world.

There was an odd sense of contentment she attained from washing their dessert plates. It was a comfortable thing to be doing. Only now, this instant, she realized her mother's presence at the sink must have been reassuring to everyone who had witnessed her there.

Familiar scents lingered in the kitchen. Banana-bread pudding, most recently removed from the oven, sat on Ethan's table—probably still lukewarm, hours later. Walter had eaten two pieces with appreciative nods, a form of speech all its own. He wasn't particularly chatty, though he responded well to Zoe's questions—not always to her greatest satisfaction, but she supposed he had a right to keep some things to himself.

She wondered what Ethan was doing right now . . . wondered

what it might be like to live here on the island again . . . if not indefinitely, perhaps long enough to get to know him a little better.

She pictured Ethan standing in her driveway and wished she'd had the nerve to ask him to stay . . . maybe next time?

If ever there was a next time.

She had a role to play in that, she realized.

Really, where else did she have to go? Of all the places Zoe had traveled, none had ever felt so much like home. She was forced to confess that there was nothing inherently wrong with Sullivan's Island. To the contrary, it was one of the most sublime places on Earth to be. Must she give it up because of a few bad memories?

Truth to tell, leaving the island hadn't won her any peace of mind. Without a doubt, the strongest parts of her were rooted here, in this place.

The flowers in the vases were wilted, making a bit of a mess. Zoe plucked out the droopiest of the blooms, leaving only the ones that remained firm, mainly because their presence meant that someone out there remembered she existed—and not only remembered but actually cared. These folks had taken time out of their busy days, despite the fact that they hadn't seen her in years, to pay respects.

In his house across the way, Walter stopped to peer out his window, peering back at Zoe over the sweet myrtle bushes she'd hacked nearly to the ground.

Sometimes, when Zoe was a little girl, she and Hannah would scour the base of the bushes for blackberries growing in the brambles at its feet. Sometimes they'd brought in enough for Nana to put into a pie. And sometimes they'd sat, plucking at the vines and stuffing blackberries in their mouths, turning their lips and tongues a bruised shade of blue.

The taste of blackberries was so distinct—like raspberries, only sweeter and tarter both at once. They were always best straight from the vine, warmed by the sun, but the ripest of the batch seldom made it inside. Lovely and fragile, they burst when you tugged them. Once they were done picking berries, their fingers had been filled with itchy little thorns from trying to separate the brambles.

Yet another great spot for blackberry hunting was on the weeded slopes of the Mound. Around the Mound's perimeter were dense tangles of underbrush, girding thick bamboo forests where she and Hannah had chased each other along meandering paths to the surrounding drumbeat of hollow bamboo shafts. It was somewhere near there that Zoe figured Hannah and Gabi had discovered their secret hideaway, somewhere along the web of tunnels—long before they were sealed.

From his window, Walter Donovan gave Zoe a subtle wave, and she smiled and waved back.

ALL ALONG ATLANTIC AVENUE, the porch lights were dark. Despite a waxing moon, the night was black. Inside Zoe's bedroom, she leaned against a stack of pillows, pressing the phone against her ear, contemplating the need for light-retaining blinds. Right now, with no lamp in the bedroom, she was not in breach of the island's lighting laws, but even a low-wattage lamp might put her in danger of a fine. Tomorrow she would look into that, which prompted her to ask, "What would you think about me staying in Charleston, Nick?"

It was only once she posed the question that Zoe realized she had a stake in her brother's answer.

"In the house?"

"Maybe." If he needed money, Zoe would be forced to take the possibility off the table. She had funds, but not enough to immediately cover his half of fair-market value. "How would you feel about that?"

"Well," he said. "The girls would love it. So would Beth."

There was no protest at all, no hesitation, no mention of money.

A tiny blossom of hope flowered at the thought of starting over, so close to her family. The simple fact that they had kept the house after all these years, even knowing the rising property values, was proof enough she wasn't ready to let it go . . . maybe Nick wasn't either.

Kingdom wasn't exactly the nicest house on the block, but there was something to be said for being a little fish in a big sea.

What about you? She wanted to ask Nick. But it wasn't in her to be so direct. Despite his not mentioning it, there was money at stake, and not just a little. She'd heard one of the neighbors sold a beachfront lot with a small house for nearly two million. Kingdom wasn't on the beach, though it was near enough to warrant a decent selling price.

"If I stay and we agree on a price, maybe I can pay out your share as rent?"

Outside, Zoe could hear the shrill mating call of frogs. The sound intensified in the silence that ensued.

"I thought you hated the house, Zoe."

Zoe's shoulders tightened, her sister's voice whispering at her ear. *"What will you do when you grow up, Zoe?"*

"I'll move away as soon as I can."

Hannah's ghost—a memory—lifted her knees, hugging bare legs as she peered out from the dormer window up in the attic. Moonlight turned her lips a ghostly blue. *"Not me. I'm gonna stay forever."*

Her brother was quiet on the other end of the line.

Zoe swallowed hard. "It turns out maybe I don't."

Even as she spoke the words, Zoe realized it was true. It gave her a sense of pride to see the difference she had made in the short time since she'd arrived, and then, having vocalized as much, the tension rolled off her shoulders.

"We don't need to sell the house if you don't want to, Zoe. If you wanna keep it, we can work it out . . . if that's what you're asking."

"What about the girls? I know you wanted to send them to Bishop England" As far as private high schools went, Bishop England was still one of the best.

Nick was quick to answer. "The girls are fine where they are. Besides, we're not Catholic." There was a note of laughter in his voice.

Zoe laughed. "It's not just Catholics who attend and you know it."

"No, but who the hell wants to sit through mass if you don't have to? Can you imagine my girls squirming through Latin sermons?" He emitted a chant that was complete gibberish as far as Zoe could tell, ending with, "*In nomine Patris!*"

Zoe laughed once more. "I don't think they even use Latin anymore, Nick, but okay. I'll figure it out and I'll let you know as soon as I can."

"Is that Aunt Zoe, Daddy?" she heard Anna ask. Nick must have nodded, because Anna called out, "Hi, Aunt Zoe!" And then she wanted to know, "Why are you talking so dumb, Daddy?"

"Dumb, eh?" he asked.

Suddenly Anna squealed, and Zoe detected a bit of rough and tumble against the receiver.

Zoe imagined her brother tickling his eldest child. For all that she could tell, Nick was a good dad, giving the task a singleness of purpose that defied his own deficient upbringing. Both their parents had clearly been running on empty and Zoe was a poor substitute for a mother. The phone hung up abruptly during their horseplay and Zoe smirked.

They weren't finished with their conversation, so Zoe started to redial her brother's number. He rang back faster than she could punch in the first two digits. Grinning, she automatically answered the phone. "Hey, if that's your way of changing the subject..."

A fierce silence shrieked from the other end of the line.

"Nick?"

"No, Zoe. But it's nice to hear you laugh."

Chris.

Zoe's heart thumped against her chest.

Call waiting beeped through, signaling her brother's return call.

"Whassup?"

The question was casual, as though nothing had ever happened between them. Zoe held her breath, waiting for a verbal assault. Her voice remained trapped inside her throat, as though Chris' hands were actually squeezing her windpipe.

"I've been worried about you," he said, more a complaint than an accusation. "I wanted to be sure you're all right."

"I'm fine," Zoe replied, feeling sick to her stomach.

"Nick said you were in the hospital."

She could hear the wind bellowing past his car window. He was driving somewhere. Maybe to one of his barstools. Maybe to a woman's house. *Maybe to Charleston!* The last possibility made her heart trip.

Silence raged between them, stretching into eternity.

"Yes," she finally replied.

"He wouldn't say what happened once I told him we were over."

Zoe closed her eyes, silently thanking her brother.

Call waiting beeped again, but Zoe's grip on the phone was inflexible.

"I thought about coming down, but I figured it wouldn't be a good time to air our dirty laundry. Didn't seem a good time to meet your brother for the first time."

Zoe replied with silence.

"Well, anyway, Zoe"—He said her name acidly—"It's good to finally hear your voice."

It was terrifying to hear his, but Zoe wouldn't say so and risk an unnecessary argument. She refused to give him more power over her. She tried to sound casual, but she knew there was a note of bitterness in her question. "Where are you going, Chris?"

"Me? I'm going nowhere. I'm at home."

He'd used that liar's tone, as though by the power of positive assertion, he could make Zoe believe anything he said. Those days were gone. His blinker came on, a steady *tick, tick, tick*, that lifted the hairs on the back of Zoe's nape. *Liar*, she wanted to scream.

Liar.

"So you're at home?"

"Yeah, you know the place we live—together?" he was quick to emphasize.

"Lived, Chris. I'm not coming back."

His tone veered toward resentment. "I get it," he said, snapping. "Don't worry, Zoe. If you're not into this anymore, I'm not gonna force you."

Everything he ever said was some form of lie. Zoe had learned that the hard way. Even as a means to one of his ends, complacence wasn't normal. The calm in his tone wasn't real. "There's nothing left to say, Chris."

Zoe was ready to hang up, but she hung on, hoping Chris would admit where he was going—so she would know whether to call Chief McWhorter.

So she could brace herself.

For what?

His tone was slightly more disgruntled now, quietly seething. She detected anger in the tightness of his words. "I said . . . I get it, Zoe."

She heard the F word although he didn't actually use it.

I said . . . I fucking get it, Zoe. Fuck you.

That's how he normally spoke to her, except that now he was angling to keep her on the phone. The tips of her fingers went numb and she realized she was gripping the phone hard enough to cut off her circulation.

"Look," he said. "Just give me your address, I'll send you the shit you left."

"I don't want it."

"Don't be a dumb fucking bitch, Zoe. You still have clothes here—what about your coats, your boots, perfume? Tell me where to send all your shit and I'll put everything into a goddamn box and ship it to you. If you're going to be a fucking baby about this, we don't ever have to see each other again."

He was dangling her belongings in front of her like carrots, but Zoe's resolve held. "Donate everything. Take the receipts for next year's taxes."

His tone was a little more harried now. "What the fuck? What about your mom's quilt? If you don't take that ugly piece of shit, I'm going to dump it into the trash. I don't need fucking reminders of this bullshit relationship. Did you hear me, Zoe? This relationship is bullshit."

The image of her mom's quilt laying in some dumpster somewhere made Zoe's stomach roil. However, giving Chris her address made her stomach hurt even more. She clearly heard wind whistling past his window. "Chris, where are you going?"

The sound diminished as he rolled up his window. "Fuck you, Zoe! I said I'm at home. Why are you asking me that again?"

"I'm not stupid," Zoe said calmly. "I hear your blinker."

"What the fuck does it matter where—"

Zoe ended the call, her hands trembling as she set the phone aside, too shaken to call Nick back. She rose from the bed and went to check the locks on all her doors.

20

IN THE BONES

All night long that anxious foreboding persisted, unshakable, like a feverish sweat that wouldn't burn off, even at night with the cool ocean breeze seeping into the cracks of the old house. Nana wouldn't have ignored the feeling, Zoe realized. Thankfully, she didn't share her grandmother's Gullah superstitions. She understood the anxiousness was a direct result of her phone conversation with Chris.

She went to bed, telling herself it would pass but, much of the night, sleep eluded her. She tossed about, kicking off her covers, unused to the muggy heat, but still unwilling to open windows, too unnerved for that.

For all she could tell, her sister Hannah had never spent a sleepless night, never tossed and turned as Zoe did. Hannah had slept soundly, but on nights when Zoe ran for her life from some unspeakable monster, her sister had often woken her with soft, tentative pats along the cheek.

After Hannah disappeared, Zoe had sought glimpses of her sister in her dreams, hoping to solve the riddle of her disappearance. Ironically, it was about that same time her nightmares had ceased altogether and her dreams completely abandoned her.

Thereafter, dreaming wasn't something Zoe did, although that might seem counterintuitive, if you believed, as she did, that dreams were the mind's way of solving life's little problems, because Zoe's life was rife with problems.

On the other hand, if, as Freud claimed, dreams existed to fulfill our deepest desires, this was the first time Zoe had experienced the reality of that beast. At some point, she drifted off to sleep and the next she realized it was morning. With a sense of knowing that came from somewhere other than the space she physically inhabited, she felt the morning sun warming her face. Dreaming, she realized, but she preferred to believe it was her mother's hand cupping her face. She remembered that very well, elusive as those moments were—the reassurance of her mother's caress.

Inasmuch as Marge had sometimes been removed from life, her touch had remained vital until her death, as though she could transfer the last of her living energy to her children—even toward the end, when she drifted like dead wood throughout the rooms of their house, going wherever the current might carry her. Every so often, she would blink away the stupor, and you could spy the woman she'd once been, lurking like a frightened child behind the stark blue eyes.

This instant, her mother stood before her, a soft, radiant smile playing at the corners of her lips. "It's time, Zoe," she said.

Time for what? Time to wake?

Like a defiant child, Zoe sank deeper into the sheets. Waking was the last thing she wanted to do right now. Marge, for all her foibles, was a source of joy in that instant. Zoe forgave her everything. Like her, her mother had been subject to the travails of the human condition, but her life was no longer defined by the days she had remaining, but by those she had once lived. She was no longer a dying animal, but a woman who'd given generously to the ones she'd loved—gave until she had nothing left. It was only love Zoe spied in her mother's eyes right now, love, stripped of all the conditions she'd placed on the love she bore herself.

Capturing one last glance at her mother's face, effulgent and ethereal, Zoe understood that the moment would be over in a heartbeat. It was an impression frozen in time when the act of simply turning her face might reveal her sister's hair flowing down like a golden river across the Berenstain Bears sheets.

But then her mother vanished, taking with her that beauteous smile and, in Zoe's dream, her sister sat up in her twin bed, fully dressed, peering over at Zoe.

In Marge's melancholy voice, Hannah whispered, "All the night-tide, I lie down by the side of my darling . . . in the sepulcher there by the sea, in her tomb by the sounding sea . . ."

Edgar Allan Poe.

Like mist at the break of dawn, the dream evaporated.

Zoe peeled open tired eyes, blinking at the bright morning sun. She was, indeed, alone, but not in the room she'd once shared with Hannah. She was in her parents' bedroom in the bed Ethan had lent her. On the bedside table sat a vase of tired yellow tulips. Next to that, her phone lay quietly . . . all the night long. And next to that lay her growing stack of business cards—one from Chief McWhorter, one from the carpet guys, and one from Lori Masterson-Bryant.

It was the first time in years Zoe had dreamt of Hannah in such flawless detail, and despite the fact that she could no longer conjure her sister's voice, she remembered her words on the bridge that day with unnerving clarity: *Gabi says Annabelle's father buried her down there; that's why he couldn't find her."*

Down where?

Down in the tunnels.

Convinced the dream was prophetic, Zoe bounded up from the bed and got herself dressed. She put on her shoes and rushed out the front door, lured toward the Mound, where she and Hannah had once played together as children.

Gabi says Annabelle's father buried her down there.

Down where?

Down in the tunnels.

That might explain why no one had ever found her sister's body. If Hannah had drowned, her body would have floated ashore somewhere. On the other hand, if some undiscovered tunnel remained, and if Hannah were trapped down there—somewhere—that might explain why authorities never located her body, even after months and months of searching. Zoe's recent accident was a testament to how unpredictable the barrier islands could be. Ever changing, the currents that flowed in, around, and between the islands were constantly molding and reinventing the landscape.

On the other side of the harbor, Morris Island Lighthouse fought a losing battle with the sea. Currents were so intense there that during the 1700s there had been three islands stretching four miles between Folly and Sullivan's Islands. Originally, the lighthouse was built inland on the middle island. Now, the three were one and the defunct lighthouse sat something like sixteen hundred feet offshore—a deserting Confederate soldier, marching slowly into the Atlantic.

From what Zoe could recall, most of the tunnels running beneath the island had been built beneath fortified mounds—but maybe not all?

The tunnels beneath Fort Moultrie were part of the museum. There was little to no chance any of those remained unexplored.

Driven first to the Mound, as she was on the morning of Hannah's disappearance, Zoe conjured an aerial view of the island. From end to end, Sullivan's Island was about three miles long, less than one mile wide, butted by tributaries on one side and the ocean on the other. But there were nooks and crannies everywhere.

At the Mound, ignoring the forbidding sign that warned kids off the slopes, Zoe climbed the sandy slope in front of the playground, just out of sight of the police station around the corner. A couple of teenage boys were playing basketball on a court nearby. They stopped to peer in Zoe's direction and then gazed toward the police station, as though to see who would dare defy Chief McWhorter's orders and whether it might compel legions of SIPD out of the station doors. Unfortunately, Zoe wasn't as limber as she used to be. She slipped twice on the sandy slope, breaking her fall with the palm of her hand, stabbing herself with a burr. Half expecting the kids to go running to the police, she quickly scaled to the top. Once there, she was out of view of the police station and she took a moment to pick out the splinter from her hand. In fact, she could no longer see the boys either, but she heard their ball resume bouncing on the courts.

At one time you could look over much of the island from the Mound, but now palmetto trees and sand-rooted oaks threw up visual blockades. You could still spy the Ben Sawyer Bridge through a narrow break in the trees. But the woods had grown up around the summit, blocking most of the view. Thick vines tangled at the foot of surrounding trees, meandering like leafy snakes along remnants of old World War II gun casings.

The silo, where it was once possible to peer down below into the cavernous interior, was covered with a neat layer of sod. Thirty years ago, Zoe had climbed this hill to see if she could spy the sun glinting off her sister's golden head. Now, like then, she saw nothing. Illogically she was disappointed yet again.

Gabi says Annabelle's father buried her down there.

Down where?

Down in the tunnels.

That day, while she and Hannah had stood together on the bridge, watching Hannah's hat sail away, was her sister offering her a clue? Had she arrived on the cusp of a morning dream to remind Zoe where to search?

Working her way down the Mound, Zoe scoured the brush, even knowing it wasn't likely she would happen upon a sealed-off entry to the tunnels—not after all this time. After a century of children playing over every square inch of the island, it was doubtful any unexplored territory remained. Still, she searched the bamboo groves. Then she branched out toward the marsh, peering along the banks for signs of half-submerged passages.

Gators weren't supposed to wander into brackish water, though sometimes they did. Sometimes, they used the crevices in the tidal pools and estuaries to stash food, letting it rot beneath the surface until it was soft and ready to digest. Her mom once worried that had been Hannah's fate, but Zoe's father had said no. "They don't linger in salt water, Marge."

"Are you sure, Rob? Are you sure?" It had been a rare moment of tenderness between them. Her father had moved behind her mother at the kitchen sink, setting a hand on her shoulder. "We'll find her, I promise."

But it was a promise he couldn't keep.

Zoe checked now as she did back then, getting low on her belly to inspect the banks. The smell of pluff mud was strong here. The sound of bubbles popping in the muck made her think, arbitrarily, of a witch's brew. In the tidewater below, baby shrimp waltzed amidst thin, pale reeds.

Before her sister's disappearance, Zoe had kept a diary, but she no longer used one. It seemed a sin to scribble words for posterity, when she could no longer even remember her sister's face. How dare she indulge in things that gave her joy when Hannah could no longer breathe? It felt like a betrayal. So she wrote lies for other people, chipping away at her integrity and her wholeness with every word she wrote. That's what marketing was, after all: lies. Like the ones Chris and Gabi told, only with blessings and a paycheck.

Disgusted with the choices she'd made in her life, Zoe abandoned the ripe tidewater pool, making her way toward Battery Marshall. There, encroaching on private property, she scaled the rise of another mound, half tempted to knock on the door of the restored bunker. It was an odd place for people to live, mostly beneath ground, with enormous metal doors built into one side of the hill. The front looked exactly like what it was, an old military complex, with great big white doors. On the patchy lawn out front sat two old beaten-up lawn chairs—the kind with vinyl straps that appeared as though they'd lost their elasticity years before. Their presence was completely incongruous with the concrete monstrosity behind them, which, if Zoe had the facts straight, had cost someone a pretty penny to restore. Now the price tag was something like three million. A blue-and-white "For Sale" sign sat outside with a hanging attachment that read "Lori Masterson-Bryant," along with her phone number.

She had half a mind to ask the owner if they had any inkling of old, forgotten, sealed-off tunnels. But thirty years later, that sort of inquiry probably wasn't welcome. She could imagine how that conversation might go: "Hi, I'm searching for my missing sister?"

"Oh, God," they would exclaim—and this, only if they didn't happen to recognize Zoe's face after all these years. "How? When?"

"Her name is Hannah Rutherford. She's been missing since 1986."

"Oh," they would say, with a deflated tone and a look of confusion. "I'm sorry. We can't help you."

"It's time, Zoe," her mother said.

Time for what?

By mid-morning, Zoe had scoured much of the island to no avail. Dispirited, she made her way home along the dunes were she'd discovered her sister's blue Schwinn all those years ago. She sank to her knees, in the same spot, as though, by perching herself there, she might better determine where it was her sister had gone.

Half an hour later, Zoe's cheeks and nose were sunburned, and she was sweating offensively.

Hannah's ghost never materialized.

Nothing happened, except that Zoe remembered that morning with even greater clarity. That day, she'd gone searching for Gabi and Hannah, but she never found them. Like today's exercise, her search had proved futile.

She hadn't pushed her sister into Breach Inlet as Gabi had claimed, although perhaps there was more than a shred of truth in Gabi's tale . . .

At the moment, the shoreline glistened under a seething sun. The sandbars were scarcely visible under a living, breathing tide, disappearing and reappearing.

Maybe those two had been out on a sandbar—out there. Zoe placed a hand to her brow, shading her eyes from the sun, looking hard. Maybe Gabi had pushed Hannah into the sea. Or maybe, she'd led Hannah down into a tunnel, somewhere—some place Zoe and no one else had yet to uncover. It didn't have to be anything nefarious. Half sealed, half flooded, any tunnels that remained were bound to be treacherous. What if something had happened down there—a ceiling or wall collapsed—and Gabi had left Hannah down there, terrified of what might happen if she told the truth?

Only this fact remained: her sister would not have wandered far from her bike. That much Zoe knew. Not even Gabi's adverse influence would have allowed for that, so it was more than likely that Hannah had drowned somewhere near Breach.

Picking herself up and brushing the sand from her thighs, Zoe headed in the general direction of home, the pain of her loss as fresh today as it was thirty years before. Swinging her sandals from half-crooked fingers, she walked along the beach, staying clear of the water's edge, not ready to wade even ankle-deep.

It was a terrifying feeling to be swept off your feet, when only seconds before the ground seemed firm beneath your step.

It was a bit like discovering the man you were with was not

the man he claimed to be. Zoe would never make that mistake again.

The breeze along the shore was barely there—enough to notice, but not enough to make her long for sleeves.

For the first time she imagined her life without the pursuit of answers. What would it be like? To simply live? To stop waiting. No more searching?

Once she'd made the decision to leave Chris, coming home— to the island—had seemed such a crucial part of moving on, peeling out of her past, like a butterfly discarding a cocoon. At first Zoe was sure it was all about the house, that selling it would free her at long last. But now she no longer saw the house as a decrepit husk meant to be shucked, and she realized, maybe only this minute, that she had come here to the island not to pick away at scabs but, in essence, to return to the warmth and safety of the womb, because that is what the island was to her.

Aside from her recent accident—which had merely given her a renewed appreciation for life—returning to Sullivan's was not such a terrible thing. Zoe had received a warm welcome from her neighbors who, by all accounts, should have been happy enough to see her leave. Even the memories that greeted her here were entirely welcome for, although bittersweet, they etched new, indelible impressions into her heart.

Over the years, Zoe had become a washed-out canvas, a watercolor left too long under the rain. Coming home added new dimensions, more defining brush strokes.

Lingering on the beach near the house, Zoe peered out over the coast.

Not much farther out than the sandbar where she'd gone down, a dolphin's fin emerged—and then another and another. At high tide, none of the sandbars were visible now, but she knew they were there . . . the same way she sensed her island roots.

"Where are you, Hannah?"

Hannah was already gone by the time Zoe's hormones began to rage. Zoe spent her teens in a cocoon of her own making, choosing to view her eventual escape from the island as a sort of rebirth.

Her mother was depressed, removed, although she never actually pushed Zoe away. To the contrary, she flowered in those instances when Zoe reached out to her, like a blossom seeking the warmth of the sun. It was simply that Zoe never had the maturity to comprehend their relationship, much less to nourish her mom in a way she might have needed. More to the point, Zoe was too uncertain of herself to grow under the stunting weight of such a complicated relationship. She came to resent her mother's needs—because she had so many of her own. Small things became large things when the act of culling through them felt insurmountable.

There was a boy at school Zoe had a crush on. Craig Truelove. Even his name gave the girls palpitations. He was a surfer dude, a golden boy, with teeth as pearly as the inside of an oyster shell, hair as shimmery as sand. Against all odds—at least those of Zoe's perception—he asked her out on a date. As many first dates went, it was spent on the beach. It should have been fun, and Zoe might have looked forward to a good time, but from the instant she uttered the word, "yes," it became a conduit for stress, even considering that, for Zoe, the island should have been home turf.

Zoe was a bit of a late bloomer. At sixteen, most of the other girls already had their periods. Not Zoe. Yet this she could easily keep to herself, because it necessitated only a nod while discussing cramps in the school bathroom or a quick study of menstrual products to discuss the dubious merits of each. The thing Zoe couldn't keep to herself was her A-cup breasts, which were only A-cup if she lined her bra with toilet paper.

Zoe was not a liar by nature, so she went light on the padding, giving herself a barely noticeable bump that didn't merit longing glances from boys, especially from surfer dudes like Craig.

The truth was that she never considered someone like Craig might see her as anything more than the sum of her parts. And since Zoe's parts weren't all that notable, she hadn't ever concerned herself much with what she wore to the beach, until that day. In fact, on more than one occasion, she and her friends went skinny dipping out by some of the more stable sandbars, daring each other to tie their bathing suits to bamboo posts to wave over the coastline like Confederate flags.

But this was Craig Truelove. He was a junior at Wando, with long, lean legs that could maneuver successfully through bulwarks of flesh out on the football field. He was a shoe-in for a sports scholarship to Duke, and somehow he made good grades to boot. Whenever he looked at Zoe, she melted a little right in her chair—evidenced, of course, by the dampness between her legs that often accompanied glances from Craig.

A few weeks before that day, lying alone in her bedroom, sometime in the middle of the night, with a soft breeze lifting the curtains of her window, Zoe had dreamt about Craig Truelove. In a house that was as quiet as a dusty mausoleum, she discovered her sexuality, exploring her womanhood, while imagining Craig peeking in through her window. Her fingers went deep that night, craving knowledge. Behind closed doors, the nipples of her nonexistent breasts shivered beneath a sultry summer night. She knew enough to understand how it was done, despite being unable to imagine her parents doing more than slipping numbly into their bed every night, backs toward one another, haunted eyes staring blindly into the dark.

But not Zoe; when the time came, she would be bold, make love in the light. She imagined Craig Truelove pressing her down into the sheets, his weight foreign to a girl who had not yet had her first kiss.

The next morning, Zoe was ecstatic to find blood on her

sheets, believing she'd finally become a woman right there in her bed. It seemed only right somehow that she be initiated this way —as though she had downloaded all her womanly secrets overnight.

Zoe even told her mother, who promptly offered a treasure hold of thick, unwieldy pads, all her own, to be used as Zoe deemed necessary.

Unfortunately, that one short bleed was all there was. Zoe discovered later that she'd torn her own maidenhead—popped her own cherry, as the boys so crudely put, while boasting of real or imagined conquests.

Her blood flow dried up, and along with it, so did Zoe's confidence. She was convinced her Catholic mother would discover her shameful secret, though in fact Marge seemed to forget altogether that Zoe had come running to her so breathlessly, asking for help. She never once asked Zoe if she needed more pads, or if her cramps were too much for her to bear. She simply went back to cleaning, or crocheting, or staring off into space—whatever the day's form of distraction might be.

But the day after Craig asked Zoe out, Zoe went back to her mother with tears in her eyes, and her mother rose to the occasion. Zoe wept with her head in her mom's lap, until Marge encouraged her to wipe away the tears.

"I have the thing," Marge said softly, rising from the couch. Zoe didn't care that she'd gotten the syntax wrong; she was so grateful for a solution to her troubles.

Marge left Zoe kneeling on the yellow troll-hair carpet, flitting away like a fairy godmother to fetch her magic wand—which ultimately turned out to be a size-four needle with thread in the color of Zoe's bathing suit—burnt orange.

Marge proceeded to rip up one of her own bras to remove the padding, and then, with careful stitches—to hide the evidence of their collusion—she sewed her bra pad into Zoe's swimsuit. This, her mother reassured, would solve all Zoe's troubles. Unlike toilet paper, the pad wouldn't bunch up when it got wet. It would offer Zoe just a bit of lining to give her a bit of lift, but not so much that it might be noticed by prying hands. Left unspoken was the distinct possibility that Craig Truelove might actually want to touch her breasts. This, Zoe was certain, her mother had over-looked, but she determined it was enough to give Craig some-thing he could see. Hopefully, soon, puberty would solve the rest of her troubles.

The date with Craig was a complete disaster.

As planned, they met at the beach, Craig with two of his friends and two of the prettiest cheerleaders Zoe had ever met. Both were from Bishop England High School, both were blond, and both had perfect, mature breasts.

For a long time, Zoe refused to get into the water—more because she didn't want to mess up the mud-colored hair she'd worked so hard to tame, not particularly because she had any fear over the bathing suit getting wet. Her mom had promised the suit would solve her troubles and Zoe, for once, placed all her faith in Marge.

But that's where everything went wrong.

As soon as Zoe got into the water, the pad in her bathing suit behaved like a sponge, soaking up the salt water, until the weight at her breast felt like a hunk of lead. Still, she didn't realize, until she surged up from the water—a gesture that should have been as momentously seductive as the scene from *Fast Times at Ridge-mont High*. For Zoe, however, it was nothing like that. The bloated weight of her bra liner split the delicate stitching—the ones Marge worked so meticulously to sew. Zoe's left "breast" plum-meted to her naval. The right one shifted slightly. Zoe realized in horror that her padding had betrayed her and sank back into the water. Craig never seemed to notice. He was too busy flexing his muscles for the girls up on the beach and looking to see who else might be ogling him.

Once immersed, Zoe repositioned her errant "breasts," but

whatever confidence she'd had in herself—and in her mother—was lost.

All she could think about after that was the traitorous lining of her suit and somehow securing enough privacy to discard them. But that came with its own set of potential problems: What if she reemerged from the water with vanished breasts and Craig Truelove should happen to notice? What then? Would they whisper about it endlessly at school? Would she become a pariah? A faker? A pretender? A liar?

What the hell were you thinking, Zoe?

She might live out her teen years without ever scoring a single kiss and the only finger that would make third base would be her own.

What if she managed to slide *them* out of her suit into the water and *they*, Benedict Arnolds as they had already proven to be, should float back to the surface and remain there, like flotsam from a wreck at sea?

Dear God.

What if she threw them into the dunes, and one of those cheerleaders with the long batting lashes should stumble upon them there? Zoe would forever be known as the girl who stuffed her suit. They would pass the story down through the ages, whisper to themselves. *I always knew there was something wrong with Zoe Rutherford. Didn't you? You know they say she killed her sister, because she was jealous that her parents loved Hannah best.*

And that was the crux of it all: guilt over Hannah. Deep down, Zoe realized she *was* jealous of Hannah—Hannah who was probably dead.

PERHAPS THE GREATEST tragedy of that day on the beach was that Zoe withdrew from her mother. Marge became her consummate scapegoat, responsible for everything, from failing to protect them from their father, to allowing Hannah time and space to vanish from their lives. And maybe Zoe had been furious at her sister as well, for leaving Zoe alone. The island had became her crucifix, and the memories, each and every one, were like iron spikes keeping her fastened inexorably to the cross. Slowly, painstakingly, Zoe had drawn them out and discarded each, one by one, until all that was left was the bloody shell she had become. But she'd had it all wrong; memories were not constraints. They were the building blocks that made her the woman she was—the good, along with the bad.

Marge was not the cause of Zoe's problems, neither was her father. They'd simply been two broken people trying to find their own way.

Mere days shy of forty, Zoe was discovering that home was not so much a place, but she had choices to make. Wherever Hannah was now . . . the only thing Zoe knew for certain was that her sister no longer had any choices remaining.

"It's time, Zoe," her mother's voice echoed through her mind.

The best advice Marge ever gave came from somewhere beyond the grave. It was time for a lot of things, but mostly, maybe it was time to let her sister go.

21

THE BOO HAG

The events in Zoe's life seemed more connected now. If she had never left the island, she might never have appreciated the beauty she would return to. If Chris were not abusive, she might not ever have been lured back home. If she hadn't left Baltimore, she would never have plummeted into the same cold depths her sister must have found. Ultimately, if Zoe never found herself in the riptide, she might not have remembered anything at all.

Over the years, she had forgotten the way Hannah's eyes crinkled at the corners—that mirthful squint that shuttered the whites of her eyes. Zoe missed that face, with the smattering of freckles at the bridge of her nose, always more pronounced with a bit of sun. It had been years now since she could picture her sister's countenance with such perfect lucidity. Simply being here had opened the door to her memory.

A sandpiper hopped along beside her in the burning sand and, although Zoe commiserated with its plight, she refused to don her sandals, telling herself that it was past time to develop calluses. If, in fact, she meant to stay here on the island, she couldn't spend her days and nights pandering to the ghosts from her past. Living alongside them was one thing, but they should no longer dictate her future.

In the dream, her sister spoke of a sepulcher. Rather than an ancient, half-submerged tunnel, it could simply be a metaphor for the house, but the house wasn't a tomb because it had walls and a roof. It was a tomb because Zoe had buried her memories there. It was a tomb because the house had been deprived of life.

Zoe could change all that.

Her stride became more sure-footed the instant she spied Walter Donovan working on her front porch steps. The sight of him gave her a warm feeling. Consequently, any fears she harbored about Chris faded as she considered the house, not in terms of curb appeal, but in terms of her own personal tastes.

The white exterior needed a new paint job, but instead of white, a pale shade of gray might better suit the old bungalow. It would go well with the haint-blue ceiling of the porch—a perspective only those invited inside could see, but nevertheless an important aesthetic consideration.

The driveway might also benefit from a new layer of crushed shells, in keeping with her granddad's wishes. He'd always said he loathed blacktop and refused to "kill his plot of land with a bunch of old tar." On the other hand, her father had never felt strongly one way or another, though he'd left the driveway as his father and his grandfather intended—for the same reason her mother had kept the blue ceiling of the porch.

The tops of the windows were another matter entirely. Zoe didn't see the need to keep those blue any more than she intended to place bowls of salt throughout her house, but she had to admit there was a certain nostalgia to the tradition that offered a distinct bond with her past—one she no longer felt the need to discard.

Tossing down her sandals, Zoe slipped her feet into the safety of her shoes to avoid sandburs and made her way across the scrubby yard. "If you're going to work on the stairs without me, you're gonna have to let me pay you."

Walter didn't bother to look at her. "I work better alone."

"Yeah, but . . . how do you expect me to know how to fix things later, whenever they break?"

"The stairs won't break," he said, and once he was done tightening the screw he was laboring over—still without the benefit of an electric screwdriver—he finally turned to acknowledge Zoe. For an instant, his eyes brightened with a warm spark of something that looked suspiciously like joy.

She broadened her smile, realizing that her neighbor, not unlike her, simply needed reminders to view the world differently. She had no idea what troubles Walter Donovan had endured, but she knew his youth couldn't have been easy with parents like his. In the end, everyone had a cross to bear. As far as Zoe's was concerned, it was past time to lay hers down.

After a moment, Walter scowled, as though sensing his own delight and finding fault with it. Grunting, he returned to working on the porch, slamming another riser against the stringers in evident frustration. Zoe tried to imagine the child he must have been. His niece had looked so much like him, especially with that taut set to his jaw.

Zoe sat down beside him in the grass to watch him work. She leaned back on her elbows, bearing her head backward to bathe in the afternoon sun.

The distant scent of pluff mud filled her lungs. If she didn't love that smell, precisely, she didn't hate it either. She lifted her gaze after an instant to find Walter studying her, his gray eyes as uncertain as an offshore storm.

"So," he said, turning his back to her, shielding his expressions from her knowing gaze like a reticent little boy. "Where'd you run off to this morning?"

Zoe watched him turn the screw with careful precision, hesitating to answer, mainly because the truth necessitated mentioning his niece—a subject that, according to Zoe's experience, brought out the worst in Walter Donovan.

"I went for a walk."

He nodded, still with his back to her. "I saw you."

Zoe furrowed her brow. "You must have been up early?"

"Yep," he said, still torquing at the screw. He eyed her over dirty spectacles. "The sun ain't caught me abed in fifty years."

Zoe grinned. "Is that how old you are?"

"No. It's just a saying."

Zoe knew that. He didn't seem to realize she was teasing. "Lucky for me you're an early riser," she said quickly. And that was true; if he hadn't been up on the morning she went into Breach, she might now be resting at the bottom of the sea, right alongside Hannah.

Walter gave her a curt nod and thereafter gave his rapt attention to the screw he was turning. Long minutes stretched by without either of them speaking.

"I had a dream," Zoe said after a time.

"About?"

"My sister." Zoe eyed him circumspectly, watching his reaction, to gauge whether or not he might be open to discussing Gabi. "And, of course . . . Gabi."

"My niece?" Zoe detected curiosity in his voice, although he didn't acknowledge her with his gaze.

"More like something Gabi said."

Clearly reluctant to pursue the conversation, yet curious nevertheless, Walter muttered. "What might that be?"

Now it was Zoe's turn to waffle. She wasn't sure whether she wished to remind him about his niece's accusations—if in fact he'd ever known about them. It had taken her half a lifetime to get over Gabi's accusation, and she wasn't entirely certain she was over it yet. However, this felt like the right time to talk about it. "Not sure if you know . . . she told Chief Hale I killed my sister."

Zoe watched Walter's reaction. His shoulders tensed slightly, although he tried to appear casual. Zoe didn't mean to put it so bluntly, but there it was, as plainly said as ever spoken.

Walter quietly tapped at the flat end of a new screw with the butt of his screwdriver. "Did you?"

"No."

"Then why would Gabi say so?"

Zoe stared at Walter's back. "Honestly, Walter, that was something I hoped you'd be able to help me figure out."

He turned his face in profile, making half an effort to look back at Zoe—as though he meant to, and then determined he didn't want to. "Well, I don't know anything," he said after a moment.

But he did.

He knew *something* . . . what, precisely, Zoe couldn't say. Merely the mention of his niece made the muscles in his jaw clench and unclench. She sighed. "That makes two of us."

He gave Zoe his back, once again concentrating on the screw.

Zoe decided he might be more amenable to talking if she explained how much Gabi's accusations had wounded her. "They sent me to a shrink, probably to see if I'd confess—at least that's how I perceived it at the time."

Still Walter said nothing, though he didn't stop her from talking and Zoe felt a bit as though she were seated in a confessional, waiting for absolution from a priest, except that, here, there was no screen between them. Neither was Walter quick to turn and judge her with his gaze. He simply listened, keeping his back to her as he continued to work on the stairs.

"Honest to God, they had me so confused by the time I walked out of those sessions, I second-guessed everything I knew. It didn't help all that much that my dad seemed to believe them."

"Them?"

"Gabi," Zoe said, clarifying.

As soon as Gabi had spoken the words, doubt spread over the island like a noxious fume. It wasn't long before Zoe spied the same uncertainty in every pair of eyes she'd looked into. Conversations had always carried a bit of an edge: *Did you see Brittany Spears trip over Michael Jackson? What makes her think she can dance? What are you wearing to the prom? Did you really kill your sister?*

Walter Donovan's forearms flexed with barely restrained violence toward the screw. Zoe wanted to believe he felt incensed on her behalf. "What about your mother?"

Zoe shrugged. Marge had always claimed she didn't believe Gabi, but she'd only ever defended Zoe in the privacy of her bedroom, behind closed doors. "They fought. A lot."

"About what?"

It was the first time in Zoe's life she'd ever opened up so thoroughly. "About me, I suppose. But at least it gave them something to talk about. If they weren't arguing, they didn't seem to have much else to say."

Walter sat quietly, listening intently, moving from one screw to another, until the riser was firmly in place and he was ready to mount another.

On the other hand, seated beside him, Zoe felt as though she might come undone. Every turn of his screw left her a bit less composed. Even after the morning's epiphany, she felt as though he were unscrewing the lid from Pandora's box and whatever calm she'd found on the beach was dissipating fast.

"Exactly how did my niece claim you . . ." He paused for a moment, letting the question form in the space between them.

He couldn't even say it.

Did he believe her?

Frustrated, Zoe ripped a grass blade from the ground. "She said I was pissed because they didn't want me tagging along. She said I fought with Hannah, chased them both out onto the bridge, where I shoved her over the side."

"Her, meaning Hannah?"

"Right."

It was an elaborate story, with Hannah smashing her head on the way down, but no amount of inspection of the bridge had ever produced a drop of her sister's blood, nor any other evidence. No torn fibers of Hannah's clothing, no telltale scrapes, no witnesses . . . none except Gabi, who'd sworn on her Bible that it was "God's truth."

"So is it true?"

Zoe bit the inside of her cheek. "Not one word."

"You're sure about that?"

Zoe frowned. His tone didn't appear to hold judgment. Maybe he was responding to something in her voice?

Zoe didn't recall any of it happening the way Gabi had claimed. No matter how hard she tried to recapture it as memory, it simply didn't exist. She knew it now with more certainty than ever. However, the simple fact that Gabi had said so had planted tenacious seeds of doubt that even now wanted to sprout in Zoe's head. "Yes, I'm sure," she said..

"You don't sound so sure."

"Well, I am."

"So tell me . . . what were you out there searching for, Zoe?"

Zoe tensed. "I needed air."

His tone took on the tenor of a counselor. "So it's only a coincidence your sister died out there as well?"

Zoe lifted a brow. "As well?" She laughed nervously. "Last time I checked, Walter, I was still breathing. Thanks to you."

Walter Donovan nodded soberly.

Zoe furrowed her brow, considering that night again.

Maybe she hadn't misjudged the shoreline? She remembered feeling water around her ankles and had never once considered she was way off base. She guessed she must have followed a sandbar attached to the beach while the tide drifted in, separating her from dry land. It had been dark that night. Not even the stars had provided light and she'd barely discerned their reflection on the sea, probably because the water hadn't been all that still. In retrospect, the whitecaps should have given her a clue she was in trouble, but she had been so distracted by her thoughts, and then, after realizing where she was, her only consideration had been to get back to shore.

"They never found your sister?"

It was a rhetorical question, Zoe realized, but she shook her head anyway. It was no secret they'd never recovered Hannah's body. "No."

"You know . . . there are places along the inlet where the currents act like a tidal jet, spewing everything they catch out to sea."

The tension in Walter's shoulders eased as he settled back on his rear to fasten the remaining screws on the riser he was mounting. "Back when I was in the navy," he said. "We ran operations out near Antarctica. There are deep bottom currents out there, moving quick as eight inches per second. One day we lost a man overboard," he said. "You understand much about biology?"

Zoe shook her head.

"A body in the drink begins to sink the instant air in the lungs is replaced with water. Stays down until bacteria in the gut and chest cavity produce enough gas to float it back to the surface—something like twenty-four hours in warmer temperature. In cold temperature, could be longer. Your sister drowned in December, didn't she?"

Zoe nodded, wondering where the conversation was leading.

"Anyway, so we never found that guy's body," he said. "But they did find his dog tags in the belly of a shark out off the coast of Australia. That's how far the current took him."

Zoe lifted her knees, hugging them. "So you think currents here are that fast?"

Even as she asked, she remembered the force of the riptide that had dragged her back and knew they were.

He lifted one shoulder in a half-shrug. "Maybe . . . you recall those boys they rescued out near Cape Fear a few years ago? They drifted something like six days before someone found 'em and brought 'em back. Those kids put the boat in here at Breach. They got caught up in a riptide and the rest is history."

Zoe thought about her sister out there . . . somewhere . . . It had never appealed to her to believe that truth, but neither did she wish to believe her sister had met a fate like Etan Patz. Considering the circumstances—and the facts—it was far more likely Hannah had drowned. And while Zoe might never learn if Gabi had had a hand in her sister's death, it was quite possible she did. "My sister's death haunts me every day of my life," Zoe confessed.

Walter cast her a glance. "You two were close, I'm guessing?"

Zoe focused once more on the image of Hannah's face.

"Not everyone is so lucky," Walter said, picking up another screw and tapping it into the riser. "Gabrielle wasn't. My sister killed herself when Gabi was four. Gabi was the one who found her."

Zoe winced.

"Her dad never wanted much to do with her, claimed she wasn't his."

Zoe tried to picture the little girl next door. Possibly Asperger-ish, Gabi was quiet around her grandparents, maybe frightened of them. Even if they weren't cruel to her, she must have been terrified they would send her away. Ultimately, that's exactly what they did.

"You could say Gabi was a throwaway."

"What about you? You must have cared about her."

His gaze turned to meet Zoe's, hard as steel. There was no love there, not grief nor even regret. Uncomfortable with his gaze, Zoe shrugged. "I assumed she went to live with you. There was no one else."

He continued to stare at Zoe for a long, unpleasant moment before returning his attention to the porch steps and his screw.

He said nothing more, merely sat there, torquing the screw, and Zoe realized she must have inadvertently upset him.

It was possible Walter Donovan had nothing to do with raising his niece, that Gabi had somehow ended up in Baltimore without her uncle's knowledge, at least until her death.

"Ain't nothing worse than an unloved child," he said sullenly.

Zoe knew it to be true. Even as bad as her own life must have seemed at times, it was probably never as bad as Gabi's. Her mother, for all her shortcomings, had loved her. So had her grandmother and her grandfather. Her relationship with Nick was complicated by her relationship with her dad. Whatever her dad had felt about her, he was just one man.

Daunted by the topic, Zoe changed the subject, swallowing past the thickness in her throat. "So, tell me, how is it you have enough time to work on my stairs? Are you retired?"

"Mostly. Sometimes I help out at the women's shelter."

Zoe tried to picture an altruistic Walter Donovan, without his grumpy attitude. The image eluded her, in spite of the cashier's claim that he never came through the grocery line without donating a few bucks.

"I need adhesive," he complained.

Zoe took it as her cue to exit the conversation. She stood, slapping the grass off her palms. "What kind of adhesive do you need?"

"Stair tread adhesive, that's what it's called."

Zoe studied the front garden. It wasn't too late to plant a few roses. She could put them in tomorrow while Walter finished up the stairs. Conversation wasn't easy between them and it certainly wasn't light, but it gave her a good feeling to think about working side by side with her neighbor. It felt as though she were mending fences her parents had failed to mend. "Tell you what, I'll grab some first thing in the morning. Why don't you take a break, Walter?"

Walter peered up at her, his scowl not quite so pronounced,

but Zoe could see where time had etched lines permanently into his face. Both of them could use a bit more to smile about. "If you won't let me pay for the stairs, then at least stay for supper. I've got more than enough to share."

Walter's lips slid over his teeth as he considered Zoe's offer. He glanced over at his own house, as though to gauge what pressing thing might be awaiting him there, then back at Zoe, his pale gray eyes examining her.

Zoe tilted her head. "Come on, Walter." She clapped her hands together. "There's pie, roast, mac and cheese, ambrosia salad . . . you've got to be hungry."

Still, he hesitated.

"There's more bread," Zoe teased.

Finally, his pupils dilated and Zoe smiled. It was a long moment before he replied. "All right, but I gotta finish the one I'm working on."

"Great!" Zoe exclaimed. "I'll get dinner started. Come on in when you're ready."

He gave Zoe another nod, and she left him to finish up, more than grateful that he'd taken on the responsibility of her stairs. She had forgotten how ingrained Southern chivalry was—so much so that even someone like Walter Donovan seemed a slave to it. After living so long with Chris, it was something she might never get accustomed to again, and she certainly would never take it for granted.

HUMMING SOFTLY, Zoe slid a casserole dish full of macaroni and cheese onto the stovetop, next to a platter containing the rump roast. Most of the food had been delivered in disposable containers. Those that weren't bore tape on the lids, with names and addresses written in Sharpie, so she could return the containers once they were empty. Feeding Walter would bring her closer to that goal, and just to take it up a notch, she was going to challenge herself to return each dish with a handwritten thank you.

These were now Zoe's neighbors and she wanted to make things right. Like long-lost family, so many had come to wish her well during her recovery.

Unfortunately, there weren't many get-well flowers remaining, although a few endured. Zoe gathered the survivors—yellow and white daisies, chrysanthemums, purple statice, baby's breath, and one slightly weepy tulip. She placed them together into a single vase, and then set them on the kitchen table, off to one side. No candles, since, first of all she didn't have any, and because this wasn't meant to be romantic. Once Walter came in and the casserole dishes were just a touch cooler, she would place everything on the table, family style, suitably spoiling any romantic notions that might be erroneously conceived. Walter was more her father's age. Still, she had never intended to lead Ethan on; so it was better to play it safe.

She washed the empty vases and put them away in barren cabinets, intending to find a better place once the need arose. The cabinets were all outdated, and she thought she might replace them soon. She washed a small saucepot she'd bought yesterday at HomeGoods, filling it with water for tea and placing it on the stove.

The house had come a long way. The kitchen was no longer overwhelmingly gold, more the shade of wet sand. The Ice Mist trim unintentionally matched the kitchen table, giving the room an airy feel. At this point, most of the rooms remained empty, but it was easy enough to imagine a cozier space filled with familiar things. Maybe tomorrow she would call Nick to let him know she'd made her decision and planned to stay.

Starting over wasn't as difficult as she had imagined. Whatever she didn't have, Zoe could easily buy. No material thing was worth the heartache she'd endured. Aside from her mother's quilt, there wasn't much she'd left behind that she would miss.

There was more than enough stored up in the attic to provide a sense of history and place if that's what she needed to feel at home.

In fact, her Nana's sewing machine would make an interesting conversation piece. Zoe could bring it down and set it up in the guest bedroom and maybe learn to use it. Or—she reconsidered, remembering Anna's and Parker's pillows—if Beth wanted the sewing machine, Zoe would gift it to her. The girls might enjoy learning to use it and it would make Zoe intensely happy to spend more time with Nicky's girls.

She imagined picking the girls up from school, taking them out shopping or maybe out for a treat. There was a little old-fashioned ice cream shop down on Main Street in Summerville. Beth had taken her there one Sunday after Nick proposed, determined to introduce Zoe to her little town, her friends, her park, her post office, and all of Summerville's quaint little shops. There was a keen sense of pride Southerners engendered for the place of their birth—something Zoe was generally lacking although it was never too late to start. She and Beth were not at all alike, but that didn't mean they couldn't find common ground. It would be nice to have a sisterly figure in her life. But that didn't mean she was replacing Hannah—she could never replace Hannah.

And then there was Nick. Her brother craved more of a relationship, Zoe sensed, but she also knew her brother had spent most of his life shying away from their dysfunctional family; getting close to him would take a bit of work. It should be worth it in the end.

Tonight, she felt like celebrating. Regrettably, that meant drinking the remainder of Ethan's wine as well as eating his bread, since that was all she had on hand. Pulling the cork out of the bottle and setting it down on the counter, Zoe found two red plastic cups—the last two in the house—in case Walter might want some too. Tomorrow, she would buy a real set of glasses—and dishes. She set one cup aside on the counter, pouring the other half-full, and then set the bottle on the counter next to the glass, before returning to the task of reheating casserole dishes. To top everything off, she placed the remainder of the banana-bread pudding into the oven to heat while they ate. Walter seemed to like it a lot.

Only one thing continued to bother Zoe . . .

Lifting up her cup and sipping at her wine, she retrieved her cell phone from her purse, staring hard at the numbers on the pad. If she called *him* and he should happen to answer, what should she say?

Where are you? Please don't tell me you're on the way.

Contemplating her reasons for calling, Zoe took another a sip of wine as she reconsidered ringing Chris's phone.

Enough time had passed by now that perhaps he wasn't driving down from Baltimore after all. If he were coming, wouldn't he have been here by now? There was no way to tell what calling him might prompt him to do; but some part of her needed to know.

Zoe couldn't stand the feeling of waiting for the other shoe to drop. At least this way, if she spoke to Chris, she might get a sense of what he intended to do. She was stronger now; ready to handle whatever he had to say. Zoe took another sip of wine, putting the cup down on the counter, turning her attention to the phone.

Was she so screwed up that, with everything quiet on the home front, she had to seek out drama?

He couldn't hurt her anymore—not so long as he stayed away. And she wasn't alone, she reminded herself. If she needed anything, Walter was right next door.

The sound of water boiling made her consider setting down the phone . . . but she didn't. Zoe continued staring, swiping at the display every time it went black, nibbling pensively at her bottom lip.

Her hands tingled as she pressed her index finger over the first digit. Her heart pounded as she pressed the four, one, zero . . . ever so slowly, each with overwhelming uncertainty. The next seven numbers flew off the tip of her finger. And then, once the number was dialed, she lifted the receiver to her ear and waited, her heart tripping against her rib cage as she listened to it ring.

One.

Two.

Three.

Zoe told herself to hang up, but the phone remained firmly attached to her ear. A woman's voice answered. "Hello?"

Zoe blinked in surprise. Bewildered by the unexpected female voice, uncertain what to say, she said nothing. She stood in her kitchen, thoughts scattering.

"Hello?" She sounded young. Not that Zoe cared one way or another. It would be easier if Chris had already replaced her. She simply hadn't expected a woman to answer his phone. In eight years, Zoe had never dared to answer Chris's phone.

"Hello?" the woman said again.

Zoe wracked her brain, thinking over the past few weeks, trying to remember if there were telltale signs Chris was already seeing someone. It wasn't easy to tell with him. He was the only guy she'd ever known who could sleep with two women at once and look both in the eyes and say, "I love you" without hesitation. Still, it seemed more lately that it was Zoe who was avoiding him.

The woman's voice had a singsong quality. "Baby, someone's on the phone, but no one's saying anything."

It was a long, awkward moment before the other person in the room responded. "Goddamn it!" Zoe heard Chris say, before his voice became muffled. It sounded as though there might be a scuffle over the phone, and then Zoe heard a rude dial tone. Stunned, she pulled the phone away from her ear, checking the number she'd dialed. It *was* Chris's. For all that she'd sat worrying, it didn't appear he was coming after all.

"Everything okay?"

Startled by the question, Zoe turned to find Walter Donovan standing in the threshold of her back door. Behind him, the position of the setting sun blinded her, illuminating him in profile, casting his face into shadow. In silhouette, he was a lean, youthful man, and for an instant, her eyes played tricks on her as he morphed into Chris.

She gave a startled gasp and, shaken, tossed the phone down on the counter. It rattled across the Formica. "I'm fine," she said quickly, trying hard to sound composed. Her stomach roiled. "Come on in, Walter, pour yourself a glass of wine. I'll be right back," she said.

Darting out of the kitchen, Zoe ducked into the hall bathroom, turning on the light. Flipping open the cold water on the faucet, she dipped her hands beneath the cool stream and splashed water up onto her face, then stared hard at the woman's face in the mirror.

Chris wasn't coming.

That was the good news.

Only a few weeks with Zoe out of the picture and already he had some girl quick to answer his phone. If Zoe knew him—and she did—the poor girl would be young, but she would have a damned good job and she was no doubt ready to do whatever it took to keep Chris happy. He had that way about him—a way of making you believe you were lucky to have him, when all the while it was the other way around.

Zoe blinked at the mirror.

She wasn't judging; she'd been there once upon a time, and while there was a part of her that wanted to warn the poor girl to run while she still had the chance, there was also a chance she wasn't as screwed up as Zoe. Maybe Chris could be a different man with someone else. Maybe he deserved that chance. Didn't he?

Zoe wondered who the girl might be—wondered if it were someone she knew. The voice didn't sound familiar—which came as little surprise since Zoe had long suspected Chris hid aspects of his life. He was a bit of a grifter.

Whatever . . . she should count her good fortune that she was out of the picture. Who cared if the bastard inherited everything she'd owned. Zoe had already decided those things weren't important on the day she walked out the door.

"So now walk away," she told the woman staring back from the depths of the bathroom mirror.

There was a healthy pink on the bridge of Zoe's nose, a smattering of freckles, not unlike Hannah's. The sun had begun to tinge the ends of her hair with a faint hint of strawberry blond. The scar on her forehead was healing as well. No longer was there a pronounced ridge where the stitches were. It was pink and fading, blending with her skin. She touched the area with a fingertip and the skin turned white around the stitching, leaving a thin white line.

The first time she spied herself this way, she'd thought how ugly she must be. But Ethan mustn't have thought so. Eventually, the scar would fade, but the lessons she had learned would remain. Never again would she compromise herself that way.

Zoe peered into her own blue eyes. Her pupils were wide enough to drive a freight train through, but she blinked, and a small, tight smile turned the corners of her mouth. "Nobody can break you if you don't wanna be broke," she said aloud.

Her Nana's words.

Everything was going to be all right.

No.

Everything was *already* all right.

With a sense of wonder, Zoe turned off the faucet and made her way back into the kitchen, embarrassed to have left Walter alone for so long.

He was standing at her sink. Already, he had the kitchen faucet halfway dismantled and was brushing at the seal with a thumb. "Your sink leaks," he said.

Zoe smiled. "I know. I was going to call a plumber."

"No need. It just needs a good cleaning."

Zoe's gaze fell on the two empty glasses, one as yet untouched. She moved across the kitchen. "How about a glass of vino, Walter?"

Walter grimaced as he pulled a long thread of hair from the dirty seal. He must have sensed her need not to drink alone. "Sure," he said, although without much enthusiasm.

Relieved, Zoe snatched the bottle off the counter, filling Walter's cup first, before topping off the other. She handed one to Walter.

"Thanks," he said, and set the cup down on the counter while he finished cleaning the seal. Zoe downed her glass, pouring herself another, feeling like a lush. But hey, she needed to take the edge off. She hadn't touched a drop of alcohol in months— probably in protest over Chris's drinking, but now seemed a good time to indulge.

"Everything okay?" he asked again.

Zoe forced a smile. "More than okay."

"Who was on the phone?"

Zoe gave him a half-hearted wink. "No one important. In fact, no one at all."

So why did the very thought of no one make her stomach hurt?

Walter peered at Zoe over the rim of his glasses as she set her cup down to check the oven. Her stomach heaved in protest over the sudden movement. Wondering if he could tell how weak her legs felt as she crouched, Zoe connected a hand to the floor to keep from toppling over. The instant she opened the oven door, a wave of heat smacked her full in the face. The scent of warming banana bread was sweet enough to make her mouth water, but she felt suddenly and violently sick to her stomach.

"Must have been *someone*. You don't look so good."

Zoe didn't feel so good either. She shut the oven door with a thump and struggled to regain her feet, moving awkwardly to the kitchen table. She pulled the chair out to sit down, fighting another surge of nausea.

Narrowing his gaze, Walter studied her much the same way he had earlier in the day. "Why don't we do this another time?"

For a moment, Zoe couldn't find her voice to speak. Her mouth began to salivate and her head spun. She had an odd metallic taste in her mouth, similar to something she'd experienced only once before after a bad can of sardines. She sat straighter, hoping the feeling would pass, but it didn't.

"Zoe?" he said firmly. "Will you be okay?"

Zoe blinked hard. "I'm fine."

At the hospital, they'd cautioned her to take it easy, to watch for neurological indications. But this had come on so suddenly, after hanging up the phone with Chris. It was only stress, she reassured herself, and tried to shake it off. "I'm fine," she said again.

"Allright," Walter said. "Let me get out of your way."

Except he stayed.

With painstaking slowness, he pieced her faucet back together as Zoe waited impatiently for him to leave. The sick feeling intensified, until all Zoe could think about was getting Walter Donovan out of her house and going back to her bedroom to lay down.

While Zoe fought to keep herself together, he seemed to work in slow motion, taking an inordinate amount of time to set everything back in working order. As grateful as she was for his solicitousness, all she wanted to do was get him out of her house, now, before she puked all over the floor in front of him.

"I hope you don't mind," she said, rising uneasily from the kitchen chair. The entire kitchen listed in front of her. Pulling open the oven door, Zoe dragged the banana-bread pudding out of the oven, burning her thumb. "Ouch," she said, dumping the tin on the counter. Another fierce wave of nausea assaulted her.

"Why don't I just go?" he said quietly, setting the faucet pieces down on the counter, quietly, precisely. *Clap. Clap.* In Zoe's head, the sound each made were like cannons exploding. "The leftovers can wait for another day." His voice sounded slow, like a forty-five record slowed to thirty-three.

A full-on case of vertigo set in. The kitchen floor began to whirl, the gold in the tiles looking like moving fan blades. The refrigerator danced in her peripheral and, once again, Zoe thought she might puke. Stumbling over to the counter, Zoe tried to keep it together long enough to wrap something up for Walter to take home.

"Here . . ." She swallowed hard. "At least take some bread pudding," she insisted. And then, after handing him the plate with trembling hands, Zoe ushered him out the back door. To her relief, he went without complaint, with assurances that she would call if she needed anything at all.

Zoe didn't need anything. All she wanted to do was lie down. She'd never realized how much all this tension was affecting her.

She had friends who'd had anxiety attacks, never her. But it made sense after everything that had happened over the past few weeks.

With Walter gone, Zoe managed to remember to check the stove and then she staggered back to her room, trying not to gack along the way. She clutched the corner of the wall in the living room—where Nicky had broken the vase—stabbing her palm against a light switch, a bare metal pin she'd yet to replace the dimmer switch on. She passed the hall bathroom, thinking hopeful thoughts. If she could get into bed . . . lie down . . .

"This too shall pass," she said aloud, so it would be true.

The hall was already dark as it was the only part of the old house without access to windows. Zoe floundered, reaching for lights. She felt inordinately tired, barely able to hold her lids open. Her body vanished beneath her; she was floating along the hall, a disembodied head. Somehow, she made it to the bed and fell atop the covers, worrying as she fought another savage rush of vertigo. Outside, the sky turned from twilight to black. The wind lifted, twisting oaks into moving beings.

Sleep, she told herself.

Go to sleep.

It will pass.

As a child, there were times Zoe had awakened in the middle of the night with a terrifying sense that something lurked beneath her bed. She felt that way now, but she couldn't move. She closed her eyes, feeling as though she were trapped in a disjointed dream. Her arms were leaden, locked at her sides, her feet as heavy as cannon balls. The scent of pluff mud grew strong —*maybe it was the Boo Hag?*

Somewhere in Zoe's subconscious, she understood the way sleep paralysis worked, but fear crawled underneath her skin like tiny maggots as she sensed rather than saw a shadow slip in through her bedroom door. Like a cartoon reaper, the shadow fell across the wall, rippling along the moving curtains. She tried to turn her head to see who was there, but she couldn't move at all. Inside the prison of her ribs, her heart hammered to be free.

It's only a dream, Zoe; wake up!

As a child, there was never anything beneath her bed, no matter how many times Zoe had looked. No matter how afraid she was, that's all it ever took. *If you look at the Boo Hag, you'll see she's not really there. It's just your imagination, Zoe.*

Look. Look at the boo hag.

One, two, three—look.

Look now.

No matter how she tried, she couldn't catch the Boo Hag's face. It loomed outside her peripheral. Again she tried to scream as the Hag settled on her bed, staring down without a face. It whispered her name. "Zoe . . ."

Zoe struggled to respond; no sound escaped her frozen lips.

"*Ever wonder why women float face up, men float facedown?*"

The voice was low, distorted, but Zoe understood every word.

Even realizing it was only a dream, she shook her head, terrified where the question might lead. Except for the Boo Hag, Zoe envisioned the room precisely as it was: The open window; drapes, white, snapping with a scrappy breeze; the bed posters, rising tall, like spectators at a sacrifice. The closet was a dark hole, a demonic mouth. Inside, indistinct forms wriggled in the shadows, their shackles ringing, holding them back.

Oh, God. Wake up, Zoe.

Once again, she sensed rather than heard the Boo Hag speak, the voice oddly familiar. And male. In *all* Nana's stories, the Boo Hag hads been female.

"Women carry weight below the waist," the boo hag said. "Men up top. It's all about gravity, Zoe. Do you understand what I am saying?"

Eyes closed, throat tight, Zoe tried to move her fingers, and then her hand, to place it on the Boo Hag's chest, push him away. *Wake up,* she commanded herself.

Oh, God. Please.

The hag's face was only inches away now—an alien form without features, a burning, fetid whisper at her ear. *"Love is gravity, Zoe; d'ya wanna die?"*

Liquid terror shot through Zoe's veins. Any minute she would open her eyes, and then she would laugh at herself for being afraid of a folktale.

Rough fingers lifted the hair from her neck. Those same fingers brushed her forehead, caressing her scar, touching it reverently. She felt a kiss on her skin, sweet and gentle. *"Wanna see your sister, Zoe?"*

Somewhere in the distance, she heard the murmur of the ocean. The scent of sweet myrtle filled the air, barely detectible past the Boo Hag's breath. And then came a little pressure around the neck. Slight at first, then a bit more pronounced.

She was choking.

Suffocating.

Couldn't breathe.

Couldn't move.

Couldn't scream.

Zoe was drowning. *Again.* Her pulse pumped through her face. Her eyeballs were near to bursting. White light detonated behind her lids and suddenly Hannah appeared in a vision, arms outstretched.

Hannah.

Zoe tried to call her name, even though she wasn't really there. She realized that, even though it was a dream. "*No, Hannah,*" she tried to say. "*Not today.*" But the words bounced inside her head, like a metal piñata full of nails.

A metallic clang boomed through Zoe's brain. Suddenly, the grip loosened around her neck and she heard a distant voice as she gasped for air.

"*Zoe!*"

More rapping.

"*Ms. Rutherford?*"

Liquid fire ripped across the skin of Zoe's neck.

As swiftly as Hannah appeared, her sister vanished again. So, too, did the Boo Hag. The dream faded and Zoe drifted into a cold, dead sleep.

22

Relieved to wake to bright morning light, Zoe winced against the thrumming in her head. It was the worst hangover she had ever experienced—hands down. Her mouth felt like cotton, her eyes burned—painful—as though her eyeballs were far too big for her sockets.

Doing her best to clear the fuzziness out of her head, Zoe sat up, realizing only then that she must have slept all night without covers. The white spread was rumpled, but otherwise made, the edges tucked neatly beneath the pillows. A spot of blood on the bed caught her eye. Instinctively, she moved her fingers to her nose, feeling for dried blood. Sometimes, when she was a little girl, she'd suffered nosebleeds along with her night terrors.

"Damn," she said.

For a moment, she sat, dumfounded. Could it be she had some sort of infection after inhaling all that seawater? The nurse had said it was possible, although Zoe had felt fine after being dispatched from the hospital. As far as she knew, she was on the mend. But this morning, she felt worse than she had the morning after her accident. Her lungs burned. Even her tongue ached.

Feet dangling limply over the side of the bed, Zoe stared groggily at her closet.

It no longer appeared quite so demonic. It was mostly empty, with a number of blouses dangling from metal hangers. The rest of her wardrobe remained either in her suitcase or in boxes in the spare room. Now that the house was painted and they would no longer be in her way, she could unpack them later this week.

The ungodly jangling she'd heard in the closet must have been the hangers, but the windows were closed, not open as she recalled from her dream—but that's exactly what it was, she reminded herself, a weird, awful dream.

She must have eaten something bad, she decided. But whatever, she would take a few aspirin and be good as new—if not, she would call the doctor later in the day.

Moving slowly, Zoe slid off the edge of the bed, cautiously connecting her feet to the floor, and then she stood, stumbling into the master bathroom, tasting something awful in her mouth. Clearly, it was past time to brush her teeth.

Flipping on the light switch, Zoe peered at herself in the mirror and found her skin paler than the walls.

This bathroom still needed to be painted. Zoe planned to use the blue. There should be more than enough left over. These bathrooms were small in comparison to the bathroom she'd left out in Baltimore. Here in the master, there was barely enough room for a toilet, a sink, and a curtained tub, which Zoe felt compelled to look behind—just in case. This morning, she felt violated, although she wasn't sure why. Shoving the vinyl curtains aside, she inspected the raw enamel of the empty tub, and turned again to peer at her bloodless face in the mirror.

She might look like death, but she was very much alive, judging by the pounding in her head. Unlike yesterday afternoon, her skin looked wretched, the scar on her forehead stood out like an angry red flag. It was only then that she noticed the fine red line on her neck—like a delicate necklace. Zoe checked her nails, deciding it was past time to trim them, and then made her way to the kitchen, thirsting for water.

The mess that awaited her there reminded her that not everything had been a dream. The banana pudding lay overturned on the counter. It sat halfway beneath the tin, looking particularly unappetizing. The roast had formed a dry crust and the grease had solidified in the pan. The cheese on the macaroni looked more like dried snot and the wine sat open, smelling sour, filling the room with an acrid scent.

Zoe lifted the bottle to her nostrils, wincing, and then poured the remainder of the wine into the sink, certain that Ethan had inadvertently gotten his revenge.

Tossing the empty bottle into the trash, Zoe set about cleaning the kitchen, hoping Walter wouldn't come over before noon. She'd promised to get him the adhesive first thing in the morning, but she was moving like a turtle without much incentive to step it up.

Half an hour later, after a shower, she felt marginally better—enough to brave a trip to Southern Lumber to get the stair tread adhesive for Walter. She found the car keys in the bedroom, and her purse in the kitchen, next to her cell phone.

She left the cell phone—disgusted by the fact that she'd bothered to call Chris at all. She stumbled out the back door, dreading the possibility of finding Walter already at work out front, because then she would be forced to talk.

Thankfully, Walter was nowhere to be found. Grateful for the reprieve, and realizing he must have purposefully meant for her to sleep in, Zoe hurried to her car before Walter could catch her outside. She had already gotten that he was an early riser, so he could be itching to finish the job he'd started.

Or maybe he wasn't, and the longer she delayed getting back with the adhesive, the greater the chance he would walk away and never finish? In any case, he'd done enough that even if he left Zoe to finish the stairs on her own, she could handle the job just fine. All that was left to do was to set the treads, seal the wood, and then paint the stairs. If she wanted rails, she would hire a carpenter to do it right. She was glad now that she'd spent a little more for the cedar rather than buy poplar that would rot within a year.

Backing out of the driveway, she spied the silver Camry parked in Walter's driveway and considered bringing home donuts as a bribe. That way, at least she would have a reason to knock on his door. Praying her headache would be gone by the time she returned, Zoe pulled out onto the road.

THERE SHOULD BE an old rule related to Murphy's Law that said when you most want to avoid folks that's when you inevitably run into them.

Once, when Zoe was fifteen, she gave herself "highlights," using a grocery store variety hair-dye kit. The results had been devastating.

She'd missed Hannah most at times like that, when she might have hidden under the bed and bribed her sister to make the trip to the store. Asking Marge to go had been out of the question. By that point, their mother-daughter relationship had been destroyed.

It became clear through Zoe's teens that she had become a hot button for her parents. Even when Zoe had managed to keep herself out of her father's ill graces, somehow, behind closed doors, in their room, most of the grenades they'd lobbed at each other had Zoe's name written all over them.

There were times when Marge had come to Zoe's defense and Zoe could sense the underlying cause for her righteous anger had had little to do with Zoe. For example, much later, toward the end, when Marge suspected Robert Rutherford of cheating, rather than confront him about his late nights at work, she'd wanted to know why he'd continued to pick on Zoe more than he did Nick. Of course, by then Nicky had long defected from Zoe's camp, realizing that, at least under their dad's roof, Zoe was destined to remain on the losing side. Their relationship, from that point onward, had become complicated. Although Nick might have privately rooted for Zoe, publicly he kept his distance and his opinions to himself, even when she was in the right.

"I don't know," he would say. "I didn't see what happened."

Zoe's frustration would be more than evident in her tone. "Yes, you did, Nick. You were there."

Once, out of spite, Zoe bought him a set of those ugly monkeys, one with a hand over his eyes, another with a hand over his ears, the last with a hand over his mouth: See no evil. Hear no evil. Speak no evil. She'd found the statue at a drugstore and set it on his dresser, without an explanation, and never told him they were from her. If he'd ever understood their meaning, he never let on, but she'd later found the monkeys in the kitchen trash. She'd emptied her plate of grits over the ugly bastards and shut the lid, because, truthfully, she hadn't wanted her brother to change; she loved him, for the most part, exactly the way he was.

Nicky learned early that if he allowed Zoe to champion him, or if he took up for Zoe under any circumstances, his life became all the more difficult for the effort. Like Pavlov's dogs, their father had slowly trained him to respond accordingly, and under Robert Rutherford's roof, "accordingly" meant that whenever he'd gone on the rampage, and if Zoe was his target, it was easier—and safer—to put blinders on and walk away. As a teen, this process had never escaped Zoe. Yet this lesson was one Marge had never heeded behind closed doors. She'd continued to champion Zoe there, while Zoe was forced to listen from her bedroom, resenting her mom and wishing she would just stop.

In retrospect, Zoe was certain her mom had been so unhappy she didn't know any other way to live. She recalled sitting behind her own closed doors, staring bitterly at her sister's empty bed, while her parents' voices had bounced off the yellow walls.

"*Just stop!*" she'd shouted one day. "*Just stop!*" Zoe had picked up a plastic AM radio and hurled it against the bedroom wall, smashing it to pieces.

So, on this day she'd dyed her hair, Zoe was forced to make the trek to the store to find a suitable shade to hide the bleached-out strands. She'd gone with a beach towel on her head, because back then she hadn't owned any hats. She'd run into, of all people, Lori's brother, Bobby, whom she'd recently broken up with. He'd smirked at the sight of her, shaking his head, judging her and finding her lacking.

Now, once again, she faced his sister in the hardware section of Southern Lumber—without her baseball cap on, so of course, her scar was front and center. Lori's gaze fixed on the scar the entire time she spoke. "Hi," she said to the scar on Zoe's head.

Zoe fought the overwhelming urge to cover the injury with the canister of adhesive she held in her hand. "Hi."

"Crazy running into you here."

"Yeah, crazy."

Dressed in a pair of skinny jeans, with three-inch heels and a neatly pressed white button-down shirt, carefully tucked in, this was apparently Lori's version of dressing down. Her lipstick was the same shiny coral shade that matched her manicured nails. Her lips, perfectly glossed, continue to move but her gaze remained fixed upon Zoe's forehead. "We don't see each other for like twenty-some years, now it's twice in two weeks."

Zoe forced a smile. "Crazy, huh?"

Rolling her eyes, Lori held up a set of keys in her palm. "I'm here to make keys for one of my clients, because some idiot left without returning the originals to the lockbox. I'll probably get stuck paying for all new locks. Luckily, Mr. Southern's a friend of my pop's, so I'm pretty sure he'll probably give me a good price, but still it burns me up."

Zoe cast a longing glance toward the cash register. "Yeah, I'm sure."

"You know, chances are good it's all good, but I just wouldn't feel right if I made up new keys and didn't tell them about the ones I lost. But damn it, I just forked over a thousand bucks for my daughter's teeth. Luckily, my clients are in Europe for a month."

"That's a blessing, I guess," Zoe said, peering once more in the direction of the register. "So you must be working today." She didn't much care, but it felt like the right thing to say. Her head was still pounding. Conversation was the last thing she wanted.

Lori shook her head. "Nah, not really. I'm taking the week off, after last night's news—didn't you hear? My hubs says he hates the thought of me traipsing about town with that cray-cray on the loose, so I'm gonna take some time and be with my kids while they hunt that bastard down."

Zoe shook her head, confused. At times, it was a blessing living without TV or radio in the house. She didn't have to listen to the nightly news broadcast every robbery and every rape. Even in Baltimore, she'd rarely watched TV, but here she hadn't so much as cracked her notebook to check her emails. Judging by the rapid-fire phone calls Chris had made over the course of the past few weeks, she probably had near a dozen drunken, angry emails—some begging, others bitching—all spamming her inbox. Just in case there was some kind of work emergency, she was monitoring messages from her service, but nothing else.

"What news?"

Lori leaned in, mouth dropping open. "OMG, girlfriend." She spelled it out; just like that, as though their conversation were a text message. "You didn't hear? They discovered a body." She nodded, looking a bit unhinged, pointing at her feet. "Right here!"

Zoe's brows knit.

Lori kept on nodding. It was difficult, in that instant, to tell if she was horrified by the prospect or whether the news titillated her. "Everyone's been speculating for *months*, but *finally* they found some poor girl's body out near Breach—ain't no damned way the police can deny it now. There's a cray-cray out there, killing girls."

Illogically, Hannah's face entered Zoe's thoughts. It had been far too long since Hannah's disappearance for her to be a recent victim; still, her heart did a little backflip against her ribs.

"They haven't found the other two yet, but seems to me that's what happened to them as well. Don't you think?"

Unconsciously, Zoe put a hand to her forehead, as though to steady her thoughts. "Did the police actually say that, Lori?"

Lori sneered. "Well, no, but you know how tight lipped they can be. I know someone who works with Isle of Palms Police. He said that's what they're all thinking too. The others are buried in the marsh. Either that, or the guy's settin' bodies loose near Breach, so they'll wash out to sea."

A shudder ran down Zoe's spine.

Lori leaned in again, pressing her manicured fingers gently against her cheeks. "And get this, you won't hear it in the paper, but he supposedly raped that girl; so if they catch the bastard, they've got his DNA."

No matter how hard Zoe tried not to think of Hannah, she kept picturing her sister's face.

"It's true," Lori persisted. "Poor thing apparently got tangled up in the reeds. Some kid found her after school. I think her name was Susan, maybe. Her grandma used to teach at the elementary school. Maybe you knew her. Last name is Bayles. Pretty little thing, all messed up with drugs."

Zoe blinked as Lori's hand went to her shoulder. "Anyhow, Zoe, you take care, honey."

Zoe didn't know Susan Bayles, or Susan's grandmother, but last night's stomachache returned with a vengeance.

"Oh, God—I almost forgot. I heard about what happened to

you. I'm so sorry I haven't been by to see you yet. Looks like you've been through hell, poor thing. Is there anything I can do to help?"

Zoe reached up unconsciously to finger her scar. "No, no, I'm good," she said. "Everything is good."

"All right, well, you've got my card, right?"

Zoe nodded.

"If there's anything at all—anything—please don't hesitate to call. And—oh!" she said, spinning back around as she turned to go. "I told Bobby you're in town; he wants to see you. Think about that and let me know, okay?"

Zoe nodded, feeling dazed.

"Great," Lori said, mistaking Zoe's nod. She made a happy, little scrunchy face. "He'll be so pleased."

Zoe didn't have the wherewithal to take it back. She went through the motion of saying goodbye, watching Lori's lips move, but not truly hearing anything more she said. Zoe paid for the adhesive and went dumbly out the door, pausing at the newspaper dispenser. It felt as though it were 1986 all over again with news about her missing sister. Filtering through the change in her purse, she found seventy-five cents, and set her bag on the ground to open the dispenser and pull out a copy of the *Charleston Tribune.*

Three faces were laid out in order of their disappearance, three two-by-three black-and-white photos. All three had hair a little darker than Zoe's, but she didn't recognize any of the names. None of the three girls were Hannah, but the third face was vaguely familiar.

The headline read: BODY DISCOVERED AT BREACH INLET. Beneath that headline, Zoe read the first line of text: *The discovery of a body near Breach Inlet provides gruesome new clues as to the possible whereabouts of two local women . . .*

Her gaze skidded back to the third picture.

The girl was youngish, with dark-blonde hair, all one color, not striped with that chalky pigment some girls now smeared in their hair—like that teen she'd seen at the grocery store the day before her accident. In the photo, the girl wasn't wearing thick eyeliner that looked as though it had been applied before a drinking binge, but Zoe was certain it was the same person. She picked up her bag and took the paper to her car, tossing it into the passenger seat, front page upright, along with her purse and the bag with her purchases. All the way home, she gave the paper furtive glances, considering the last time she'd seen the girl: talking to Walter Donovan through his passenger-side window.

PEOPLE WENT MISSING ALL the time. Old men sat in their cars out in parking lots of drugstores and simply forgot the way home. Runaways disappeared for weeks on end, sometimes returning to their families, sometimes not.

For Zoe, the idea that people went missing was far more ordinary than for most. How could it not be, when her own sister had walked out the door one morning, never to return?

Foremost in her mind—always—was that one missing person, her sister. Therefore, upon returning to Sullivan's, after living in Baltimore, where folks turned up missing every day, the idea that there might be two more women out there, somewhere, who hadn't made it home, didn't immediately resonate. It was an egocentric view, perhaps, but those girls weren't Zoe's problem. Hannah was Zoe's problem, and even after a lifetime of trying to make sense of her sister's disappearance, Hannah had taken a backseat to Zoe's travails with Chris.

Only now, having seen that girl's face in the paper—the one who'd stood in front of Zoe at the grocery store . . . mere inches away, so that Zoe might easily have fingered the pink, chalky strands of her hair—once more, it came uncomfortably close to home.

Zoe tried to recall the girl's demeanor . . . aside from the goth-girl makeup there weren't any clues that may have given her pause . . . not enough to think she might have walked out of the store and straight into oblivion, as Hannah once did.

"*It's not always about you, Zoe*," she heard Chris say—this to any number of occasions that had cropped up between them. If he cheated, it wasn't about Zoe. If he lied, it wasn't personal. If he was simply in a bad mood, "*It's not about you, Zoe.*"

But, yes, it was, Zoe demurred, because she internalized everything. If he cheated, it must have been because she wasn't good enough. If he lied, it was because she'd made him feel defensive. If he was in a bad mood, it was because she couldn't make him happy. Along that same vein, if her sister didn't make it home, that too must have been Zoe's fault.

But perhaps Chris had been more right than Zoe realized. If he cheated, maybe it was because he didn't have what it took to remain monogamous. If he lied, maybe it was because he didn't hold himself to a higher standard. If he was in a bad mood, maybe, just maybe, it was because he had regrets, and maybe those bad moods were proof he had a conscience after all.

More importantly, when her sister didn't make it home . . . maybe there was nothing at all Zoe could have done to change that fact.

Still, she was loath to compare Hannah to Susan Bayles. They were not at all alike. Hannah had been a bright, sunny child; Susan was a dark, doleful teen. But then . . . Zoe remembered the girl's purposeful gait as she'd walked out the grocer's door—that backward glance as she and Zoe made eye contact. There'd been nothing in the depths of that gaze that hinted at Susan Bayles's impending death. They were the eyes of a bored teenager, to be sure, one who, given the chance, had sought to make herself useful.

In Zoe's head, she replayed the moment Susan ducked out of the grocery store, hurrying toward Walter Donovan's car, and then she'd stood there, animated, speaking with Walter through his passenger-side window. And then she replayed the scene over and over in her head while she drove home from the store.

How did Walter and Susan know each other?

At home, Zoe pulled out her notebook, did a bit of digging.

One of the missing girls—Heather Rodriguez—had disappeared on her way to work. She'd lived in North Charleston—a twenty-two-year-old with expressive black eyes. She'd had an abusive boyfriend—a situation not unlike Zoe's, in that she worked two jobs to support a lazy, hot-tempered jerk. At the time of her disappearance, the boyfriend was questioned, though he was never arrested. His friends had vouched for his whereabouts on the night that Heather disappeared. She had been missing now for four months.

The second girl, a waitress, was Sara Kelly. She'd gone missing two months after Heather, after a late-night shift, somewhere between where she'd worked and lived in West Ashley. Her apartment door had been discovered ajar, but the nineteen-year-old was nowhere to be found. Everyone assumed she'd made it home only because her car was sitting in her assigned parking space. No one had seen her arrive home or leave again. More digging revealed the girl lived in transitional housing.

A prick of something close to fear sidled down Zoe's spine.

The last girl—the one Zoe recognized—was Susan Bayles. At fifteen, Susan had been recovering from a recent drug overdose, living with her grandmother and grandfather on Isle of Palms—a story that sounded eerily familiar. Her body was the only one as yet recovered. It was found, they said, with the head nearly severed, possibly with some kind of wire. The cut was so deep, so fiercely done, that it had nearly severed Susan's head from her shoulders.

Another shiver raced down Zoe's spine as her fingers sought the skin of her neck.

She thought about Gabi at age nine, with those greasy

pigtails, and her too-tight T-shirts, and wondered whether she'd grown up to be anything like Susan Bayles. It wasn't certain they'd met the same fate, but Lori's words rang in her head: . . . *that's what they're all thinking too. The others are buried in the marsh. Either that, or the guy's settin' bodies loose near Breach, so they'll wash out to sea.*

Those boys in the boat . . . despite the fact that it wasn't their intent to go off that day, had found themselves dragged out to sea. Zoe understood, especially now, how strong those riptides could be. Walter Donovan had known precisely where to intercept her.

You know . . . there are places along the inlet where the currents act like a tidal jet, spewing everything they catch out to sea.

Walter was MIA this morning. His car was parked in his driveway. He never made it over to work on the stairs. That suited Zoe fine.

What day did Susan Bayles go missing? That's what Zoe wanted to know. She searched reports online, trying to pin down the precise day Susan had disappeared. Specifically, she wanted to know: How soon after their encounter at the grocery store did Susan meet her end? If Zoe had the slightest culpability for putting the girl in harm's way . . .

She was getting that feeling again, deep down in her gut . . .

As with Hannah, she'd had a chance to make a difference. Instead, she might have inadvertently pushed a girl to her death with a stupid lie about razor blades.

Zoe thought about the girl standing next to Walter's car door window, talking in such an animated way, and a pang returned to the pit of her gut.

But, no, Walter had driven away, leaving Susan to sulk her way across the parking lot and then down the street.

But that was the thing that bothered Zoe—the fact that Susan's attitude had changed after Walter drove away. The fact that she had known his name when Zoe said it meant little on its own; it was a small town. Everyone knew everyone. In fact, she didn't have to know Walter's name to remember he was the one who'd stood in front of Zoe in the grocery line. But Susan had known Walter, judging by the ease of their conversation, and what did Walter say he did for a living? He helped out at the women's shelter.

That's what he'd said.

Separately, everything might be unrelated. When you put together the whole picture, it felt . . . *wrong*. Some part of Zoe wanted to pick up the phone, call Chief McWhorter, but if she was mistaken, she could destroy a man's life.

There was no proof.

In the *Tribune* Zoe found the date of the girl's disappearance: Monday, in fact . . . the day before Zoe's accident. Walter had been up early that morning. Zoe had set out to walk the beach around 3:45 a.m. Shortly before that, she'd heard a car door open and close outside her bedroom window. Was it Walter?

Why would he have gotten home so late?

Or perhaps he'd been leaving?

Zoe paced the house, periodically checking locks. It was entirely surreal to consider that the man next door might be responsible for two missing girls and one dead one . . . and if he had killed her—them—what about Hannah?

What were the odds?

More confusing yet: Why would Walter bother to save Zoe if she were the type of girl he might prey upon? If he'd killed that poor girl, and he'd been there at Breach, disposing of the body, why would he leave unfinished business to save Zoe?

Did he decide to kill her before or after he'd saved her life?

If she called Chief McWhorter to ask him these questions, would he think Zoe was grasping at straws, still searching in vain for long-lost Hannah?

Zoe pictured Walter Donovan's face, trying to remember what she'd thought of him the first time they'd met—and before that day, when she'd spied him walking from his house to his car. He had that limp. She'd thought him harmless, lean, and frail. It was only after she'd met him that she'd considered him anything else . . . and yet, she remembered the way Susan had spoken with him, her hands dancing . . . and, yes, there'd been laughter on her lips. Zoe could see her smiling from where she'd stood at the register.

But then he had driven away.

Susan never got into his car.

As the hours ticked by with no sign of Walter, Zoe was grateful not to have to face him—because now how could she?

She walked into the hall bathroom, flipping on the lights, staring at herself in the bathroom mirror . . . the fine red line encircling her neck.

It wasn't thick enough to be a scratch.

Nor was it deep enough to be the slice of a knife.

Love is gravity, Zoe; d'ya wanna die?

But that was a dream, Zoe reassured herself as she flipped off the bathroom light. She made her way into the kitchen as the phone rang. It was Beth, her brother by proxy. "Hey you, how're you holding up?"

"Fine," Zoe said. She didn't want her brother to believe her decision to remain in Charleston would bring unwanted drama, but she was relieved for the lifeline. "I'm so glad you called. I was up in the attic and found my grandmother's sewing machine. I thought maybe the girls might like to have it."

The sun was going down. The sky looked battered and bruised—the color of abuse. Susan Bayles's face flashed through Zoe's head, pale-faced, with dark, smeary makeup . . . or maybe just black eyes.

Sometimes I help out at the women's shelter.

Zoe blinked away the sting of tears.

"Really Zoe, you know the girls would love that, though I think you should keep it,"

Zoe felt like gagging. She clutched at her stomach. "Nah, it's yours. I don't sew. I love the pillows the girls made for me and can't help but wonder what more they might make—for me, of course." She forced a laugh. "It's all about me, really," she joked.

Beth laughed as well. And then, inevitably, she brought up the news. "I'm sure you heard about that poor kid they found up there."

"Yeah," Zoe said. She wanted to say more. Maybe, if she spoke to Nick . . . if her brother thought it could be something, maybe she would call Chief McWhorter. "Hey, Beth, is Nicky around?"

"Nope. He's working late tonight. He wanted me to call and let you know that you should expect a package, probably tomorrow."

"A package?"

Beth's voice was full of remorse. "Yeah—God, Zoe, I'm so sorry. I hope you won't hate me. I made a bad call. I didn't realize until Nick told me later that he didn't think your break up with Chris was all that amicable. Well, Chris called to get your address, he said there was something he needed to return to you; so I gave it to him." Her voice was tight, full of apprehension, like a little girl's. "I hope it was okay."

The sick feeling in Zoe's gut intensified. Her silence must have conveyed everything she couldn't say.

"Oh, Zoe. I'm so sorry," Beth said again. "Really. He sounded so sincere on the phone. I just didn't know."

"It's okay. Don't worry about it."

"Are you sure? Nick was so upset with me, though I hoped it was only him projecting—you know how he can be."

Zoe didn't anymore, and that fact didn't help the sense of disorder she felt. "It's fine. Don't worry about it, Beth."

"Okay, well, I'm really sorry," she said again. "I'll let you go, Zoe, but please take care, you hear? You sound exhausted."

"I will. Don't worry, Beth." Zoe didn't want to get off the phone, but she couldn't think of a reason to keep Beth on. "Hey, if you're up to it, I'd love to see the girls this weekend."

"Sounds good to me." There was a note of relief in her voice. "I'll call Thursday to make plans. You get some rest."

"Okay," Zoe said woodenly.

"Bye now."

"Bye." Zoe ended the call, pressing her thumb against the "call end" button. The cellphone display and the microwave clock gave the room an eerie blue light.

Zoe leaned over the sink, gagging a little. The faucet remained in pieces at the edge of the sink, the black seal dark against the pale enamel, the metal faucet head reflecting LED light. Zoe glanced at the clock on the microwave: It read 8:10 p.m. The sun was setting later this time of the year, rising earlier, around 6:00 a.m. From the hours of 3:00 a.m. to 6:00 a.m., the sky was dark enough for Zoe to have misjudged the shoreline, certainly dark enough to conceal someone following along the beach . . . definitely dark enough to dispose of a body from a boat out on the water . . .

Zoe realized with a sickening sense that she had no idea how exactly Walter had fished her out of the ocean.

Zoe's hands shook as she reached up to open the blinds. Across the feral yard, Walter Donovan's house remained dark. She had begun to believe he wasn't home, but the light in his bedroom blinked on, a dim beacon across a sea of patchy grass.

The sweet myrtle bushes were growing back now, inching upward, conspiring again to block the view. Another month or so and they would be right back where they were before Zoe cut them down.

Not right away, but after a time, as Zoe watched, Walter's blinds separated. She could see him peering out between his blinds. All she could see through the shadows, through the silhouetted shafts of sweet myrtle, were the whites of his eyes.

Zoe's knees felt weak. She stood, realizing he spotted her too . . . standing alone . . . in the shadows of her kitchen, where only yesterday he had stood, dismantling her faucet piece by piece. She'd left him there . . . where he could have drugged her wine.

Her gaze shifted to the lidless trash, where the cork-free bottle peeked above the edge.

After a moment, Walter waved. Zoe spied the movement of his hand, a shadow as it flit along the blinds. She lifted a hand to wave back, but it floundered, finding purchase at her neck . . . across the new red necklace she wore.

It was only a feeling—that same feeling she always managed to ignore.

Walter Donovan looked tired across the way, his shadow slumping as he peered out from his window at Zoe.

It could be last night had been nothing more than a bad dream . . . he might be a kindly old man who was nice enough to fix her stairs . . . could be he was only fishing out there, like he said, and nothing more . . . but what if . . . what if someone had intervened on the day Hannah disappeared?

Zoe was grateful to Walter for saving her life—equally as grateful as she was for all the things Chris had done for her throughout the years. Not all their times had been bad. But simply because Walter Donovan had saved her life and then fixed her sink didn't mean he wasn't capable of taking a life.

Zoe could play it safe, wait a day or two . . . the paper said they were working on leads. Whoever killed Susan Bayles didn't mean for the body to be discovered . . . and there was DNA.

It was difficult to say how long Walter stood, staring back across their yards—seconds, minutes, perhaps longer—but Zoe sensed it down in her bones.

Someone said—long ago—so long ago she couldn't remember who, Nana, or maybe her dad—but it had stuck with her all these years, because instinctively, she had understood it to be true: In those moments, before you closed your eyes one last time, it was never the things you did you found cause to regret . . . it was the things you didn't do that haunted you in the end.

What would Walter Donovan regret?

His blinds snapped shut, and Zoe sensed, more than saw him back away from the window. His light was never on so early and she knew he'd settled in for the night. Somehow, he wanted her to know that too.

Zoe moved purposefully toward the back door, trying the lock again, finding it secure. With her cell phone still in her hand, and the display lighting the way, she moved quickly to each window throughout the house, each door, checking and rechecking locks, pulling doors tight, before retreating to her room. Once there, she sat on the bed, staring straight at the closet, listening to the soft jangle of metal hangers.

She flipped on the flashlight built into her phone and pointed it at the stack of business cards that waited on her nightstand.

What if she was wrong?

What if she wasn't?

Flipping through the cards, Zoe found Ethan's card and turned it over, peering at the scribbled number with the flashlight on her phone. She dialed Chief McWhorter's number. His phone rang. He didn't answer. Zoe left a message: "Hi, this is Zoe Rutherford. I have information pertaining to the death of Susan Bayles."

Zoe hung up, turned off the flashlight on her phone, and set the cell phone down beside her on the bed. The idea of sitting in a lit fishbowl didn't appeal to her at the moment. It was a small town. Sirens were already wailing by the time the first ring pealed from her phone.

23

CLOSURE

In the center of the kitchen table sat a four-by-nine-inch white envelope. Zoe studied the coffee stain on one end, where a cup must have been placed haphazardly, half on, half off the paper, maybe a little disrespectfully, as though the contents were not valued.

But for Zoe, what lay inside could be life changing . . . if she chose to accept it.

It could be that everything was a coincidence.

Could be nothing was.

The truth fell somewhere in between.

This much they did know: Walter Donovan killed his niece. He'd strangled her with a piano wire, leaving the girl nearly decapitated—the same way he'd left Susan Bayles. FBI records in Baltimore revealed six more unsolved cases, most occurring between 2003 and 2006, one during 1997. Altogether, including Hannah, there were at least eleven possible deaths attributable to the "harmless old guy" next door.

The stained white envelope begged for Zoe to open it. For some reason she couldn't seem to reach out and touch it, despite it sitting mere inches away.

Chief McWhorter leaned against her kitchen counter, arms crossed, as he waited for Zoe to process all the information he'd given her. Next to him, the faucet remained in pieces.

Crossing her arms as well, Zoe dug her fingernails into the soft flesh of her biceps. "Do you believe him?"

Chief McWhorter shrugged, then alternately shook his head. "I don't know, Zoe. Seems improbable." He pointed at the envelope. "We looked into every angle."

"And?"

"At the time, he was doing a second six-month tour of duty in Iraq."

Closure was within her grasp—so close. Chief McWhorter seemed so ready to snatch it away. "You said he came back in December? What day?"

He scratched his chin, a gesture borne of discomfort more than physical need. He seemed to sense her desperation. "The eighteenth."

Zoe pressed her fingernails deeper into her flesh. "Hannah went missing on the twentieth—that's two days. He might have come here."

Chief McWhorter shook his head, but slowly, as though he didn't wish to disagree.

How screwed up was that? That both of them were hoping the words in that envelope could be true, that Walter Donovan took her sister, and strangled her with piano wire, then jetted her body out to sea.

"They returned him to Washington Naval Base, not Charleston."

Zoe blinked away the morbid scene forming in her head. "But... what if they lied for him?"

"Why would they, Zoe?"

"To protect one of their own—he's a war hero, right?"

Once again Chief McWhorter shook his head. "Turns out, he

fell off a ship deck, shattered his femur. He couldn't climb ladders anymore, so they gave him an honorable discharge."

"Honorable discharge," Zoe said, staring at the white envelope. How did a serial killer get an honorable discharge? She wasn't sure what to believe. If Walter Donovan killed her sister, as he said he did, at least then she would know the truth. On the other hand, if Zoe didn't accept Walter's confession, she must also accept that she might never know what happened to Hannah. Thirty years later, it was a closed case that would never again be reopened. Zoe eased her fingernails out of her flesh, tentatively placing her hand on the table. The envelope remained unsealed. It would be a simple matter for her to open it and read Walter Donovan's confession.

"There was something else," Chief McWhorter said somewhat uncertainly, halting her fingers' approach to the envelope. "We're not certain what it means."

Zoe met his gaze, hoping for a reprieve. "What's that?"

"He was adamant we tell you something, Zoe—said it was important. He said he'd made a mistake, but he wouldn't say what it was. He said you'd understand."

Zoe furrowed her brow. "What is it?"

She and Chief McWhorter locked gazes. In his eyes, Zoe spied his son, and she wished, illogically, that she could hold Ethan's hand. "He said to tell you 'gravity wins over all.'"

Zoe's chest constricted. "Gravity wins over all?"

"Does that mean something to you, Zoe?"

Zoe swallowed. She gave a little half shake of her head, not entirely certain. Her gaze returned to the coffee-stained envelope lying upon her table.

"Are you sure, Zoe?"

Ain't nothing worse than an unloved child, Walter Donovan had said.

Love is gravity, the Boo Hag whispered.

It gave Zoe a shudder, sensing a connection she couldn't put into words. All her life, she'd clung to the things she believed defined her—the good and the bad. Always, the good in her life seemed to serve as a temporary scab, while the past lay festering beneath, raw and ready to bleed. Zoe took comfort in that pain because it was familiar. For some reason, even now, she couldn't seem to get words out of her mouth, even to tell Chief McWhorter that she'd allowed Walter Donovan into her house, into her life. Perhaps if he hadn't already confessed, she might feel compelled to pull the wine bottle out of the trash and offer it to the police, but her hand went to her neck, tugging at the collar of her blouse. "Yes, I'm sure."

Chief McWhorter shoved off the counter. "Well, all right. Whatever you decide to do with that, it's your copy," he said. "We have the original on file."

Walter Donovan's confession and cryptic message left Zoe with more questions than answers, but she reached out, shoving the envelope away as Chief McWhorter moved toward the back door and put a hand on the knob to pull it open. "Oh, yeah," he said, "with all the hoopla, I forgot to say. I hope you don't mind. I came onto your front porch the other night, turned off your porch lights."

Zoe blinked up at him.

"Not sure if you remember, there's an ordinance."

Zoe blinked again. "May till October?"

"That's right," he said. "I called for you first, but it was early. The lights were out, so I figured you musta been gone. I didn't think you'd mind too much if I popped in and flipped off the lights for you, save you a fine."

Zoe nodded dumbly.

Chief McWhorter screwed his face. "I hate to do it, but next time there'll be a fine."

Zoe nodded again. "I understand."

Chief McWhorter smiled at her warmly. "Anyway, I saw you fixed up those stairs. Nice job, Zoe. Welcome home."

"Thanks," Zoe said.

Chief McWhorter stepped outside.

"Hey, Chief?"

He turned around.

"Will they keep him behind bars?"

"Yup. Even without Hannah, we've got more'n enough to give him a one-way ticket to Lieber."

Death row.

"At least two of those confessions are solid."

The one that wasn't sat on Zoe's table.

"Thanks."

"No sweat. Take care now," he said, and then he left Zoe staring down at Walter's gift.

Zoe barely heard the back door close.

When the front doorbell rang moments later, she thought Chief McWhorter had returned to whisk the envelope away, thereby saving her from having to make a difficult decision. But it was UPS. The man handed her a rectangular package. Zoe took the package and let the screen door slam shut behind her, noticing the return address: Christopher Mays, 221 Fairview Lane, Baltimore, MD 22201. She set the package down onto the seat of her grandmother's rocking chair and poked a thumbnail into the tape on one end, breaking the seal. Peeling back the tape, she pried open the box lid.

Nestled inside, folded neatly, lay her mother's red-and-white quilt. Zoe pulled it out of the box and held it up, shook it out. There was no note, only the quilt. For a moment, Zoe merely held it, reveling in the way it felt in her hands—the scratchy yet soft feel of old, many-times-washed crochet. Lifting the blanket to her nostrils, Zoe inhaled deeply, searching for familiar odors. It smelled musty from having been tucked away so long. No hint of her mother's scent survived—not even the smell of nicotine. She cast the blanket over the rocking chair to air out, fingering a few of the squares as she stood contemplating the last years of her life. She touched a burnt-orange square—a piece of the bathing suit she'd never again worn after that day on the beach. Another square—a pimply white material—brought to mind a pair of Marge's polyester slacks. The memory made her smile. Another square, a bit of cloth from someone's faded pair of blue jeans, maybe Hannah's—each square a potential memory. Some she might easily unlock, some maybe never, but each one a part of her life. Clearly, the quilt was Chris's parting gift to her. This one Zoe could accept. That other one—the one sitting on her kitchen table—she could not.

Without thinking about where she was going, Zoe found herself beneath the attic door, reaching up to pull it open. Moving by rote, she tugged down the door and ascended into the attic, going straight for the plastic pencil box nestled atop the pedals of her Nana's sewing machine. Taking the box, she brought it back downstairs and set it on the kitchen table, next to the white envelope. She stared at it a long while, trying to muster the courage to open it once and for all. There was no telling what the box might hold—Hannah's kindergarten photo, the one with both missing front teeth. Zoe had always loved that photo. It was the perfect portrait of the precocious child she had been. But maybe it contained some odd memento of their childhood together. A bunch of seashells they'd uncovered, while combing the beach. Might even be Zoe's diary, which she'd lost and never found.

Swallowing hard, Zoe peeled back the electrical tape from the plastic box—electrical tape, because what else would the daughter of an electrician use to seal her secrets? After all these many years, the tape was gooey from the attic heat. She tore it away slowly, peeling it off, then attempted to flick the tape aside. When it wouldn't release her fingers, she stuck it to the table. Then, once the lid was no longer encumbered, she pressed her fingers against the sticky surface, popping open the lid.

Inside lay two blue-and-white bicycle streamers.

Zoe's throat constricted.

That day, Zoe knew exactly where to find her sister's bike because she'd discovered it earlier in the day. Hannah and Gabi were nowhere to be found, but her sister's pale-blue Schwinn sat looking as abandoned as Zoe felt. Furious with Hannah, and wanting her to feel the pain she was feeling, Zoe had ripped those streamers out of her sister's handlebars and considered throwing them out to sea—except that she'd understood how much the bike meant to her sister. So instead, Zoe took the streamers home, intending to return them later. Later never arrived.

Now she remembered.

Everything.

Tears filled Zoe's eyes.

Later, she told no one.

Later, she'd hid the streamers in a pencil box.

No one would ever know about the lapse of character she'd displayed out on the dunes—not even Hannah. But Zoe knew. She'd tucked away the ugly memory, along with the bicycle streamers, concealing the evidence she'd been afraid would raise more questions, yet never able to bring herself to throw them away. She never told anyone, and secretly feared Chief Hale would discover the box and consider it proof of Zoe's guilt.

How did you know where to find the bike, Zoe?

Because Zoe had hurled that bike down into the sand, burying the rubber handlebar at least two inches deep so that sand spilled from its interior once she'd lifted the bike to walk it home. Tears blurred her vision as she stared at the twin streamers in the pencil box. "It's time," she said quietly.

Time for what?

Time to let go.

Reaching across the table, Zoe took Walter's confession, tore the envelope in two and shoved it into the pencil box along with the streamers, snapping the lid shut. Chief McWhorter was right.

Chances were that Walter did not kill Hannah, and she already knew what the envelope contained. Chief McWhorter had already told her. For some reason, Zoe nicked a pity artery in a monster, and perhaps he only wanted to gift her with peace of mind. Or maybe it was just his last sick joke at her expense, leaving her with a blow-by-blow description of a savagery that would give her nightmares the rest of her life. But did she really need to know how someone like Walter imagined the final moments of terror in a young girl's death? No. Peace of mind wasn't going to arrive as a gift bestowed by somebody else; it was a decision you made. As of right now, she decided that she had closure. Hannah was dead—however it happened, she wasn't coming back. Some endings, she realized, simply were not neat. Maybe closure happened the instant you put a hand over the rearview mirror and stopped focusing on the past.

Picking up the box up from the table, she walked over to the trashcan and shoved it facedown into the trash.

Right about now, she owed Ethan McWhorter a phone call.

ACKNOWLEDGMENTS

Many thanks to Michelle Boubel for fielding my criminally minded questions and sometimes macabre muse. Thanks also to Lou Aronica, without whom I would never have stepped out of my comfort zone. Thank you, Lou.

ALSO BY TANYA ANNE CROSBY

MAINSTREAM FICTION

The Girl Who Stayed

The Things We Leave Behind

Redemption Song

Reprisal

Everyday Lies

ROMANTIC SUSPENSE

Leave No Trace

Speak No Evil

Tell No Lies

DAUGHTERS OF AVALON

The King's Favorite

The Holly & the Ivy

A Winter's Rose

Fire Song

Lord of Shadows

THE PRINCE & THE IMPOSTOR

Seduced by a Prince

A Crown for a Lady

The Art of Kissing Beneath the Mistletoe

THE HIGHLAND BRIDES

The MacKinnon's Bride

Lyon's Gift

On Bended Knee

Lion Heart

Highland Song

MacKinnon's Hope

GUARDIANS OF THE STONE

Once Upon a Highland Legend

Highland Fire

Highland Steel

Highland Storm

Maiden of the Mist

THE MEDIEVALS HEROES

Once Upon a Kiss

Angel of Fire

Viking's Prize

REDEEMABLE ROGUES

Happily Ever After

Perfect In My Sight

McKenzie's Bride

Kissed by a Rogue

Thirty Ways to Leave a Duke

A Perfectly Scandalous Proposal

ANTHOLOGIES & NOVELLAS

Lady's Man

Married at Midnight

The Winter Stone

ABOUT THE AUTHOR

 Tanya Anne Crosby is the New York Times and USA Today best-selling author of thirty novels. She has been featured in magazines, such as People, Romantic Times and Publisher's Weekly, and her books have been translated into eight languages. Her first novel was published in 1992 by Avon Books, where Tanya was hailed as "one of Avon's fastest rising stars." Her fourth book was chosen to launch the company's Avon Romantic Treasure imprint.

Known for stories charged with emotion and humor and filled with flawed characters Tanya is an award-winning author, journalist, and editor, and her novels have garnered reader praise and glowing critical reviews. She and her writer husband split their time between Charleston, SC, where she was raised, and northern Michigan, where the couple make their home.

For more information
Website
Email
Newsletter

Lightning Source UK Ltd.
Milton Keynes UK
UKHW011028120620
364896UK00002B/99/J